THE PROPOSITION

"To us." David lifted his glass.

She clinked her glass against his and took a sip.

"There will be an us, won't there, Kate?"

"It seems to be heading in that direction," she said quietly.

"Then what's the problem?" David was exasperated. "We're both consenting adults. We're attracted to each other, maybe even more than attracted, so there's nothing to stop us."

"You're married." Kate looked at him intently.

An incredulous expression flitted across his face. "I've explained that. It means nothing, has nothing to do with us! Look, Kate, I adore you. I want nothing more than to make love to you. Right now."

"Please, David, all I'm asking for is a little time," she pleaded.

"Okay," he said with reluctance, "but as a closing argument, let me say that I think we could have a wonderful relationship. I'm not without influence in Los Angeles. I could help you in many ways. And you could help me."

"That almost sounds like a business proposition," Kate said with a small laugh.

He had the grace to look embarrassed, shrugging his shoulders. "We'll play it any way you like—as long as you play."

Mistresses

Trevor Meldal-Johnsen

PINNACLE BOOKS
WINDSOR PUBLISHING CORP.

PINNACLE BOOKS

are published by

Windsor Publishing Corp.
475 Park Avenue South
New York, NY 10016

First printing: May, 1988

Printed in the United States of America

For three women: To Marcia, for her generous help from conception to completion; to Lydia, for her wise counsel and guidance; and to Sherry, for her enthusiasm and support.

Prologue

December, 1986

Hollywood

Angie was the last to leave the funeral. A forlorn figure in a fashionable grey suit, she stood alone, unable to move from the grassy knoll, looking down at Joel's grave. She had thought about buying something in black, but she had to be careful with money now. Joel was gone, and her lover had thrown her out on the street. She owned nothing except a splendid wardrobe and a couple of pieces of jewelry.

Finally, as if uprooting herself, she lifted her head and turned to look away. Below the marble-dotted hill at Forest Lawn was the concrete-encased Los Angeles River, and just beyond it, behind a tall fence, transplanted in time, a small turn-of-the-century town. There was a village square, the pointed spire of a country church, a general store, a saloon.

She stared uncomprehendingly for a long time before realizing she was looking at the Burbank Studios' back lot. She raised her eyes and saw that two miles away, rising from tumbling rows of houses, the Verdugo Hills hung suspended against a piercing blue sky like a studio painting. It was an unusually clear day for Los Angeles, although the sky was overcast and the light wind had a chilling bite to it. Joel would have liked it, she thought. He always complained about the smog.

This was all so unreal. One day, she and Joel had made love, chasing each other naked around his downtown loft, laughing like children, and she had left with a smile on her lips. The next day, they found his mangled body on the sidewalk, where it had been tossed like a useless broken toy.

A woman walked purposefully up the hill toward her, a veil covering her face. Angie turned back to look at the grave, wondering who it was. All of Joel's friends, musicians mainly, had been and gone, intent on holding a rousing wake. She had been invited but had put them off. They were nice enough, but she felt it would be somehow improper to do anything but mourn. Besides, she had too much to think about.

The woman stopped two feet away from her and stood there without speaking, looking down at the small marble headstone.

Joel Buck
1953–1986
"Let There Be Music"

Angie felt the tears well up and swallowed. Joel had given her the first album he had just cut with his group. She'd never be able to listen to it without thinking about the headstone. "Let There Be Music." It was all he really cared about, that and her, of course. After years of struggle, playing small clubs in LA and the rest of California, nickel-and-diming it, the group had finally made it. Now Joel wouldn't be around to enjoy any of the rewards.

She sobbed then, a thick sound that caught in her throat.

"You were a friend of his?" the woman said, taking half a step toward her. She had a gentle voice, but Angie couldn't see her face through the veil.

"Who are you?" Angie said.

"His sister."

"His sister?" Angie asked, surprised. Joel had mentioned a sister to her but said they hadn't seen each other for about three years.

"Yes," the woman said. Her voice sounded tired. "I just flew in. The plane was late. . . ."

"Well, Miss Buck, it was just a short ceremony," Angie said, her voice consoling. "Just a few of his friends."

"I'm sorry I missed it," the woman said dully.

"I'm Angie Cox. Joel and I . . . we were friends."

The woman swept the veil away from her face. Yes, Angie could see the likeness in the mouth and eyes. A beautiful face, like Joel's, though five or six years younger, she guessed. The same auburn hair, firm but full mouth, sparkling green eyes, a small upturned nose. She felt drawn to that face. It was something of Joel, something that brought her closer to him than anything else had that day.

"I need a drink," Angie said. "How about you?"

They found a place called Dimples on Olive Street, where all the major film studios' logos were featured in stained glass in the windows. Inside, portraits of actors and actresses hung on the walls. Angie ordered a screwdriver and Joel's sister ordered a B & B. She twirled the small snifter glass for a moment, and then lifted it to her mouth. Suddenly she spoke, lowering the glass before tasting her drink. "What happened to Joel, Miss Cox?" she asked.

Angie was surprised. It wasn't a question she wanted to answer. "You weren't told," she stammered. "Someone must have contacted you."

His sister waved the question away. "I spoke to the police. They said he had surprised a burglar, there was a struggle, and Joel either fell or was thrown from his apartment window. They said it was probably a junkie. That the neighborhood was rife with them."

"Yes, that's what happened," Angie said. She twisted her fingers together and then stopped, suddenly self-conscious. She couldn't show her fear. Not now.

The woman shook her head. "The detective I spoke to was thoughtful enough to say that, for a musician, it was just as well he died in the fall. He said all the fingers in both his hands were broken."

"So?" Angie said, sounding defensive and quickly looking away.

"I asked him about it. He seemed annoyed. As if I was

complicating his life. The policeman said it probably happened when he hit the sidewalk. It seems very unlikely to me. Both hands!"

"Well, that's what the police told me, too," Angie said. "When I arrived at the apartment the next morning, they'd already taken his body away." She paused, shook her head, and reached for her glass.

She took a long swallow of vodka while the other woman studied her. Angie was a blonde, with tell tale dark roots in her well-groomed hair and a full figure that would one day turn to fat, but for now was voluptuous and probably very attractive to men. Her clothes were expensive, and she wore diamond stud earrings of at least a carat each. It was hard to imagine Joel with her, but then it was impossible to understand other people's attractions, even her own brother's.

Of course, Joel had always liked almost everyone. It was one of the qualities that drew people to him. He had a capacity for forgiveness. When he looked at people, he saw their best, even if they didn't deserve it. He was also generous, lighthearted, and modest about his considerable talents. He was an innocent, a true innocent, without a hateful or vindictive bone in his body.

She remembered the last time she had seen him, about three years ago. She had come to California to visit him. Broke at the time, he shared a one-bedroom apartment with another musician and looked as if he ate once a week. Yet he had consoled and encouraged her during that confusing period. She had just broken up with a lover and was uncertain about the direction of her life. Joel had been like a bubble of invigorating air, lifting her out of herself and sending her off with fresh purpose.

Since then, they had both been too busy to make time for a trip. She had come out a couple of times on business, but in each case he had been touring. Instead, they had talked regularly on the telephone. God, how insignificant that precious time that had kept them from seeing each other seemed now! She would never see him again.

She looked back at Angie, whose eyes flickered away. Angie wasn't telling her everything. She knew that much.

The difficulty meeting her gaze, her shifting hands—the woman was afraid of something.

"Joel was my only family," she said, her voice gentler. "We didn't see each other often enough, but we loved each other."

For the first time since hearing the news in New York the day before, she allowed the tears to appear in her eyes. They rolled down her face, all the more poignant in her silence.

"I loved him, too," Angie said, her voice shaking. Somehow it sounded like a protest. She looked into the tear-filled eyes of the beautiful woman opposite her and saw the pain there. And the question.

"I loved him," Angie said again. "But I can't do anything about it. I'm all alone now. I have to think of myself."

"So we both loved him. And we're both alone." The woman reached across the table and grabbed Angie's hand with surprising ferocity. "You have to tell me what happened. I'm owed that. I need to know."

Angie pulled her hand away and looked down, her eyes stinging painfully. How could she tell her that she was responsible for Joel's death? How could she tell her anything?

"Look at me," the woman hissed, anger in her voice now. "Joel is all I had in the world. You'll go off and find yourself another man. Goddamnit! Do you expect me to go and find another brother? Another family?"

It was true, Angie thought passively. She would find another man. She'd have to. She had always been with a man of one kind or another. It was her staff, her survival.

"Tell me," his sister ordered, the dim light of the bar glinting in the tears on her face.

Angie was confused. The empathy she felt for this grieving sister, the insistence, were both compelling. What harm would it do to tell her? She was just a woman from New York. She couldn't do anything about *him,* anyway. Perhaps it would give her some peace to know the truth. But, God, it was dangerous. If he somehow found out that she had talked to anyone . . . God, maybe this woman wasn't even Joel's sister—in spite of the physical similarities, the apparent grief. She could have been sent by him to find out how much talking she would do.

"Tell me."

Angie looked at the mouth, now firm with determination, the unflinching green eyes. "How do I know you're even Joel's sister? I don't know who the hell you are. You could be anyone. Why should I trust you with my life?"

The woman looked thoughtfully at her and paused before speaking. "Joel had a scar on the right side of his stomach from having his appendix removed at the age of six," she said. "He had another scar on his right knee from falling out of a tree when he was twelve. He also broke his leg then. He had a Fender bass guitar that he named Angelique. And he met you about a year ago, in a club called the Lamplighter, where he was playing."

"He told you that?"

"Sure. We talked very frequently on the telephone. He mentioned his girlfriends. The one before you was named Franchesca."

"If I tell you anything . . . Why should I trust you?"

"Because I don't want to hurt you. All I want to know is who did this to Joel. I loved him and you were his friend. Why should I betray you?"

"Yes," Angie said uncertainly.

"Listen, do you believe I'm Joel's sister?"

"Yes," Angie said, meeting her eyes. "Nobody else could know all that stuff about him."

"Well, I swear to you on his grave, on his death, on his life, that whatever you tell me, no one will ever know you did. Never! And if you ever need help, I'll help you."

Angie nodded, convinced. She had sworn on his grave, endowing her word with sanctity, and there was no doubt she loved her brother. "Joel was killed and I know who was responsible," Angie said, letting the words fall out, shocked at the sense of relief they brought.

The woman didn't seem surprised. All she said was, "Yes?"

"I was the mistress of . . . a man. Very wealthy. A big deal in this town. He gave me everything. But I fell in love with Joel and I'd been seeing him. The guy found out. He sent a couple of people to see Joel to scare him off. I know, because this man told me about it just before he kicked me out of my apartment."

"They did more than scare him off."

"Yes. My ex-lover came back to my apartment an hour later, when I was packing, and said the men had overreacted. They were just supposed to break Joel's hands and beat him up." She stopped and sobbed, her face painfully twisted. "They—they were overzealous, he said. But that it didn't matter anyhow. He said that Joel was a nobody, and who would care, anyway. He said that if I ever told anyone this, I'd end up like Joel."

"Did you tell the police?" the woman asked, her face frozen.

"Didn't you hear me?" Angie said, wiping her eyes. "Do you think I want to end up dead? What's done is done. It's my word against his. Do you think the police would believe me? He is one of the most powerful people in town, in the country, for Christ's sake!"

"So you're just going to forget it ever happened," she said disdainfully.

"I want to live," Angie protested fiercely, leaning closer to the woman. "Don't you?"

"What's the man's name?"

Angie fell back in her chair and shook her head resignedly.

"I can find out, Angie. You've told me enough. Why don't you make it easy for me?"

The woman was calm now, her face unreadable except for the resolve that filled it. Angie felt as helpless as a fish being drawn to shore. She could fight, but the hook was deep in her, and sooner or later she'd end up on the sand. It was preordained, unavoidable.

"What are you going to do?" Angie asked faintly.

"I'm going to get something that's very rare in this world—justice," the woman said.

"What can you do? What can anyone do?" Angie said, bitterly. "You're like me—nothing. He's, he's . . . Geez!" It was ridiculous even to think about it.

"I'll get my justice," the woman said, certainty strengthening her voice. "Now tell me the name."

For a moment, Angie believed her, but then the fear and helplessness filled her again. She couldn't, not with her own life at risk. The hell with justice.

She stood up suddenly, bumping the table and spilling some of her drink. "No," she said. "No name. I've told you too much already. I can't tell you anymore. I'm sorry, but I can't." She turned and half ran from the room.

The woman didn't follow her. It wouldn't do any good at this stage. Obviously, she had learned all she would from Angie for now. She sat alone at the table and took another sip of her drink. It would take time, but she would do what had to be done. The pain in her eyes was replaced by resolve, a light that filled her face.

CHAPTER ONE

June, 1987

Beverly Hills

"Jasmine! For Christ's sake, hurry up! We'll be late."

Allan Silver drained the drink she had poured for him, putting the glass down heavily on the black lacquer coffee table. Jasmine didn't bother answering him, just continuing to hum some tuneless popular song to herself in the bathroom.

He looked at his Rolex again, admiring for a brief second

the way his tanned skin glowed against the gold strap. He'd paid for that tan, just as he paid to keep his stomach flat. About five feet ten inches tall and in his mid-forties, he tended to put on weight easily. Twice a week, his personal trainer came to his office at Elixer Studios and worked him till he begged for mercy. Another day a week at the tanning salon, two mornings of racquetball, and he looked like a man half his age. It was well worth it. Appearances were important, particularly in business.

And then there was Jasmine. She helped keep him young, with her wild beauty and unpredictable behavior. He paid for that as well, of course. Jasmine's apartment, the car, the clothes, the jewelry—all came out of his pocket. Luckily, as president of one of the hottest movie studios in town, he had deep pockets. Deep enough to keep both wife and mistress in the manner to which they had grown accustomed. It was the price—and the perk—of success.

Jasmine's apartment was as eclectic in appearance as she was in character, Allan thought, looking around. Antique Chinese screens clashed with pop posters, colorful Kashmiri throw rugs were offset by glass and chrome tables. Fashion magazines were strewn over one of the coffee tables and on the floor. Records sat on top of the already-filled cabinet. A sweater hung over the back of a chair. When they first met, it had bothered him that the apartment was never tidy. But after prompting her a few times to straighten it out, he had given up. It was part of her charm, he told himself.

So was her lateness, but this was too much. He glanced impatiently at his watch again. "Jasmine!"

Jasmine looked critically at her olive-skinned face in the mirror and rubbed her full lips together, smoothing the lipstick. She winked at herself. She'd kept him waiting long enough.

She swept out of the bathroom, smiling radiantly. "I'm ready, darling!" She twirled once, totally aware of the effect she created.

He couldn't help but grin. She never just got dressed; she put on a show.

She was twenty-four and Chinese-American, with a slight slant to the eyes, the long strong legs of a dancer, and the smallish bust of her Oriental heritage. She was tall, almost his height, and that came from the American side, he guessed. As always, she wore silk. Dresses, suits, underwear, nightgowns, even the sheets on her bed—silk. A bow to her Oriental legacy.

This time she wore red and black. Black blouse, a flowing red skirt, and a red jacket with padded shoulders. A small red silk flower highlighted her long black hair. A silver and turquoise bracelet circled her left wrist.

"You look beautiful," he admitted grudgingly. He rose and faced her, suddenly aware how plain he must seem in his black tux beside this bird of paradise. "But if we don't leave now, we'll be late."

Jasmine came and stood inches away from him, a playful pout on her lips. "So?" she said. She swayed forward, not quite touching him, but close enough for him to smell the Opium perfume and feel the warmth radiating from her body.

"We can't be late," he said.

She lazily touched his groin with her slim hand. "All work and no play could make you a dull boy."

He was tempted. God, she could turn him on. A smell, a touch, a taste, and he was like a slave to her sexuality. "I—" he said, and then couldn't think of what he had been about to say.

She moved her hand in small circles and smiled, watching his reaction. A small hiss escaped his lips and he lurched toward her. She put her hand against his chest, the smile disappearing, her mood suddenly changing. "Come on," she said, taking his arm. "We'd better hurry."

He shook his head and walked to the door. She was a most exasperating and complex woman.

Jasmine smiled to herself as she walked out ahead of him. Allan needed a touch of unpredictability to keep him on his toes. And she knew exactly how to do it. The key was never to let him forget she was a woman, a desirable woman, and never to let him take her for granted.

Downstairs, the driver touched his cap and opened the door of the limousine.

"Thank you, Doug," she said, sliding into the seat.

She leaned back a moment, enjoying the feel of leather against her shoulders and the soft, cushiony comfort beneath her. The car began to glide forward.

"Champagne or coke?" Allan asked.

"Champagne!" she said, throwing her head back.

There was the clink of glass, a soft plop, and then the hiss of bubbles.

He handed her the glass and then touched his to hers. "To us," he said.

She sipped it slowly, allowing the splendid bubbles to tickle the back of her throat. Allan sighed and stretched his legs out.

"A hard day?" she asked solicitously.

"Mmm. A bitch," he said.

She took another luxurious sip of champagne. Outside the lights glittered, cars sped to their destinations, people stood in lines by movie theaters. She could see it all, but none of them could look in through the tinted windows. It gave her a sense of power, and of pride. They were on their way to a political fundraiser for some young Democratic hopeful who was smart enough to woo the Beverly Hills business and film community. Like everything else, in politics you went where the money was. She'd learned a lot about the power of money since she had been in LA.

She had come a long way for the daughter of a San Francisco produce merchant. She'd arrived in Los Angeles immediately after graduating from high school. There was nothing for her back home. There never really had been. Even though her mother's father had been a California miner of German descent, her parents were more Chinese than American and still believed in the old ways: the law of the patriarchal family, the smell of incense and the mumbling pleas to placate countless gods and spirits. If she stayed, she would have followed in their footsteps, with long hours of hard work for her father and, ultimately, some marriage to an approved husband who would have made her work just as hard. She wasn't made for work. She was made for a life like this.

She had always been different. Her friends were mainly American, not Chinese, and she had always rebelled against the accepted way of doing things—whether Chinese or American. She tended to act without thought of consequences, the sure road to ruin according to her teachers, guidance counselors, and disapproving relatives. But their opinions had never influenced her. She firmly believed that people were here to act, not to think and deliberate while the world passed them by.

When she came to Los Angeles, she dropped her last name of Yang. From now on she would be Jasmine, a symbol of her new life, a mysterious and beautiful woman with no last name and no history, free to create whatever future she wished.

Compared to some girls in Hollywood, she'd been lucky. There was no shortage of beautiful, willing, talented women here, but she'd landed an agent, Ted Shield, gotten a few small roles in television movies, met the right people, and finally met Allan, who took her under his wing. After that, she had stayed in casual contact with Ted because every now and then Allan would arrange a part for her in a feature film. Nothing too demanding, but at least she worked. In the meantime, he totally supported her. What's more, she thought, he loved her in his way. If it weren't for his wife, Elena, lurking in the background like a vulture, ready to strip him to the bone if he screwed up, he would have married her by now.

Sometimes, she wasn't too sure if she would marry him, even if she had the chance. He was handsome, wealthy, and successful, but there were times when it didn't seem quite enough. While he amused her, even impressing her with his wealth and influence and business acumen, somehow he didn't thrill her to the core of her being—which was how she always imagined *the* love affair of her life would be. Not being an introspective person, however, Jasmine didn't think about it too much. It was a hypothetical situation, not a real choice to be faced. The present arrangement had its advantages. He was good to her. All she had to do in return was love him—and be available when he needed her. She was grateful for the independence it provided her, financially, at least.

She put her glass down on the bar and then, sliding toward him on the long seat, reached her hand out and touched his leg.

"What?" he said, woken from some thought.

Deftly, she unzipped his pants and slid her hand inside. "I want this," she said, making her way through the folds of his underpants and grasping his penis.

"Jasmine!" he said. "We'll be there in fifteen minutes!"

She took the glass from his hand and put it down. Then she grabbed his hand and put it on her knee, from which her skirt had conveniently risen.

"And you want this," she said, ignoring his objection. She pushed his hand up her sleek thigh and heard him gasp as it met her silky pubic hair.

"You're not wearing panties," he said weakly.

"They just get in the way," she said.

"You're not wearing panties," he said again. He looked away and rolled his eyes. "We're going to the Bel-Air Hotel and she's not wearing panties."

Jasmine ran her fingers over his now-exposed penis, which began to react predictably. He looked at the driver, but of course Doug could see nothing through the glass barrier, shaded except for a rearview mirror space. Besides, he'd been trained to ignore everything that went on behind him in the limo.

She bent forward, her long hair falling over his lap, and ran her tongue along his growing hardness. "Mmm," she said, "I missed this today."

"God, Jasmine!" he said, torn between desire and caution.

She laughed and took it deep in her mouth, wetting the entire shaft and then withdrawing three-quarters of the way. She sucked the tip so hard he felt like it would fly off. "God, Jasmine!" he said, running his hands through her hair.

She suddenly withdrew and sat up. "No!" she said.

"What?" he asked, confused.

Her lips were wet with his spillage. She licked them and smiled widely. "I want more," she said.

And then she swung one leg lithely over his and pivoted so that she was crouching over his lap, facing him, her mouth on his, her tongue thrusting into his mouth.

He reacted instinctively, his hips rising, and as he did so, she lowered her body and he slid up through her warm, flowing juices until he was encased in her, gripped in a rhythmic motion as she rose and fell, her hands gripping his shoulders, her head thrown wantonly back, a laugh caught in the long lines of her neck.

It was madness, delicious madness. He glanced sideways out the window and then back at her, his testicles tightening, the heat growing in both of them. She was panting now, her face distorted, her eyes unseeing.

"We're almost there," he said, suddenly panicked.

"We're almost there," she said, chanting it. "We're almost there. We're almost there. We're almost there!"

And then she screamed, "We're there!" And he felt the clutching spasms create an unbearable friction, spurting out in almost painful pleasure.

The limousine coasted to a halt in front of the hotel.

"We're there," she said, falling against him.

Kate Buchanan sat in the rear seat of the taxi from the airport, looking dubiously at what was about to become her new home. In the distance, lights stretched in an unbroken carpet to the Hollywood Hills before scattering into a border of blackness. She counted three stars in the sky; the rest had been doused by the reflections of the city and the impurities that clogged the air. Tall palm trees stood like sentinels on either side of the road. Reaching upward for seventy-five or eighty years, they had withstood the elements and the derision of visitors and natives alike, becoming with time as much a part of the city as the hills, the ocean, and the hundreds of miles of freeways that connected it all.

Los Angeles was very different from the concentrated hustle and bustle of Manhattan. But in spite of her trepidation, she had plunged ahead. In the past six months, according to plan, she had given up her apartment in Soho, her job at the Dotson Gallery, and all her belongings, except for a few art objects she had put in storage. She was arriving with the clothes on her body, two suitcases, and about four thousand dollars she had managed to save. Luckily, through a contact at the gallery, she had a furnished apartment waiting for her in West Hollywood, which would be available to sublet for six months at a fairly nominal rent—nominal by New York standards.

The cab took La Cienega Boulevard toward the hills. Traditionally known as gallery row, it was close to the Beverly Hills and Hollywood money. Some of the names she recognized from earlier trips, some were new. She'd been out West a couple of times before on buying trips and knew that, in spite of the ornate lettering on the galleries, it was not really the center of the art scene in Los Angeles anymore. New areas had come up in Venice and Santa Monica and West Hollywood and even in downtown Los Angeles, where artists rented cheap warehouses to live and work. It was an ever-changing arena.

The cabbie stopped in front of the address she had given him. It was a small, quiet street a few blocks from Melrose Avenue, with two-story stucco apartment buildings, many of them houses that had been made into fourplexes.

Quickly, he opened her door and carried the suitcases up to the front porch for her. He wondered if the attractive auburn-haired woman was yet another movie hopeful. She sure was pretty enough.

After paying the driver, she took the keys from the envelope in her bag. One for the front door, the other for the apartment, number four, upstairs.

There was a slightly musty smell inside, but the walls were clean, the once-expensive carpets were still in good condition, and the stairs were made of glowing red wood.

It looked well cared for and comfortable, which is what she had been told.

The suitcases grew heavier with each step, but finally she stood outside the door, a thin sheen of perspiration on her forehead and her breath short. She opened the door and stepped in, dragging her suitcases behind her, fumbling for the light switch and clicking it on.

The apartment was enormous compared to her place in New York, which had cost three times as much. There was a large living room, furnished in comfortable modern furniture, a spacious kitchen with a butcher block in its center, a breakfast nook off to the side, a bedroom with a double bed and two wooden dressers, and a bathroom with a tub and a separate shower stall. The telephone was connected and the refrigerator was stocked with a few basic necessities, including a bottle of California wine.

After looking around quickly, she poured herself a glass of wine, fell into a billowy cotton-covered armchair in the living room, and took her shoes off. She stretched her toes and feet and sighed. The five-hour airplane trip and three-hour time change had taken its toll. She was tired.

Besides, it hadn't been easy, not any of it. Not quitting her well-paid job, not giving up her home for the last few years, not leaving a secure present for an entirely uncertain future. But once she had made up her mind she hadn't hesitated. She had set a moving date six months ahead and had begun to disassemble her life. It was the least she could do for her brother. She owed him that. Joel would have given up his life for her, if necessary. There was no way she could have carried on, acting as if nothing had happened.

She would simply have to contend with the fact that what she intended to do scared the hell out of her. She likened her situation to someone entering a dark tunnel, only to find the entrance had been blocked. Secure in the knowledge of an opening at the other end, however, one had no choice but to move forward, slowly, cautiously, with much trepidation, but also with faith in the ultimate outcome.

She had attained step one of her plan, and in spite of her

exhaustion, the thought satisfied her. One step at a time. At the end of the road, justice waited.

"Yes, I know it doubled, but the stock will go higher," Page Peters said into the telephone the following afternoon. She listened for a moment, and then added, "I know that pigs lose, but I don't want you to sell GDO until twenty. I also think it's going to go to twenty-five, but I want the sell order at twenty, is that clear?"

When her stockbroker understood her perfectly, she hung up and looked at the papers on the table. She had bought 666 shares of the stock at $7.50, and it was now at $15. When it went to $20, her $4,995 investment would be worth $13,320—minus broker's commissions, of course. Not bad, she thought with a self-satisfied smile that was quickly replaced with a frown that marred her smooth, rounded forehead.

It was still peanuts compared to what she wanted and needed and had worked for. So far, after seven years of scrimping and saving and using her brains, she had a grand total of $247,000 in real estate, $75,000 in stocks, and roughly $50,000 in liquid assets. But the real estate was illiquid, the stocks could go down the toilet in one trading session, and the $50,000 in cash would keep her in food and lodging for about nine months. She needed more money and she needed it faster than it was coming in.

Page's apartment was as organized as she was. The living room, filled with antique turn-of-the-century American furniture, looked as if it had never been touched by human hands. It would be fruitless to try and find a speck of dust. Besides the mantle above the fireplace, which held some small African wood sculptures of excellent quality, and the coasters on the tables, everything else was in glass cabinets. The bedroom, which also doubled as her office, was equally spotless, its design marred only slightly by the small desk and file cabinet in one corner.

Tall, slim, with elegant features and soft brown hair that tumbled gracefully to her shoulders, Page had a particular beauty that automatically bespoke breeding and wealth. Insecure men found it intimidating; self-confident men were drawn to it. In both cases, she had learned to use it for her purposes, the prime one being to look after Page and see that history never repeated itself. She had started life with both breeding and wealth, but the wealth had deserted her before she had had time to enjoy it. If others continued to think of her as wealthy, it was more a result of hard work on her part than reality.

Although just on the wrong side of thirty now, Page had never really recovered from the shock of poverty. The only child of an affluent New York family, she had first known need at the age of fourteen when her father killed himself after his financial improprieties at the banking firm where he worked were discovered. What he did with the money he embezzled was a mystery. He left his family virtually nothing, and her life changed overnight.

Not only was she forced to fend for herself, but she had to shoulder her mother. The widowed Clara was totally unprepared for the real world. Shopping, bridge, and cocktail parties had nothing to do with the disasters now facing her: bankruptcy, eviction, and a bleak future. Page took care of her then and took care of her now. Only a few months earlier, she had brought her out to Los Angeles and placed her in an expensive Westwood Village nursing home, where she visited her at least once a week.

Page learned to despise weakness and incompetence and to hate poverty. Self-taught in the nuances of culture, she made the most of her beauty and strong native intelligence. Untrained and relatively uneducated, she worked as a waitress, secretary, and office manager. Page became a master at the art of making do with nothing. She invested almost every spare penny in her appearance and maintained a few family contacts from better times to enable her to mix with the wealthy.

She swore that one day she, too, would be rich. But she knew she wouldn't do it by working for someone else.

In 1983, at the age of twenty-six, she became the mistress of a well-known Houston businessman. A self-made man who had generated millions in oil and real estate deals, he met her at a New York dinner party. His rough edges included a blowsy, loudmouthed wife, and he fell hard for the elegant Page. When he was due to return to Houston a month later, he asked her to come with him. She put him off for three months, and then joined him.

He provided her with an apartment, a car, clothes, and a generous allowance. In return, she slept with him, but her main duty was to accompany him discreetly to certain meetings and events where he felt the need for a little class. It lasted four years, until his wife discovered where he spent all those afternoons away from the office and went after his balls with a 12-gauge shotgun. Succeeding only in blowing an oak door apart, the woman threatened an extremely expensive and newsworthy divorce. The man was a pragmatic businessman. He gave Page $5,000 and sent her on her way.

Page came to Los Angeles and looked up a man who had cast a longing eye at her, a business associate of her Houston lover. Within a month, she had the same arrangement with him. Things could have continued in the same vein forever, with her totally depending on one man after another, but instead she had met Elsa Bennet. She was still dependent on men, but at least she could see a different future, thanks to Elsa.

Elsa was sixty, as ugly as sin now, and rich. She took a liking to Page and became her informal advisor. Elsa had come to Hollywood from Holland more years ago than she cared to tell, and she had been the mistress of a leading film producer for fifteen years; ten years before that, she had been the mistress of a real estate developer. She was a "professional" mistress, she often stated proudly, and her advice to Page was simple: "You must approach this as a job, and you must learn to leverage your investment."

Under Elsa's tutelage, Page became adept at skimming every penny she could from her lover. She had an arrangement with certain Beverly Hills establishments to charge her twenty percent over the cost of everything she bought—and refund the surcharge to her, in exchange for her patronage. And piece by piece, she sold the gifts of jewelry and replaced them with inexpensive replicas. Finally, she saved and invested as much of her allowance as she could, putting much of her money into real estate and the stock market, under Elsa's knowing guidance.

The rest she had put into her own business venture, the Peters Public Relations Agency. Elsa had invested in the company as well. Even her lover had put some money up. He saw the agency as a way to keep her occupied, a toy for her to play with when he wasn't around. Page saw it as much more, as a way to peddle influence and maintain contact with that elite circle of the wealthy and powerful. Through hard work and intelligence, she had quickly built it up from a two-man operation to a staff of five account executives plus half-a-dozen secretaries. It wasn't making her rich, but it had other benefits.

The affair with her businessman had lasted until fairly recently—six months ago, to be exact—when she met Jason Thomas and became his mistress.

There's rich . . . and then there's *very* rich. The other two men had been rich, but Thomas was very rich. It was a matter of how many zeroes you could put on your millions of net worth. Thomas had zeroes to spare. Where the others had a few millions, he had tens of millions, perhaps even hundreds, for all she knew. He owned half-a-dozen television stations, radio stations, three daily newspapers, and half-a-dozen magazines. In addition to that, he had perfected the art of greenmail, raiding other companies and gaining enough stock to threaten the status quo, which he did until his interests were bought out at an immense profit to him. But it wasn't just the money that attracted her. From the moment they met, she saw him as a man who knew power and how to wield it, and that intrigued her more than anything.

She first saw him at a Malibu cocktail party, a tedious event filled with the self-conscious movie business crowd. She was there with her current lover, and Thomas was with his wife, an attractive yet somehow vapid blonde with a bright, nervous smile.

Jason was tall and lean and devastatingly charming. His

smile had a slightly sardonic edge, his gaze was disturbingly direct, and he spoke emphatically, even when saying nothing of importance, all of which gave him an ability to dominate any discussion he was involved in. He said no more than two dozen social words to her, but it was enough to cause a tingling on the back of her neck. The next day he called her unlisted phone number, that night they had dinner, the next they went to bed, and two days later he provided an apartment for her.

He was generous to her, but even more important was the information she gained. It didn't seem like much, just a word here and there. The solicitous and loving mistress, she would ask him about his day at the office, and occasionally he would drop the name of a company into which he was buying heavily. But that was all she needed. As soon as he left the apartment, she'd make the necessary calls to her stockbroker. She had done it three or four times so far, virtually doubling her money. She had told nobody except Elsa who, as a result, had also done very well for herself.

Jason had been helpful with the agency as well, sending a number of important clients her way. In fact, among the current roster of fourteen clients, eleven had come directly on his recommendation.

Page looked at her watch. She had an appointment with her acupuncturist in forty minutes, and then she had to meet Jason. First, however, she had to rush over to Elsa's and share her latest news. She knew exactly when Jason planned to make his announcement about the GDO stock. Right now it was climbing on takeover rumors, which he had cleverly planted. When the announcement clarifying his intentions was made, it would tumble ten points. By that time, he would have made his profit, but so would she and so would Elsa.

Page, casually dressed in a beige knee-length linen skirt, a pink silk blouse, and comfortable low-heeled shoes, drove her silver Mercedes 250SE into the underground garage of a high-rise apartment building just off Wilshire Boulevard in Beverly Hills. Elsa had the penthouse suite. She had lived there for ten years, ever since she had bought the building.

Elsa's maid, Maria, a thin, self-effacing Spanish woman, opened the door for her.

"How are you, Maria?" Page asked pleasantly.

"God be thanked, I am still alive," Maria said, as she led Page down a small hallway to a living room of enormous size, with a domed ceiling and windows that looked out on the city. The walls were adorned with art deco paintings, highlighted by a few Erte sculptures. Surprisingly, however, the room was dominated by an enormous thirty-six-inch television screen against one wall. All the furniture faced it.

Elsa reclined on a billowy white couch and waved a languid hand at Page, without taking her eyes from the screen. She had a satellite dish on the roof, and when she wasn't making money, she spent her time flicking from one channel to the other, making tapes of movies, on expensive VCR equipment, she would never have the time to see. Television was her weakness; she was a true addict.

Page sat in a comfortable armchair and waited, studying her friend. Elsa had once been beautiful; she had the pictures to prove it. A lissome redhead with long legs and a prominent bust, she had started her career as a calendar girl. The bust was now enormous, as was the rest of her body. Her rounded face ended in folded chins, which became layers of neck and then shoulders, although it was hard to discern where one ended and the other began. And yet, her skin still glowed and her eyes were as bright as they had ever been. She also happened to have one of the most astute financial minds Page had ever known.

"I'll tape it and watch it later," Elsa said, pushing a button on her remote control. After a momentary whir of machinery, the screen went dark and she turned her attention to Page.

"So, my sweet, so nice of you to visit an old woman," she said cunningly.

It was a game they played. Elsa berated her for not visiting often enough, claiming that while she may be member of a boring and obsolescent generation, she still deserved a little attention. And Page would counter with flattery and excuses.

"I wanted to tell you about the GDO stock," Page said brusquely. She didn't have time for Elsa's games right now. "Put your sell order at twenty. We're going to make a killing."

"It won't go higher?" Elsa asked.

"Yes, it will, but take your profit at twenty. It could turn around fast. There are too many hands in the pot."

Elsa nodded and looked appraisingly at Page. "You have come a long way since I first met you," she said, an edge of pride in her voice. "You know that, don't you?"

Page was surprised. "Because of this stock? It's elementary, and very easy when you have inside information. Besides, anything I know, you taught me."

"Every teacher looks forward to the day when the student becomes the teacher," Elsa said.

Page laughed. "That day is still far away, Elsa, my dear. I think you still have a few tricks up your sleeve."

"Perhaps," Elsa said, lapsing into a thoughtful moment of silence. "Would you like a drink?"

"I can only stay a moment longer," Page said.

"I have an interesting property I ran across. It's in Encino," Elsa said. "I should be able to turn it around in three months for a one-hundred-thousand-dollar profit. Are you interested in putting something in?"

"How much?"

"About fifty thousand dollars, I should think."

"Not now. Perhaps in a few months," Page said.

"That will be too late."

Page suppressed annoyance, not at Elsa, but at her own inability to act. "Then I will just have to wait for the next opportunity."

"There will be more," Elsa agreed.

Page rose. "I just wanted to say hello and tell you about the stock. I really have to go now."

"And when will you visit this old woman again?" Elsa asked.

"Soon. I promise," Page said with a bright smile. She

came over to Elsa and kissed her on the cheek. "My master calls."

"Are things going well with you and Jason?" Elsa asked, reluctant to end the conversation.

"Yes, fine. He's just been very busy with this GDO deal. But he's going to make out like a bandit. I'm meeting him in a little while."

"Treat him well," Elsa reminded her. "For now, he's your bread and butter."

"For now," Page said.

As she drove, her conversation with Elsa was still in her mind. She regretted missing out on Elsa's latest deal. Having to accept crusts when all around her people had entire loaves of bread to waste was difficult. She had to do something spectacular to get ahead of the game. She was in too vulnerable a position, depending upon the largesse of others. Jason had been a wonderful help in the expansion of her public relations agency, by sending high-caliber, high-ticket clients her way. But they were clients whom *he* had power over, not her. If ever things soured between them, he could just as easily see that they left. She had to find a way to one day become financially independent. And that meant depending on nobody.

She swung into the parking lot of the acupuncture office. The treatment was for both stress and cosmetics, and would take thirty-five minutes. She would still have time to get home and change before Jason arrived to take her to Allan Silver's party. In the meantime, while she lay on the table like a prostrate pincushion, she would have time to think more about her financial problems.

Selena Carter was bored. Past experience had shown this to be a dangerous condition, but Selena never acknowledged the past—or experience. "The only way to live is in the present," she often said, which justified her behaving as outrageously as she wished, when she wished.

David had not called, nor had he returned her calls, in spite of the fact that they were supposed to go out that evening to a screening. His bitchy secretary had simply said he was "in meetings."

At three o'clock, her patience exhausted by the prospects of an evening alone, Selena made a final call to his office. "You hairy-legged cunt," she said to the secretary, "you tell him to call me and call me soon." The woman hung up.

They had been going out for a year. David Ross was president of an investment banking firm and married, which didn't bother her. He was attractive and considered a catch. Besides, she was rich and didn't care what anyone thought. Unlike her friend Jasmine, she was not financially dependent on anyone. She hadn't known wealth until relatively late in her twenty-five years of life, but she had grown used to it. She had no reason to be Ross's mistress other than because she wanted to. The very fact that their relationship was illicit was what had first attracted her. The ordinary and mundane were not to her liking. She was in it strictly for the kicks. That was how she lived her life, how she liked it.

David's only fault was his inordinate need for discretion. They could never go to any event where there would be photographers, nor could he take her places he was obliged to take his wife. He had an "A" list and a "B" list of restaurants and clubs—one for the wife, one for the girlfriend. Except for nights like this, it didn't normally bother her. But nights like this had begun to bug her more and more lately.

She looked across the room at the telephone, but it remained obstinately silent.

"Fuck," she said, taking a last toot of coke from the silver box on her mantle.

There was a small rush, but it didn't seem to help her mood. She looked around the apartment. With two bedrooms, a living room, and a dining room, it was large and comfortable. Art posters from various museum exhibitions and modern Italian furniture created a bright, casual effect. Half-empty glasses of liquor dotted the living room and clothes were scattered in every room. It was a mess. Right now, the apartment felt confining, giving her a surge of panic. Fuck David, she'd go out herself.

She called Jasmine. Out of all the women in their crowd, she was the only one Selena could stand. Jasmine wasn't as wild as she was, but at least she had a sense of adventure. Maybe they could go out and cruise a few bars, she thought as the phone rang. But there was no answer, just the stupid machine. She slammed the phone down, leaving no message.

She sat at a loss for a moment, her thoughts turning inward. She hated thinking about herself, hated remembering who she had been. But sometimes, like now, she couldn't help it. Selena vividly remembered the flight from Denver.

The sky was clear and most of the time she stared out of the window, trying to imagine what her life would be like from now on.

The nice talkative businessman sitting beside her had a daughter her age, he said. Concerned, he warned her about the perils of Los Angeles, particularly for a girl as young, attractive, and alone as she was. Then he rubbed his knee heavily against her thigh. She ignored him and concentrated on watching a thousand miles of America flow like an ocean beneath them.

A beautiful girl of nineteen, tall with a wide mouth, quick to smile, and eyes the soft brown of a spaniel's, she was used to the attentions of men, older and younger, men she'd never thought would make a pass at her but who somehow always did. She didn't invite their interest. It was just that she was "so damn beautiful," as her mother used to say, usually with a sigh of regret, as if looks were a curse that the both of them would have to bear.

Her mother had been dead for six months. Her father had left five years earlier and was somewhere in Texas, working on the rigs. He hadn't been back in touch since sending a check once, three months after his leaving. There were no other children, no relatives. It was easy for her to leave Denver, her dead-end secretarial job, and her dead-end boyfriend Rory, with his pickup truck and mangy dog and baseball cap that said Smith Motors on the front.

She'd been going with Rory since high school. He loved her and wanted to marry her, he said. She slept with him and took to the sex part of it like a bird to air, but the thought of marriage clutched her chest with a premonition she couldn't explain. She had the same feeling in nightmares where she tried to walk forward and yet, step after slow and pained step, she stayed in the same place. Life with Rory would be just like that.

Not that she didn't like him. Hell, he treated her okay most of the time and made her laugh when he wanted to. But all he could talk about was fishing and hunting and football, and when he was drunk, which was every Saturday night without fail, he would say the stupidest things and get into fights over nothing that mattered, embarrassing her in front of everybody, and she simply saw no point to it.

She wasn't any saint herself. She had a smart mouth, and every now and then she felt things build inside her until she threatened to break and she did something that totally shocked Rory and their friends, like strip at a party in front of everyone. But she knew, thinking of the smooth rich people in the office building where she worked, that things could be different—*should* be different for her. She didn't think of herself as particularly smart. She enjoyed movies and read books and even went to a few plays, things that none of Rory's friends did, but she knew that wasn't any big deal. She just wanted better.

She had left Denver without saying good-bye to Rory. She had placed a note on the table in his apartment saying she was leaving town and that she was sorry things hadn't worked out. She took a last look at him on the bed. He was snoring, his mouth opening and closing like a fish, sleeping off the beer from the night before, his forehead clammy with it. She knew then she wouldn't miss him. She went back to the apartment she shared with Maggie from her office and packed one suitcase of essentials. And then she went to the airport and caught the Western Airlines flight to Los Angeles.

Even after the 747 landed and she sat on the airport bus, gazing at the tall, thin palm trees and more traffic than she had ever seen in her life, she still didn't know why she had picked LA, except for the fact that she knew it would be different. About as different from Colorado, she imagined, as anything could be.

And then she arrived in Hollywood and, clutching her suitcase, went to Grauman's Chinese Theater where she mingled with the tourists, enjoying their excited chatter and watching them place their palms reverently against the concrete prints of the famous. It was wonderful. All of it.

After two hours of aimless wandering, she realized it was already four in the afternoon and that she would have to find a place to stay. She'd saved three hundred dollars, but for all she knew it would have to last her a long time, so she would have to be careful of what she spent. She had no idea where to start looking, so she bought a *Los Angeles Times* and went into a coffee shop, a tacky remnant of earlier days. Rickety plastic partitions separated booths with red cracked vinyl seats. But it seemed warm and friendly and touched with the same mad excitement of the boulevard outside.

"Coffee?" the waitress asked, placing a menu in front of her.

She was hungry. She hadn't eaten breakfast and the meal on the plane had been little more than a snack. She ordered a cheese omelette and attacked the newspaper while she waited.

Rooms were much more expensive than she had expected. Apartments were impossible. Four hundred dollars for a single! She should have saved more money before leaving, she thought, feeling a twinge of fear.

"Where'd you come in from?" the waitress asked, looking down at her suitcase. She was an elderly woman, lined face, overweight, but with shrewd eyes.

"Denver," Selena said.

"Looking for a place, hey?"

"Yes, but I had no idea they'd be so expensive," she said.

"This is LA honey," the waitress said, not unkindly, and moved away.

She turned to the employment section. Wages for secretaries and receptionists were a little higher than back home and that was some consolation. She couldn't waste any time before looking for a job though. At this rate, her money would run out in a couple of weeks.

The waitress was back. "You interested in sharing a room?" she asked. "One of the girls just lost a roommate. If you like, I'll talk to her."

In a few minutes another waitress came to the table and slid into the seat opposite Selena. She had a sharp thin face and black eyes. Bright red lipstick made her mouth look bigger than it was, but she was not unattractive. She looked about twenty-two.

Her name was Sara, and Selena moved in with her—for a month. She got a secretarial job with an insurance broker, and when he offered an arrangement—an apartment, a bonus now and then, in return for sexual availability—she took it.

Over the next year there were two more men. Both supported her, but barely. They were not particularly wealthy or generous. And then there was the surprise in the form of a telephone call from a Mr. Duncan.

"I've been trying to find you for months. Finally had to hire a detective," he said in a heavy Texan accent. "I'm a lawyer."

"So?" she said. She'd learned to distrust most men, particularly lawyers.

"I'm afraid I have some good news and some bad news," he said. "Your father is dead."

"So, is that the good news?" she asked, feeling nothing. The man had deserted her. He was a stranger.

The lawyer choked. "No, that's the bad news. The good news is that your father was George Carter."

"Yeah? Thanks for the hot flash," she said sarcastically.

"I understand you've been out of touch for a few years," the lawyer said patiently.

"The bastard deserted us," she said.

"Well, George Carter came here to Texas, honey. He worked on the rigs for a while and then he started leasing oil wells. In four years he became a very wealthy man here in Houston."

"My dad?"

"Yep. And he left it all to you."

She took the phone from her ear and looked at it. Then she looked around her small bed-sitter, with the tattered secondhand furniture and the prints with their edges curling on the walls.

She jerked the phone back to hear Mr. Duncan ask if she was still there. "How much?" she asked.

George Carter had left her about three million dollars—after taxes and attorney's fees.

Within two months she had dumped her lover and moved to Beverly Hills and an entirely new social life. She had never had a father to speak of, but she had his money. She was rich, and she soon learned not to give a shit about anyone. . . .

The doorbell interrupted her thoughts. "Jasmine!" she said, opening it, her morose-edged mood deserting her. "I just tried to call you."

"I thought I'd take a chance and drop by for a few minutes. I was shopping at I. Magnin."

They walked into the living room and sat. Selena immediately launched into an energetic recounting of her latest sexual encounter, describing the whole event in explicit detail.

She giggled and concluded, "His dick was hard from the moment I met him to the moment I left him. It was hard when we were first dancing, and it was hard after we fucked. I'm talking hunk here. You should have seen him."

Jasmine rolled her eyes. "God, you take chances. What if David had shown up?"

"David was otherwise occupied," Selena said derisively. "I'm not going to sit around and wait for him."

As usual when together, they discussed men, money, and parties, in order of importance. They had met two years earlier and struck up an immediate friendship that became an erratic relationship, due mainly to Selena's undependable nature. Sometimes she would see Jasmine almost daily, but then there were times when weeks would go by with Selena nowhere to be found.

Selena lolled on the couch, wearing only shorts and a skimpy T-shirt cut off just below her breasts. Jasmine in tight blue jeans and blouse looked formal in comparison.

Selena returned with vigor to her subject. "The guy's dick was this long!" she said, holding her hands apart.

Jasmine laughed. She couldn't help but enjoy Selena's company. While she zestfully enjoyed her own sexual escapades, she still felt restrained compared to the wild abandon with which Selena entered and left relationships. She also admired her independence, which was something Jasmine did not possess. Selena had money. She was with David because she wanted to be. Yes, David was married, but she was his girlfriend, not really his mistress according to strict definition. She took virtually nothing from him.

"You want a joint?" Selena asked, rolling over so her feet touched the floor. She rolled back in almost the same motion and said, "Shit! I forgot. I'm out. Ronnie is coming over soon with some more stuff."

"I've got to go," Jasmine said. "You're coming to the party tonight?"

Selena knew Allan Silver's wife was still away and that he had invited a few of his close friends to his house, ostensibly to view some X-rated outtakes featuring a well-known female star who was stoned out of her mind at the time of filming. David had told her that the star also happened to have the hots for the leading man and had needed little encouragement to demonstrate her ardor before the camera after most of the crew had left the set.

"I thought so. David mentioned it a few days ago, but I haven't been able to get the bastard on the phone today."

"I'm sure he'll call, so I'll probably see you there," Jasmine said, rising.

Selena waved her hand while her friend let herself out. In spite of her energetic recounting of her adventures, she felt inexplicably down. Yeah, Greg, the guy she had met at Trumps had a big dick, but he hadn't known how to use it and it had been like fucking a machine.

She turned her face into the pillow and closed her eyes. She sometimes thought she was turning into a machine herself—a rich machine, but a machine nevertheless. Hardly anything gave her real pleasure anymore. It was like getting stoned: The first time was always the best. From that point on, you kept taking more and more to try and get the same high. And you never did.

"Cheat!" she said aloud. Life was the Big Cheat. It promised and never delivered. She had always thought that wealth would end all her problems and anxieties; in reality it seemed only to intensify them. There were times like this, when she was alone in her apartment, that she felt as if she were momentarily resting in the eye of a storm. Beyond her small protective cocoon, the elements were raging against her.

She hated these thoughts. Where the fuck was Ronnie when she needed him?

CHAPTER TWO

Jason Thomas pressed the buzzer on his desk. Within moments his secretary, Janice, entered his office, carrying a stenographer's notepad.

"I want you to take a couple of letters and then get Gordon in here, please," he said.

A trim woman in her fifties, her hair tied in a severe bun, she nodded and sat opposite him. She had been with him for seven years and knew him as well as anyone—certainly better than his wife, to whom he had been married for twenty. She was his protector and, in effect, his memory, but she still called him Mr. Thomas and treated him with diligent formality.

He looked out the window of the Century City office and composed his thoughts. A fog was rolling in from Santa Monica, obliterating what would have been a spectacular sunset.

"All right," he began, and dictated the two short letters.

When she rose to go, he said, "I'm leaving in half an hour. I'd like those for my signature by then, please."

"Yes, sir. I'll get Mr. Chesterman up here now."

A minute later the phone on his desk buzzed quietly. "Send him in," he said, after picking up the receiver.

A short, corpulent man walked hurriedly into the office and sat opposite him without waiting for an invitation. Chesterman was vice-president of business affairs for Jason's daily newspaper group. It was a hot seat, but he had held it for three years, longer than any of his predecessors.

"Tampa is giving us a problem," Jason said, without greeting him. "Ad revenues are down for the second month in a row. What the hell is going on there?"

"The ad manager says it's editorial, and editorial says it's advertising sales," Chesterman said.

"Well, get someone the hell down there. I don't care who's blaming who. I need to know what's happening."

"I sent Foster yesterday. I'll get a preliminary report from him by the end of the day."

"Good," Jason said, relaxing in his chair, a pleasant smile coming to his lips. "Whoever is screwing up I want out of there immediately, okay? I don't buy newspapers to lose money."

"It shall be done," Chesterman said. "Anything else?"

"No, that's it." His smile melted away. "Don't let these things drag on this long in the future. You should have spotted a problem source weeks ago."

"Yes, sir," Chesterman said. He'd learned not to argue or justify with Jason Thomas. Excuses didn't wash with his boss. The man expected miracles and it was Gordon's job to perform them. He got paid well to do it. If he didn't, he'd get fired, just like anyone else in the company.

"Anything else?" Jason asked.

"No, sir. Nothing pressing."

He rose and left the room. Jason glanced at his watch. He hadn't seen Page for a couple of days, and he was looking forward to it. She had a way of helping him relax, a geishalike quality to her, that left his mind and body calmed.

He signed the letters Janice brought him and told her he was leaving. She knew better than to ask where he was going. She knew, of course, that he had a mistress—she personally took care of the bills—but she was under stern instructions never to divulge Page's phone number or ever call him there. Her number appeared on the telephone bills, but nowhere else. Instead, he wore a beeper in case any emergencies came up.

He took Olympic Boulevard into Beverly Hills, enjoying the comfort of his Rolls Royce Silver Cloud and the envious stares of other drivers. He found driving a pleasure, except during rush hour. Although he employed a full-time chauffeur, most of the time his wife, Sharon, used the driver. In fact, she both hired and fired the chauffeurs. They had gone through an inordinate number in the last few years. The latest, a blond young man named Adam, had to be performing well, he thought sardonically. She had kept him for six months now.

The fact she was having yet another affair didn't bother him. He hadn't touched her for two years. She had to know he had other interests, just as he knew of hers. All that mattered was that she keep them discreet. In this town, little more than a village really, discretion was important.

Sharon had loved him once, as he had wanted her to, but it had always been just a marriage of convenience for him—a business marriage, which gave him ownership of his first newspaper, one that had been in her family for three generations. She was pretty when he had first met her. Not beautiful, to be sure, but pretty in that bland cheerleader way. All long legs and blond hair, naive in all matters nonsexual, and with a frantic desire to please. Not much going on upstairs, but since then, she had gotten smarter. But she had also gained lines of dissatisfaction around her mouth, and cellulite and sagging breasts, problems which innumerable beauty salons and health treatment centers had addressed to the eternal benefit of their profit margins. In her search for happiness, she had also, at one time or another, been a devotee of Rosicrucianism, Nicheren Soshu, Transcendental Meditation, and EST. He didn't care. He hadn't married her for her brains or her beauty, just her newspaper.

Since then, he hadn't looked back and she couldn't complain. Although he had used her, he had parlayed their money into millions. She had access to wealth her family had never even dreamed of. The fact that it didn't seem to make her happy wasn't his problem. If she wanted enlightenment and eternal peace of mind and body, she would have to find it elsewhere. It wasn't what he provided. He might not be one of the most sensitive men around, but he was certainly one of the most notable.

And he was notable. His media holdings gave him an exposure he couldn't buy. At first, he had used the newspapers and magazines to promote himself, but then he realized that the media game in general was like a school of frenzied fish: They fed on themselves. The newsgatherers became the newsmakers. Media magnates and media hirelings were just as susceptible as anyone else to the cult of celebrity. And an unspoken, seldom considered agreement had permeated the business: They were not only stars but starmakers, and deserved just as much coverage as anyone else. He had to do nothing except demonstrate his power by wielding it. Now he was as well known in important circles as some movie stars. Soon, if all went as planned, he would be even better known.

He reached Page's condominium in Westwood. Jason had paid for the extra parking space, and he drove through the security gates unhindered. Two minutes later she opened the door, discreetly closed it when he entered, and then kissed him, her breath smelling of mint and persimmon.

She went to the bar in the living room without consulting him, pouring a Scotch on the rocks with a twist of lemon while he sat in the Ames chair and stretched his legs.

She gave him his drink and then sat in the chair opposite him, a glass of white wine in her hand. They sipped their drinks in silence.

"Aah," he said, when half the drink was gone.

"How was your day?" she asked solicitously.

She wore a cream-colored satin gown that fell in tantalizing folds over her body, hinting at swells and hollows. The expression on her face was serene and untroubled.

"Fine," he said. "The usual business problems, but everything is going as planned."

He wasn't talking about the GDO stock, she knew. That was just doing business as usual. The most important thing to him at the moment was the new Thomas Wing of the Rex Museum. He had contributed most of the money for the new building and raised the rest from business associates. It would immortalize his name for generations to come, he had told her more than once.

He was a handsome man, she thought abstractedly. The aquiline nose, firm mouth, tanned skin, and lean, casual body combined to make him look more like an actor than a businessman.

"You need some attention," she said, unwinding herself gracefully from the chair and moving behind him.

She began to rub his neck, kneading the taut balls of muscle that were always there at the end of the day, rolling them in her strong fingers until they dissolved in groans of pleasure and appreciation.

"Enough," he said finally, reaching back to clasp her hand. He swung her around and led her to the bedroom.

He made love to her with his usual cool expertise. She had given up wondering how a man so handsome could be so lacking in passion. His lovemaking was mechanical, all technique and no substance. He said the right words, but the warmth that crinkled his eyes so attractively was all facade; behind it was an almost inhuman observer. There was no doubt he enjoyed sex with her on some level, for it left him relaxed and contented, but sometimes she thought he would have attained the same result on a racquetball court. Sex was just another form of exercise. At first it had bothered her, but over time she had grown to accept it for what it was—nothing to do with her.

When they finished, he lay with his hands behind his head and silently stared up at the ceiling. She rested her hand on his chest, enjoying the warmth. They never talked much. She suspected that was one of the things he appreciated about her. She never demanded anything, including conversation.

"We have to go soon," she reminded him. They had been invited to a private screening of some film or another at Allan Silver's home. Silver's wife Elena had just left for Europe so, for once, the men could bring their mistresses.

They showered and dressed, each having another drink. She knew from experience that Jason would have one more drink that evening and then stop. He kept himself to three Scotches, no matter what the situation. His discipline was one of the things she admired.

She chose a black skirt, a simple Brooks Brothers white cotton shirt with a quilted Hermès blazer, red suede pumps, her gold-plated Gucci watch, and gold hoop earrings. They all combined to give her a look of quiet elegance, which she knew Jason appreciated.

As they were leaving, he stopped her just before she opened the door, his hand on her arm. "Something I wanted to mention," he said casually. Then his hand tightened and his voice became icy. "The money you're skimming off your living expenses. That has just ended. Do you understand?"

She opened her mouth to protest, automatically, but stopped. There was no point. He knew. How, she had no idea, but it didn't matter. He had all kinds of security people working for him. He had probably noticed the bills and had someone check them out.

His hand was hurting her arm now, but she said nothing, just looked back at him. His eyes had narrowed. There was nothing in them, just an emotionless someone looking out, someone who lived according to a ruthless code she couldn't even begin to fathom. It frightened her and she felt an overpowering need to shake, but she held her body steady.

"If you need anything, ask me. But don't cheat me. Do you understand?"

"Yes," she said, a tremor to her voice in spite of her intention to show nothing.

"Very good," he said. He released his hold and held out his arm for her to grasp. "Shall we go?" he said, his voice perfectly pleasant.

She realized then that at that moment she had been more frightened than she had ever been in her life. She had heard him speak harshly to people on the telephone, but she had never seen him this cold and hard. She took his arm and walked casually beside him, her legs suddenly weak.

Her earlier thoughts about vulnerability returned to her. Not only could this man destroy her business, but if he wanted to, he could be ruthless enough to destroy her. She was in a terrible position. She had no safety net, no viable fallback alternative. She had to change her situation and she had to do it soon. The only problem was that she had no idea how.

"Beautiful weather we've been having," Jason said.

"Yes," she replied, her voice calm now. "It's supposed to stay this way all week."

Selena had finally heard from David, and he had indeed invited her to watch the screening at Alan Silver's house that evening. But, citing business pressures, he had asked her to meet him there instead of picking her up. That added to her irritability and she had kept the conversation terse and abrupt.

She needed to get high.

As if in answer to a prayer, Ronnie appeared at the door.

"Oh, thank God! Come in!" she said.

Briefcase in hand, Ronnie looked like a Wall Street banker. In his late forties, with distinguished silver temples and a sedate gray three-piece suit, he adopted the solicitous and conservative manner of a professional, fitting, he had said more than once, his self-declared status as "Dealer to the Stars."

"And how is my favorite customer today?" he said, placing the briefcase on the dining room table and carefully unlocking it. "You look a little pale."

"I'm fine now, Ronnie," she said, her depression lifting. "What have you got today? I'll take one of everything."

"Voilà!" he said, opening the briefcase.

The deceptively deep briefcase was neatly divided into a dozen compartments. Half of the display consisted of cocaine in one-ounce and five-ounce plastic bags. Other compartments held bottles of pills—uppers and downers; there was a section of neatly rolled joints banded in packs of ten; a little "crack"—rock cocaine; amyl nitrate for a sexual rush; and an assortment of half-a-dozen other fashionable drugs.

A greedy glint in her eyes, Selena reached for one of the larger bags of coke, followed by two packs of grass, a handful of Quaaludes, two bottles of other pills, and a vial of morphine.

"That's all you want today?" Ronnie asked.

"I guess I might as well get more of that," she said, taking another bag of cocaine.

"Very good," he said, snapping the briefcase shut.

He eyed the pile of drugs on her table, mentally calculating the total.

"I'll get some cash," she said, going to the bedroom. She returned, a bundle of bills in her hand. Eagerly, she began to peel off hundred dollar bills until he held up his hand.

"Thank you very much," he said, sweeping the money from the table to his pocket.

"Do you want a toot?" she asked, picking up one of the bags of cocaine.

"Thank you, but no," he said politely. "I've got places to go and people to see."

As soon as he left, she went back into the dining room and opened one of the bags with trembling fingers. She didn't bother with the normal rituals, just stuffed her nose as fast as she could. Within minutes, there was color in her cheeks and a sparkle to her eyes. In an hour, after more cocaine, a few pills, and a joint, she was flying.

She dressed quickly, putting on a long, bright red skirt

with a slit up one side that revealed her thigh when she moved, a wide pink sash around her waist, and a flowing long-sleeve blouse of a darker but similar color. An emerald bracelet on her left wrist, matching emerald earrings, a hasty makeup application, and she was done. Quickly stuffing a small bag of cocaine in her purse, she left the apartment.

The man who entered the elevator with her murmured a polite greeting and paid no further attention to her. Athletic, good-looking even with the small black moustache, he simply stared at the flashing lights indicating the passage of floors.

What a waste, she thought irritably. She might as well be invisible, for all he cared. Half the men she met these days were homosexual. Her building was filled with them. Somehow she always felt personally slighted by their attitude. She was used to admiring glances from men; when they didn't come, she wondered what she was doing wrong.

Selena left the elevator without speaking to him again, but she put an extra sway in her hips, just to show him what he was missing.

She wouldn't go directly to Silver's house. She'd stop in at a couple of places and check out the action. Serve David right if she was late. Selfish bastard! She'd go find an adventure on his time.

Kate Buchanan had spent most of the day trying to find Angie Cox. Now she was both exhausted and disappointed. The woman had literally disappeared. She had started with a telephone number Angie had given her after the funeral. It had referred her to another number, then another, and finally to one that was disconnected with no referral.

She had found an address on a letter among Joel's belongings. At about eleven in the morning she had gone to a large duplex apartment in Beverly Hills and the manager had eyed her questions with disapproval.

"She no longer lives here, darling," he had said, looking slyly down his nose at her.

"When did she move out?" Kate asked.

"Who *are* you?" he asked, cocking his head effeminately to one side.

"Her sister," Kate lied. "I've been in Europe and lost contact with her."

"Oh. Well she moved about six months ago to an apartment somewhere in Hollywood."

"Did she happen to leave a forwarding address?"

"I don't know if I still have it."

"Well, could you look?" Kate asked. "We haven't seen each other for over three years, and I'd really like to find her."

The manager rolled his eyes and sighed. "Well, all right," he conceded. "Just wait here."

He came back three minutes later with the address written on the back of an envelope. "It's on Wilton Place," he said. "Not exactly the same kind of neighborhood as this."

Kate thanked him and, after consulting her Thomas Guide map, drove her rented car down Melrose to Wilton Place. She found the apartment easily. It was in a large building that had been modern ten years earlier but already looked like a shabby relic, with peeling paint on the walls and overgrown shrubbery in the front.

Angie had left about two months earlier. "We had to ask her to leave," the manager said, a woman in her fifties with gray hair, washed-out blue eyes, and a disapproving line to her mouth. "The noise was just terrible," she added.

"Did she leave a forwarding address?" Kate asked.

"Not with me. Good riddance, too."

"Is there anyone here who might know where she is?"

"Girl upstairs might. They were neighbors. Although she's a nice girl, unlike that—"

"Is she in now?"

"Doubt it. She works."

"What's her name?"

"Brenda. Brenda Dalrymple. Nice girl, not like that other one."

"Could you give me her phone number?"

"It's in the book," the woman said, and closed the door in her face.

On the way out, Kate noted that B. Dalrymple was in Apartment 206. When she got home, she found the number in the phone book and tried calling it, but all she got was an answering machine. She left her number and the reason she was calling.

She spent the rest of the afternoon buying groceries and a few other items she needed for the apartment. Then, at five-thirty, she began calling the Dalrymple woman again with no luck. At eight she gave up, leaving a final message, "Call me, please, no matter how late it is."

She was tired, still not recovered from the trip. One more night of good sleep and then she'd start a fresh attack. Sooner or later she'd find Angie, and then Angie would lead her to the man who had Joel killed.

Then what? She didn't know yet, had no idea how she was going to bring about this justice she so desperately wanted. All she knew was that she owed it to Joel and that she would find a way. It had been enough to bring her three thousand miles to Los Angeles, and it would be enough to keep her going.

She soaked for forty-five minutes in the tub and then collapsed into bed. She dreamed of her brother. Someone was smashing his guitar over his hands. Joel was screaming and calling out her name.

Allan Silver lived in the hills above Ventura Boulevard, in Encino. Although scorned in the seventies as hopelessly suburban, the better parts of the Valley had become a favorite enclave of the nouveau riche in recent years. Silver's home was a sprawling ranch-style building, with more rooms in it than he and his wife would ever use. French doors in the living room opened onto an enormous patio, which covered almost a quarter of an acre. At its end, situated on the edge of a cliff that dropped into nothing, was an Olympic-sized pool tiled in black. Beyond was a breathtaking view of the San Fernando Valley.

They were all there—the men Page privately thought of as the Los Angeles Mafia: Jason; Allan; David; Ted Benson, who owned a chain of regional magazines; Stodding

Watson, the status-conscious director of the Rex Museum; Michael Wadler, president of one of the largest brokerage firms in the city; and one or two others, including the editor of one of the largest daily newspapers in Los Angeles.

Perhaps Mafia was too strong a word, she thought, as she looked around. But they looked out for each other, these men. They were all involved in each other's deals and represented a maze of financial interests. She also knew for a fact that a number of them were involved in trading stocks with insider knowledge through their connections with each other, a definite crime in the books of regulatory authorities such as the SEC. But, as Jason had explained to her once in a rare revealing moment, "Everybody does it."

Most of them had women with them, not their wives, of course, but girlfriends of the moment or mistresses of some duration. She'd seen some of these men with their wives at events where her social calendar had collided with theirs. At those times she had never ostensibly been with Jason. One never mixed mistresses and wives; it was more lethal than mixing drinks. But the men behaved differently on those occasions, conservatively subdued. Now they were imbued with a kind of schoolboyish glee, a slightly inane backslapping jocularity that hinted at shared irresponsibilities.

The only one who didn't share this probably unconscious character shift was Jason, which probably explained why he was the most powerful of them all, the one the others looked up to. He maintained his warily charming stance at all times—whenever she had seen him, at any rate.

They were all powerful, successful men, leaders of one kind or another. Yet somehow Jason dominated them. Perhaps it was his ruthlessness. She wasn't sure. But she knew that there was some unspoken agreement among them that Jason was the most powerful. Or the most to be feared.

She thought back again to the moment he had confronted her with the knowledge of what she was doing with the expenses. She had always known there was a dangerous edge to him but had never been the recipient of his anger before, an experience she did not want repeated.

"Deep in thought?" Jasmine asked, sitting beside her on the couch.

"Just looking at the boys," Page said.

They had known each other for five or six months, but their relationship had never passed beyond the point of idle social gossip. As Page had limited patience with idle gossip, their conversations had generally been brief.

Jasmine, on the other hand, admired Page, although she had never shown this admiration in any overt way. Page's obvious breeding, which allowed her to maintain a cool composure in all the circumstances in which Jasmine had seen her, was so unlike her own more tempestuous personality that she marvelled at it. Page never showed her true feelings, her contributions to the men's conversations were always intelligent without being obtrusive, and her calm seemed unshakable. This aura of East Coast royalty sometimes made Jasmine feel like a barbarian. She tended to find herself uncharacteristically deferent in Page's presence.

Jasmine looked across the room to where Jason, Allan, and David were huddled together, discussing business no doubt, always the main topic when they got together. Jason was talking; the others were attentive.

"Are you happy with Jason?" Jasmine asked, her eyes now on Page's face.

The question surprised Page. Jasmine rarely asked personal questions. Bright and totally superficial chatter usually fell from her lips, seemingly without conscious thought.

Not knowing how to answer, she asked instead, "Are you happy with Allan?"

"Of course," Jasmine said. "He's a doll. I'm very lucky." She looked fondly across the room at her lover.

"Yes," Page said dryly. Personally, she couldn't stand Allan. He had about as much depth as the Los Angeles River, a concrete aqueduct that swelled only when it rained three or four times a year. How he managed to run a major studio and actually turn out a hit movie every now and then was totally beyond understanding. She assumed that the decision-making machinery was so competently in place that nothing he said or did actually affected the final outcome.

Either that, or his existence was based on the fact that if you threw the die enough times, sooner or later you came up with doubles.

"Oh, there's Selena," Jasmine said.

Selena stood in the doorway, a smile plastered on her face, a barely perceptible wobble to her knees. Even Page, who never touched drugs, could see she was stoned out of her mind. Selena saw David, ran across the room, and kissed him enthusiastically. The other two men stepped back with amused expressions. She spotted Jasmine next, waved gaily, and came over, sitting heavily on the couch beside them. Her bright red skirt was darkly stained near her knee, as if she had spilled a drink there.

"When's the movie start?" she asked, throwing her head back dramatically against the cushions. She didn't wait for an answer, but continued, "Geez! I shouldn't have stopped on the way here."

"Where did you go?" Jasmine asked.

"Stopped in at Barney's. Saw some people." She tapped her bag. "I scored some great blow from Ronnie today. Want a taste?"

Jasmine looked over at Page. She was ignoring them, staring intently at a painting on the opposite wall. Page did not approve of Selena. She had made that clear on numerous occasions before by her lack of response to Selena's sometimes frantic effort to be the life of the party. And she almost certainly didn't approve of Barney's, one of the many sleazy Hollywood clubs frequented by dope dealers, hookers, and members of the elite who had more money than good sense.

"Maybe later," Jasmine murmured.

Selena leaned across Jasmine and tapped Page on the arm. "Want a toot?" she asked.

"You know I don't," Page said with icy disinterest.

Selena raised a hand to her mouth and giggled, a shrill, inane sound.

"Excuse me," Page said, getting up and going across the room to join Jason.

"Stuck-up bitch," Selena said, looking after her.

"She's okay," Jasmine said. "She's just a little . . . I don't know . . . different, I guess." She put her hand on Selena's arm. "Don't be too hard on her."

"Stuck-up bitch," she muttered again vindictively, looking at Page across the room. "Serve her right if Jason kicked her out on her ass one day. I don't know what he sees in her. She's probably a shitty lay, anyway."

"Come on, she's a classy lady. That's what he sees in her. He'd never kick her out."

Selena raised her eyebrows and laughed coldly. "When the fuck were you born? Yesterday? Do you really think these guys give a shit about anyone but themselves?" she asked.

"Allan cares for me and I care for him," Jasmine replied stiffly.

"Jesus," Selena said disbelievingly. She slumped on the couch for a moment, closing her eyes, and then raised her head, the conversation already forgotten. "Wanna come to the bathroom with me and get high?" Her eyes could barely focus.

"Later," Jasmine said. Sometimes Selena was just too much to take. Most of the time she was fun, but when she got this stoned she became a pain in the ass. And she'd been doing it more often lately.

Jasmine was rescued by Allan's announcement that the movie was about to start. "Come on," she said to Selena.

"I'll be there in a while," Selena said disgruntedly. "I'm off to the bathroom for a little refresher."

The screening room was in the north wing of the house. The projection machines and video equipment were state of the art, the seating luxurious. In a pinch, the room could hold about twenty-five people.

When everyone but Selena had straggled in and seated themselves, Allan stood to give a short introduction. "As many of you have invested in this film, I thought you would like to have the opportunity to see what won't be on the screen in your local neighborhood movie theater when the movie is introduced." He grinned and added, "I assure you that, in spite of what you are about to see, your money was well spent."

There were a few chortles from those who knew what was coming and then a strained silence, broken only by a sudden fit of coughing by one of the men.

The room grew dark as the lights dimmed, and then the beautiful face of Andora Dover faded onto the screen, filling it with the famous icy blue eyes and full red lips. Her pink tongue caressed the underside of her top lip and the eyes grew heavy, as if seeing nothing. The camera held the shot.

Page was not particularly interested in movie stars, but even she had been unable to ignore this phenomenon Andora was in all the magazines and trade papers, and Page recalled what she had read.

Andora had been what people in the business liked to call "catapulted into stardom" a short two years earlier. Although only in her early twenties, she had been cleverly promoted as the reigning Goddess of the Sophisticated Eighties, after making four movies in quick succession. She was helped by her beautiful face and lush body, undoubtedly one of the most perfect in Hollywood, but as Page looked at the image on the screen, she knew it was the camera's ability to capture the sensuous mix of utter lasciviousness and youthful innocence that had caught the public imagination. Andora was the girl who didn't but could—if only you knew the right button to push, and Page could easily believe that every man imagined pushing that button.

The shot held on her face, revealing lines of tension around her mouth. Slowly, almost imperceptibly, a sound began. At first it was only a quiet rhythm and difficult to distinguish, but then it rose until it became apparent that the sound filling the room was the panting of the beautiful Andora.

Her mouth moved then and her words boomed out, "Harder, baby. Do me harder, baby. Come on, lover. Give it to me."

And then the camera gently pulled back to show Andora being passionately fucked in her dressing room by her leading man, Clive Baxter.

There were a few uncomfortable chuckles from the audience, but it soon grew into loud laughter.

Allan poked Jason's arm and said loudly, "She was stoned out of her fucking mind. Didn't know which side was up. But she knew she wanted to get laid by Clive, and when I suggested to her they record it for their own pleasure, she insisted it be done by professionals. Apparently she already has a collection of her men on videotape. Nothing like this quality."

"They did it in front of the crew?" Jason asked.

"Just the cameraman. The lights were already set up. We closed down the set."

"And got extra prints made."

"Hey," Allan said, spreading his hands. "If a guy can't do favors for his friends, what can he do?"

Page snuck a sideways glance at Jason. His face showed no emotion as he watched. She was totally unaroused herself. She thought the whole affair tasteless, but as long as Jason watched, she would sit there as well.

Andora was now wrapping her long legs around Baxter's hips, her whole body shuddering, whimpers of pleasure coming from her lips. Baxter was dutifully pumping her, sweat pouring down his face.

Jasmine reached over and put her hand in Allan's lap. His cock was threatening to burst free of his trousers. He hardly noticed her, all his senses focused on the screen.

She looked around for Selena, but she wasn't in the room. God, she thought, talk about stoned! She'd never seen Selena this high before. And now she was out there doing more.

Back on the screen, Andora and Baxter had changed positions. Now she was on top, her ample, perfectly proportioned breasts bouncing enthusiastically as she whipped her hips against him.

Maybe I'd better check on her, Jasmine thought uncomfortably. Selena had been gone a long time.

"I'm going to the bathroom," she said to Allan, who merely grunted in reply, his eyes fixed on the movie.

She looked in the closest bathroom. Empty. Selena had

probably gone to the one nearest the living room. Quickly, she walked through the house. Selena was probably too stoned to move, sitting in the bathroom and staring at wall-paper patterns. David would be pissed if she was too far gone. Selena had been pushing her luck lately. This was a wild crowd in its way, but that was only behind closed doors. Discretion was important. Jasmine had heard a couple of the men discuss Selena's behavior in unflattering terms.

Ah, the bathroom door at the end of the hall was closed. She had to be in there.

"Selena?" she said, knocking loudly. "Selena?"

No sound. She knocked again, but there was no response.

She grabbed the handle and turned it, pushing on the door. It swung open.

Selena was crumpled on the blue carpet, her skin white and bloodless against the brilliance of her red skirt.

"Christ!" Jasmine said, dropping to her knees beside her. "Selena, for God's sake."

There was no movement. Selena's eyes were closed, her mouth partly open. Desperately, Jasmine felt her wrist for a pulse. She thought there was something but couldn't be sure.

An empty vial sat on the toilet tank beside a syringe and a bottle of pills.

"Christ!" she said again, running frantically through the house to the screening room.

She burst in just as Andora was coming for the third time, screaming at the top of her lungs and beating her fists against Baxter's chest.

"Allan!" Jasmine shouted. "It's Selena! Come quickly. I think she's dead."

Andora was left writhing without an audience. "In the bathroom!" Jasmine cried, leading the way.

Jason, Allan, and David crowded around the limp body on the floor, while the rest of the party filled the hall.

"It's all right," Jason said loudly, looking up. "We'll take care of it. Everyone go back." The crowd obeyed the authority in his voice and began to straggle off in a buzz of muted comments.

"I'll call an ambulance," Jasmine said, turning.

"The hell you will. Not here," Jason said sharply, his words stopping her. "We've got to get her out of here."

"If she's alive, she needs treatment," Jasmine said.

Jason ignored her. He put a hand on David's shoulder. "Get a couple of chauffeurs we can trust. We'll have them take her back to her apartment. I'll have one of my men there to take care of tidying up. She can't be found here with all of us."

"But she'll die," Jasmine said shrilly.

"She's already dead," Jason said coldly. "Now get the fuck out of here and go back to the party."

"Go on," Allan said. "We'll take care of her."

"But—" Jasmine began.

"Go on!" Jason said. "Do as you're told!"

Her eyes fixed on the tableaux in the bathroom, Jasmine took a couple of steps backward. She wanted to rage and scream, but instead she just moved slowly away, her face almost as white as Selena's.

CHAPTER THREE

Kate threw the "View" section of the *Los Angeles Times* on the coffee table. The Aquarian horoscope for the day warned, "Ingenuity will be necessary in situations that could be risky."

"Hell!" she said aloud to herself. "So what else is new?"

The newspaper had left her fingers blackened with ink. She went into the kitchen and used dishwashing soap to remove it.

Three frustrating days had passed since she had arrived

in Los Angeles, and still she hadn't been able to speak to Angie's ex-neighbor, Brenda Dalrymple. For all she knew, the damn answering machine had sent her messages on to the great message graveyard in the sky. Either that, or Miss Dalrymple wasn't interested in answering her calls.

For lack of anything better to do, she had in the meantime waylaid the mailman outside the apartment building on Wilton in an attempt to get Angie's forwarding address from him, only to find that she hadn't left one.

Actually, it hadn't been easy. When she first approached him with her question he'd acted as if he were about to call the FBI in because she was tampering with the mail. She'd had to blink her not-unattractive eyes and tell him a sad story before he loosened up.

"She got a bunch of bills and they were returned to sender. Must have made them happy," he said, adding philosophically, "Happens all the time."

The thought that Brenda Dalrymple was her only lead disturbed her. If Kate couldn't contact the woman, or if she knew nothing about Angie, then Kate was left with limited alternatives. She could place an advertisement in the "Personal" section of the *Times, LA Weekly,* and *Los Angeles Magazine,* but it could draw the wrong kind of attention. After all, Angie had been very afraid of her mystery man, so advertising her interest in Angie's whereabouts wouldn't be wise. Besides, if the choice of seeing Kate were left up to Angie, who knows what she'd do. She was upset and scared enough the last time they had met to make Kate doubt that she'd even reply.

Kate dried her hands and returned to the living room. If Brenda didn't work out, there was only one real alternative left—professional help. She could hire someone to track Angie down. She'd come into contact with detectives before, although they had specialized in stolen and forged art, but she knew they had ways to follow a paper trail, inside contacts who could give them addresses on traffic tickets, automobile registrations, unlisted telephone numbers. But it would be a costly and time-consuming alternative, and she hoped to God she could avoid it. She wasn't exactly flush.

At moments like this, doubts seized her. Her "plan" of step one: finding the man who had Joel killed and step two: creating a suitable revenge, had all kinds of contingencies attached to it.

In devising it, she had realized that the second step would be where the real planning occurred. But she had bravely told herself that once step one had been accomplished her natural intelligence would enable her to move forward from there. So far, her intelligence hadn't even helped her accomplish the first step. Right now it didn't matter a damn that her IQ could have gained her membership in MENSA. What she needed was a break.

As if to answer her wish, the telephone rang. It was Brenda Dalrymple finally returning her half-dozen messages, explaining that she had been out of town. She was sympathetic, apologetic, willing to help. The question was, was she *able* to help?

"I'm trying to reach Angie Cox," Kate said. "Do you happen to have any idea where she lives now?"

"Are you a friend of hers?"

"Yes. She and my brother went together."

"Oh, well I don't know where she moved to. I haven't talked to her since she left."

Kate repressed a sigh. "Do you have any idea where she works?"

"Works?" Brenda asked, humor in her voice. "I don't think she ever has. I'm sorry, I don't think I can help you. We weren't really friends, you know. Just neighbors who talked to each other every now and then. Had a couple of dinners, you know."

"What about places she goes to?" Kate said quickly, desperation in her voice. "Any place where she hangs out?"

"Well, there was a club she mentioned a few times. I guess she used to go there a lot. It was . . . I'm sorry, I can't remember the name offhand."

"Where was it? Near you? In Hollywood?"

"Uh, West Hollywood, I think. I'm sorry, I just can't— Oh, I know! The Twilight Zone. That was the name. Like the television show."

"No other place I'd be likely to find her?"

"Not that I know of."

Kate thanked her and hung up. She looked in the telephone book and saw the Twilight Zone was on Santa Monica Boulevard. It was eight o'clock, early for club life but worth a try.

She dressed quickly, putting on a casual cotton skirt and a T-shirt. One of the things she liked about Southern California was the acceptance of casual, comfortable clothes in all but the most formal situations.

As she drove through the heavy traffic, she realized suddenly that it was Friday. She had lost track of the days since leaving New York and the discipline of having to show up at a job every day.

That was another thing she'd have to take care of soon, she thought—get a job of some kind. But it wouldn't prove too difficult. Her work at the gallery in New York had given her a number of West Coast contacts. At this rate, with the car rental, the apartment, and all the other incidental expenses, her paltry nest egg wouldn't last too long though.

She almost missed the small blue neon sign on her left, so she turned down a side street, parked the car, and walked back.

The Twilight Zone had an unpropossessing front but inside was cavernous. There was a stage on which a band was setting up, a small dance floor overhung with a battery of colored lights and surrounded by tables, and a long, wooden bar where all the action was. Seemingly a singles crowd, men and women in their twenties and thirties jostled around the bar like bees to honey. This was not exactly Kate's kind of place.

She reached the bar through the entanglement of bodies and ordered a glass of white wine from one of the three bartenders. The patrons were faster than the help. Before her drink arrived, a man in his mid-thirties inserted himself beside her and introduced himself.

"Hi! My name's Bart," he said, demonstrating a facile grin that crinkled up the corners of his eyes.

"Hi," she said. The bartender put her wine down on the bar in front of her.

Bart wore tight white jeans, a pastel blue shirt, and a white cotton jacket. "Haven't seen you here before," he said.

Normally Kate wouldn't have given Bart the time of day. She intensely disliked the modern bar ritual between men and women. But on this occasion she smiled pleasantly and said, "Are you a regular here?"

Bart shrugged and grinned again. "I come pretty often. Good crowd. Good music."

"I'm looking for a friend, Angie Cox. Do you know her?"

"Angie? Angie? No, I don't think so. What's she look like?"

"Blond, pretty, well-dressed, what some people might call flashy."

Bart threw his head back and chuckled. "You've just described half the women in the room!"

It was true, Kate thought, sipping her Chablis and looking around. Half the women were blond, although ninety percent of them had dark roots. They ranged from the elegant to the trashy, from secretaries and office workers to the wildly hip. The same went for the men. Some wore jackets and some wore chains, their sexuality either hetero or homo. There was no sign of Angie Cox though.

"Don't see your friend, huh?" Bart interjected.

"No. Does this place get busier later on?"

"Packed," Bart said. He looked at her appraisingly and leaned closer. "Do you want to score a little blow?" he asked.

"From you?" Kate asked.

He shook his head. "No, but half the guys in this room deal. I'll fix you up if you like."

And get a cut of the action, she thought to herself. Dope pimp. "Thanks, but I don't need to," she said pleasantly. She had tried smoking grass once at college and had fallen ingloriously asleep. Drugs weren't for her.

"I need to find my friend," she said. "Do you know

anyone here who kind of hangs out all the time, who would be likely to know all the regulars?''

"Billy there," he said, inclining his head at a tall black man who sat with two women at a table near the bar. "I'll go ask him. What's her name?"

"Angie Cox," she said. "Thank you so much."

"Be right back," he said, making his way through the crowd.

"How's your wine?" the bartender asked. He was young, maybe twenty-two. Tanned, handsome, thin blond hair. Everyone's idea of a California surfer.

"Fine, thanks. Has Angie been in tonight?" she asked.

"Wouldn't know. I've only been working here a few days," he said.

"Oh," she said.

"Hey, baby," a voice said behind her.

She turned to see the man called Billy.

"Hear you're seeking Angie," he said. "You a working girl too?"

"Working g—?" She stopped, suddenly aware of what he meant, and almost blushed. "No. She's just a friend of mine from way back."

"Sorry to hear that." He scanned her body. "You're a prime-lookin' piece, baby. I could help you make a fortune."

He was handsome in a flashy way, his features almost Caucasian, but there was a cruel twist to his mouth that she didn't like, and his eyes held none of the warmth in his voice.

"A fortune?" she said, resisting the urge to throw her drink in his face. Now was not the time to make enemies.

"A grand a night, baby," he said, leaning a little closer. "Billy will take care of it all for you."

"Well, thanks, but that's not my line," she said.

He clicked his tongue sadly. "Too bad, baby. Hate to see good stuff go to waste."

"You know Angie?" she asked.

"I know everyone," he said arrogantly. "You known her long?"

"Quite a while," she said. "When does she come in here?"

"Round 'bout midnight. Depends on business."

"Does she work for you?" Kate asked.

Anger flashed in his eyes. "Free-lance. Dangerous way to go. Woman needs a man in this town."

"You've offered your management services, I take it?" she asked, a hint of amusement lurking at the side of her mouth.

"You ask a lot of questions," he said, his voice growing surly. Apparently Billy didn't like to be laughed at. "Who shall I say was looking for her?"

"I'll be here myself," Kate said, meeting his stare. "Thanks for your help."

"Pleasure's all mine," he said ironically, backing away.

Angie a hooker! Kate thought as she drained her wine. A long way down from being mistress of what she had called "one of the most powerful men in the city." But not inconceivable. Maybe pleasing men was all she knew how to do. It was, in a way, a logical progression if times got hard, and apparently they had for Angie.

"Was he a help?" Bart appeared at her elbow again.

"Yes. Thanks for doing that," she said.

"Can I buy you a drink?" he asked.

"No, thanks, I have to go," she said, suddenly making up her mind. If she encouraged him further, she'd never get rid of him. She knew the type. Besides, she hadn't eaten since noon and the one glass of wine was going to her head already. She'd leave, grab a bite somewhere, and then return.

"Can I take you somewhere?" he asked hopefully.

"No, you've helped enough already. Thanks," she said, slipping off the stool and throwing the strap of her bag over her shoulder. "I'll see you later."

"Can I see you again?" he asked, his voice dropping away as he watched her retreating back. She hadn't heard him, or had chosen not to. He shook his head regretfully, admiring her long slim legs and the way her hair bounced on her shoulders. Some woman. What the hell was she doing looking for a friend in a place like this?

Kate wondered the same thing as she went out into the cooling night air. It wasn't her kind of scene and they weren't her kind of people. She was out of her depth, heading for trouble, cruising for a bruising. Who the hell was she to pursue this ideal of justice? Who the hell cared except her? There was nobody left to care. What was she? Some kind of vigilante?

All the doubts and reservations that she had so often pushed aside in the past months crowded in on her now. She felt suddenly inept, stupid, some naive and unrealistic Don Quixote tilting at windmills.

She saw a restaurant called Theodore's and went in. She was seated immediately at a quiet corner table and ordered an omelette and another glass of white wine, ignoring the few curious stares at the pretty young woman eating alone. She was used to eating alone. She hadn't been a hermit in New York, dating occasionally, but there had been no serious relationship, not since college where an intense love affair had ended disastrously.

God! She hadn't thought about him for a long time, she realized. Damon O'Reilly had been a brilliant student, a talented painter, and a handsome, charming man with a silver tongue. In the wisdom of hindsight, "man" had been the primary incorrect assumption. He was really little more than a spoiled boy. Wanted everything his way. Immediate gratification. It had been wonderful at first though, passionate, exciting—heady stuff. Then he had begun to experiment with drugs. He started with grass, moved on to hash, then coke, then LSD, then heroin, sinking ever-deeper into his own mind, growing more difficult, emotional, even violent.

At first she had fought it, matching him in volatility, the two of them known to their friends for their knock 'em down, drag 'em out fights. But it was physically and emotionally exhausting and ultimately unproductive. She had finally broken it off, motivated by a nagging sense of self-preservation. Later, she heard that three years out of school he had gone straight, joined a born-again Christian group, married his high school sweetheart, and became a stockbroker in his hometown of Chicago.

That had been a sad moment. Oh, she was pleased he had quit the drug scene, but the trade-off was that he had become a cliché. He had deserved better.

The waiter brought her wine, a crisp dry Fume Blanc. After the sweet jug wine in the Twilight Zone, it was doubly delicious. Why was she thinking of an old sweetheart now? she wondered.

Probably because she was inspecting her motives. She had done a lot of that before breaking up with Damon. But, in the end, it had been the correct decision. Just as her decision now would ultimately prove to be right. It was right when she made it after Joel's funeral and it was right now. All she had to do was persist, show a little backbone, not let the barriers stand in her way, ignore those niggling little voices of doubt.

The omelette was thick and moist, and as she ate she began to feel better. She had to remember to look after herself, eat properly, sleep, exercise. She wouldn't be able to accomplish anything in a half-dead state.

By the time she finished her meal and started to sip on a cup of strong aromatic coffee, she had regained her certainty. She had the intelligence, courage, and will to do what needed to be done. All she had to do was take one step at a time.

She looked at her watch. Almost eleven. Time to stroll back to the club and wait for Angie. If she didn't show up tonight, Kate would return on the next day and the next and the next—until she found her.

When she arrived back at the Twilight Zone, there were five people standing in line ahead of her. The doorman greeted her and ushered her in, remembering her from earlier.

Bart had been right. The club did get busy and it was, indeed, crowded. Bodies were packed in like sardines, gay, chattering sardines. The air was clogged with the blue haze of countless cigarettes. Glasses clinked and rattled and every now and then shattered. Peals of high-pitched laughter swooped around the room like frantic birds. The band played soft rock, which still managed to be loud.

Kate stood near the bar and gazed around the room, slowly growing accustomed to the darkness, for the lights had been dimmed. There was no sign of Bart, for which she was thankful, nor was the tall black pimp anywhere in sight. Unfortunately, neither was Angie.

"Hey, how you doing?"

She turned to see a short bald man who wore a bad toupee and five gold chains tangled in the folds of his neck. He grinned up at her, obviously delighted to see her. Then across the room at the other end of the bar, she caught a glimpse, first of blond hair, and then of Angie's profile.

"Excuse me," she said to her admirer, and took off.

Angie stood with a drink in her hand, her eyes scanning the crowd. She had changed since the last time they had met. She looked harder, tougher, thinner even.

"Hi!" Kate said when she reached her side.

Angie looked at her without recognition for a moment, then realized who she was and said, "Hey! What are you doing here? I thought you lived back in New York?" And then the full memory of their last meeting returned, for the social friendliness left her voice and was replaced by suspicion. "What are you doing here?" she repeated.

"I was in town and thought I'd look you up to see how you're doing," Kate said.

"How did you find me?" Angie asked, the wariness growing in her voice.

"The apartment you used to live in on Wilton. A woman—I guess she was your neighbor—told me that you came to this club."

"Oh," Angie said. She noticed Kate didn't have a drink in her hand. "Well," she added grudgingly, "I suppose that since you're here, we might as well grab a seat." She spied an empty table for two. "Come on, she said, leading the way. "There'll be a waitress along in a moment and you can get a drink."

As soon as they sat down, Kate said warmly, "How have you been since I last saw you?"

"Not bad, not good," Angie said. She snagged a passing waitress and said, "What do you want?"

"A glass of white wine, please."

Angie gave the order and then said, "What are you really doing here?"

"What I said. Truly," Kate insisted. "I had to come into LA on business and thought I'd look you up."

"Why? What do you care how I'm doing?"

It was a good question. Kate gave it some thought before answering. She looked down at the table. "You're the only person I know that knew Joel in recent times. I cared for Joel, he cared for you. I miss him. I thought seeing you, talking to you, I—I thought it might help."

Angie's voice softened. "It's over. He's gone. What's the point of rehashing old stuff?"

Kate shook her head. "He was my brother. I loved him. I'm not going to forget him."

Angie smiled grimly at her foolishness. "Yeah, well, I loved him too and I'm not going to forget him, but I ain't going to carry my grief forever."

The waitress returned and handed Kate her wine. She took a sip and put the glass on the table.

"I'll have another vodka," Angie said.

After the waitress left, Angie said, "I'll tell you one thing. I've really learned to appreciate Joel since he's gone. He was a fucking saint compared to the men I've met since then. Men are bastards to the core."

"What makes you say that?" Kate asked.

Angie hesitated, then looked defiantly back at her. "My new profession, honey. I don't give it away anymore. Men have to pay for it."

"Oh," Kate said.

"Hey, as mistress of a rich man, I was nothing but a glorified hooker," Angie explained. "And I was good at it. This way, I still get the money, but I don't depend on one man. I have a client list as long as my arm. And they're all assholes."

"Well, if you don't like it, isn't there anything else you could do?"

Angie looked at her mockingly. "What? Work as a clerk in a department store? I never finished high school, honey. I'm qualified for shit. The only thing I know how to do real well is make a man feel good." She ran her hand down the front of her body. "Men like this, and they're willing to pay for it. I'm not cut out to be a housewife, wiping some snivelling brat's nose and putting the slippers out for the old man and taking a two-week vacation in Hawaii every year. So, I do what I do, and I make enough to keep me satisfied."

Her tone was assertive, challenging, but in spite of the words, Kate sensed that there was more than a little self-loathing in the new Angie.

"It sounds like hard work," Kate said carefully.

"Jesus, let me tell you, it is!" Angie said, a genuine smile appearing for the first time. "I have one john who makes me wear about five costumes—leather, French maid, jungle girl, you name it. He has to find out which one gives him a hard-on. It varies, depending on his mood. Jesus, I feel like a fashion model on parade!"

Kate laughed. "Weird!"

"That's nothing," Angie said. "Another guy has to be tied up and raped to get off. I've learned more knots than a Boy Scout."

They giggled like schoolgirls, and then the waitress brought Angie's drink. She took the glass and gulped half of it down. "I tell you," she said, looking morosely into the drink, "I never thought it would come to this. I never did."

Kate touched her hand sympathetically. "It's a different life from when you were with Joel, isn't it?"

"Yeah, and different from before. I had everything, went to the best restaurants, met the best people, jewelry, clothes, you name it. Then I had to fall in love with your fucking brother and blow it all."

"Do you regret meeting Joel?"

"Yeah. Yeah, sure I do. If we hadn't met, he'd still be alive and I'd still be living high on the hog."

"You can't blame yourself," Kate said. "Joel would never blame you."

"Well, like I said, he was a fucking saint," Angie replied bitterly.

The short man with gold chains who had spoken to Kate at the bar came to the table. "Hey, do you wanna dance?" he asked her, his voice still filled with perpetual cheer.

"Fuck off, asshole," Angie interceded.

He backed away from the table. "Creep," Angie said. "That's all I meet these days."

"Some of your . . . clients must be wealthy men. I mean to afford—?"

"Sure, they are," Angie said gloomily. "But it's different. To them I'm a whore. They pay by the hour. There's no respect. Back when I was with . . . that other guy, I at least had respect. Sure, he paid me, but I was his mistress. I belonged to him. And all the others knew it. They all had their own mistresses. It was understood. They all treated the women with respect.

"We used to go places, take trips, go to where the best people went. I mean, these are educated people I'm talking about. Opera, ballet. I mean, they collect art and stuff, you know. His buddy, Dave Ross, he's an expert on art. Has a collection you wouldn't believe. Goes to every opening in the city. I used to love that. You'd sip champagne and walk slowly around the room, staring at the paintings like you knew something, and the salespeople would hover around you, and . . ."

She stopped and shook her head. Tears lurked in the corners of her eyes, Kate noticed. But the pity she felt for the fallen Angie was hard to sustain in view of the excitement that gripped her. She had a name. Dave Ross. A portion of her mission had been accomplished. It would be easy enough to find out who he was, if he truly was a well-known local collector. And when she found him, he would lead her to the man who had Joel killed.

"Do you still see any of these people?" she asked.

"You kidding? I was kicked out on my ass. I don't want to end up like your brother. I stay away from them—even the women." Angie drained her drink and then looked shrewdly at Kate. "Hey, how come you haven't asked the name of the guy? Last time I saw you that's all you wanted to know. Come to your senses?"

"I guess so," Kate said. "There's really nothing I can do about it."

"Damn right," Angie said. "Be like banging your head against a concrete post. People like you and me, we're nothing. People like him have it all." She looked at her watch. "I have to meet a trick in twenty minutes. You wanna come to the bathroom for a toot?"

"No, thanks," Kate said.

"Right, I should have known," Angie said with a sad smile. "Your kind, straight as an arrow. You don't know shit about what life's really like."

"I know enough to stay away from coke," Kate said.

"It keeps me going," Angie said, rising. "Whatever gets you through the night, right? Hell, I take anything that gets me high. What else have I got?"

"I don't know," Kate said.

"I like you," Angie said, standing above her. "There's something about you that's so like Joel it frightens me." She fumbled in her purse and handed Kate a card. "There's my phone number. If you want to get together next time you're in town, give me a call."

"Okay, I will," Kate said, standing. "Good luck, Angie. I wish you well."

"Huh!" Angie said. "If I counted on my luck, I'd be dead. See you."

She turned and walked toward the bathrooms, disappearing in the crowd.

Kate put the card in her purse and snapped it shut. She had what she had come for—the name that would lead her to the man she sought. And poor Angie, poor Angie had nothing.

It would be Angie's revenge as well, she thought as she walked toward the exit. One dead man, one ruined woman. Whoever he was, she would make sure he paid in full for both.

* * *

Page sat alone in her office, working on a press kit for a client who was about to release a new line of cosmetics for men.

It was a difficult account. In truth, all that set these cosmetics apart from others on the market was their incredible expense, due mainly to exotic ingredients such as skin-rejuvenating tissue found only in the stomach lining of calves. This posed somewhat of a public relations problem. While the hook of the story was the ingredients, one couldn't exactly play up the fact that the primary one came from little baby cows. The solution was, of course, to emphasize in the press releases the less controversial yet almost equally exotic ingredients. After that, she had to just hope for the best and handle any snide media comments when they came up.

Page was dressed in jeans and T-shirt, an outfit she normally wouldn't be caught dead in, but this was Saturday and nobody important would see her. The small suite of offices was usually crowded with hectic people, but today it was quiet. She had the largest room, the only one with huge windows overlooking Wilshire Boulevard, and she found she could enjoy it when the telephone wasn't ringing and account executives weren't bursting in with crises for her to handle.

In this room, which looked more substantial than it was, she met clients. She had furnished it with a comfortable couch and armchair, a glass-topped desk around which she could hold meetings, and an imposingly large desk behind which she sat when necessary.

Page sighed to herself and started a new file on the computer. While she enjoyed the challenges she faced in her field, there were times when the fees just didn't seem large enough to make up for the aggravation. This particular client had given her nothing but problems. The president of the company, Bob Messinger, was a prima donna, an actor who had provided the financing and his name to the line of emollients, skin fresheners, creams, and oils that made up the collection. Messinger of Hollywood, he called the line.

Messinger was a pain in the ass. He never paid his bills

on time, demanded the impossible, didn't follow Page's advice unless it fit in with either his preconceived notions or the counsel of his live-in boyfriend, and bitched when anything went wrong, even if it was his fault. And yet she had little choice but to grin and bear it. Jason had graciously referred Messinger to her, and the truth was, when he did pay his bills, the fee was almost large enough to cover the rent for the very expensive address her office occupied.

She stopped typing, looked at her gold watch—another gift from Jason—and saw it was time to go. Lucky Jason was tied up for most of the weekend, she thought. She wasn't seeing him until Sunday afternoon. She'd be able to return and finish the job either tonight or Sunday morning.

She rode the elevator down to the parking garage, walked toward her little Mercedes, and pressed the remote alarm control. Slipping into the seat, she started the car, then chose a tape and put it in the cassette player. Within minutes, she was heading down La Cienaga Boulevard toward the Santa Monica Freeway, the strains of Bruce Hornsby filling the car.

It was a beautiful day and traffic was commensurately heavy. The crowds were heading for refuge at the beaches. If the temperature edged into the nineties, there'd probably be half-a-million people scrambling for a piece of sand.

She found herself thinking of Selena's death as she drove. She hadn't liked the woman—an irresponsible fool whose demise had simply been a matter of time—but the attitude of the men that night gave her food for thought. Selena could have been a dog for all the compassion they had shown. Their only interest had been to protect themselves. It gave a new perspective to her own precarious position. Mistresses were apparently expendable items.

As she did every Saturday afternoon, she took the San Diego Freeway north and exited on Wilshire Boulevard, driving toward Westwood Village. She drove along a couple of small streets and stopped in front of the Chateau Rouge. As the name implied, it was a gay red five-story building, with striped awnings hanging over a long porch that overlooked the street.

After parking on the street, she took a small package from the back seat of the car, then strode down the sidewalk and up the front steps.

"Hello, Miss Peters," the lady at the desk called out. "I think she's in the rec room."

"Thanks," Page said, breaking her stride long enough to ask, "How has she been this week?"

"Oh, about the same. She seems to be doing well," the woman said.

It was the usual answer, and Page wondered why she bothered asking the question.

The recreation room was a combination living, television, playing (table tennis, cards), and crafts room. People suffering various degrees of physical and mental deterioration wandered in and out, some purposefully, others aimlessly.

Page saw her sitting in a large wicker chair in a corner by herself, a magazine open on her lap.

"Hello, Mother," she said, dropping to her knees beside her and planting a kiss on the soft, feathery cheek.

"Hello," her mother said vaguely, not looking up from the magazine.

She was a shrunken woman, as thin as a bird, her features sharpened over the years, with bright blue eyes that skittered nervously around.

Page pulled another wicker chair over and sat beside her. "What are you reading?" she asked.

"Do you know that six out of ten husbands cheat on their wives today? I don't know what the country has come to," the old woman said. "Why, in my day, there was such a thing as fidelity, and loyalty. I remember when it came out that Billy Waxman had been cheating on his wife, why everyone in our set just cut him dead. Cut him dead. He deserved far worse, of course. His wife Irma was a lovely woman. I remember when we used . . ."

Page listened to her chattering with one ear. She had brought Clara Peters out to the West Coast four months earlier. Before that, she had been in an old folk's home in New York, but Page felt that as necessary as they were, these places were ultimately nothing but warehouses for the aged and wanted her mother closer so that she could give her some personal attention.

The only person she had told about her mother was Elsa. She had not mentioned either her existence or her presence here to Jason or any of her friends or employees. It was a personal matter. Elsa was the one who had recommended this place. "The best of a bad lot," she had said, adding the somewhat callous statement that she thought it was better in today's world for most old people to die young.

"I brought you a present," Page said, diving in during a pause in her mother's monologue.

"Oh, a present! I love presents," she said, a greedy gleam appearing in her eyes.

Page handed over the small box and watched her mother's tiny liver-stained hands struggle with the ribbon.

"Here, let me help," she said, removing the ribbon.

Her mother tore the paper off and opened the small box to see the pair of sterling silver earrings nestled inside. "Oh, they are lovely," she said, lifting one out. She held it against her ear and said coyly, "Do they suit me?"

"Perfectly," Page said. "You can try them on in your room and look in the mirror."

"Oh, thank you so much," her mother said, putting the earring back in the box and closing the lid.

She stared down at the box in her lap for a long moment, and then turned to Page. She looked at her face, her clothes, the purse on her lap, glancing away and then back again.

"Who are you?" she asked.

On the drive back to the office, Page thought back to that moment. The familiar dread had clutched at her stomach. It had been nine months since her mother had stopped recognizing her and she was no more used to it now than she had been the first time. She was terrified seeing her mother's once-alert mind crumble.

As always, she had answered her mother's question with, "I'm Page, Mother. Your daughter."

And, as always, Clara had looked blankly at her and then, her eyes shaded with memory, said, "Your name is Page too. I once had a daughter named Page. She was a lovely girl. All the young men used to come by to see her. And then—then something happened. She became one of those women. You know, a w—h—o—r—e. She gave herself to men. For money, you know. I haven't seen her since that happened. She could be dead for all I know. It's such a shame. She was a lovely girl once."

A car cut in front of Page, dangerously close. She leaned on the horn and gave the driver the finger. It was a pointless gesture, but visits to her mother always left her feeling this way.

"Goddamnit!" she said aloud to herself. "Godfucking-damnit!"

She almost turned on her windshield wipers before she realized it was a beautiful, cloudless day and that she was seeing the road through the haze of tears streaming down her face.

"You're such a bunch of bastards," Jasmine said vehemently, her arms folded across her chest as she paced back and forth in her living room.

Jasmine's apartment was messier than usual, but that was the least of Allan's worries. He sat uncomfortably in an armchair, a drink on the table beside him. He felt like an errant child enduring a parental tongue-lashing. Jasmine wore a tight pale pink cotton T-shirt and blue jeans and was, as usual, stunningly beautiful, her long black hair hanging down her back, her cheeks flushed. Unfortunately, she was also angry.

"I'm the only one who had the decency to show up at her funeral," she continued. "Shit! David didn't even care enough to send flowers."

Allan spread his hands helplessly. "He had no choice," he explained again. "You know that we couldn't be associated with what happened. The scandal could have hurt us all."

"So you just took poor Selena back to her apartment and left the body there to be found by some stranger. Shit!"

Allan shuddered. What they had done was criminal, a criminal conspiracy. If Jasmine blabbed on about it . . .

Jesus! Worse yet, if Jason and the others found out she was blabbing . . .

"Jasmine, we weren't responsible for the fact she was stupid enough to OD and kill herself. She was already dead, for Chrissakes. All we did was take the fucking body back to her apartment. I couldn't have her found like that at my house. My wife and kids away, the scandal. Jesus! Surely you can see that."

"God! But it was so—so callous!" Jasmine said, unfolding her arms and clenching her fists. "It was like she was nothing. She was a person, just like you and me. A little compassion and respect wouldn't have been out of place."

"Well, maybe it could have been handled better, and maybe David should have sent flowers, but that's not our problem, sweetheart. That's between David and his conscience."

"He's an asshole!" she said, sitting heavily on the couch.

Allan felt relieved. He knew the signs. She was running out of anger, calming down. He got up and sat beside her, putting a hand on her leg. "But you know I love you, don't you?" he said.

"Yes," she said. "I know you do. The whole scene just pisses me off."

"It's over and done with," he said. "There's nothing we can do about it now. It was a terrible tragedy, but it's done."

Tears began to run down her cheeks. He put his arm around her and pulled her against him so that her head rested on his shoulder. "Come on, baby," he said.

"I really liked Selena," she sniffled. "She was crazy and wild, but I really liked her."

"I know you did. So did I," he said sympathetically.

Jasmine began to giggle, a fact that didn't surprise him. He was used to her mercurial moods. "Do you remember the time she drove her car into Billy's swimming pool? God, that was hysterical."

Allan shuddered. Bill Seidelman, a well-known and powerful Hollywood producer, had not been amused. He had banned Selena from ever coming to his home again. And as Allan had introduced Selena and David to Bill in the first place, he had lost a lot of points over the matter. David, of course, had been mortified and ended up paying for all the cleanup. The girl must have been a great lay for David to put up with her for so long, he thought.

"Listen," he said to Jasmine, "I've got a little surprise to cheer you up."

"What?" she said, moving her head to sit upright, the tears mysteriously drying.

"I've got to go to London next week to negotiate a joint production venture. Why don't you come with me? It'll do you good to get away for a while. We can see some plays. When I'm in meetings you can go shopping and exploring. We'll stay at Claridges, of course."

"Oh, that would be wonderful!" she said, clapping her hands in delight. "Can we go boating on the Thames? I've always wanted to do that."

"Anything your heart desires," he said generously.

"When?" she said, alarmed. "When are we going? I have to do some shopping, get my hair done, pack. Is there time?"

"Tuesday. The flight leaves in the afternoon. We arrive in London early in the morning."

"Oh, you're so good to me," she said, leaning across and kissing him lightly on the cheek. "What can I do to repay you?"

She ran her hand down his chest as she spoke, skillfully unbuttoning his shirt.

"What you always do," he said, smiling.

She slipped her hand below his shirt and began to stroke his chest. He felt stirrings of passion and noted that her nipples were hardening beneath the tight T-shirt.

"What I love to do," she murmured, nibbling at his skin.

Thank God, he thought. The danger was over. With the prospects of a trip and then five days in London, far away from here, she'd forget all about Selena.

Her hand crept down and worked on his fly. He moved his hips conveniently forward to allow her access.

This was what it was all about, he thought, looking forward to the approaching pleasure. Fuck Selena, fuck everyone. Jasmine took him to another place where nothing else existed.

"Love you, baby," he said as she lowered her head. He put his hands in her silky hair and gave himself up.

CHAPTER FOUR

Sharon Thomas walked past the Picasso, past a small Rodin sculpture in the living room, past a priceless collection of Chinese pottery and the T'ang horse, and past a cabinet filled with dainty Japanese netsuke. She noticed none of it.

The art was all Jason's. Her taste was more inclined toward the American moderns that filled their Santa Barbara home. Art as decoration, Jason scornfully called it. Here, in the Bel-Air house, where Jason often brought clients and other businessmen, his taste ruled. She often suspected that he had bought the house up north not so much for a retreat they could use to get out of LA, as he had claimed, but simply to give her something to decorate other than his precious Bel-Air residence.

She went through the French doors to the patio and stood among the lush hanging plants, looking out at the grounds. She wore only a white chiffon dressing gown. Beneath it she was naked.

Tall and blond, her skin had lost the pink luster of youth and her body some of its firmness, but she had retained the long shapely legs and large breasts that had first attracted men when she was in her teens. She still enjoyed admiring glances when she entered a room.

Her eyes narrowed when she saw Adam, her chauffeur.

He was lying beside the pool, his slim, tanned body clad only in brief bikini pants. It was Sunday, supposedly his day off. When Jason was home, Adam kept to the servant's quarters, but on days like this, when her husband was tied up elsewhere with business, she gave him the run of the house. It was all part of keeping the help happy, and the special services Adam provided made his happiness important to her.

"Adam!"

He looked up lazily and lifted a hand in acknowledgment.

She felt a flash of resentment. Why did she need him? At forty-five, although still attractive, she was fighting a losing battle against gravity. She needed his youth to remember her own; he, apparently, needed only her money. "Get your ass in here!" she said sharply.

He rose slowly and ambled toward her, a towel dragging at his side. It was quite an ass, too, she thought as she watched him. Tight, firm, young. The wide shoulders and flat stomach helped complete the picture of a twenty-five-year-old Adonis.

"You need to go somewhere?" he asked when he was about ten yards away.

Her eyes were drawn to the bulge of his crotch. It shifted from side to side with the motion of his legs, and for a brief moment, it seemed to have such a life of its own that she imagined it growling at her. As he grew closer she saw the full outline of his flaccid penis, compacted in a half-moon shape by the tight silk briefs.

"No," she said, her throat dry, her heart thumping at her chest, her irritation with him disappearing as it always did.

He noticed the direction of her eyes and smiled, a quick, sly smile, certain of the power behind it. "What can I do for you, ma'am?" he asked, ironically polite.

Her tanned hand touched the coiled shape, feeling the warmth the sun had given it. "I need a massage," she said.

He glanced sideways at the patio chairs and said, "Out here, ma'am?"

She squeezed her fingers suddenly, pinching his bulge,

bringing a gasp of surprise from him. "Inside," she said, removing her hand and turning.

He followed her into the house, his earlier insolent playfulness absent. Every now and then she had to remind him who was boss. Physical intimacy unavoidably bred a certain familiarity, but there was an unspoken line she did not encourage him to cross. She paid him, bought him clothes, provided a lenient work schedule, and it was not something she ever allowed him to forget, except in the bedroom, and even there, she was the final regulator of their activities.

She led the way up the stairs. The cook was in the kitchen, the maid had finished making up the bedrooms. They would be uninterrupted.

When they reached the bedroom, she turned, allowing the gown to fall open. Her skin was a golden brown, except for bikini marks that seemed painted on in white. Adam swept the door closed with one hand and came toward her, dropping his towel on the floor. She backed away until she felt the pressure of the bed against her legs. He came closer, still not speaking, and touched her breast. She had large brown nipples, and he ran a finger around one of them, gauging her reaction. Then he put an arm around her and pulled her to him, his face nuzzling her neck.

She pressed against him, her pelvis automatically lifting to meet his, and noticed his penis still wasn't hard. God! She couldn't even give a kid a hard-on anymore. Her earlier irritation flashed back, but she immediately suppressed it as she ran her palm firmly over his bulge. Then she swung him around so his back was to the bed and pushed him over. Before he could react, she fell to her knees and lowered her head, taking his penis in her mouth through the silk briefs, wetting them with her saliva, and grunting with pleasure at the sight of it unwinding and growing, straining against the thin material until it poked out the side.

Now he couldn't ignore her. Now he was excited. Now he was dealing with the best little cocksucker from Houston, Texas and probably all points west. Now he was thrusting up, his beautiful vacuous face contorted with a pleasure that breached pain.

"Now," she said, ripping the briefs down his leg and climbing over him, her own face flushed with exhilaration. "Now," she said, lowering her body until her saturated sex captured him, surrounded him. This was the moment she loved, when surprise colored his face.

"Now," she said, bouncing as joyfully as a child on a trampoline.

It lasted about three minutes, and then he groaned once, went as stiff as a board, and ejaculated.

She rolled off him and away to the other side of the bed. He lay there as if shot, his eyes closed, his penis already soft.

She reached beside the bed for a cigarette and lighted it, inhaling deeply and blowing the smoke up toward the ceiling. Shit, she thought, too fast, too selfish, too young. No staying power at all.

She looked over at him. So damned beautiful though, and so damned young. She wondered what he thought, if anything at all. His features were perfectly symmetrical, entirely unmarred by character or intelligence. She sometimes thought him inhuman, her own little robotic sex machine.

She had met him at the beach. He was surfing virtually full time then, and still did whenever he had the chance. It was the only time she had ever seen enthusiasm on his face. He had come in and plunked his board on the sand beside her, still wet, his muscular brown body shining like a shield in the sun. She had offered him a joint, then herself, and then a job. He had taken them all.

She wouldn't keep him much longer, she admitted to herself for the first time. She knew the signs, both his and hers. In the beginning he had at least pretended passion, now it was almost too much of a chore, and soon it would be. She, on the other hand, was beginning to feel the need for added stimuli. His skin-deep beauty wasn't enough to keep her occupied much longer. She had explored virtually everything he had to offer.

"Adam?"

He grunted.

"Time to go," she said, stubbing her cigarette out.

He rolled obediently off the bed and stood. He picked his briefs up from the floor and looked at them. Instead of putting them on again, he held them in his hand and wrapped his towel around his waist.

"Will you be needing me again today?" he asked.

"No, that will be all," she said.

She watched him leave, and then reached for another cigarette. She held it in her hand without lighting it. Such a bummer, she thought. Jason was an asshole, Adam was a nothing, and she couldn't find satisfaction, never had been able to. All she had was money, and there were still things it couldn't buy. She wanted to cry, really wanted to, but it was no use. She hadn't been able to cry for years—not for herself, not for anyone.

Jason walked gingerly around piles of bricks and broken masonry, critically examining every phase of construction. Even though it was Sunday, the curator of the Rex Museum, Stodding Watson, was with him, a pleased expression on his face.

Watson had good reason to be pleased: The new wing of the museum would elevate it to the status of the Los Angeles County Art Museum, the Norton Simon Museum, and the Getty. And the thirty-million-dollar extension, which had started as his dream, was becoming a reality mainly because of Jason Thomas's generosity, influence, and persistence. Which is why the new wing was going to be named the Thomas Wing.

"How far behind schedule are they?" Jason asked, stopping at what would be the sculpture room.

"Just a few weeks, which isn't bad. In targeting the opening, we allowed for a two-month delay, which is more par for the course in construction these days, I'm told."

Jason nodded. He had chosen the contractor himself, and as the company had done three office buildings for him in the past, with the promise of more to come, they were working to please him. God knows what would have happened if he had left it to the museum administration. Watson and his staff knew art, but what they knew about business wouldn't have got the first brick laid.

A tall, slightly bowed man with distinguished graying temples and a gregarious manner, Watson was not without charm. He could be termed a "social climber," but Jason did not underestimate his abilities. Stod, as his friends called him, knew how to coax money from wealthy patrons, particularly socially conscious and elderly widows, and he knew how to get the right kind of publicity for the museum. But he was not a detail-oriented person, preferring to think in terms of the broad picture, a trait that was both an asset and a limitation. His main concern was his vision for the future, of which this wing was a large part, and he hired a very able staff to take care of the day-to-day details of running an art museum. If Jason had had any doubts about Stod's basic intelligence, they were laid to rest when the curator approached him to help raise money for the new wing. Stod knew that Jason was a man who got things done.

More through luck than intelligence, Watson's approach happened to coincide with Jason's recognition that, although he had abundant wealth and power, what he still needed was a higher and more acceptable social profile among the people who really counted in Los Angeles—the old money families. These included the original landowners, the financiers who opened up California, the media kings whose holdings overshadowed his, the oil barons, from families who scorned Bel-Air as a "pretentious development for the nouveau riche," flouting addresses in Pasadena, San Marino and, of course, Santa Barbara.

Jason's response had astounded and delighted Stod Watson. Jason proposed that he alone put up half the thirty million dollars needed for the new wing, raising the rest himself from business associates and other museum donors. Furthermore, he would donate some of his valuable collection to be displayed in the new building. All he wanted in return was that the wing carry his name and be called the Thomas Wing.

Although he never mentioned it to anyone, Jason saw it as more than an entree into new levels of society; he saw it as a form of immortality. His name would be enshrined forever as a cultural benefactor.

Stod didn't care about the name, only about the increased space and stature the wing would bring him. It was a marriage made in heaven.

The two men began to walk back toward the main building and Stod's office. The courtyard was crowded with the usual Sunday visitors—tourists, young families, old European immigrants, dwellers of the barrios and slums who sought brief spiritual elevation through contact with timeless art. A magician performed in one corner, drawing a large group of admirers. Ten percent of what went into the hat was donated to the museum. Stod never missed an opportunity.

Jason looked at his watch. He was planning to spend a couple of hours with Page and then take her with him to a business dinner.

"Jason, have you decided yet what pieces you are going to donate to the wing?" Stod asked.

Jason shook his head and smiled. "I want to surprise you," he said.

"Of course," Stod said, hiding his frustration. He knew every piece in Jason's collection and there were a few that he was determined to have. "Should you need any help with your decision, I would be delighted to assist in any way I can."

"Thank you," Jason said, knowing exactly what Watson was thinking.

He also knew exactly what pieces he would donate. The truth was, only a small percentage of his collection was museum quality—paintings he wasn't that proud of and three sculptures. What he planned to do before the wing opened was to acquire a stunning and invaluable work. He had no idea yet what it would be or where he would find it, but it would be a coup that would set the tongues of the art world twaddling from London to New York and immediately establish the wing as an international presence. It would be an Old Master or Impressionist work. That much he knew. Needless to say, it would also establish him.

To do this, he was prepared to spend between five and seven million dollars, additional money he was planning to raise among a few close associates. He had already discreetly put the word out to a few art dealers he trusted in Los Angeles, New York, London, and Paris. Soon, something would turn up.

It was a tremendously exciting venture, to seek out and secure something so unique it would be virtually priceless. To discover perhaps an unknown Rembrandt or Matisse, or an ancient Greek statue. He didn't really care what it was, only that it be one of the great art objects of the world.

An impossible task? Not when you had money. And not when you were Jason Thomas.

And that little surprise, he thought with some satisfaction, would put Stod Watson on his ear. Not to mention the rest of the art world.

Whenever she was asked about her name or her past, Jasmine grew either vague or enigmatic, depending upon what the situation called for. "Jasmine who?" men would say at parties. "Just Jasmine, darling," she would reply. "Just Jasmine." They would eye her exotic Oriental beauty and ask exasperatedly, "But who are you? Where are you from? How did you get here?" And she would evade their eyes and glance across the room and say, "I am who I am. Why are you so hung up about the past? It's meaningless." And then the cunning, "If we dwelt on the pain of the past, where would we be today? How could we create a future?" Then they imagined bound feet, servitude, torture in Chinese prisons, starvation in Macao, and God knew what else. It was a good game. Nothing kept men as interested as a large measure of beauty mixed in with a dash of mystery.

And yet, as she sat alone in her apartment this Sunday afternoon while Allan was occupied with his weekly Family Day, Jasmine found herself dwelling embarrassingly and morbidly on her past. It wasn't anything new and was unavoidable. It happened every Sunday. She had nothing to do, nobody to see, nowhere to go. She sat alone in her West

Hollywood apartment, brooding as fixatedly as any middle-class hausfrau, and realized again that she hated Sundays.

She thought of her family and the stifling life she had led with them, tradition-bound, superstitious, parochial. They had not been poor—her father made a good living—but they might as well have been. Spending money had always been anathema to him.

She cheered herself up by thinking how far she had come with nothing but her wits, her beauty, and her natural understanding of men's emotional needs.

She had met Allan in just that fashion, snaring him by being enigmatic. It had happened at a party at some producer's house, a man named Kenneth Draper, who was reputed to get his financing from members of the Colombian Mafia. Judging by the generous mounds of white powder filling strategically placed crystal bowls for the guests, there was probably some truth to the rumor. She had just finished a minor role in his latest film, a martial arts "B" movie in which she ended her life as the victim of some evil Fu Manchu. Her demise did not occur, however, without torn bodice and the exposure of some silky thigh. She thought she had made a good impression.

She knew who Allan was, of course. As head of Elixer, he was a public figure in the business. Apparently he was putting in an appearance because Draper was releasing his next film through the studio. As he told her later, he hadn't intended to stay long—until he saw her.

When they were introduced, he held her hand a moment longer than appropriate and complimented her on the part she had played in Draper's film. "Why haven't we seen you before?" he asked.

The slim, handsome man impressed her as well, not only because of his looks, but more immediately because of his obvious power and influence—two attributes of some value to an ambitious actress. Acting jobs were few and far between in Hollywood's competitive environment. She knew as well as anyone that talent had little to do with success. There were a thousand talented and beautiful girls up for parts every day. It was more important who you knew.

She smiled at his question without answering it, waiting for the next one.

"Your name?" he asked. "Is that all you go by?"

"Yes, just Jasmine," she answered.

"It's very beautiful," he said. "As you are."

It was virtually all they said, apart from a few polite social remarks. The next day he called and invited her to dinner.

They went out four times before she slept with him. By then the hook was set. He found her charming, sexy, and fascinating. She told him almost nothing about herself, in spite of his numerous curious questions. He wasn't even sure if she was American-born.

When she finally slept with him, it was an incomparably sensual experience. She was both demanding and gentle, wanton and innocent, consistently contradictory, in keeping with the mysterious image of her she had created in his mind.

After the second time, two days later, he asked her to be his mistress. "You can't safely sleep around these days," he explained. "And, frankly, I don't know about you, but I'm past the point of casual fucking. My family, my position . . . Until I met you, there was no one I wanted to be with, anyway. Now I want you. And I want you to be mine. I can't marry you. I already have a family. But I can love you and look after you."

Loving her and looking after her meant that he would pay for her apartment, he would get her work when she needed it, he would provide an allowance for expenses. He didn't say it, but she knew there would also be gifts.

It was almost too good to be true. In exchange for a continuing liaison with a man she found immensely attractive anyway, she would gain a security she hadn't been able to achieve on her own and probably wouldn't be able to for years. All he wanted in return was her love and her loyalty. She had suppressed the immediate inclination to jump up and down for joy.

"None of that is necessary," she said wisely. "I don't want your money. We can just see each other when you like."

"Look, the money doesn't matter. It's unimportant," he said. "But I love you and that's my way of committing to you."

He didn't have to say that it would also be her way of committing to him. She would indeed be his. She would see no other men in her capacity as his mistress, bought and paid for.

"I'll think about it," she said, and proceeded to give him the best head he had ever had in his life.

After two days, in which he pressed her for an answer, she finally agreed. They celebrated with a weekend in Puerto Vallarta.

That had been a year ago. In the intervening time, they had both lived up to their agreement and created a workable relationship. She had been loyal and affectionate, always there when he needed her, intuitively able to satisfy him with passion when necessary, or compassion when appropriate. He, in turn, had provided the material benefits he had promised, with the additional perks of gifts, travel, and entree into circles she might never have entered.

She had grown in her way to love him, she thought. He was by no means a perfect man. At times he was selfish, dominating, emotionally unreliable, but he was kind to her, he adored her, and he was exceedingly generous.

It was only lately that a demon of dissatisfaction had begun to whisper in her ear. Only since Selena's death.

The loss of a friend alone hadn't disturbed her but also Allan's and his friends' reaction. They acted as if Selena had never existed for any of them. Her name was never mentioned, their lives were all unchanged by her departure, the dreadful waste had taken nothing from any of them. Selena had proved herself truly expendable.

The only difference between Jasmine and Selena was that Selena had had money of her own. She, on the other hand, was dependent on Allan, more now than she had ever been. She hadn't pursued her career with any aggressiveness to speak of, only cursory courtesy calls to her agent; the parts that came her way literally fell into her lap through Allan. She did them and waited for the next one. Her career had no momentum. Neither had she saved anything. All she had was a vast wardrobe and a handful of jewelry.

What if? . . . No, Jasmine thought. Allan loved her, just as she loved him. He would marry her if he could. He had said so many times. He would never just toss her out like Angie had been or desert her if she was in trouble. He wasn't that kind of man.

She wished she could call him now, hear his voice, console herself with his murmured affections. But it wasn't possible. It was Sunday, and he was with his family.

And she was alone.

She began to halfheartedly tidy up the living room, shoving some records back into the cabinet. One of these days she'd file them by category or, at the very least, by artist.

Maybe she should tidy up the kitchen or vacuum the living room. They could both use it. Wasn't that what Sundays were for?

The hell with it! She would go shopping, she decided suddenly. Shopping always cheered her up. She would buy some clothes for the trip to London, nothing extravagant—Allan was sure to buy her clothes while they were there—but something comfortable to travel in. And perhaps something new and different to wear while she was shopping in London.

Opening the Sunday paper, she began to scan the advertisements, looking for something that would catch her eye and spark her imagination.

Allan Silver skillfully turned the steak over with long-handled tongs and said to the other men, "The secret is never to pierce the meat. Gotta keep those juices in there."

Sunday afternoon was family time. He religiously maintained it as the one day he spent time with his wife, Elena, their two sons, Daniel and Robert, and family friends, no matter what business pressures existed. Somehow this commitment justified his hectic existence outside of the family on the other six days—and his philandering with Jasmine.

Today, David Ross was there with his wife, Pat. To round out the party, his neighbors, Peter and Alice Chalmers, had come with their teenage daughter, Olivia. Chalmers was an entertainment lawyer and they had done business together in the past.

The men stood around the barbecue pit, while the women lolled on lounge chairs beside the pool. His thirteen-year-old son Daniel swam, while Robert, who was fifteen, sunbathed beside Olivia, who was six months younger yet ripening rapidly and suddenly worthy of Robert's undivided attention.

Ross and Chalmers began to toss a tennis ball at each other while Allan cooked.

"The kids are playing," Elena said to nobody in particular.

In her mid-thirties, she was a still beautiful woman, with dark hair and honey-brown skin. She had come to Hollywood as an actress at nineteen, struggled for a year, and then met Allan. Nothing if not pragmatic, she ditched her dreams of stardom, married him, and settled for a life of luxury instead. At the time he had simply been a fairly successful, by no means wealthy agent, but she knew ambition when she saw it and hitched herself to his rising star.

She sipped at her vodka tonic and said, "I saw Donna Marks at Giorgio's yesterday. She looked like shit."

"I heard she has AIDS," Alice Chalmers said.

"The way some of these actresses sleep around, I wouldn't be surprised," Pat Ross said.

Unlike Alice who was blond, verging on voluptuous, and pretty in a Barbie-doll way, Pat was blond and plain. A tall woman with sharp, angular features, thick curved eyebrows, and a mouth too small for her face, Pat looked as if she had spent her life around horses. Her hips were broad and her thighs muscular, but she had surprisingly tiny and dainty hands with long slender fingers.

"Whatever she has, it isn't good," Elena said. "She looks like she's dropped about twenty pounds, and she didn't need to."

"God, I could drop twenty pounds," Alice said. "Well, ten maybe."

"Anyone like another drink?" Pat asked, standing.

"I'm fine," Alice said.

Elena just shook her head. She didn't offer to pour. Pat had been around their house enough to help herself at the bar.

"She sure puts them away," Alice said when she was out of earshot.

"Only on Sundays," Elena said. The truth was, Pat drank like a fish every day, usually starting at lunchtime, sleeping for a bit in the afternoon, and then picking it up again before dinner. She never got really drunk, just sodden. But Alice wasn't really a close friend, just a neighbor, and Elena didn't feel like discussing Pat's problem with her.

As far as Elena could tell, Pat's main problem was David. She couldn't figure out what held that marriage together. It certainly wasn't sex. Judging by the few comments Pat made, there was none. David apparently had a mistress for that, according to Pat. When Pat had divulged this over lunch the week before, Elena had laughingly suggested that Pat take a lover. Pat had looked wryly at herself and said, "Who'd want me?" It had been such a sad comment.

She knew Allan had other women. Hell, as head of a studio, he had pussy pushed into his face all the time. But at least he didn't neglect her. They made love twice a week regularly, which was more than enough for her. Truth was, after all these years, their sex had settled into a pretty mechanical rut. Comfortable, but there was nothing spontaneous or exciting about it any more. Hadn't been for years. Any more than twice a week and it would have been a chore to be avoided.

Occasionally, she found herself wondering about his affairs, but it was never with concern, just idle curiosity. They didn't threaten her, never would. The situation was acceptable as it was. He would never leave her for anyone else; he took his family responsibilities too seriously for that. This predictable stability was the most important thing in her life.

Perhaps David had a similar sense of obligation to Pat. Why else would he stay with her? Not that she wasn't a nice person, she reminded herself quickly. It was just that they had so little in common. David was flashy, Pat plain. He was glib; beneath her dull exterior, she was intellectually curious. He was, in spite of his eminently respectable position, little more than a quick-buck artist, a man who believed in expediency; she came from a wealthy family where money was acquired in a more genteel manner. Still, she had supported him steadfastly throughout his career, and no hint of their marital problems ever surfaced. Or had until now. Maybe that was enough to keep them together.

Pat's other problem was their daughter, Pamela, who Elena had never met. She was about twenty and a student somewhere back East, apparently living her life from one scrape to the next. Every few months her escapades occupied Pat's energies.

Pat came out with her drink and sat heavily in her chair, spilling a little in the maneuver. "Goddamnit!" she said, drying her leg with a towel.

Pat never swore—unless she was drinking heavily. The rest of the time, she was the perfect investment banker's wife. Conservative, charming, socially aware. Generally, she only let her hair down among friends.

"Allan's going to London next week," Elena said to her. "Would you like to come up to Santa Barbara with me? We could stay overnight at the El Encante. Do some shopping."

"Maybe," Pat said. "There's supposed to be a marvelous new gallery there that I've wanted to see."

"What's happening in London?" Alice asked.

Elena rolled her eyes. "Film business. He has to meet some Italians and Germans, or is it English? I don't know. Something about a joint venture in China. I don't know."

"Oh, I've always wanted to go to China," Alice chimed in. "I've been trying to get Peter to take me for two years. He's always too busy. Do you know, we haven't had a real vacation for almost three years! Last year, Olivia and I had to go to Hawaii by ourselves. It was so boring."

"This year you'd have your hands full. She's grown up a bit," Elena said, looking at Olivia and her son. He was telling her something and touching her hand as he spoke.

"It'd be nice to get out of this damn city for a couple of days," Pat murmured, her mind still on the possibility of Santa Barbara.

"I'll call you tomorrow and we can set something up," Elena said. She looked over the expanse of lawn at the barbecue pit and saw the men were ladling meat onto plates. "Looks like the food's on. I'd better get the salad."

"I'll help," Pat said, getting to her feet.

They walked toward the house and Pat said, "You know I told you that David has a mistress?"

"Yes?" Elena said.

"I think he's given her up."

"Why? What makes you think that? Did he say something?"

"No," Pat said. "Last night he fucked me."

Later, after everyone had left and the boys were in bed, Allan and Elena stood side by side in the bathroom. He wore pajamas and she one of the sheer nightgowns she kept for these nights. She brushed her hair while Allan gargled.

"Does David have a mistress?" she asked suddenly.

Allan stopped gargling and spat into the sink before answering. "Why on earth do you ask that?" he said.

"Pat says he does. Or did."

"I've no idea," Allan said. "He's never said anything to me about having something on the side like that."

"Half the men in this town do," she said spitefully.

It was too close to home. Allan reached for a towel and dried his mouth. "Talking about sex," he said, "did you notice Robert and Olivia. Pretty soon he's going to be slipping over the fence and into her bedroom."

"I know, her hormones are bursting out all over," Elena said.

David put an arm around her and cupped her breast in his hand. "Talking about sex, are you going to stop brushing your hair long enough to come to bed?"

She put down her brush and smiled, following him into the bedroom. But her eyes were thoughtful. His reaction had been curious. Something in his voice. Maybe it was just boy's honor, a code that forbade telling tales out of school.

He sat on the bed and patted it. "Come to daddy," he said.

Yes, that was probably it, she thought as she walked toward him. Something to do with the men sticking together against the wives. Childish, but totally predictable among these men.

She sat beside him and rubbed his chest, her thoughts forgotten now. They each had their duty to do.

CHAPTER FIVE

Kate felt a strong sense of accomplishment. First of all, it hadn't been that difficult to find out exactly who David Ross was. Art circles, even in a city as large as Los Angeles, are incestuous, with important collectors well known to the major galleries. After wondering for a while which course to take, Kate discovered that all she needed to do was call a business associate, Madge Bernstein, the owner of Friars, a well-known gallery on Melrose Avenue. Madge had all the answers.

David Ross, she learned, was a well-known investment banker, president of his own company, Ross and Company, Inc., with offices in Los Angeles, New York, and London. He was wealthy, married, and a patron of the arts—a term that brought a wry smile to her face. It had lost the original meaning of a wealthy patron who financially supported individual artists. Today it meant someone who bought expensive art, often merely for investment purposes. More important, she learned that Ross had been invited to an opening that week at Friars, a retrospective of three major California artists.

"Is he likely to come?" she asked.

"Oh, yes. I'm sure he will. He collects Breer's works," Madge said. Breer was a reclusive oil painter, one of the three artists exhibiting. The second was a watercolorist, the third a sculptor.

Kate's luck was running well. Madge's next question was to ask what she was doing in Los Angeles. "I heard you'd left Wallace Dotson's gallery. Do you have a job here?"

"I decided to come out to where the sun shines," Kate said lightly. "I don't have a job, but I'm looking. That was the second reason for my call. Do you know of anything?"

There was a slight pause, and then Madge said, "Well, I happen to need some help myself." She added hurriedly, "Of course I can't pay what you were earning in New York, but if you're interested, we could talk about it."

By the end of the conversation, Kate had a job, starting the following morning, Tuesday. She had accomplished two goals with one telephone call, hence her self-satisfaction.

She arrived at the gallery bright and early, wearing old jeans and a T-shirt, knowing from experience how involved and messy preparations for a show could get. Madge, short, plump, and energetic as a beaver, was already there, her mop of red hair disappearing behind crates as she talked. Every now and then she lifted the ends of her red sweatshirt and wiped her forehead with it.

"The show is tomorrow?" Kate asked, incredulously eyeing the chaos.

Madge popped out from behind a large packaged painting and slapped a mat knife into her palm. "Tomorrow night we open. Half of Breer's paintings only came in this morning. I'm usually not this late."

Kate carefully cut the string around the painting and then the tape that held the cardboard. "How did you land Breer? Have you met him?"

Breer, the only name he was known by, was something of a mystery in art circles. As far as Kate knew, nobody had ever met him. He disdained publicity, turned down all interviews, and never attended his own shows. When he appeared on the scene about five years ago to almost instant acclaim, he had issued a written statement explaining that his art spoke for itself. "If the work is good, it will stand on its own without the cult of personality and image to help it." Naturally, the tantalizing mystery had simply added to the question of personality and stirred a debate as to whether he was truly exhibiting extraordinary integrity or simply a marketing genius.

"He wrote me a letter out of the blue and asked me to exhibit his works. About a year ago. Of course I accepted," Madge said. "But I've never met him, never even spoken to him."

"Amazing," Kate said. "I guess your reputation preceded you."

Friars *was* well thought of in art circles, thanks entirely to Madge's diligence since she had become sole proprietor four years earlier. Originally, it had been owned by her plastic surgeon husband as an investment, the business simply plodding along under the management of others. Then the good doctor fell in love with a nineteen-year-old actress who wanted her nose done, and after the dust cleared, Madge owned, among other things, the art gallery as part of the divorce settlement.

At first she had thrown herself into the gallery as a form of therapy, a way to put the ugliness of the divorce out of her mind. But then she had discovered a competence for business she never knew she possessed. After the usual trial and error during a lengthy process of self-education, she managed to create one of the most viable galleries in Los Angeles.

Kate finished unwrapping the painting and leaned it against the wall. It was a landscape: a hilly village, whitewashed houses as close together as teeth, winding roads, a hint of azure ocean in the background, all done in the bold, colorful strokes that were Breer's trademark. The scene was alive and vital, yet imbued with a curious tranquility.

"This is incredible," she said, awed.

Madge stood beside her. "He's an incredible talent."

"It looks like Greece—or Spain," Kate said.

"They're all island scenes," Madge said. "The Mediterranean, Catalina, the islands off South Carolina, Indonesia, Australia."

"A travelling man," Kate said enviously.

"Apparently so."

Kate began to open another package, an unfamiliar excitement gripping her. There was a lot of art she liked, but possibly even more that left her cold. This feeling of discovery, of *recognition* was rare. She had felt it the first time she had seen Cezanne's paintings as a child, and again when she had first seen Monet's water lilies. But modern artists seldom evoked such strong passions, which every dealer hoped for and all too rarely experienced. This artist Breer, whoever he was, did it for her. She had seen photographs of his work before and had admired them tremendously, but photos seldom did a painting justice. They had been a validation of his technique for her, but this—seeing the paintings as they were meant to be seen—created an emotional response.

The morning turned out to be a delightful journey of discovery. Each of Breer's paintings plucked a different string, touched another chord. None of them bored her. This man saw things, showed her colors, tones, shapes, scenes, beauty she had never seen before. By one o'clock she was exhausted by her own high-flying emotions and gratefully accepted Madge's invitation to lunch.

Madge drove through the bustling downtown traffic to a small Thai restaurant on the south side of Wilshire Boulevard. Kate was unfamiliar with the cuisine and Madge had to guide her through the menu, warning her which items would probably be too spicy for her palate.

The inevitable question came after they ordered, but Kate was prepared for it.

"What's your interest in David Ross?" Madge asked.

"Oh, a friend of mine in New York knows him and suggested I look him up. She said he might be able to help me find a job, but that's not necessary now," she said lightly.

"Oh, I see. Well, I suppose he's a good person to know.

Very influential. Very involved in the new Thomas Wing of the Rex Museum. You've heard of that, of course?''

''Yes. I read about it. Jason Thomas is behind it, right?''

Madge sipped on her Thai iced tea. ''Ross is a good friend of his. Helped raise a lot of the money and donated some himself. He'll probably come to the show.''

''I see.''

''Thomas may show up as well. I hope so. He's filthy rich. But I don't think he's too fond of Breer's work. Anyway, if that whole gang turns up, it'll be quite a show, in more ways that one.'' Madge smiled. ''They'll all come with their mistresses, very exotic-looking young ladies.''

''Mistresses?'' Kate asked.

''Oh, yeah,'' Madge said. ''Everybody who's anybody in LA has a mistress—at least in those circles.'' Her eyes narrowed. ''There are certain places they can take their women, you understand, where there won't be television cameras and newspaper photographers and paparazzi. An art show is pretty low-key. You never know. Sometimes they bring their wives, sometimes their mistresses. I've learned never to address anyone as Mrs., unless they're introduced first.''

''Ross and Thomas both have mistresses?''

Madge shrugged. ''Who knows? Things change all the time.''

She shifted the conversation. ''I think New York's days of glory as the center of the American art world are fading,'' Madge said. ''With the new wing of the LA County Art Museum, the enormous finances the Getty has, the Norton Simon and the Rex growing at such a pace, Los Angeles has suddenly in the last few years become a major player. On top of that, sitting on the edge of the Pacific, this is, or soon will be, the most vital economy in the world.''

''I know. It's very exciting,'' Kate said, adding untruthfully, ''that's one of the main reasons I was willing to move out here.''

Madge sighed. ''I don't like to talk about my failures, but I came this close to getting Breer exhibited in the new wing." Her thumb and forefinger almost touched, to show the distance.

"Really? What happened?"

"Well, I showed Stodding Watson, the director of the Rex, Breer's work, and he loved it. One of the rooms in the new wing is going to contain the solo work of a contemporary artist. I thought, and so did he, that Breer would be a perfect example of fine contemporary work. Then, he changed his mind—like that!" She snapped her fingers.

"Do you know why?"

"Apparently Jason Thomas didn't agree with Watson's judgment. He wouldn't tell me more than that. But, it's Thomas's wing, and he has some influence over what is chosen to appear in it. I guess he didn't think Breer was well-known enough."

"God, that's too bad. It would have made Breer's career. I mean, I'm sure he does well, but he's not considered a *major* artist and he should be."

"Yeah," Madge sighed. "His paintings would have tripled in value."

"And your commissions," Kate added slyly.

"Talking about money, I've been thinking about expanding into authentication, offering it as a service," Madge said. "You'd be well qualified to run the department, if you're interested."

"I'd be interested in talking about it more."

"We'll get into it more after the show," Madge promised. "Anyway, I'm glad you moved out here. I think you'll do very well for yourself."

"I'm sure I will," Kate said firmly. "I have no misgivings about it."

Madge beamed, oblivious to the true meaning behind Kate's words.

"How much did you make on the GDO stock, my dear?" Elsa asked, lying on her couch, clad in a long oriental robe, a glass of peppermint schnapps in one hand.

Page sat opposite her, slightly distracted by the flickering television picture on the other side of the room. Elsa had, however, turned the sound down in deference to her visitor.

"About eight thousand dollars," Page said.

"I made fifty thousand dollars on that deal," Elsa said. "It was a good tip you gave me."

"You sold at twenty?"

"Yes, just like you said. It began to slide at twenty-four."

"I know. It's somewhere around twelve now."

"And how go things with your man?" It was a question Elsa always asked.

"Fine, I suppose," Page said enthusiastically, sipping her drink and putting the glass down on the table. She didn't particularly care for schnapps, but as it was all Elsa drank, she usually had it when visiting her.

"Is something wrong?" Elsa asked shrewdly, her bright eyes fixed on Page.

Page shrugged. "I don't know. I don't like depending on him so much. He's unpredictable . . . he's a dangerous man, I think."

Elsa smiled and said, "Dangerous men are the only ones worth knowing."

"Easy to say," Page said.

"Are you afraid of him?" Elsa asked seriously.

"Sometimes."

Elsa nodded. "It's a good thing you recognize both those facts. What are you going to do?"

"Do?" Page asked, surprise in her voice. "Nothing. There isn't anything I can do. I'll continue. And I'll keep making money as fast as I can, no matter how painfully slow it seems."

"You see money as your freedom," Elsa said, a strangely troubled expression on her face.

"As you've always told me, it's the only way to be independent," Page said.

"Yes, I did. But it's not the most important thing in life."

"Elsa, what are you going on about?" Page said, impatient at the turn the conversation was taking.

Elsa shrugged and her entire obese body seemed to wobble. She waved a languid hand at the room. "I have bought everything I want," she said. "There isn't anything else I need."

"So?"

"But there are things I long for."

"Like what, Elsa?"

Elsa looked down at her body, and when she spoke, her voice was morose. "I am an old woman now, Page. I'm bored with making money. There's no purpose to it anymore. More and more I find myself longing for youth, for adventure."

"But you've had enough adventures to fill a book," Page said, trying to sound encouraging.

"Had," Elsa emphasized. "Now I'm supposed to grow old gracefully and die."

"You need to get out more often. See more of the world," Page said.

"*Ja.* Once I created the world. I was a participant. Now I'm supposed to see it, turning my head from side to side like a cow put out to graze."

"Elsa, stop it. You're depressing me," Page said.

"I never had enough adventures. I should have had more when I had the opportunity," Elsa said. "I just don't want you to make the same mistake. Make your money, but don't forget to have your adventures."

"Elsa, why don't I take you down to Venice. We can walk along the beach, look at the locals. It'll do you good."

"It hurts my legs to walk," Elsa complained. She looked at her glass and raised her voice. "Maria! Another schnapps, please."

"You're hopeless," Page said, a smile appearing.

"Just don't you become hopeless," Elsa grumbled, looking fondly at Page. "You have never wanted to borrow my money. You let me invest in your business, but that's all. I want you to know that if you ever need it, it is there for you."

"I appreciate it, Elsa, but I'll be fine," Page said, glancing at her watch. "I have to go. I have dinner with a client."

"Is the business going okay?"

"Yes, but I'll have to figure out another way to make my fortune."

"If anyone will, you will," Elsa conceded.

Page got up and kissed her on the cheek. "I'll come and see you again soon."

"You promise, my dear, but how often do I see you? Not often enough," Elsa complained.

"I'll come soon. And, Elsa, you really should go out more often," Page said, looking down at her.

"I have everything I need here," Elsa said.

"Except adventure," Page reminded her.

Elsa waved, a dismissive gesture.

The late June weather in London was unseasonably warm. According to the newspapers, which apparently took the state of the weather very seriously, the mid-eighty-degree weather constituted a heat wave. To Jasmine it felt like stepping on the plane in California on Tuesday and getting off the plane in California on Wednesday.

It wasn't what she had expected. Gloomy old London was as bright as a button. Its inhabitants filled the rolling green parks and clogged the sidewalks. Traffic moved at a snail's pace through the narrow streets, but nobody seemed to mind. The English, who normally grumble more than any people on earth, were unusually cheerful. And Jasmine, who had never been abroad before, was like a kid in a candy store.

Claridges was everything Allan had told her it would be. It was like stepping into the eighteenth century, with its high ceilings and powder-puff plaster and gracious service. Guests sat in the lobby, sipping tea and cocktails, discreetly watching the new arrivals. And their suite was the size of a huge apartment, its emphasis on comfort rather than style.

Right after they showered and changed, she insisted that Allan take her for a ride on a double-decker bus. As his first appointment wasn't for a few hours, he readily agreed, captivated as usual by her infectious enthusiasm.

Boarding a red double-decker near their hotel in Mayfair,

they took it to Picadilly Circus, which was close to where Allan had a late lunch appointment with a group of Italian and English filmmakers. But they didn't make it five blocks before Jasmine spotted a string of small boutiques. "Look, look at those!" she said, pointing a finger. "Let's get off and see!"

Allan examined his watch. He still had time to kill. He'd experienced shopping expeditions with Jasmine before, however, and knew he'd probably end up leaving her at the stores and catching a taxi to his appointment. She was, as a T-shirt he'd once seen stated, "Born to Shop."

"Okay," he said. After all, he'd promised her shopping in London and this was as good a time as any to start.

She pulled the cord and they lurched down the stairs. She twirled around the pole in the doorway and spun off the bus as it stopped.

"Come on," she shouted gaily, and started walking back toward the stores.

"Oh, I love London," she said as he caught up with her. "I've only been here a couple of hours and I love it already. Look! A fish and chip shop. It's so—so—"

"English," Allan said dryly.

"No. Quaint. I meant, quaint."

"You should see the villages just outside of London," he said. "They're like movie sets. We'll take a day, rent a car, and drive out along the Thames. If you think this is quaint, wait till you see some of those towns."

"How many times have you been here?" she asked, stopping and taking his arm.

"I don't know. Fifteen or twenty times, I guess."

"God, I envy you," she said. For a moment there was a look of stark hunger on her face, but then it disappeared.

"I have something for you," he said. He reached into his jacket pocket and withdrew his wallet. "You need something to shop with."

She expected him to hand her money, perhaps a few hundred dollars, but instead he took a credit card from his wallet and gave it to her. "For you," he said. "It has a credit limit of four thousand dollars. Don't spend it all in one place."

She took the card and hugged him. "Thank you, Allan. Thank you."

She looked down at the card again and, for the first time, saw the name imprinted on it.

"Yes," he said, with a satisfied smile at her expression. "Just Jasmine. You don't know how much trouble it took to arrange that."

For the rest of the day Jasmine thought she had walked through the pearly gates. Allan left after an hour to keep his appointment, and the day was hers. She lunched alone at the Coconut Grove on Barrett Street, conveniently close to the wonderful shops on Oxford and Bond streets. She went to department stores and boutiques she had only read of—Selfridges, Liberty's on Regent Street, Dickens & Jones, and Fortnum & Mason. She bought boots of English leather, sweaters of Shetland wool (although it was summer, she was thinking ahead), and counted her discovery of a store called So Sari the coup of the day. It featured Indian and Thai silk, and in spite of the name, saris made up only a small portion of the inventory. The majority of the stock consisted of fashionable silk gowns, skirts, scarves, jackets, and robes. By five o'clock she had bought more than she could carry. When her taxi drove up to the front of Claridges the doorman had to assist with her packages.

There was a message from Allan saying he would pick her up at seven for dinner—a "business" dinner, which indicated that he didn't want her to dress or behave too outrageously.

Jasmine was disappointed. She had planned to model her clothes for him—without underwear. A little reward for his generosity. It would have to wait. Duty called and left her just enough time to shower, dress, and make her face and hair beautiful. She wore silk as usual. A skirt that showed six inches of her legs above the knees, a loose turquoise blouse, and a cavalier scarf that fell halfway down her back.

Promptly at seven, Allan arrived and, after kissing her cheek, jumped into the shower and changed his clothes, all in less than ten minutes. By 7:15 they were inside a roomy London taxi, heading for their destination in Belgravia.

"We're meeting three men," Allan said. He leaned back in the seat, closed his eyes for a second, and rubbed his forehead. "There's Peter Willoughby of Acton Films, Sergio Morino of Morino Films in Rome, and his production man Elan Vittorio. Willoughby is a real English gentleman, on the outside. Beneath that, he's as tough as nails. We're going to his London home for dinner. He also has an estate in the Cotswolds. Morino is a self-made Italian tycoon. Very full of himself and theatrical. He's also an old lech. And I don't know enough about Vittorio. But I want you to be nice to them, particularly the Italians. Very nice."

"How nice is that exactly?" Jasmine asked, not liking his emphasis.

"Oh, God, come on," Allan said with an angry sidelong glance. "I'm not asking you to sleep with them. Just be pleasant with Morino. Flirt with him if you have to. He loves beautiful young women."

"Is that why you invited me to London?"

"Of course not," he said mollifyingly. "I invited you because I wanted to be with you. I'm just asking you to be your normal charming self."

"I didn't need to be reminded of that," she said.

"Jesus! Forget I said anything," he said, and stared out of the window.

They drove in an uncomfortable silence for five minutes, and then Jasmine moved closer to him and touched his arm. "I'm sorry, Allan. I'm not trying to be difficult, but it's you I love. I don't want to flirt with anyone else."

Allan shook his head. "I know. I guess I'm just nervous about the deal. The Italians are the ones with the contacts to the Chinese. It's not in the bag yet, there are a few problems to iron out, and there's a lot riding on it."

"Don't worry," she said. "I'll be nice to your Italian."

"Just be yourself," he said. "That's nice enough."

The Italian turned out to be a large, jovial man in his sixties, with a huge mane of gray hair, a booming voice, and a habit of gesturing theatrically when he spoke. With him was a tall, striking black woman introduced as Vanessa. She spoke with a London twang, but deep below it were traces of sleepy West Indian beginnings.

His assistant, Vittorio, was dark, slim, and intense, everything Jasmine imagined a sophisticated Italian to be. When he spoke, which was not unless addressed directly, it was with a quiet cultured voice. He was accompanied by a pretty blond young Englishwoman named Audrey, a Londoner by her accent.

Their host, Peter Willoughby, was as Allan had described, a suave English gentleman, with thin blond hair, pale blue eyes, and a solicitous manner. With him was Stephanie Ambrose, who was introduced as his assistant. Jasmine knew immediately, intuitively, that they were sleeping together. Stephanie was brunette and beautiful, but with a hard, determined mouth. She wore expensive clothes—a Chanel one-shoulder black silk crepe cocktail dress—spoke with a cultured British accent, and acted as if she owned the house, treating the butler with a disdain certain people normally reserve for their own servants. The butler, an elderly gentleman overflowing with reserve, treated her with unfailing politeness, which nevertheless did little to conceal an icy eddy below the surface. Apparently he disapproved of his master's choice. Compared to the other two women, however, she was a class act. Jasmine was willing to bet that the Italians' women were one-night stands, actresses perhaps, or even professionals provided by one of the many London escort services.

If this was a business dinner, it was not obvious. The talk was wide-ranging and social, never touching on the project they were all in London to discuss, even though much of the conversation was about the film business in general. A getting-to-know-you business dinner, Jasmine realized after a few minutes.

Probably to a greater degree than any other business in the world, the film industry was built on personal contacts. You did business with people you could work with. If you liked them, so much the better. If you trusted them, it was a miracle. Luckily trust was not a prerequisite. Allan had once explained to her about a business associate of his whom she knew and didn't like, "Of course I don't trust him, but I know exactly how he'll try and shaft me. There's no mystery to it. I can deal with a man like that. All I have to do is remember not to bend over with my back to him." She suspected that his relationship with the men here tonight was similar.

They sat in the living room before dinner and had drinks. The furniture was French provincial, the paintings seventeenth and eighteenth century English on large canvasses. There was a landscape, some hunting scenes, and portraits, presumably of Willoughby's bewigged ancestors. The drinks were served on silver trays by the butler, and appetizers of pâté and Russian caviar were placed discreetly before them.

Morino began to talk about an actor they all knew. Once a major box office star who had commanded about two million dollars a picture, he was now a three-hundred-fifty-seven-pound recluse on a Greek island. "He was the most difficult son of a bitch I've ever had to deal with, but he had a genius," he said, waving his arms expansively. "I speak to his agent who tells me that he wants one million dollars for the part. It is only a cameo, a small part. Who wants to see an elephant all the way through a movie, hey? And his genius?" He shrugged expressively. "All he has left is his name. And it is not worth a million dollars. I offer him two hundred thousand dollars for two days shooting, and his agent says yes. He comes to the set a day late. He wants—" Morino began to count on his fingers. "His own trailer, a case of Dom Perignon, a waterbed, a chef to prepare his meals, the pretty assistant camera girl to be sent to his trailer, and the script changed. I say, 'You are crazy!' He threatens to walk. I say, 'Walk,' and he walks. Some things are not worth the pain."

"Indeed," Willoughby said. "If only we could make films without actors."

Allan darted an uncomfortable glance at Jasmine.

"Actors and writers," Morino agreed. "Every gray hair on my head comes from actors and writers!"

"What about women?" Allan asked.

Morino grinned and put his hand on Vanessa's thigh. "They keep me young. Without love, my life would be empty." He looked appreciatively at Jasmine but spoke to Allan. "It is obvious that you too have an appreciation of beauty."

"Jasmine is an actress, a good one," Allan said.

"Such an exquisite face," he said to her. "If you would come to Rome, you would be a major star."

"But you don't like actors," Jasmine said tartly.

Willoughby interceded graciously. "Present company excepted, of course. Besides, we were only talking about those well-known stars with reputations for being difficult."

"Of course," she said. "Producers, on the other hand, are never difficult."

"Touché!" Morino said. "Brains as well as beauty."

"Surprise!" she wanted to say, but bit her tongue. Something about these men irritated her. Perhaps it was their wealth, their attitude toward the people with whom they did business, their proprietary attitude toward their women, or a combination of all these factors. Without exception—even including the silent Vittorio—they all had an attitude of possessiveness, as if the world and all it contained was theirs by right. Even Allan was that way, she realized, although he did a better job of hiding it. Perhaps it was an integral part of power and wealth, just as shame was an essential element of poverty. Whatever it was, she found herself particularly disliking it this evening.

Shortly before dinner, she had a chance to talk to the formidable Stephanie.

"You're very pretty," Stephanie said, envy in her voice.

"Thank you," Jasmine replied.

"Have you been to London before?" the Englishwoman asked.

"It's my first time here," Jasmine said.

Stephanie looked at her with something close to pity in her eyes. "You've never been here before?" she asked.

"No, but I love it. I went shopping today. The stores here are marvelous."

"If you can afford them," Stephanie said. "I'm sure, however, that Allan takes good care of you."

Jasmine fought down a surge of resentment at this intrusion. "Just as Peter does of you, I guess," she said pleasantly.

Stephanie arched an eyebrow. "We're women in a men's world," she said. "We do what we have to in order to take care of ourselves."

"You look as if you were born with money," Jasmine said.

"Come on, luv," Stephanie said with a smile, her voice breaking into a harsh accent. "I was born in the East End without a pot to piss in. I've made something of myself, that's all. Just as you 'ave, I bet."

Jasmine was surprised. "Your accent—?"

"I started as an actress, just like you, luv. If you want to be a toff, you have to talk like one."

Jasmine sat beside Morino during dinner, his girlfriend sat on his other side. The main course was roast lamb and Yorkshire pudding, both superbly prepared. The potatoes and vegetables were disastrously overcooked, but the wine, a rich Bordeaux, more than made up for this flaw.

Between mouthfuls, Morino regaled them with stories about his tax problems. Apparently, he and the Italian government were not seeing eye to eye on the subject and they were threatening to confiscate his seaside villa. "They have no idea what it is to work for money," he said. "Like governments everywhere, hey?"

It was a source of common grief. Allan and Willoughby chimed in with their own complaints.

Jasmine ignored the conversation, concentrating instead on the excellent lamb and mint sauce. Just then she became aware of a stealthy hand trying to push its way through the slit in her skirt. It was Morino, intent on Allan's words, chuckling at all the right places, his hand busy beneath the tablecloth.

Jasmine reached for the mint sauce and spooned half of the bowl onto her plate. Then, casually, slowly, she lifted her plate with her right hand, leaned toward the Italian, and tipped the entire contents into his lap.

"How could you do that?" Allan asked in the taxi back to their hotel. "How could you?"

Allan was furious. Morino had been furious. She had been furious—and still was.

"He was an asshole," she said. "He was trying to grab my cunt under the table. Don't you care?"

"That's beside the point," Allan said. "You could have handled it without making a fucking scene. You embarrassed him!"

"Don't you think what he was doing embarrassed me?" she asked, unflinchingly. "Don't you think it embarrassed you?"

"Oh, Jesus," Allan groaned. He continued talking, more to himself than her. "I'll have to make it right tomorrow. I'll talk to him, apologize."

"Didn't you apologize enough tonight? Christ, what are you going to do? Get on your knees?"

"Cut it out," Allan said, his voice rising. "You've done enough damage for one night."

Jasmine looked at him across the vast distance that had opened between them, her mouth compressed. "Why don't you just sit on it, Allan," she said, and turned her head to face the dark London streets.

Attendance at the Friars' art show exceeded Madge's expectations. More than seventy percent of the people invited showed up—LA's stellar society and art crowd—which was some kind of record. Madge was atwitter, buzzing around excitedly, answering questions, introducing people to the two artists who were there—the watercolorist and the sculptor—not at all daunted by the fact that most of the crowd wanted to see the work of the mysterious Breer.

Kate was ready. She was dressed to create an impression. In the few hours between the final preparations and the start of the show, she had rushed into Beverly Hills, brandishing her sole credit card like a weapon, and raided I. Magnin and Neiman-Marcus. Her spoils included a velvet-trimmed black lace dress with a plunging back that hugged the curves of her body and ended just above the knees. She wore dark silk stockings, new high-heeled black shoes and pink coral earrings. She was almost nine hundred dollars poorer, but the striking blend of sexuality and elegance she had attained was worth it.

This glamorous beauty with the soft pink lipstick and glowing eyes was a different Kate. When she arrived at the gallery just before opening, Madge had stared at her without recognition for a full ten seconds. Her first word was "Wow!" The second thought she expressed was, "God, I hope you don't detract from the paintings! All the men will be watching you instead of looking at the art."

And they were. Eyes kept sliding in her direction. As soon as it became obvious that she worked at Friars, she became the target of questions, many of them with no point except the opportunity to talk to her. She was gracious, charming, and helpful, neither encouraging nor dismissing the attention. She worked the room like a pro, guiding people toward the art that interested them and handing prospective buyers over to Madge.

Like the crowd at a New York opening, it was affluent, but there was a distinctive California flair. The men were dressed more casually, the women more flamboyantly. Half the conversations seemed to be about film or television, the other half about money, with the odd mention of art thrown in. A couple of college students Madge had hired acted as waiters, dispersing an inexpensive but acceptable California jug wine, crackers, and cheese. Madge was not one to waste money on peripherals.

Wisely, she had kept the work of the three artists separate. The small reception area contained only one sculpture. Three rooms led off of it, one for each of the artists, the largest reserved for the work of her star artist, Breer.

Kate was talking to a dentist and his wife when David Ross arrived. Dr. Wirtschafter and his wife both had perfect teeth, expensive clothes, luscious tans, an overly friendly manner, and an equal ignorance of art.

"We have a teakwood liquor cabinet on one wall and a big blank space next to it," the woman was saying, gesturing with her hands. "The wood is so dark and gloomy, you know. We need something to lighten up that corner and set it off. I just can't make up my mind which would look better, a painting or one of these sculptures."

Her husband nodded his head rapidly while she spoke, trying not to stare too hard at Kate, but obviously taken by her looks.

Kate half listened, watching Madge greet the tall man with lightly graying temples, and knew instinctively that it was Ross.

"Why don't you look around a little longer, visualize the space, and maybe something will come to you," she suggested. "I'll check back with you in a little while and answer any questions you might have."

She left the glowing couple and chose a path across the room that would take her past Madge. As she passed, Madge grabbed her arm and said, "Kate, this is David Ross. Kate has just joined our company. I believe you have some mutual acquaintances."

"Oh, really," Ross said, one swift glance taking her in from head to toe. "How do you do?"

"I used to work in New York at the Dotson gallery," Kate said with a brilliant smile. "I've heard your name mentioned."

"I'm lucky to get her," Madge said. "She was Wallace Dotson's whiz kid. She's forgotten more about acquisition and authentication than I know."

"Really?" Ross said, impressed.

"Oh, excuse me," Madge said, turning her head, and left to meet another arrival.

"Madge is too kind," Kate said modestly.

"How long have you been out here?" Ross asked. He was a handsome man, in his mid-forties, she guessed. Thick eyebrows topped gray eyes, a long straight nose, and a mouth that was a degree too corpulent. The cheeks, too, were beginning to lose their definition, giving his face a slightly bottom-heavy appearance.

"Just a few days," she said.

"And are you enjoying California?"

"More and more," she said, amusement creeping flirtatiously into her voice. "I find the people here fascinating."

"You have—er—friends out here?" he asked. The slight hesitation emphasized the true question: Did she have a particular friend?

"No, I just got tired of the weather in New York and thought it was time for a change. Luckily, I had met Madge before, and she offered me a job. I have a few business contacts like her here, that's all."

"Well, it won't take you long to feel at home," he said.

"I suppose not," she replied. "Right now I feel a little lost. In New York my life centered around a few blocks, it seemed. Los Angeles seems so huge, so decentralized."

She could tell by his appraising eyes, the tilt of his body toward her, the warmth that had entered his voice, that he was both intrigued and attracted.

"I'd like to learn more about you and show you something of Los Angeles, but I'd better look at Breer's work before it's all snapped up," he said regretfully.

"You collect Breer?" she asked, lightly touching his arm and leading him to the room where the Breer paintings were displayed. She knew he was aware of her closeness and that he was enjoying it.

"A fine artist and an excellent investment," he said a trifle pompously. "His work will double in price in the next year."

"I agree," she said. "That's very astute of you."

"When it comes to money, I am very astute," he said, for the first time allowing humor to enter his voice. "I'm an investment banker by profession."

"Yes, so I've heard. And a generous patron of the arts," she said. They reached the room and stood in the doorway. "I'll leave you to it. Just ask me if you have any questions."

"I'd like the opportunity to talk longer with you," he said. "Could I call you some time?"

"I've also heard that you're married," she said bluntly.

He shrugged. "Kind of. It's a relative term, a complex situation."

Like being relatively pregnant, she thought, but all she said was, "I see."

"I'd still like to see you. Over dinner perhaps?"

"Perhaps," she said with a smile and turned away.

She was still smiling as she walked back into the crowded reception area. The investment in her appearance had paid off in spades. He'd call her within a day. She'd bet her dwindling finances on it.

CHAPTER SIX

The house was strangely silent. No sign of the maids or the gardener, no trace of Sharon or her chauffeur, even though the car she normally used—the Jaguar—was sitting in the driveway. Jason took his jacket off in the living room and tossed it over the back of the couch.

He needed a drink. His Florida newspapers were still giving him trouble. The revenues had been sliding steadily over the past few weeks and soon he would have to take drastic measures. He disliked drastic measures. Not because of any qualms about the ugliness involved, but because they were always born out of necessity, they shed blood, which was always messy, and there was never a guarantee they would work. He preferred to plan ahead and have the steps unfold in an orderly progression as anticipated. Drastic measures were always the result of bad business, the solution to a problem that should never have happened in the first place.

He'd planned on going to the Breer art show this evening, but the business problems had kept him at the office. He scowled and poured himself a Scotch—a Glenfiddich single malt—lowered his face to the glass to inhale the aroma, and then took a small sip. Ah, that wonderful smoky peat flavor! There were no other whiskeys worth the name except those that came from Scotland.

Back in Texas, when he was younger and poorer, he had drunk bourbon, a harsh, biting, strong drink without subtlety. It had no purpose except to get the drinker drunk, or so he thought. He had since met bourbon drinkers who would argue to the wall against that premise. The discovery of Scotch was one of the great moments of his life. It had signaled a new era, a connoisseur's appreciation of pleasure. Since then there had been many gastronomic pleasures—caviar, truffles, a regal wine with superb food—but none had compared to that first drink of Scotch.

He sat on the couch, took another sip, and leaned back. There was an uncomfortable knot in his shoulder. He should have gone to Page's instead of coming home. The woman had magic hands. They were somehow able to melt away his pains and tensions. But he had stayed away tonight on purpose. He was becoming too dependent on her for his relaxation, a situation he intensely disliked. Dependency upon others was a sign of weakness, and weakness was a flaw he could never afford to indulge himself in or expose for others to see. The decision not to visit her was a simple act of discipline, which served to reaffirm his strength.

Perhaps a shower would help. One of the benefits of this house was a bathroom the size of some living rooms. The tub became a spa, complete with adjustable water jets, and the shower also had about eighteen adjustments to choose from.

He drained his drink and put the empty glass on an end table, enjoying the warmth of the alcohol as it traveled down his throat. Yes, a shower would help, then he'd make phone calls to a number of his executives. They expected to be called at odd hours at their homes. The myth among his staff was that he never slept, and he did nothing to discourage it. It helped create the aura of omnipotence.

Walking up the curved stairway to the upstairs, he stopped at the halfway point. A noise. What was it? A rhythmic slapping sound that seemed to come from the bedroom. He resumed his upward progress, a little faster, his brow furrowed.

The noise grew louder as he approached the closed bedroom door. And then a voice—Sharon's. A groan. What the hell was going on?

He opened the door and stood there, taking in the bizarre scene. The chauffeur was lying facedown on the bed, naked, a pillow beneath his hips, his white ass sticking into the air. Sharon stood beside the bed. She wore only panties. In her hand was a belt, which she was using across his ass.

"And, Adam, this is for getting a hard-on without my permission," she said. Crack! The belt came down. Not hard. Not enough to raise welts, but raspberry patches on the white skin showed that she had been active. It was enough to have her trembling with excitement, however.

"What do you think you are doing?" Jason asked, his voice cold and calm.

Sharon whirled around, her eyes wide. Adam struggled upright.

Sharon recovered quickly. She smiled and said throatily, "Just a little game, darling. Would you like to join in?"

Jason stepped into the room, walked up to her without speaking, and backhanded her across the face. The force of the blow sent her stumbling backward three steps, and then she fell into a sitting position.

"You have fifteen minutes to get your belongings together and get off this property," he said to the young man. "You're fired as of now."

"What the hell do you care?" Sharon asked from the floor. "What the hell do you care about what I do?"

"I don't," Jason said. "Not at all. You can do what you like, as long as you're discreet. But never, never do it in front of me."

He turned and left the room. "Bastard!" he heard Sharon shout behind him. "Fucking bastard!" she said, and then began to sob.

Jason walked out of the house, straight to his car. In moments he was heading down Overland Street toward Westwood, following his earlier inclination. The bitch was getting out of hand, he thought, still furious. One of these days he'd have to deal more severely with her.

Divorce was always a possibility—God knows he'd thought of it often enough—but now was not the time for the scandal that would certainly accompany it. Not when he had so many unfulfilled plans. Sharon essentially lacked class and she would make sure it was a messy and loud divorce. The woman could be a prime bitch if she wanted to be. Bad publicity now could interfere with everything he was working toward. He'd just have to keep a tighter rein on her. Maybe have some of his security people keep an eye on her.

He was still musing over the problem when he pulled into Page's garage. The knot in his back had worsened and now radiated a remorseless throb of pain. Soon it would graduate into a full-fledged migraine.

Page was shocked to see him. "Jason! I wasn't expecting you," she said. She peered at him through the half-open door.

"Do you have company?" he asked unapologetically.

"No, of course not. Come in," she said, stepping aside and opening the door. She wore a long robe that almost reached her bare feet. "It's just that you normally call before coming over."

"I was just passing by and came on impulse," he said, walking in.

"Well, I'm glad you did," she said, recovering her composure.

He went directly to the armchair and slumped into it with a wince of pain. Page poured him a drink and handed it to him. "You look as if you need this," she said.

"Can you rub my back?"

She stepped behind him and started on the upper shoulders. "You're tighter than a drum," she said, kneading at the stiff muscles. "Is anything wrong?"

Jason shook his head. He never discussed his personal or

married life with Page—or anyone else, for that matter. Business talk was fine—he enjoyed teaching her—but discussion of the problems he was having with his wife would expose a vulnerability he would rather obscure. The fact was, he had married the stupid cunt for her family money. He had always known she was wanton and undisciplined. It was no surprise that she was teetering near the edge of disaster now. He had known it would happen, and it had happened before. As usual, however, her timing was atrocious.

Page's hands moved lower and found the spot. He grunted with pain and she withdrew.

"You're going to have to lie down and let me get at that," she said.

They went into the bedroom, where he took off his shirt and lay face down on the bed. She hung it on a hanger, then sat beside him and resumed her massage.

"The Medical Milestone stock I bought six months ago is finally moving again," she said. "It went up five points this week."

"Sell it just before the fifteenth," he said.

"Why?" she asked, alert.

"Just do it," he said. "It'll run up some more, perhaps another ten points, and then nose-dive on the fifteenth."

Page sighed silently. He was not in an expansive mood. Usually he enjoyed telling her of his manipulations, but apparently not tonight. Obviously there would be some announcement on the fifteenth, perhaps of sagging profits. No matter, she would take her profits before then—and tell Elsa to do the same. She'd be able to analyze what happened afterwards.

"Thank you," she said. "I'll get a nice profit out of that."

She dug deeper into his back and he groaned. She ignored his pain and worked more on the spot, feeling the knot gradually loosen and then melt down.

"How's that feel?" she asked.

"It hurt like hell," he said, sitting up. There was sweat

on his forehead. He moved his arms and then his torso. "Feels better though."

"It'll feel a little bruised till tomorrow."

He lay back, placing his arms behind his head and looking up at her through half-closed eyes. "What's under the robe?" he asked.

"Just me," Page said. She put her hand on his stomach and let it rest there, enjoying the warmth, the feel of the soft hair.

"Take it off," he said.

She unsnapped his pants and pulled the zipper down, then she stood up and let the robe fall to the floor. She had long slim legs, a high waist, a flat stomach, and small, perfectly shaped breasts, accented by disproportionately large brown nipples. It was the nipples that excited him more than anything about her body. Not only their size, but their color contrasted shockingly with her pale white skin. Compared to the rest of her—sedate, classy, almost demure—they were blatantly sexual.

He tugged at his pants, lifting his hips so that he could remove them. She leaned down and pulled them from the knees until he was naked. His penis, already hard, pointed up at his stomach.

"Come here," he said.

He took her without ceremony or foreplay, entering her after only one kiss.

She was still dry and his penis seemed larger than it had ever been. She wanted to cry out with the pain of it, but instead she clasped her hands around his back and let him pump at her with jackhammer force and, yes, she thought, a kind of mindless hatred. He had done this only once before. Afterwards, bruised, hurting, and bewildered, she had cried. This time she wouldn't.

The hatred he was projecting wasn't directed at her. She just happened to be there. She knew from before that it would soon be over. Tomorrow, he would send a gift. All she could do for now was to just grit her teeth and bear it.

It wouldn't last forever.

* * *

Madge's show had been a tremendous success. Half of Breer's work had sold and further orders were expected to trickle in over the coming days. The other two artists had also sold well, although their prices were not up to Breer's standard and the dollar amounts didn't compare. But Madge was almost gleeful as she toted up the accounts.

Kate was adding the names of new guests from the opening to the mailing list when the telephone rang. She was sitting at a small desk in Madge's office, name cards divided into neat piles in front of her—those already on the list, those to be added.

"It's your friend, David Ross," Madge said with an elfin grin, her hand over the receiver. "Take it here. I'm going to check things out front."

Kate sat at Madge's desk and picked up the phone. "Hello?" she said, thinking she had won the bet with herself.

"Hi, Miss Buchanan, this is David Ross."

"David Ross?" she said, and hesitated. "Oh, yes, Mr. Ross, how are you?"

"I'm fine, thank you. Have you thought over my invitation?"

"Your invitation? Oh, you mean your mention of dinner? No, I haven't, I'm afraid."

"Well, I hate to put you on the spot, but how about dinner tonight?" he said.

She decided to end the game. If you kept a fish on the line for too long, you were liable to lose him. She couldn't afford to lose this one.

"All right," she said. "Where and when?"

There was a pause while David gathered his wits. "I thought we could eat at Nicky Blair's. Have you been there?"

"No, I haven't been here long enough to get around much."

"I think you'll like it," he said. "Can I pick you up at seven-thirty or eight?"

"Eight would be fine," she said, giving him the address of her apartment.

"I'm looking forward to it very much. See you then," he said, and hung up.

She took advantage of Madge's high spirits and asked to leave work early. She couldn't wear the same clothes she had worn at the opening, and the wardrobe she had brought with her from New York was limited, to say the least. Clothes had never before been high on her priority list. She'd have to buy something else for this first date. Once again, she thanked God for her credit card.

She went into Beverly Hills again. This time, however, she was more cautious and searched out the sales racks. She settled for a simple body-hugging red cashmere dress and a flowing cape of the same color. But this was still Beverly Hills, and even though the outfit came from the sales rack, it set her back almost three hundred dollars.

But it was worth it, she thought later, as she applied the last of her makeup and stared into the bathroom mirror. Trying to look at herself objectively (something she always found difficult) she saw what some people would consider a beautiful woman. Silky auburn hair fell to her shoulders, red lipstick, almost matching the dress, accentuated her full mouth, glowing green eyes stared back at her. And the dress, though simple, did nothing to hide the flowing lines of her body.

She was attractive, she admitted to herself. Enough people had told her that before. But until now, it had never been important to her, had never been something she had remotely considered using to her advantage. She had always felt sorry for women who depended on their beauty to get ahead. Now, ironically, it was her most valuable tool if her scheme was to work. Shortly before eight, she fastened the cape around her neck, twirled once with a satisfied smile, and went to wait in the living room.

David arrived right on time. She stepped into the hallway and closed the apartment door. He took her all in with that swift encompassing glance of his and complimented her on her appearance.

"Thank you," she said, taking his arm.

Her eyes widened when she saw the long white limousine

double-parked in the street. The driver opened the door for her and then, when she had climbed in, walked around and opened the other side for David.

"I hate driving in Los Angeles," he said, by way of explanation. He opened the bar and asked what she would like to drink.

"A dry white wine, please."

She watched as he poured it. He was casually dressed in comfortable wool slacks, an open-necked cotton shirt, and a light blue jacket, looking altogether more relaxed than when she had met him the previous night. She noticed a tiny scar on his right temple, tufts of hair on his knuckles, a slight twitch of his jaw muscles as he poured the wine—the details that came with quiet observation.

He poured the same for himself, then handed her a glass. "Cheers!" he said, lifting his glass. "May Los Angeles be all you hope it will be."

The wine was chilled to perfection, a bone-dry fume blanc with a faint hint of oak.

"This is lovely," she said. "I presume it's a California wine."

"It's from the San Luis Obispo area, just less than two hundred miles up the coast. One of my little finds," he said with some satisfaction.

"You appreciate wine?"

"I appreciate everything of quality," he said, "be it art, wine, or your beauty."

She smiled a little uncomfortably at his effusiveness.

"I'm sorry if I'm coming on too strongly for you," he said hurriedly. "It's just that . . ." His voice trailed away.

"Every woman enjoys compliments," she said. "What were you going to say?"

He smiled, a quick, almost boyish grin that she assumed he had used to devastate women before. "It's just that you so seldom meet people—women that is—who make such a strong impression. You had an impact on me the moment I saw you. It's so rare, one can't let moments like that pass by."

Kate sipped her wine and met his eyes with hers. "Well,"

she said, lowering her glass, "I must admit to a certain attraction when I saw you."

He smiled again. "I'm glad that's the case," he said, reaching for the wine bottle and pouring a little more into each of their glasses.

"Tell me about your business," she said, settling back in the comfortable seat.

By the time they reached the restaurant, she had heard more about investment banking than she could understand. He sensed her confusion and summed up. "We're the real capitalists," he said. "We provide money for business and industry, very often risk money with a commensurately high return."

For Kate, one clear fact stood out in his exposition: David Ross was very wealthy.

Blair's, expensive, fashionable and though always busy, was not too loud. David was greeted by name at the door and they were shown to a table against a wall.

"What would you like to drink?" he asked when they sat.

"Some more wine would be fine," she said.

"A bottle of the '85 Firestone Chardonnay, please," he told the waiter, without consulting the wine list.

Kate scanned the menu.

"The seafood here is excellent," David said.

"I'll try the grilled red snapper," she said, and closed the menu.

"Ah, a woman who makes up her mind instantly," he said admiringly.

"Many of us do," she said tartly.

"You're right. It was a chauvinistic remark," he admitted. "So, what about you? I've been talking about my business so far. What do you intend doing here? Knowing Madge as I do, it seems that you left a high-paying job in New York for a low-paying job in LA."

Kate shrugged. "I wanted to get out of Manhattan. I knew I could get a job here. I'd developed enough contacts."

"Do you have family back there?"

"No," she said. "I'm alone. My parents died when I was young. There's really nothing back there for me."

"An unhappy love affair recently?"

Kate smiled. "No, nothing like that. I just needed a change. I've always liked LA, in spite of the bad press it gets in New York. It suddenly occurred to me one day that I didn't need to spend another freezing winter or sweltering summer with the huddled masses."

"Well, New York's loss is our gain," he said, lifting his empty glass in a silent toast.

The wine steward arrived and poured a taste into his glass. David swirled it, sniffed it, tasted, and smacked his lips appreciatively. "Excellent!" he said.

The conversation over the next hour ranged from business to art. Over coffee, Kate veered it into a more personal direction. "Your wife? You said your marriage was 'relative.' What do you mean by that?"

David looked down at the table. "My wife and I haven't been intimate in more than two years," he said, with pain in his voice. "We are still married, we live in the same house much of the time, but there is nothing left between us, nothing at all."

"Why aren't you divorced then?"

He sighed. "It's difficult to explain. Very complex. There are legal and financial reasons and there is also the matter of—I suppose you could call it loyalty. My wife bore our daughter, raised her. For me to desert her now—well, it just doesn't feel right. Instead, we have an understanding. She goes her way, I go mine."

"A modern agreement," Kate said, not hiding the sarcasm in her voice. And an old story, she thought to herself. It was amazing that men still used it.

"I suppose it is," he said, and added defensively, "It's the only way to cope with a difficult situation."

"I'm sorry," she said. "I'm in no position to judge you. Besides, it's none of my business."

He reached across the table and put his hand over hers. "I'd like it to be your business," he said. "I'd like everything I do to be your business. And everything you do to be mine."

She removed her hand. "You're moving a little too fast."

"I'm sorry," he said, "but I want you to be a part of my life. I knew it when I saw you and now, after talking to you, I know it even more."

"I've never had an affair with a married man before—on principle," she said.

"Don't think of me as married, just think of me as a man."

Kate shook her head slightly, her eyes worried. Inside, she marvelled at his practiced smoothness. The earnestness, the emotion he put into the explanation about his wife. The man had apparently been through this scenario a time or two before.

"Let me give you some time," he said. "But as a closing argument, let me say that I think we could have a wonderful relationship. I'm not without influence in Los Angeles. I could help you in many ways. And you could help me. I need someone like you to help me balance my life, to share with."

"That almost sounds like a business proposition," Kate said with a small laugh.

He had the grace to look embarrassed. "We'll play it any way you like."

Kate shook her head again.

"Just think about it," he said hurriedly. "Think about me, and let's have dinner again tomorrow. Get to know each other better. Talk some more."

"All right," she said, allowing relief to enter her voice at the out he had given her. "We'll have dinner tomorrow."

She let him kiss her at the door of her apartment, pressing her body against his just long enough for him to know what was available, and then pulled away. "Thank you for a wonderful evening," she said breathlessly.

"I hope it's the start of many." He touched her hand, turned, and walked away.

Kate closed the door and walked into the living room, removing the cape and throwing it over a chair. From her window, she watched him enter the limousine, her face unreadable.

David could hardly contain his excitement as he sat alone in the back of the limo. He wanted to sing, to dance, to act like a teenage boy again.

Kate was really something special. Beautiful, intelligent, and classy. A sophisticated young woman. Everything that Selena hadn't been. She was just what he needed.

Selena. Her death had been most unfortunate. No, he corrected himself, tragic. He'd been fond of her in a strange way. For one thing, she'd always been able to surprise him. He remembered the night he had arrived at her apartment, only to find that she had another visitor—a woman. At first he had been peeved, but then when it became clear that what Selena had in mind for him was double the fun, he had been intrigued and grateful. He'd never forget that night, a collage of bodies and mouths, a disappearance of identity.

It was too bad about Selena. Even sad. But a surprise to nobody. Some people clearly had death as their next destination and Selena had been one of them.

Since Selena's death, he'd resorted to fucking his wife once or twice. He'd even thought about approaching one of his assistants at work—an act that would have been a violation of his own policies. Desperate measures. But in this day and age, with AIDS hanging over everyone's heads like the sword of Damocles, you couldn't get your rocks off when the fancy struck you. It was one of the things that had worried him about Selena. She was wild and self-destructive enough to fool around indiscriminately, even though she was supposed to be his mistress. But, unlike Jason with Page, and Allan with Jasmine, and some of his other friends with mistresses, he had never owned Selena. She had her own money and had never been dependent on him. Kate, on the other hand, needed him. Madge Bernstein probably paid her shit. And with her taste in clothes, she no doubt needed more money.

He remembered the feel of her body against his. Firm,

young, beautiful. He imagined how she'd be in bed, that long auburn hair scattered over a pillow, those full lips parted in passion. God, it was exciting! He hadn't felt this way in ages. What luck to come across her. If he played his cards right, he'd have her. He had to have her. Women like that simply didn't appear every day.

Allan knew how to please Jasmine. On Friday, he cut his business in London a day short and told her to pack her bags.

"We're going home already?" she asked.

Fences had been mended since their argument after the disastrous dinner, but a small wall of resentment still existed between them. Nothing serious, but enough to create a few strained silences every now and then.

"No, a side trip on the way home," he said.

"Really?" she asked, a smile dawning. "Where are we going?"

"A surprise," he said coyly.

When they checked their luggage in at the airport, she saw they were taking a flight to Paris.

"Oh, Paris," she said, hugging Allan. "I've always wanted to go there."

"No, not Paris," he said. "We're just changing planes there. Paris is filled with fucking tourists in the summer."

"Where then? Where?"

"You'll see," he said enigmatically.

The flight landed at Nice, where a rental car was waiting. They drove west through small villages, shady groves, and along majestic cliffs footed by an ocean so blue Jasmine could hardly breathe.

Finally, they drove over a hill and below them was a bay, a stretch of white sand, a small town of multistoried white buildings, a harbor filled with dazzling yachts.

"We're here," Allan said smugly.

"Where?" she asked.

"St. Tropez, or St. Trop, as the locals call it."

"Oh, my God!" she said.

As they checked into the venerable Residence de la Pinede,

Allan explained with more than a hint of self-satisfaction that he had gone through heaven and hell to get reservations. "You normally have to book about a year in advance to get a room during the season, but I pulled every string there was."

"It's beautiful," Jasmine said. And it was, a gracious building surrounded by shady trees and fronting a semi-private beach.

They walked through the small town, stopping at a sidewalk cafe for coffee and joining the hundreds who watched each other watching each other. Half-a-dozen languages filled the clear air, and everywhere there were signs of affluence. St. Trop was no place for travelers on a budget.

Allan noted that wherever they were, Jasmine still managed to turn heads. No matter how cosmopolitan the setting, and St. Trop was about as mixed a crowd as could be found anywhere, the exotic edge to her beauty commanded attention.

Jasmine, on the other hand, was almost oblivious to the effect she created.

"I can't believe this," she said. While people had always thought her exotic because of her looks and heritage, she had always thought of Europeans as the true exotics, always wanting to travel there. France, for a reason she could no longer remember—perhaps a magazine article or a film she had seen when younger—had always exemplified European sophistication for her. Now she was here and it filled her with a childlike thrill.

They went to the beach after lunch, a sparkling ribbon of white sand, a gentle ocean swell, and topless women soaking up the sun.

"You can take your top off if you like," Allan said, settling himself into a beach chair with the Hollywood trades that had mysteriously appeared at the front desk for him. "This is France. Nobody minds."

She stretched out her towel, removed her bikini top, and lay on her stomach. This was heaven. This was what she was born for.

She lifted her head lazily and regarded Allan through one

eye. He was scanning the *Hollywood Reporter* with practiced skill, turning the pages with the ability of a speed reader.

He had more than made up for his earlier rudeness, she thought fondly. She'd have to reward him. Tonight she'd give him a fuck to remember, something hot enough to scramble his brains.

With that thought warming her body, she fell asleep.

CHAPTER SEVEN

"I want to take you somewhere," David said after they finished dinner.

"Where?" she asked.

It had been, in his estimation, a delightful evening. Kate was as beautiful as ever, and he had been at his most charming. He found it hard to believe his luck in stumbling across her. The rapport between them was building into something stronger, something he hoped would be more permanent. It was their third date. On Thursday he had taken her to Nicky Blair's, on Saturday to Scandia's. And on this Monday evening they ate at The Bistro, where he enjoyed pointing out the famous scattered throughout the restaurant: actors, studio bosses, agents—the Hollywood powermongers.

"Some friends of mine are having a party tonight. I thought we could drop in. I think you'll enjoy meeting them."

"Oh, that would be nice. Who'll be there?" She sipped the strong Colombian coffee, thankful for the relief. Her throat had suddenly gone dry now that she was faced with the prospect of getting closer to her goal.

"Jason Thomas, who I mentioned to you before, Allan Silver, the president of Elixer Studios. Oh, and Stodding Watson, who's curator of the Rex Museum. I'm sure you'll have a lot in common with him. Maybe another dozen people. It's just a small gathering on Jason's corporate yacht."

"A corporate yacht?" Kate asked, trying not to sound impressed.

"Yes, it's down in Marina del Rey. He uses it for business meetings, as well as pleasure."

"He must be very wealthy," Kate said.

David smiled condescendingly. "That would be an understatement. He's very successful at everything he does and has amassed quite a fortune in the process."

"Magazines mainly, isn't it?"

"And newspapers, radio, television, real estate, art, speculation. Jason has his fingers in a lot of pies."

When she put her cup down it clanked noisily against the saucer. Easy, she told herself. "You've been friends a long time?"

"Oh, yes. We're also involved in a number of business ventures together. He's quite a remarkable man, as you'll see."

"Well, I'm looking forward to meeting him," Kate said.

She was mostly silent during the drive to the Marina, listening to David's conversation with one ear, answering automatically when necessary, her thoughts on the party ahead.

One of David's friends—one of the men she would meet tonight—would in all likelihood be the man responsible for Joel's death. The prospect of discovering who both excited and alarmed her. How would she react? she wondered.

It was a rhetorical question, she knew. She had no choice but to react as planned, to be as cool as ice and give nothing away, not a clue, not a blink of the eye. She would discover which of these men had killed her brother, and smile and shake his hand. And then she would formulate her plan to ruin his life.

* * *

Marina del Rey was a modern singles paradise. David explained, slightly tongue in cheek. Tall condominium towers lined the oceanfront, interspersed with restaurants, bars, and trendy shops. Yuppies lived there, together with the divorced and hopeful of both sexes. Airline crews liked it because of the proximity to Los Angeles International Airport and the loose lifestyle. Dope dealers liked it because of the concentrated wealth among their potential clientele. Developers had made their fortunes there.

And yet, Kate perceived a sense of aimless affluence about the place, a transient insubstantiality, in spite of the imposing buildings. One day they would be gone and all that would remain was what was there in the beginning—the ocean.

The Marina itself covered about five square miles and housed about six thousand boats of all types and sizes. Day fishing craft, family weekend cruisers, ocean-cruising yachts, ranging in value from thousands of dollars to millions, were crammed beside each other into slips, giving the entire area the appearance of a hatchery for boats.

It was a calm night, and as they drove into the parking lot, the water danced with the lights of a thousand portholes. If Kate had not been feeling so nervous, she would have appreciated the beauty. As it was, when they got out of the limousine, David stood beside her and said, "Pretty, isn't it?"

"Yes," she said.

She was wound up. She needed to relax, be her normal sociable self. She took three deep breaths and felt their calming effect as the tangy sea sir entered her lungs.

"No smog down here. The air is wonderful," David said, misinterpreting her action.

"It's lovely," she said, taking his arm.

"We go this way." He led her through a gate and onto the dock.

He glanced sideways at her profile as they walked. Straight nose, long lashes, the curve of her full lips—she was a lovely picture. Her hair blew back and exposed the diamond studs in her earlobes. They glittered like the lights on the water. He couldn't help but smile at the beautiful lady walking beside him. What a prize!

Kate's mind was elsewhere. Although this boardwalk was concrete, it triggered a rare childhood memory of a wooden dock, cracked and creaking boards beneath her feet, the smell of salt and oil, her father's leathery hand encircling hers, Joel running ahead of them. Their time as a family had been so short that the memories were few and far between. A handful of moments like these existed, submerged in webs of time, brought from the depths and disentangled by strange associations. They were precious when they came.

Kate chided herself as they walked. This was no time for reminiscing. She had to be both alert and calm, a curious state of balance her Tai Chi Chuan teacher had demanded during her college days. Perhaps those lessons would come in handy now.

"It's over there," David said, pointing.

The ship was a hundred and forty or fifty feet long, she guessed, a gleaming giant with long sleek lines, tall masts, the dominant impression one of rich dark wood and gleaming brass melded with perfect workmanship.

"Wow!" Kate said. She knew nothing about boating, but it was clear that the craft made the others beside it look like rubber dinghies.

"It's a Scandinavian-made Fed ship. A hundred and fifty feet of luxury," David said. "It has half-a-dozen passenger cabins and a crew of between twelve and twenty, depending upon the number of guests. Worth millions, of course."

There were a few people on the deck, but most of the activity seemed to come from inside the well-lighted main lounge—voices, soft music, the occasional laugh. When they reached the gangplank, a uniformed guard recognized David and touched his cap. Kate noticed that he wore a side arm.

"Good evening, sir. Welcome aboard," he said.

"Thank you." David took Kate's arm as they walked up to the deck. "There's a full-time crew on this boat at all times," he said to her. "Jason is not the type to be kept waiting. If he wants to set sail, he wants to be able to do it at a moment's notice."

There were perhaps twenty people in the lushly furnished lounge. A few stood, but most sat in small groups. Modern modular furniture, white and cushiony, was arranged to seat clumps of six or seven at a time. Mahogany and brass gleamed against each other. Kate caught a vague impression of faces, and then a tall, lean man in charcoal-gray slacks and a baby-blue open-necked shirt rose and came quickly toward them.

"David, so glad you could make it." He shook David's hand and looked questioningly at Kate.

"This is Kate Buchanan. Jason Thomas," David said.

He shook her hand. "Now I can see why you're late." A quick grin changed his tanned face. "Welcome aboard," he added to her.

Thomas was a man of authority, Kate surmised. It came through in his self-assured voice, in an aura of power that permeated his manner, in the piercing directness of the dark brown eyes. He was also handsome, not like a movie star, but more like a politician who had developed in his face those qualities of strength voters loved so much. It was there in the firm set of his mouth, in the leanness of his face, and in a body that demonstrated no trace of self-indulgence. Altogether an impressive package.

"This is a beautiful boat," she said.

"A ship, Miss Buchanan," he corrected her, humor taking the edge away. "This is a fairly large seagoing vessel. It could take us around the world if we wished."

"A beautiful ship." She corrected herself with a smile.

"David tells me you're interested in art?"

"It's my line of work," she said. "I work at Friars Gallery and before that for the Dotson Gallery in New York."

"Ah, I know them both," he said. "In what area? Sales?"

"Authentication and acquisitions," she said.

"She has a Masters," David interceded. "Apparently she was quite a star in New York."

Jason gave her a thoughtful look, then waved at the walls.

"This is my corporate art. I have a private collection that's quite different."

Kate swiftly took in three of the paintings closest to them. "A Pollock, a de Kooning oil and, who is that? Lichtenstein? Very nice."

"Yes," Thomas said, his tone impressed. "Is contemporary art your area of expertise?"

"Not really. I don't even particularly like it. I probably know more about the Old Masters and Impressionists than anything, but one has to follow the market, you know."

"My God, David?" Jason said, genuine admiration in his voice. "Where did you find this young lady? Not only is she beautiful, but she has intelligence and taste!"

David simply beamed, while Jason said conspiratorially to Kate, "I loathe abstract art myself. My private collection consists mainly of Impressionists. You'll have to see it sometime."

"I'd love to," Kate smiled.

"David, why not introduce Kate to the others while I get you both a drink. What would you like?"

"A dry white wine would be nice," Kate said.

"Same for me," David said, and led her to the nearest group.

An extraordinarily beautiful Eurasian woman was talking animatedly. "And after London, the food in France was really something! I ate so much I have to go on a diet now." She stopped and looked up as they approached. "Hi, David!" she said gaily. She was a glittering creature, her silky long hair shining as brightly as her deep blue silk shirt.

The man sitting beside her stood and shook David's hand. "Hey, babe. Good to see you." He took Kate in and added, "And your gorgeous lady."

"Kate, this is Allan Silver, and this is Jasmine," David said. He pointed to a woman who was still seated. "Page Peters." And then to a man beside her, who rose, "Stodding Watson." And to another man, "Michael Wadler. And this is Kate Buchanan."

"Pleased to meet you," she said. People shifted around to make room for them, and she and David sat. It was accidental, but they looked like a perfectly matched couple. Both wore bone-colored light wool slacks and jackets. The only difference was that instead of the cream shirt David had on, Kate wore a pearly green silk shirt that added a sparkle to her green eyes.

She found herself beside the woman named Page.

"I gather you had a good trip," David said to Allan.

"The best. Even got some R and R in. We took off from London and spent a couple of days in St. Trop."

"Your first time overseas, wasn't it, Jasmine?" David asked.

"But not my last," she grinned. "I've got the travel bug now."

Allan groaned. "I've created a monster."

Kate examined the faces while they talked. Jasmine was vivacious, talkative, probably in her mid-twenties, perhaps something of an airhead, she thought ungenerously. Page, on the other hand, had that sedate Grace Kelly beauty about her. A listener, not a talker, her face, though attentive, giving away nothing of her thoughts.

As for the men, Silver was the typical Hollywood type, obsessed with his appearance and the impression he created on others. Someone who had hustled all his life, she guessed. Probably grew up in the Bronx. She noted that while he wore a wedding ring, Jasmine did not. Stodding Watson—she recognized his name as the curator of the Rex—could only be called distinguished and charming. Even white teeth, a ready chuckle, and, judging by the way his eyes darted around the room, an opportunist. The final man in the group, Michael Wadler, seemed to be in his mid-thirties. Dark hair, slim build, a cheerful persuasive voice, perhaps a salesman of some kind. Was one of these men responsible for Joel's death? It was too soon for speculation, too dangerous. Patience, she told herself.

A waiter appeared with their wine on a tray. She sipped her drink slowly, as Jasmine continued to describe her trip, and looked around the lounge. All the women were attractive, all the men seemed affluent, ranging in age from mid-thirties to early fifties. Successful men who had already achieved a great deal.

There was a lot of financial power in this room, she realized. She saw Jason Thomas approach another group and join in their conversation. She took note of the attentive respectful expressions on the faces of the people around him when he spoke. And there was none more powerful than Mr. Thomas, she thought.

She realized suddenly that someone was watching her and turned her head quickly to find Page Peter's cool blue appraising eyes on her. Page didn't look away but smiled, "And where are you from, Kate?" she asked. "I detected an East Coast accent in your voice."

"I just moved out here from New York."

David interrupted. "Stod, you and Kate have a lot in common. She has a background in art. Works at Friars Gallery."

"Oh, I was just there, looking at the Breer paintings," Stodding said, raising an eyebrow. "A remarkable talent. Did the show go well?"

"Excellent," Kate said. "Breer is very much in demand."

The conversation turned to art. Stodding proved extremely knowledgeable, Page interjected with a couple of perceptive comments, Allan Silver and Michael Wadler were interested but obviously possessed only laymen's knowledge, and Jasmine, for once, merely listened, apparently out of her depth.

During the next hour, Kate followed David's lead and worked the room like a professional. She met half-a-dozen equally impressive people, confirming her earlier impression of a gathering of considerable financial power. There was a congressman, a banker, a city councilman, a real estate developer, a shopping mall tycoon, magazine publisher Ted Benson, and Senator Corbett Donnelly.

When she spoke to the senator, she found Donnelly's charisma was undeniable. He had a smile like a floodlight and an attentive way of listening that made the speaker feel they were the only two people on earth. His opposite was Benson, the magazine publisher. He was more taciturn than most in the room, a distracted man whose mind seemed always to be on other more important matters. The shopping mall tycoon was gruff, with a loud laugh. A bulldozer personality, he stripped her with his eyes, even while he patted his girlfriend on the fanny.

She sensed that it was important to David that she made a good impression on them all, as if their opinions of her were significant to him in some way. She was charming to everyone, determined to pass this unspoken test. He, in turn, treated her with a mixture of boyish pride and tentative possessiveness. "Look what I've pulled off," his attitude seemed to say. "She's gorgeous and she's mine."

It wasn't true. They hadn't even made love yet, but he obviously felt it was preordained—simply a matter of time.

Although naturally observant, her powers seemed even sharper tonight. She missed nothing about every person she met, took them all in, formed quick judgments, filed the information away to be assimilated fully later.

One particularly interesting fact emerged. None of the men were there with their wives—*if* they were married. All the women were attractive, younger, and apparently single. She remembered what Madge had said about this particular crowd and their mistresses, and it was obviously true. Of course, it made sense. Men like these probably had another and entirely different social life, one in which their wives were involved. The wives in all likelihood knew each other, sat on the same committees, belonged to the same clubs, lunched together. If one wife attended the gathering in this room, the word would be out. These men were all involved in a sexual conspiracy, a shared deceit.

Which one of these men had been Angie Cox's lover? She had no idea. It could be anyone in the room—except David. His name had only been mentioned by Angie as someone who was a member of the circle her boyfriend/lover/master belonged to. Influential? Powerful? Most of the men here would fall into those categories. How often did these men change their mistresses? How incestuous a group was it? Did they hand the women over to their friends when they were ready to discard them? Too many questions. Too many to ask or answer on this night.

Page, she realized, was with Jason. Stodding Watson was unaccompanied. Homosexual perhaps? Another unanswered question. Michael Wadler (who she learned was president of a large brokerage house, confirming her hunch that he was in sales of some kind) was with a young blond actress named Cindy. Jasmine and Allan. The senator and an auburn-haired young lady of indeterminate occupation named Ellen, who had outstanding legs and a wild laugh. The liberal congressman was with Diana, a black woman. And so it went, the pairings gradually becoming clear to her but bringing her no closer to what she needed to discover.

Jason Thomas began to hold court, the politicians among his audience. His subject: the crucial need for a new multilevel entertainment complex in West Los Angeles. Construction had been proposed some months earlier. No-growth proponents were fighting it. "As usual, they are not concerned with the prosperity or jobs it will bring, only how it appears against the skyline," he said. "The majority of people in the area are far wiser. They want it."

Kate then realized the purpose of the entire party. It was a low-key lobbying effort, with the politicians as the targets. Thomas, although he never stated it, obviously had a financial interest in the proposed complex. Probably half the men in the room did, and the support of those who didn't was being enlisted.

David chimed in his support of the project in the measured professional tones of a banker. It was, he stated, a financially sound investment, promising exceptional returns. So, Kate thought as she listened, they also want more investors. Or maybe that's the carrot being dangled in front of the politicians. One thing was certain: The real business would be conducted later behind closed doors. These were the preliminaries, the warm-ups.

She wandered away from the men and went out on deck. Jasmine and the blonde Cindy were discussing the film business.

"Even giving good head can't guarantee a part anymore,'' Cindy was saying with surprising cynicism for one so young. She couldn't have been more than twenty.

Jasmine erupted in laughter and said, ''Things are tough all over, kiddo.''

''Are you an actress as well?'' Kate smiled tentatively as she joined them.

''Yes.'' Jasmine turned and instantly assessed Kate, then continued, ''I do some movies, some television.''

''I guess it's a tough way to make a living,'' Kate said sympathetically.

Cindy snorted. ''Who said anything about making a living? If we had to make a living doing this, we'd be starving!''

''Some people do,'' Jasmine said guardedly.

''It helps if you're going out with the head of a studio,'' Cindy said, attempting a smile to soften her words. She was a little drunk, Kate saw, and probably hadn't meant to say it.

''You do what you can do,'' Jasmine said, unabashed.

''Have you been acting a long time?'' Kate asked.

Jasmine shrugged, as if to indicate the irrelevancy of time. ''Three or four years. I don't work at it as hard as I should.''

Cindy looked at her empty glass and giggled. ''Oops, time for a refill,'' she said, and walked back inside.

''She's drunk,'' Jasmine said. She turned and looked out at the water. A thin sheen of oil discolored it. ''Have you known David long?'' she asked.

''No, less than a week.''

Jasmine became silent, her thoughts turned inward.

She really is beautiful, Kate thought, looking at her profile. There was no trace of the earlier gaiety on her face now. In repose it was inscrutable, except for a tiny tug at the corner of her mouth, giving it a downward slant, a trace of self-indulgence.

''He used to go with a girlfriend of mine,'' Jasmine said finally.

''Oh? What happened?''

''She died.''

"I'm sorry," Kate said. "I hadn't heard anything about it. What happened?"

"It doesn't matter. She's dead. I shouldn't have mentioned it. It has nothing to do with you."

"No, that's all right."

Jasmine turned to face Kate, her eyes troubled. "I shouldn't have mentioned it," she repeated. "David wouldn't like it."

"It's okay. I won't say anything."

There was a moment's silence, and then Kate said, "Would you like to have lunch sometime next week?"

Jasmine looked surprised, then she smiled with a touch of embarrassed pleasure. "Sure." She flipped her black hair over her shoulder with her left hand and several silver bracelets clinked down her arm. "That would be great. Can I call you when I know my schedule?"

"I work at Friars Gallery during the day. You can reach me there."

"I'll call you tomorrow," Jasmine said. She excused herself then and went back into the lounge, leaving Kate alone at the rail.

She stood there, listening to the soft lick of the ocean against the sides of the ship.

"Hey! The girl is hot!" Alan said enthusiastically to David.

"Where did you meet her?" Jason asked.

"At the Breer show, at Friars," David said, obviously pleased by their attention. The three men stood together in a small group, out of earshot of the rest of the guests for the moment. Allan had his hands stuffed in his pockets.

"Do you know much about her?" Jason asked.

David looked startled by the question. "Enough. She's new out here."

Jason smiled. "Well, she's certainly an improvement over Selena."

"Are you banging her yet?" Allan asked with a crude grin.

It was a typical comment from him, offending no one.

David simply raised his eyebrows and said, "A gentleman never tells."

"Yeah, but I was asking *you,*" Allan said.

"She's very bright. Very knowledgeable about art," Jason said thoughtfully.

"Yes, I know," David agreed. "A useful friend to have."

"Yes, well"—Jason glanced around the room—"back to the senator."

"Is it going well?" David asked.

"I think so," Jason said cautiously.

"Who fixed him up with the hooker?" Allan asked.

David was surprised. "The girl he's with?"

"Sure," Allan said. "I'll bet she charges five hundred dollars a night."

"A thousand," Jason said with a slight smile. "My people arranged it. He'll be spending the night aboard. In the best stateroom, of course. I'm sure it will be very enjoyable."

"And he'll be very grateful," Allan said with a snigger.

"You should see the briefcase she always carries with her," Jason said. "Every sexual aid known to man."

"Oh," David said, trying to keep his face bland. He should have known. Sometimes he felt out of his depth around these guys. It was a long way from the conservative banking circles in which he had started his career twenty years earlier.

"Well, I'd better find Kate," he said. "We should be moving on."

"I saw her go out on deck," Jason said. "I hope I have the chance to meet her again."

"Oh, you will," David said with conviction. "I'm going to be seeing a lot of her."

When he took her home this time, Kate invited David into her apartment for a nightcap. It was a calculated act, one she didn't have much choice in making. David was a big boy and couldn't be led along much longer. Since their first date, when he had proposed a "relationship," he had been the perfect gentleman, allowing them to get to know each other, as he had suggested. He had kissed her only when the unspoken invitation was there. But on those few occasions, she had felt his excitement, literally felt it pressing against her. The guy was as horny as a teenager.

She had known it would come to this sooner or later. Naturally, she had hoped it would come later, the later the better. She was not anxious to sacrifice her body for this mission of hers. But was she prepared to? It was the question she had asked herself and answered when she'd first met David and embarked on this scheme. And the answer had been yes. To come this far and have qualms about going to bed with an attractive man to further her goals was ridiculous. Or so she had told herself.

"Nice place." David cast a cursory eye around the apartment. He stood in the middle of the living room, waiting to be told what to do.

"Sit down and make yourself at home," Kate said. "What can I get you? I have wine, and wine, and wine."

"I guess I'll have some wine," he said, choosing to place himself on the couch.

"What did you think of my friends?" he asked as she walked away.

"Very impressive collection of people," she said, turning her head.

"You impressed them, too."

She posed in the doorway to the kitchen and gave a small curtsey. "I'm honored."

She returned a few moments later with two glasses of wine, handed one to David, and sat on the couch, close to him but not touching.

"To us." He lifted his glass.

She clinked her glass against his without speaking, and then took a small sip.

"There will be an us, won't there, Kate?" he asked, putting his glass on the table, looking intently at her for an answer.

"It seems to be heading in that direction," she said with a small noncommittal shrug.

"You don't seem thrilled by the possibility." He sounded hurt.

"I'm sorry. I don't mean to make it sound like that. It's just that it's happening so fast." She put her glass on the table as well.

She had made up her mind in that second. The thought of the actual reality of sleeping with him was suddenly dreadful. In theory it was fine, but in practice? She would try and put him off for just a little longer.

"You're very attractive," she continued, in what she hoped was an admiring tone. "Physically, mentally, in all ways. But you're sweeping me off my feet, and I'm not used to it."

"You've thought about it?"

"Of course. I've thought about little else since we met."

He spread his hands. "Then what's the problem? We're both consenting adults. We're attracted to each other—perhaps even more than merely attracted, speaking for myself—and there should be nothing stopping us."

"You're married."

David allowed an incredulous expression to flit across his face. "I've explained that. It means nothing, has nothing to do with us!"

She put her hand out and placed it over his. "David, I'm sorry, you'll just have to be patient with me. I've never had an affair with a married man before. The idea takes some getting used to."

He put his other hand over hers. "Kate, I adore you. I want you. Right now, I want nothing more in the world than to make love to you. Do you know what you're asking?"

"I'm asking for a little time."

"I'm not a very patient man."

"You've been wonderfully patient and understanding," she said. "And I'm very grateful."

"A little time, huh?"

She nodded.

"All right." He released her hand. "I'd better go." He lumbered to his feet. "Will I see you tomorrow?"

She rose to stand beside him. "Give me a couple of days to sort things out, David."

He put his hands on her shoulders and pulled her toward him. "You're making me crazy, you know that, don't you?"

She lifted her face, parted her lips. With a groan he lowered his head and kissed her, his lips hard, his tongue exploring. He pulled her body against his, ran his hands down her back, forced her pelvis against his so that she could feel him hardening against her.

She drew her head away, fighting for breath. For a long moment they stared at each other. David's eyes fogged with passion, and then he released her and stepped back.

"Soon," he said, his voice tight.

"Yes, soon," she answered.

He turned and walked out of the apartment.

She stood in the center of the room, her breathing still heavy. What kind of woman am I? she wondered, dismayed at her reaction. She had felt his passion, had genuinely responded to it. A slave to the automatic passions of her body.

"God!" she said, suddenly feeling helpless, speaking aloud, the sound of her voice grounding her. "I hope to God I know what I'm doing!"

CHAPTER EIGHT

"God, he's so lame! He wants to do local papers instead of a *People* magazine interview!" Brett Feltzer's complaint came in a loud aggrieved voice. His client's ignorance was a personal affront. "Next thing you know, he'll want to do local radio shows!"

Page leaned back in her chair and looked at him without amusement. Brett was one of her five account executives. He wore fashionable baggy charcoal pants, a grey shirt, and a silver tie. She was more conservatively dressed in a pale blue Pierre Cardin jacket and skirt, a lemon-colored blouse, and light blue high-heeled shoes.

Brett's "costume," as she tended to think of it, was allowable, however. He was hip. Her Hip Account Executive, responsible for her few show business and related activity clients. About twenty-seven, a communications graduate of USC, his main fault was a smug superiority that allowed him to overlook his obvious deficiencies.

"Well, get him in the local papers *and* in *People,"* she said. "He's paying us because we're the experts. So we do what's best for him, whether he knows it or not."

"Why bother? He won't appreciate it," Brett warned. "He thinks *People* is on the same level as the tabloids. We're dealing with a real dumb guy here."

Page allowed a thoughtful silence to develop before commenting. "Tell you what, Brett," she said pleasantly. "He may be dumb, but he's valuable. He pays me to do his PR, while I pay you. Who do you think is more valuable to me?"

Brett blinked and sat straighter in his chair.

"This is what you do," Page continued. "You don't waste my time criticizing the client. Instead, you do what the client wants and what I want. That way you get to keep me happy. Okay?"

"Sure," Brett said, his voice more formal. "Anything else?"

"No. That will be all for now." Page bent her head to examine the papers on her desk.

She looked up when Brett left the room and swiveling her chair to face the window. It was Wednesday, and a hot Santa Ana wind was oppressing the basin. The police said that when the dry winds were around, the murder rate climbed. Page believed it. She hated the Santa Anas; they were somehow disheartening.

A knock at the door interrupted her thoughts.

"Come in."

Anne Miles, another account executive, stood close to the door, as if ready to turn and flee at the first harsh word. She was twenty-three, pretty in a nervous way, intense, a good worker, but lacking in initiative and confidence at times—a serious drawback for someone in public relations. Still, Page had hopes for her. When she had started, six months earlier, she had hardly been able to talk to strangers. Since then, she had become very good on the telephone and had demonstrated a natural flair as a writer. The next step was to develop her ability to communicate face to face with the media and clients.

"I just talked to Mr. Perkins," she said in her gentle, hesitant voice. "He wants to announce a new acquisition. He wanted to discuss the strategy with you. He should be calling in a few minutes."

Page repressed a sigh. Perkins was another client she had gained through Jason. He was chairman of an oil company that was spreading its tentacles through leveraged buy-outs of smaller companies. Anne should have known how to handle him. A fully responsible account exec would have taken all the pertinent information, put the whole PR plan together, and presented it to Page for approval. A crucial prerequisite for a successful PR person was the ability to let the client think you knew what you were doing, even if you didn't.

"You'll have to get a press release together. Do a mailing and put it on the business wire. Make sure he's accessible to the media. It's no big deal. Check with accounts and see if his budget allows the bizwire expense. If not, make sure you get a PO from him."

"I've got all the material for the release," Anne said.

"Good. Well, write it and then let me see it this afternoon. Anything else?"

"No. Thank you," Anne said, backtracking out of the room.

What a way to make a living, Page thought. Babysitting. It was her own fault, of course. She hired these kids because they were cheap and trainable. There were moments, though, when it just didn't seem worth the effort.

She was abnormally irritable today, she realized, because the relationship with Jason was taking its toll. Always at his beck and call, always subject to his generous whims, with most of her clients his friends, always sitting on the fringes of his power was like being in a prison, in a trap. Instead of gaining her long-sought independence, she was growing more and more dependent on him. It was not a good position for her to be in and it made her nervous.

The telephone buzzed. "Yes," she said, punching the speakerphone on.

"Jim Perkins on line three, her secretary announced.

"Tell him I had to leave the office, that I discussed the strategy with Miss Miles and if he has any questions of an urgent nature to take them up with her."

She got up from her desk. She had to get out, walk, think.

"I'm out for the rest of the day," she told her secretary as she passed. "Unreachable."

She needed time for herself. As it was, her life was divided into neat compartments of responsibility to others: her business, Jason, her mother. They all took from her, demanded of her. There was no space for Page. Perhaps she should follow the advice she gave Elsa and simply get out, walk on the beach, give herself the time she deserved.

A half-hour later, she was parked in a lot beside the Santa Monica pier. She went down to the boardwalk, bought a hot dog at a fairly unsanitary-looking stand, and walked toward Venice while she ate.

The beach was crowded with other hookey players. Roller skaters, cyclists, and joggers bustled for space on the boardwalk, all trying to get a little sea breeze, escaping the stifling warm wind in the city. Half the offices in LA must be empty, she thought.

After walking for fifteen minutes, she sat on a bench and gazed out at the sparkling blue Pacific. It looked almost as calm as the sand, to the despair of the surfers who sat idly on their boards, waiting just beyond the waves. Twenty yards down the boardwalk a crowd gathered around a juggler.

"Hi!" said a girl, and sat on the bench beside her. 'Rad weather, isn't it?"

"It's very nice," Page said cautiously.

The girl was about eighteen, pretty, with long light brown hair that fell halfway down her back. She wore shorts and a halter top, no shoes. Her skin was tanned the color of honey. Page, still wearing office clothes, felt ridiculously overdressed.

"You look like you escaped from work," the girl said, also noting Page's clothes. She had a pleasant smile, an open, untroubled face.

"I did. And you?"

"School. I go to college in Santa Monica. I cut classes today."

"What's your major?"

The girl shrugged. "I haven't decided yet. Maybe journalism, maybe visual arts—TV, film, you know. What do you do?"

"Public relations. I have my own agency."

"Oh, really? That's rad. That's another area I'm interested in."

"Well, it's a living," Page said unenthusiastically. Rad it wasn't.

"Do you make a lot of money?" the girl asked with a bluntness that would have been objectionable in anyone older.

Page smiled wryly. In the young, such rudeness was graciously conceded to be an unavoidable part of an admirable curiosity. "No, not a lot, not as much as I want."

The girl looked at the expensive skirt and blouse Page was wearing, the diamond stud earrings, the two large rings on her fingers. "You must want a lot," she said.

Out of the mouths of babes, Page thought to herself. "Yes, I do."

The girl got to her feet, stood hesitantly for a moment, then said. "Well, good luck."

"Thanks," Page said. "The same to you."

"See you," the girl said, and walked on toward the juggler.

"God!" Page said, suddenly feeling old.

She had been as young as that once. Never as carefree, not that she could remember, but definitely as young. Now, as she watched the young girl, her long, athletic legs attracting glances as she passed the crowd and continued into the distance, it seemed that she was walking into a lengthening future, as limitless as the horizon. Page, on the other hand, although just over a dozen years older, saw only a diminishing future for herself, a treadmill that would grow shorter and shorter unless something changed. Correction. Unless *she* changed something. She would have to do it herself; it wouldn't just happen. Positive experiences didn't always happen to people who sat around passively waiting for them.

She clenched her jaw and told herself to be patient. An opportunity would present itself—somehow, sometime. When it did, she would grasp it.

She rose from the bench and began to walk back the way she had come.

For the third time that day, David looked at the telephone on his desk and almost reached for it. He desperately wanted to call Kate, hear the sound of her voice, and press her for a decision. But love was something like business, and when making a deal, overeagerness was a bad mistake, a sign of weakness.

He had promised to give her time to think about their relationship. A couple of days. That had been Monday, and now it was Wednesday. Surely he could call and ask her what she had decided?

"Ugh!" he said to himself, disgusted by the ruminations of his mind. He was acting like a kid. He would just have to be patient, even if it took another two days.

He didn't know what he was worrying about. She was fond of him. More than fond. He remembered that kiss before he had left her apartment, the passion between them, and he couldn't understand her reluctance. Had she been recently hurt in a love affair? Was there someone she still loved back in New York? It hadn't sounded that way.

No. She would make the right decision. She was just exercising her female prerogative to be undecided.

God, he could do so much for her. Would do so much. He had the financial ability to give her anything. He'd take over her rent, move her to a better part of town if she wanted. He'd buy her a car so she could get rid of that expensive and silly rental she couldn't afford. If she didn't want to, she wouldn't even have to work at the gallery anymore. He could provide her with literally everything she needed.

He would be able to do things for her that he hadn't been able to do for Selena. The problem with Selena had been that she had wanted nothing from him except the occasional sexual thrill and entree into his circle. Oh, he had bought her presents, and she had been delighted to receive them. What woman wouldn't be? But she hadn't *needed* them—or him.

Whether she knew it or not, Kate needed him. She deserved better than what she had now. An intelligent and beautiful woman like that deserved the best. Deserved him. He could show her a lifestyle she had never seen, except from a distance. It would be a different experience for both of them.

She would be his mistress. His. Belonging to him.

"Mr. Ross! Mr. Ross!"

Surprised, he looked around, then realized that the voice was coming from the squawk box on his desk. His secretary had been calling him for at least a minute, but he had been so lost in his thoughts he hadn't heard.

I should stop worrying, he told himself. It's going to happen. She's too smart to turn me down. It'll happen just the way I want it to.

"Yes," he said impatiently into the speaker. "What is it?"

That morning, Sharon had thrown her wedding ring into the bathtub in a fit of fury. She had wound herself up with resentment, mulling over Jason's recent treatment of her. It was a quixotic gesture more than anything else. She knew full well that the trap would prevent the valuable ring from going down the drain.

After her bath, she hurriedly tossed on a red Halston dress, climbed into the baby-blue Mercedes, and resentfully drove herself into Beverly Hills. It was yet another insult. She hated driving, but since Jason had fired Adam she had been unable to find a suitable chauffeur.

She went directly to Mr. Paul's, the furrier on Rodeo Drive. He was known to charge exorbitant prices, but he was tolerated because of his well-promoted reputation for servicing celebrity clientele.

It was a sedate store, with a front door of burnished oak and two mannequins in the small window. This was an establishment that did not need the normal blandishments and was considered a "class act." The service was personalized, discreet but always available.

Sharon went directly to the largest rack, fingering the lush fur coats while the salesman hovered a respectable distance away.

The red and brown Arctic fox was nice, but too damned cheap, she thought, looking at the three-thousand-dollar price tag. Jason was going to pay a lot more than that for his little outburst.

She touched her cheek. There was still a slight swelling where he had hit her, but carefully applied makeup had eradicated the traces of discoloration that had first appeared.

Her eyes swept around the store. His assault was worth at least a full-length mink, she thought. She strode greedily over to another rack. White mink—white for lost innocence. She reached out and withdrew a coat, pressing it against her face.

"Madam would like to try it on?" the salesman asked, stepping forward and taking it from her hands. He was middle-aged, and wore a gray three-piece suit and a black toupee.

"Yes," she said, moving to the mirror.

He placed it over her shoulders and stepped back. She enjoyed its weight, the glistening white, the luxurious rolling folds, Her hair looked like strands of gold resting on snow.

"I'll take it," she said, not even looking at the price.

The salesman hid his surprise. In Beverly Hills one never showed surprise at the customer. Just that morning a well-known female rock star had come in, accompanied by an entourage of six equally barbaric hangers-on. She had bought a mink and a sable for herself, and short fox jackets for each of the people in her group. The young savages had also smoked a joint in the store while trying on their purchases. Nobody had blinked an eye. The kids could afford to behave any way they liked.

"Your account, Madam?" he asked her, taking the coat back.

"Charge it to Jason Thomas."

"Yes, Madam," he said, looking at the price tag.

"How much is it?" she asked, not out of concern but to ascertain the extent of her damage.

"Eleven thousand five hundred and ninety-nine dollars."

Sharon nodded. Yes, that was most satisfactory For starters at least. Jason would shit.

Money was one of the many irritants in their marriage. He had always been generous up to a point, but in spite of his wealth—by all accounts immense—he maintained a tight control over her spending. Before incurring large expenses over and beyond a set monthly budget, she was required to clear them with him. It made her feel like some functionary on his staff who had to get a purchase order every time he needed new pens and paper.

That was Jason for you—businessman to the core, asshole to the limit. She had money of her own, of course, but it was all tied up in various investments. Jason had taken care of it for her when they had first married. She never touched it. It was her nest egg, her security blanket.

She signed the bill presented by the salesman, then noticed him start to box the coat. "Don't bother wrapping it.'' She took it from him, slung it over her shoulder, and sauntered out of the shop.

The parking lot attendant took her ticket, eyeing the mink and then her. He was in his mid-twenties, athletically built and olive-complexioned, with short-cropped black hair, a clean-cut college look about him.

''Do you like it?'' she asked, her voice friendly.

Normally he would have simply said yes. You didn't speak to the clientele around here with familiarity. But there was an openness about this woman, an obvious willingness to communicate. ''What did you do? Win the lottery?'' he asked, grinning and looking her straight in the eye.

Sharon leaned against the makeshift parking lot counter and dazzled him with a broad smile. ''I made a killing in the stock market, honey.''

''Really?'' Interest animated his voice. ''I'm a business major at UCLA. I'm really interested in the market.''

His pants were tight around his hips and broad shoulders stretched the red parking lot jacket.

''What time do you get off work?''

''In a couple of hours,'' he said, his eyes growing speculative.

''Maybe I could give you some tips. Why don't you meet me at the Beverly Wilshire? In the bar in two hours.''

''Sure,'' he said. ''That would be great!''

He continued staring at her, hardly believing his luck. She was a lot older than he was, for sure, but she was some lady. A little on the heavy side, but still a great body.

Sharon gave him a moment to enjoy the view, then spoke.

''What?'' he said.

''Why don't you get my car now, honey?''

''Oh,'' he said, a flush rising. ''Yes, ma'am. Right away.''

Two hours, she thought as she drove back onto Rodeo Drive. That was enough time to do a lot of damage. She'd have her total purchases up to about twenty thousand dollars by then.

* * *

Jason was not thinking of his wife, but his mistress was very much on his mind as he listened to his chief of security, Fred Porter. He had asked Porter to do a spot check on Page for a couple of days, just to make sure she was following his advice not to pad the bills. Now Porter was in Jason's office, making his report.

"Her purchases were all legit," Porter said. "She bought a dress at Morelli's, where she was padding the bill before. This time it was fine."

"Good," Jason said. He hadn't doubted his warning to her would have the desired effect, but it was wise to check anyway. "Anything else?"

"She visited a couple of places." He shrugged. "I don't know if you need the information, but I got it."

Porter had been a policeman until a slight embarrassment had necessitated his departure from the force. Something to do with the use of excessive force. He had been working for Jason for five years, and he was very thorough. Burly, with close-cropped hair and a slab of a face, he was not physically impressive, but he was totally loyal to Jason, who paid him very well.

"What is it?" Jason asked.

"She visited two women. The first was named Elsa Bennet. Here's the sheet on her."

Jason took the extended page and scanned it. "A rich friend. Who's the other?"

"Name is Clara Peters. Lives in a retirement home in Westwood." Porter took another sheet of paper from his folder and held it out.

Jason raised an eyebrow. "Relative?"

"Mother," Porter said. "She brought her out here from New York just over four months ago."

Jason took the page and placed it on his desk. "Thank you very much, Porter. You can take your man off her now."

"Yes, sir. Anything else?"

"No, that's all."

Jason sat alone in his office, drumming his fingers on the desk. Page had never mentioned a mother, let alone that she was here in LA. In fact, he could have sworn that when he first met her she said she had no family. Perhaps not. He wasn't sure.

Well, it probably wasn't important. On the other hand, perhaps one day it would be. Information had always been valuable to him. It was a matter of knowing when and how to use it.

He closed the folder and put it in the wall safe with his other personal papers.

Sharon had done enough shopping damage, so she arrived half-an-hour early at the Beverly Wilshire. She took care of some business at the desk, then went to the bar to wait for her parking lot Romeo, as she found herself thinking of him. She wore the white mink.

He arrived when she was halfway through her vodka. The parking uniform had gone; he wore slacks and a sports coat, with an open-necked shirt that showed tufts of black hair on his chest.

"Hi." He sat on the stool beside her.

"Hi, Romeo. Glad you could make it."

"The name's Jim. Jim Morris." His voice was more confident now that he was wearing civilian clothes. "I see you're wearing your mink."

"Nice, isn't it? What would you like to drink."

"Whatever you're having."

"A screwdriver," she said to the bartender.

"So, tell me about yourself," he said, leaning an elbow on the counter. "What's your name?"

"Do you really want to know? Names, history. They're all so boring."

He laughed uncomfortably. "Well, I have to call you something."

"Stella. Call me Stella."

The bartender put the screwdriver in front of him. He took a quick gulp and then put it back on the counter.

"What do you do, Stella?"

"I dabble in the stock market," she said. "My husband died and left me some money. I've tripled it in two years."

"Really?" he asked eagerly. "Do you make your own decisions or depend on a broker?"

She drained her drink, already tired of the game. "Come on." She slid off the stool.

"Where?"

She dangled a key in front of him. "Room service is so much more fun."

"You have a room here?"

"Follow me," she whispered with a wink.

They went down the hall to the elevators without speaking. She pressed the button and, when the doors opened, stepped into the elevator. "Five," she said.

Obediently, he pressed the button. She leaned back against the wall and stared at him, an amused expression on her face.

"Quite an adventure, isn't it, Jim?"

He swallowed, looking up at the lights indicating the floors. Hell! He couldn't believe this was happening to him. His buddies wouldn't believe it.

The elevator stopped and the doors slid open. When they stepped into the hallway, she handed him the room key. He looked at the number and took the lead.

"Here we are." His fingers fumbled with the key as he tried to insert it into the door. Finally, thankfully, it opened. He flicked on the light, then stood aside and let her enter.

Sharon went directly to the large queen-size bed. She sat on its edge, letting her shoes fall from her feet.

He came forward and stopped about three yards from her, uncertain of his next move.

"Would you like me to order a drink? Another vodka perhaps?"

Sharon didn't answer, just gave him a hard, demanding look. "Take off your clothes."

"What? Now? Just like that?"

"Take them off."

He let his jacket drop to the floor, then his shirt. Then, still standing, he used opposite feet to remove his shoes. His embarrassment left him, and he grew bolder as he stared back at her and saw the hungry expression on her face.

He unbuckled his belt, unzipped his fly, and tugged at his pants, allowing them to fall around his ankles. Then he stepped out of them and stood there in his socks and shorts—shorts that began to bulge visibly under her voracious gaze.

"What about you?" he asked.

"I'm not taking my coat off. I don't have to."

She unbelted the mink and allowed it to fall open. She was completely naked underneath it.

His eyes bulged. "You . . . in the bar and everything? You didn't have any clothes on?"

She beckoned him with a finger. "Are you going to stand there and ask stupid questions when you have a chance to fuck on a mink?"

Then she fell back on the bed and waited for him.

Jasmine was as gay as a bird, and as colorful. She wore a flowing silk dress in bright red and black patterns, and when she bounced into the restaurant on Melrose Avenue, she turned at least a dozen male heads.

"Hi!" she said, seating herself at Kate's table, a brilliant smile on her face. "Sorry I'm late. Traffic was terrible."

"That's all right," Kate said. "I've only been here five minutes myself."

Jasmine had called her at work on the morning after the party on the ship, arranging to meet Kate on Wednesday for a late afternoon drink instead of lunch.

"Have you ordered anything yet?"

"No, but I could do with a glass of wine. How about you?"

"The same."

The waiter took their order, and then there was a moment of silence where neither had anything to say.

Jasmine was the first to speak. "How's David?"

"I haven't seen him since the night of the party," Kate said.

"Oh."

"I needed some time to think about it," Kate explained.

"Oh, I thought—"

"—that it was further along?" Kate finished for her. She smiled. "No, not yet. I'm still in the deciding stage."

"It's wise to keep men waiting," Jasmine said, flicking her hair back with her hand. "But not too long."

"How long have you known David?"

"Oh, a year or so, I guess. He and Allan and Jason have been friends a long time."

"And what do you think of him?"

Jasmine looked uncomfortably away. "Of David?" she asked, playing for time. "I don't know. He's rich and charming and I guess he's needed someone like you for a long time."

The waiter came with their wine and placed it on the table. "The other woman you mentioned," Kate said, "your friend who died. Wasn't she good for him?"

"Selena? I loved her, but she was crazy. Wild. Too wild for David. Also, she didn't need him. She had money of her own."

What happened to her? Kate wanted to ask. But she remembered Jasmine's previous discomfort with the subject and said instead, "And you think I do?"

"God no! I don't know you well enough. But it never hurts to hook up with a man who has money and connections, especially in this town, and especially if you're new here. If it works for both of you—" She shrugged.

"If it works," Kate mused.

"If the sex is great," Jasmine said with a delicious smile.

Kate laughed. "Important point."

"Great sex is, well, you know—" Jasmine wrinkled up her nose and said, "Oink! Oink!"

They grew more relaxed with each other after laughing at that. Jasmine told Kate some of her background, how she had come to Los Angeles and how it had first been for her here. "It wasn't like you had to fuck your way into parts, but it helped if you were willing," she said. "That was one problem. The other is that half the casting directors are gay, and you couldn't fuck yourself into parts even if you wanted to."

"So did you work much?"

"Not too much," Jasmine admitted. "I've never been one for indiscriminate sex, not really. The other is that there haven't been that many parts for Chinese-Americans. Then there's also the fact that since I've been with Allan, I haven't hustled that much."

"He must be a help though?"

"Oh, yeah. He gets me a part in something the studio's producing every now and then. I could get him to help me more if I bugged him, but"—she paused thoughtfully—"I guess I hustled for work harder before I started going with Allan."

"Do you like acting?"

"Oh, yes, I love it! It's really the only thing I do well. It's just that it takes a lot of motivation to put yourself on the line like that and—"

"You've got it too easy," Kate said daringly.

"Allan looks after me," Jasmine said simply.

But for how long, and then what? Kate thought perceptively, immediately spotting the weakness in Jasmine's position. She'd have to find another Allan, or better yet, marry one. Or end up like Angie.

"Do you love him?" she asked.

"Yes. I think so. I suppose so. He has a family though. I don't think he'd ever leave them. I sometimes worry about it. I guess one day I'd like to have a family."

Jasmine continued talking. Kate was such an attentive listener; Jasmine hadn't felt as comfortable with anyone since Selena had died. Even then, all Selena and Jasmine had talked about was men. With Kate she found she could bring out the introspective side of her nature, something she rarely did.

Kate didn't say much about herself but that didn't bother Jasmine. It was pleasant for a change to be able to talk about herself with someone who seemed to understand.

Kate formed quick assessments as she listened, reading between the lines, evaluating what was not said. This beautiful woman was not dumb; on the contrary, she had a quick intelligence. But she was untried, like a metal that hadn't been forged yet. Jasmine didn't know her own potential and wasn't motivated enough to explore it. She was leading a comfortable, easy life, and she was grateful to the man who provided it. Thinking of the future probably scared her, so she tended to stay in the present as much as possible. A thumbnail sketch, Kate conceded, but probably accurate.

They finished their wine, deciding not to have more but rather to go for a walk along Melrose Avenue. There were some shops Jasmine wanted to check out.

It was getting close to five o'clock and the street was crowded with end-of-day traffic. Male drivers, secure in their metal and glass boxes, ogled the two attractive women as they stared into the brightly decorated storefronts.

Jasmine chattered away, telling her about the area. Ten years before, Melrose had been virtually unknown, a dowdy neglected street of struggling stores, no pattern to it, no identity. Then the punks had started to gather there, drawn by a few small shops that catered to their bizarre fashions. The straights came to watch the punks and finally shopowners realized that there was enough foot traffic to sustain business. In a few short years, Melrose had grown to become one of the most fashionable areas in Los Angeles, a kaleidoscope of modern culture.

Hip but expensive boutiques elbowed used clothing stores, chichi restaurants, hair sculptors, literary agents, art galleries, and bookstores. Prices ranged from outrageous to genuine bargains. At lunchtime, sleek and very expensive wives met for pasta in the expensive Italian and nouveau-cuisine restaurants, while hip kids ate hamburgers in Johnny Rocket's diner. On the weekends, kids came in from the valleys to see the latest and greatest in alternative living and show off what they had, while the remaining punkers still strutted like small groups of peacocks. Through all this diversity ran a sense of vitality that was lacking in most other parts of the city.

Jasmine was easily distracted and kept breaking off in mid sentence to enter at least half-a-dozen stores. She spent money in only one. She bought some large vinyl earrings and a belt, both done in boldly colored geometric shapes.

"Let's celebrate with another glass of wine," she said,

dragging Kate into a small restaurant. "I love shopping," she announced, collapsing into a booth.

"I see that. You could wear me out."

"It takes training," Jasmine laughed. "Like an athlete."

Over wine, Kate directed the conversation back to men. It was time to find out what she wanted to know. "That was a pretty impressive bunch of guys on the ship the other night."

"Who? Oh, I suppose so. If you're interested in money and power," Jasmine said.

"There were no wives there," Kate said pointedly.

"Hell, no! You never take wives and mistresses to the same places. Wives are for society events, mistresses for fun."

"They all have mistresses?" she asked wonderingly.

"They're all unhappily married, with wives who don't understand them," Jasmine said with surprising cynicism. "Except Allan. He keeps telling me he's happily married. At least he's not a hypocrite."

"Who's Angie Cox?" Kate said casually.

"Angie? God, I haven't seen her for ages. Why do you ask?"

"Oh, I just heard one of the men mention her name. Uh, she didn't seem to be held in high regard."

"Better believe it," Jasmine said. "She was cheating with some other guy, so Jason kicked her out. I haven't seen her since. God knows where she is now. Every now and then I wonder about her. I liked her. She was a friend of Selena's."

"Jason? She was Jason Thomas's mistress?" Kate asked.

"Yeah. Out of all those guys, he's the wrong one to cross. He didn't get as rich as he did by being a nice guy."

"I suppose not," Kate said. She couldn't help it, but her voice was shaking, her heart pumping against her chest as if ready to leap out.

"Are you okay?" Jasmine asked, leaning forward. "You look so pale."

"I'm fine. I guess it's the wine. I haven't eaten much today. I'll be fine."

"Well, then let's go and have dinner. I'm free tonight," Jasmine said happily.

"Dinner?"

"There's a Thai restaurant a couple of blocks down that I've wanted to try."

"I think I'll take a raincheck," Kate said. She was recovering her composure, her breathing growing normal. "I don't live too far from here. I think I'll just go home and lie down a little."

"Sure. Okay." Jasmine said, disappointed. Then she grew solicitous again. "You're all right now? Can you get home okay?"

"I'm fine." Kate forced a smile. "Not enough sleep, not enough food, low blood sugar." She took a last sip of her wine and stood. "It was a great afternoon. We'll have dinner soon, okay?"

Somehow she made it to her car and, clutching the steering wheel like a life belt, to her apartment. As soon as she went inside, she went directly to the telephone. She dialed the number quickly, hoping he was still at the office. His secretary put her through immediately.

"David? Hi, how are you?"

"I'm fine, Kate. How've you been?"

"Just great."

"I've missed you," he said, his voice dropping lower. "Have you been thinking about us?"

"I have. I was wondering if we could get together tonight."

"I hope you've reached a decision," he said.

"Yes, I have."

"The right one, I hope."

"Yes, I think so."

He gave a nervous laugh. "Well, that could mean anything, but I won't interrogate you over the phone. Where and when?"

"I don't feel like going out tonight," she said carefully. "Why don't you come over to my apartment for dinner. Say about seven-thirty?"

"Your apartment? I'll be there," he said elatedly. "See you then."

She heard the disconnecting click and stood there, the telephone still in her hand. Yes, she knew what she had to do. Jason Thomas was her target. There was only one way she could get close to Jason Thomas on a continuous basis. She would become David Ross's mistress.

CHAPTER NINE

Although the living room lights were on, only the soft glow of candles filled the dining area. The table was set with the best she had, which wasn't much. No silverware, just stainless steel. No Mikasa dinnerware, but nice pastel stoneware to go with the pastel tablecloth. However, in spite of her modest belongings, the candles and two bottles of red wine she had rushed out to buy—one of them already open and airing—gave the table a casual but aesthetic feeling. Atmosphere was important at moments like these.

When she bought the wine, she also purchased the ingredients for salad and for lasagna, one of the few dishes she could cook superbly. To cap it off, there was Italian bread and a triangle of Brie cheese, which was already reaching room temperature on the table.

Not that David would be overly interested in her cooking abilities. He would have other things on his mind. For that reason, she wore a loose white cotton skirt and an oversized green T-shirt that still managed to cling where it needed to. Her legs were bare, and she wore sandals. She looked, she hoped, fresh and pretty and desirable. Without the barriers of formal clothing, she probably also looked more attainable.

She was nervous, so damned nervous. Perhaps a glass of wine would calm her. Not the red, damnit! That would ruin the table. She went to the refrigerator and poured herself a glass of white wine. She didn't sip it, instead drinking half the glass in one swallow.

Could she do it? Could she pretend to adore a man she barely even liked? Oh, he was attractive, unobjectionable, even charming, but he was definitely not the kind of man she would look at twice under normal circumstances. He was probably fifteen or more years older than she was, for one thing. More to the point, could she *sleep* with a man she hardly liked? Could she pull it off?

She was using him. He was a tool. She had used him to find out the name of the man responsible for Joel's murder—and she would continue to use him to get close to that man and exact her revenge.

Jason Thomas. She should have guessed it would be him. He was without doubt the most powerful of them all—the smoothest, the most charming, the most successful, the most ruthless. She had known that much from her observations at the party. He wasn't exactly a wolf in sheep's clothing. A more accurate description would be a snake in wolf's clothing.

How could she go up against a man that powerful, a man with all those resources at his disposal? She didn't know yet, but she would find a way. It would take intelligence, planning, and courage. Tonight's action was simply another step. She *had* to do this, she told herself. There was really no choice. She'd started this journey and she wasn't about to end it, no matter what the cost. She had never been a quitter and wasn't about to start now.

Her thoughts gave her courage. She'd do it *and* she'd pull it off. All the way down the line.

The doorbell saved her from further ruminations.

David stood with a huge bouquet of flowers in his arms, a grin on his face. He too wore casual clothes—brown slacks and an open-necked blue shirt.

"I, er, got these," he said, handing her the flowers.

"Oh, thank you, they're beautiful." She took them from him and placed them on the counter. "I'll put them somewhere more appropriate later. Would you like a drink?"

"I see you have some red wine." He stood at the table and tipped the bottle to read the label. "A 1986 Bordeaus. I'll try a glass of this."

"I don't know much about red wines. I chose it by the price."

"It's a good year. I'm sure it's fine. You too?"

"Yes, please." She noticed once again the slightly pompous air that veiled David's speech and actions. And yet there was an insubstantiality about it, as if it had been hurriedly constructed as a mask or as protection.

For the first time she found herself wondering who this man was. Not who he knew or what he did, but who he really was. What had made him the way he was? Where had he come from? How had someone who entered one of the world's most conservative professions ended up hanging out with the fast LA crowd? What was his wife like? Why did he cheat on her? Before this affair was over she'd know the answers to these and the other questions that suddenly filled her mind.

He poured a small amount into each glass and handed one across the table to her. Then he held his glass up, allowing the candlelight to illuminate the ruby liquid.

"To us?" he queried, a trace of apprehension in his voice.

Kate hesitated only a second. "To us," she said, raising her glass.

He put his glass down without tasting the wine and came around the table to put his hands on her shoulders.

"Kate, I'm so pleased. You won't regret it. We'll be good for each other, I promise."

He kissed her enthusiastically then. She broke away laughing, trying to balance her glass. "My wine!"

He reached across the table, grabbed his glass and raised it. "To us," he said again.

They both drank, and then he took her hand, led her into

the living room, and sat on the couch, pulling her down beside him.

The wine was having its effect, she realized. She felt an absence of the tension that had gripped her earlier. Both her mind and body were more relaxed, a kind of loose heaviness soaking her throughout.

From this moment on, for this night at least, she would have to put away all thoughts of brothers, killers, revenge, manipulation of aging lovers, revulsion, and fear. The punch line of some obscure sexually oriented joke she had heard in college came to her: "Relax and enjoy it!" She couldn't remember the joke at all, but the punch line offered good advice. It was the least she could do.

"I want to make you happy," David was saying, breaking into her thoughts. "I want to help you in any and every way I can. You mustn't hesitate to ask me for anything, anything at all."

"I am happy, David."

He put an arm around her, holding her close to him. "There's so much we can do together. I've been thinking about it. I know you haven't travelled much. Well, for one thing, we can do that. I can make the time."

"That would be wonderful," she said.

He put a hand under her chin. "Kate, I want to make love to you," he said, his voice warm.

"Uh, there's dinner in—"

"The hell with dinner!" he said with a cavalier grin. "We can always have dinner."

"I suppose it can wait," she said with a smile.

She took his hand and led him into the bedroom. Standing beside the bed, he kissed her again. It was different from before. This time his hands pulled her body forcefully against his, roamed around her hips and cupped her buttocks, then moved up her back to her hair and down again.

She pulled away breathlessly. "I have to turn the oven down."

"Hurry." He released her, his face flushed.

She went quickly to the kitchen, peeked at the lasagna in the oven, and then lowered the flame.

On the way back to the bedroom, she realized with some surprise that she was excited with anticipation. It had been at least six months since she had made love with anyone; the last time had been in New York with a man she was sporadically dating. A casual affair. Since losing Joel, she had not felt much like love or sex. It hadn't been a priority. Although never promiscuous, she had never been suited to a life of celibacy either. It had just worked out that way for certain periods of time. She was, she thought with a chuckle, truly horny.

David had removed his shirt. He sat on one side of the bed, taking off his shoes and socks. She climbed on the opposite side and scooted across so that she was behind him. She put her arms around him, running them over his chest and stomach, and kissed the side of his neck.

He half turned to kiss her mouth, and then lost his balance and fell so that he was half on the bed. She leaned down and teased his chest with her mouth, nipping him with her teeth and eliciting small groans of pleasure.

"Stop," he said finally, pulling away from her. "Take off your clothes, Kate."

They both undressed, he staring hungrily at her body. "You're beautiful, Kate," he whispered.

She felt beautiful as she stood before him, her body tingling with a sensual feeling she had almost forgotten. Unthinkingly, she ran her hands across her stomach to lightly touch her breasts.

He was in surprisingly good condition, she noted. There were the beginning signs of a paunch and sagging chest muscles, but he was strong. His skin was smooth to the touch and his erection had risen from its cradle of curly black hair as quickly as a young man's.

She touched him and felt his burgeoning excitement. He was also, she soon discovered, a skillful lover: gentle yet demanding, concerned with her pleasure as well as his, patient, experienced enough to feel her waves and rise and fall in unison with them.

Then the moment came when their bodies blurred into one, when all was motion and sensation, when the rising and falling became simply a rising so intense and exhilarating she began to whimper, unable to see anything past the film that cloaked her eyes, able only to grow and grow and grow until finally she burst.

They rolled away from each other, bathed in sweat, silent until their ragged breathing subsided, and then David spoke, "Kate, you've no idea how good that was."

"Oh, yes, I do,"

And to herself she added, Well, that wasn't so bad. In fact, for plain and simple sex, without the enrichment and/or complication of love, it was dynamite.

She began to laugh.

"What?" David asked, unsure whether to join in or be angry. "What is it?"

She tousled his hair. "It's been so long," she said, only half lying. "I was nervous how it would be. It was such a relief, such a wonderful sensation."

She couldn't tell him what an ordeal she thought it would be, with what dread she had planned the evening, the degraded feeling she had anticipated. And what a relief it was instead to feel this comfortable physical satiation, with no emotions involved at all.

No. She couldn't tell him a word. Not who she was, or who she had been, or why she was with him, or if she would betray him, or where she was going. She was in disguise and alone, and for a second the thought gave her a terrifying lurch, like an aircraft that had hit an air pocket.

She had truly entered a life of deceit. From now on she could only tell him what he wanted to hear.

Page wore a burgundy evening dress and was putting on small gold and ruby inlaid earrings while waiting for Jason, who was going to take her to dinner with some of his business associates. He had mentioned the possibility of them needing public relations services.

She knew how the evening would go. Dinner in an expensive restaurant, with her introduced as "another business associate," someone he felt they would benefit from meeting. Never a hint of any relationship between them.

That only happened with "close" business associates. Afterwards, he would come back here and spend the night with her.

The call from the nursing home came shortly after eight, not from the director but from the attending physician.

"Your mother's having stomach pains, some internal bleeding. We thought it best to check her into the hospital," the doctor told her. "It's probably nothing serious, but they have the diagnostic equipment there to find out."

"What do you think it is?" Page asked.

"I'll know in an hour," the doctor said, refusing to commit himself.

"What kind of tests will you be doing?"

"We'll examine her intestinal tract with a scope. See what's there. She'll be sedated, of course."

"Can I see her?"

"Of course. A little later. I'm sure she'd appreciate that. Naturally she's a little scared. She's at UCLA Medical Center."

"Doctor," Page began to say, her mind racing through the alternatives. She couldn't stand Jason up. He'd be furious. She'd done it only once before, when an out-of-town client had demanded to see her, and Jason had been extremely difficult about it.

"Yes?"

"I have to go out, an important business appointment. Is there anywhere I can reach you in an hour or two?"

"Try me at the hospital."

"If I miss you, would you leave a message on my machine?"

"Of course," he said.

She hung up the phone, then picked it up quickly. She'd call Jason at the office. If he were still there, she'd ask to be excused for the evening. If he were upset, so be it. At least he wouldn't have to make the trip to her apartment. Perhaps she could arrange to meet him there after his dinner engagement.

She dialed the number and listened to the telephone ring. No answer. He'd probably already left. Damn! She had no choice now but to go to dinner with him. She couldn't renege at the last minute when he showed up at the door.

A frightening picture of her mother entered her mind. Alone in a hospital bed, the lights dim. An old lady, half her mind gone, scared and bleeding.

The doorbell rang. Page shook the image from her mind and went to answer it.

Jasmine and Allan had just made love, and she lay on the bed, her head resting on a hand, watching him as he dressed. First the shorts, then the shirt, then the watch, then the rings, then the socks, then the pants and, finally, the shoes.

"You know, you do that the same way every time," she said.

"What?" He looked at his watch. He was due home in an hour.

She rolled onto her back and lay there, half covered by a pink silk sheet, and spoke to the ceiling. "Dress. It's a pattern. You start with your shorts and end with your shoes."

"So? doesn't everybody?"

"I suppose so. I'm not making fun of you. It's just endearing, familiar. When I watch you dress I feel like we're married."

He didn't comment on that, but sat on the bed and tied his shoelaces.

"Don't worry," she said. "That wasn't a hint or anything, just a remark."

"I'm not worried. I love you, you love me, what more could we want?"

It was her turn to be silent, to think that perhaps there was more she could want.

The doorbell rang.

"Who could that be?" Allan asked. "Expecting anyone?"

"No." Jasmine got up from the bed and put on a robe.

"I'll wait in here," Allan said.

Jasmine went through the living room and hall to the

front door. She peeped through the spyhole and quickly opened the door.

"Fay, what are you doing here?"

Her seventeen-year-old sister stood there, a sullen expression on her normally pretty face, very close to tears. She wore tight stonewashed denim jeans, a T-shirt adorned with a picture of the band U-2, a denim jacket, Reeboks on her feet. In one hand she carried a small nylon overnight bag.

"Can I come in?"

Jasmine hadn't seen her sister in two years. She hugged her, pulled her through the door, and said again, "Fay, what the hell are you doing here?"

"I came to visit you," Fay said as they entered the living room.

She was smaller than Jasmine and not quite as pretty, her face flatter, the slant of her eyes more pronounced. But she had developed rounded hips and perky breasts since Jasmine had last seen her.

The obvious thought occurred to Jasmine. "Do Mom and Dad know you're here?"

Fay flopped onto the couch before answering. "No." She stared defiantly at her sister. "I took off."

"Jesus Christ, Fay! They must be worried sick. I'm going to call them right now!"

"It's a drag there!" Her words rushed out as if to stop Jasmine from doing what she had to do. "I can't stand it anymore. All they do is pick on me. I'm like a slave in that house. Work, work, work! That's all they think of. I'm not good enough at school, I'm not good enough at home. I'm not going back."

Jasmine held back the automatic rebuttal that wanted to jump out. Fay's words sounded terribly familiar, the words of a young Jasmine when she had left home five years earlier.

"They're not worried," Fay said more calmly. "They think I'm staying overnight with a friend."

"Just a minute," Jasmine said, suddenly remembering Allan. "I have a friend here. I'll be right back."

She went to the bedroom and opened the door.

"What the hell's that all about?" Allan was fully dressed, waiting, his briefcase in his hand. He had heard portions of the conversation through the door.

"It's my kid sister. She's run away from home."

"I didn't know you had a sister," Allan said curiously. She had never spoken of her family; the past had always been a closed subject between them, part of her allure.

"You want to hear my family history now?" Jasmine asked irritably. "I've got a goddamn emergency on my hands."

"Well, I've got to go," Allan said half apologetically.

"Yeah, that's fine. I have to handle this."

They went into the living room together. Fay was still sitting on the couch.

"Fay, this is Allan. Allan, Fay."

"Hi, Fay," Allan said.

"Hi," she said, her voice small.

Allan was at a loss. He shifted his feet, then kissed Jasmine chastely on the cheek. "Well, I've got to go. I'll call you later, okay?"

"Fine," Jasmine said, walking him to the door.

"She looks like you," he said.

"I'll talk to you later." She closed the door behind him, went to the living room, and sat beside Fay.

"He's a handsome dude," Fay said. "Is he an actor or something?"

"What am I going to do with you?" Jasmine ignored her question about Allan.

"You won't send me back, will you?"

"How did you get here?" Jasmine asked, again not answering the question.

"I flew down. Came from the airport on a bus. I knew your address."

"Right."

There was no choice really but to approach it head-on. Evasion would only delay the inevitable. "Fay, you know I have to call them and send you back, don't you?"

Silence.

"Fay, you're about to start your senior year in high school. You're a minor. I can't do anything else. Christ! You know that."

The lump on the couch stirred. Fay confronted her, tears in her eyes. "You could talk to them. I could stay down here with you. Go to school here."

Jasmine shook her head. "The last time I saw them or spoke to them was two years ago. You know what happened then. It was a disaster. There's nothing between us anymore. They don't want to hear from me. They think I'm Sodom and Gomorrah rolled into one. They're not going to listen to me. Be real, kid. I'm the black sheep of the family. You're their hope now, which is a drag for you, but that's the way it is."

"If you send me back, I'll just run away again," Fay said defiantly.

"Where to? The streets? You want to be a hooker before you turn eighteen? I don't think you're that stupid, Fay. It isn't worth it."

"It's not fair!"

"Life isn't fair. But that's the way it is. You have a year left, and then you have your freedom. They'll send you to any college in the country."

"I don't want to go to college."

"You should. Look at me. I didn't."

Fay looked around the apartment. The stereo, the records, the furnishings, so much finer than the dowdy garage sale remnants they had at home.

"You look like you're doing okay," she said.

Jasmine stood and looked down at her sister. "I earned almost none of what you see," she said passionately. "That guy who was here? The handsome dude? He supports me. I'm his mistress. He's married to someone else, but I'm here for him whenever he wants me to be. In return, he pays my rent, buys my clothes, my jewelry, my meals. He gives me an allowance. He bought my car, for God's sake!"

"So?" Fay asked. "That sounds cool."

"Jesus! Don't you know anything? What happens when he dumps me? What do I have then?"

Her own words shocked her. She had thought them, never head-on like this, but peripherally. Now she was saying them.

"He has a wife, a family, a career. He loves them all," she said fiercely. "What am I? A piece of ass!"

"But you're an actress!" Fay protested. "You can always support yourself," she added shyly. "I saw you in *Desperation*. You were really good!"

"It was a bit part. Ten lines. It was nothing. It wouldn't pay the rent here for a month. You know how few and far between parts like that are? *Even* parts like that?"

Fay shook her head dumbly.

Jasmine was on a roll she couldn't stop. "Forget it. I couldn't even support myself." She paused, taking a breath. "Fay, I don't know what image you have of me, but it's wrong. I'm not your glamorous big sister who escaped from home to come to Hollywood and become a major success. That's not me. Not really. Yes, I escaped, and yes, I don't regret it, but I've made a lot of mistakes and I'd hate to see you repeat them."

Fay was silent. Whether it was shock or exhaustion, Jasmine couldn't tell.

"I'm going to call them, Fay," she said. "I'll talk to them. We'll work something out. Maybe you can stay a couple of days. But there's only going to be one result. There's no way to avoid it. You're going to have to go home soon, okay?"

Fay didn't acknowledge her.

Jasmine went to the telephone, picked it up, and dialed the number she still remembered.

Her mother answered. When she realized it was Jasmine, her voice immediately became polite and strained.

The last time Jasmine had visited they had argued bitterly. Both parents thought she was wasting her life and the years they had spent raising her, shaming them with her fast living and loose morals. She had intended to visit them for three days and had left after only one, determined never to repeat the same mistake.

But now was not the time to dredge up the past. She

greeted her mother cheerfully, asking how they were doing. When the preliminaries were out of the way, she told her mother that Fay was there with her. After the initial confusion and shock, her mother grew angry and demanded that she put Fay on the next plane back to San Francisco.

"Mom, I don't think that's the best idea," Jasmine said carefully. "Why don't you let her stay a couple of days with me and then she can come back?"

"Absolutely not," her mother said, aghast at the idea. "Your father is going to be mad enough as it is. The idea of her spending time down there with you is even worse."

Big sister corrupting the morals of a minor, Jasmine thought bitterly. "Mom, she is very unhappy at home. I think a break would do you all good," she said patiently.

"There is nothing wrong at home. We love her and look after her. How can you say that?"

Jasmine looked across the end table at her sister. She was listening intently, her eyes bright.

"I know you love her, Mom, but sometimes that's stifling for a kid."

"How can you say—"

Jasmine cut in, her tone harsher, more determined. "Mom, she's here, isn't she? You've already lost one daughter—me. You didn't understand why I left home then and you still don't understand. But do you want the same thing to happen with Fay? Because, unless you get more reasonable, I promise you it will. And you're going to have to talk to Dad and make him see reason too.

"She needs a break. She's here with me, safe and sound. I'll look after her for a couple of days, show her the sights, and then send her home."

Something of what she said must have impinged, because her mother began to back down. "I don't know," she said doubtfully.

"It will be good for her, and I'll look after her, I promise," Jasmine said earnestly. "Talk to Dad about it. Do you have my phone number?"

"Yes." from the subdued tone of her voice now, Jasmine

could tell that she wanted nothing worse than to end the conversation with her as soon as possible.

"Well, call me if you need to. Otherwise, I'll call in a couple of days and let you know when she's coming home, okay?"

"Yes, I suppose so. Can I talk to Fay?"

"She's in the shower," Jasmine lied. If the two of them talked, they would both only get more upset. It would serve no purpose now. "I'll have her call you in a day or two, okay?"

"Okay," her mother said.

"All right. Talk to you soon." Jasmine hung up.

"I can stay with you?"

"For a couple of days. Right now, you probably need some food, and then some sleep."

"All right!" Fay said enthusiastically. A bright smile lit her face and she bounced to her feet. "This is really cool."

CHAPTER TEN

Page was at the hospital by eight o'clock on Thursday morning. She had been unable to reach the doctor the night before but found his message on her answering machine when she returned with Jason from dinner.

"She has diverticulitis," the doctor had said. "We don't know yet if we will have to operate or not. At the moment, she is resting comfortably and in no danger."

A mountain of useless information. She didn't even know what diverticulitis was and tried unsuccessfully to look the word up in the dictionary. The closest she could find was "diverticulum—a blind tubular sac or process branching off from a canal or cavity." It was no help whatsoever.

Luckily, when she arrived at the hospital and asked for the doctor, the nurse at the reception desk said he was there. While the nurse paged him, she sat in the waiting area and stared blankly at an empty wall.

Dr. Perkins was a small dark man with a five o'clock shadow on his chin and rounded shoulders. He shook her hand almost furtively and answered her questions absently, as if he were about to slip away at any moment. He seemed uncomfortable beside this cool, well-dressed woman.

Diverticulitis, she learned, was the opposite of having polyps. Where polyps were protrusions occurring in the intestinal tract, diverticulitis consisted of intrusions—diversions or pockets—he explained. These pockets could become impacted, infected, and ruptured. The hemorrhaging her mother was experiencing was because one or more of these pockets had ruptured.

"So what happens now?" Page asked.

"She won't be able to eat for a few days. We have her on IVs," the doctor said, shrugging. "By resting the intestine, it may heal itself. If it doesn't, then we'll have to operate, take that section of the intestine out. If the bleeding stops by itself, we'll just leave it alone."

"May I see her?"

"Yes, although she may be asleep." Dr. Perkins gave her the room number and a telephone number for his office, then as he was about to leave, he made a last warning remark. "You may find that she's not herself. Disoriented. I mentioned that I had called you, but she said she didn't have a daughter."

Page smiled grimly to herself as she took the elevator to the third floor. Her mother was being consistent to the bitter end.

The room in which her mother lay was small, sparse, and spotless. Page pulled a steel and formica chair over to the bed and sat beside her. Clara's eyes were closed, even though the television set on the opposite wall was on. An IV dripped its solution into her arm. She looked as frail and thin as a baby, her face paler than when Page had last seen her.

It was ironic how roles changed through time, Page thought. Once she had been the baby, now she was the mother, looking after her own mother. Page corrected herself; she was romanticizing. Clara had never been a mother. She had borne Page, admittedly, but in the early days when the family fortunes were still intact, Page had been cared for by nurses. Her mother had done little more than kiss her good night. After the death of her father, Clara had immediately proven her ineptitude by falling apart in all areas of her life, including motherhood. Page had looked after herself, very quickly learning that she also would have to look after Clara. It had been that way ever since.

She awoke from her thoughts to see Clara's blue eyes fixed seriously on her face. They were not as alert or as skittish as they usually were. The legacy of the sedatives, no doubt.

"Mother, how are you?" she asked, touching the veined and wrinkled little hand.

The eyes flicked away to the television set. "Nurse, could you turn up the volume, please?"

Obediently, Page rose and turned the volume higher. The *Today* show was on.

"I like Jane Pauley," her mother said. "She is married and has children." Clara had a foolish, playful look on her face, like a small child about to transgress.

"What's that supposed to mean, Mother?" Page said, rising to the bait in spite of knowing better.

"I wish I had grandchildren. I wish I had a son or a daughter."

Page sat again without commenting. She didn't want to hear how Clara had "once had a daughter." Not now.

"The doctor says you are going to be fine," she said, even though he had predicted nothing of the sort. "You have to behave and do what he says though."

Clara ignored her, fixated on the television.

God! Page thought. How could our lives have come to this?

She sat silently beside Clara, and then took her hand. It lay unmoving in hers.

At nine o'clock, Clara said, "Could you change it to channel seven, please? I want to watch *A.M. Los Angeles.*"

Page did as she was asked, then sat in silence again. After about fifteen minutes, she looked at her watch. She had to go to the office. She had made a ten o'clock appointment with one of the men she had met at dinner the previous night. He was thinking of taking his corporate PR away from Hill & Knowlton, one of the giants in the business, and giving it to a firm that was smaller and more attentive.

"I have to go, Mother. I'll be back to visit you soon, and I'll stay in touch with Dr. Perkins. If you need anything, call me at work or at home. Here are the numbers in case you don't have them with you."

She took out one of her cards and placed it on the table beside the bed. It was only a gesture. Clara had never called her, had never acknowledged her existence.

"Oh, look!" Clara said, pointing to the television. "Isn't he such a handsome young man!"

The young actor who was the featured guest was grinning, talking about the new Porsche he had just bought.

"Oh, it makes me think of Bill Evans. So handsome. He could have been famous, too. He appeared on Broadway, you know. Then there was that terrible automobile accident and he died." She looked coquettishly at Page. "He wanted to marry me, you know. But I didn't think he was reliable enough." A long sigh. "Besides, they all die sooner or later, don't they?"

"I have to go. I'll try and be back tonight," Page said firmly. She kissed Clara on the cheek and walked toward the door.

"Page!"

She span around, shocked.

Clara was looking at her, tears in her eyes, the foolish expression gone. "Page, I'm so afraid."

David Ross was a victim of the euphoria that accompanies the beginnings of a love affair. He woke on Thursday feeling years younger, sang in the shower, surprised his wife, Pat, by kissing her cheerfully on the cheek when he left for work, shocked his secretary with an irreverent playfulness, realized he was acting like a middle-aged fool, and decided he didn't give a damn.

He left earlier than usual for lunch, cancelling an appointment that had been set for two weeks, and picked Kate up outside the gallery, as they had arranged when he had left her apartment the night before.

As soon as she stepped into the back of the limo, he kissed her, ignoring the startled expression on his driver's face.

"How are you? Did you sleep well after you finally kicked me out?" he asked.

"Like a log," Kate said. "And you?"

"I missed you," he said happily. "I hated to leave."

He took her to lunch at the famous Polo Lounge of the Beverly Hills Hotel. She was surprised how plain it appeared, but this was compensated for by the fact that Donald Sutherland occupied the table beside them, Jaclyn Smith sat not far away, and they passed Dudley Moore in the lobby as they left. Although not given to star-gazing, Kate found it hard not to be impressed.

He took her back to work after lunch and arranged to pick her up again for dinner.

Dinner that night was at L'Escoffier, on top of the Beverly Hilton. Elegance was not understated here. When she was handed the menu, Kate avoided even looking at the prices. She was sure it would be terribly expensive.

David talked generously about himself during dinner, answering all those questions about his past that had occurred to her the night before. He had grown up in Seattle, Washington, where his father had worked as an engineer for Boeing. It was a comfortable middle-class family, not wealthy. He had gone to school in Los Angeles, and by the time he left college with an MBA, he also had a wife named Pat. Through contacts in her family, which was, unlike his, wealthy and well-connected, he went into the banking business, first working for others, then starting his own company. Eventually he accomplished his goal of becoming one of the best and biggest in the business on the West Coast. Now, at least on paper, he was a multimillionaire.

"Any children?" Kate asked.

David's good humor deserted him. He grimaced. "A daughter, Pamela. She's twenty now and going to school back East. She despises our wealth but takes advantage of it. One week she's a socialist, the next she's apolitical. I don't understand her."

"It's a difficult age," Kate said. She was barely seven years older than his daughter, she realized. "What's she studying?"

"Who knows?" He shrugged. "It changes so often. As far as I can tell, she's embarking upon a career as a troublemaker. Drunk driving charges, drug possession. A couple of months ago she needed an abortion."

"And you support her?"

"Well, yes. Pat thinks it's just a phase she's going through and that we shouldn't be too hard on her. I don't know."

"And your wife? What does she do?"

"Do? She was a mother. Now she shops and travels."

"Doesn't sound too bad," Kate remarked.

"Would you like coffee?"

"Please."

He signaled the waiter and ordered for them both.

"While we're on the subject of travel, can you get some time off at the gallery?"

"I suppose so. With some notice. Why?"

"I'd like to take you on a trip. Just the two of us. Get out of LA for a week."

"Where to?" she asked.

"How about Bali?"

"Bali? That's on the other side of the world! Isn't that in Indonesia or something?"

"Well, yes it is, but we live in a modern world," he teased. "They have airplanes these days. They can get you anywhere in a day."

"Bali!" she repeated. "I don't know, David. I mean . . . I don't know."

He reached across the table and took one of her hands in

his. "It's the most beautiful place in the world, Kate. Another kind of life. Romantic, tropical, different. You'll love it, I guarantee."

"When do you want to go?"

"I have some time available in three to five days. I can take a week then."

"That's not much notice for Madge."

"Maybe if I talked to her. I'm a good customer, you know."

"No!" Kate said, her reaction vehement. Then she softened. "If I decide to go, I can handle it. I'll talk to her. It is a slow period now that the Breer show's over."

"Well, then there's no problem," David said, as if the matter were now settled.

"Let me think about it."

"Sure, but only till tomorrow. I have arrangements that I'll have to make."

Kate nodded. She wasn't sure it was a good idea to leave LA for as long as a week, not now when she was so close to her prey. She needed to find out more about him, his weaknesses, his Achilles' heel. On the other hand, now more than ever, she needed to be patient. There could be no precipitous moves on her part. Besides, if she spent all that time with David, she might be able to coax from him much of the information she needed about Jason Thomas. The situation demanded further thought before she made a decision.

When they finished dinner, David said, the light of lust glowing in his eyes, "May we go back to your place?"

"Yes, let's."

"Would it be all right if I spent the entire night with you?" he asked politely. "I've made arrangements, if that's okay with you."

"That's fine," she said. "The other way is too much like eating and running."

David laughed. "I try to maintain my manners. In my circumstances, however, it's not always possible."

"I have no complaints."

"That's one of the things I like about you, Kate. No complaints."

David signed his credit card bill and, when the waiter left, reached inside his jacket pocket.

"One more thing before we leave." He took a small velvet box from his pocket and put it on the table in front of her.

"What's this?"

"You'll find out if you open it," he said, smiling.

Inside was a pair of diamond earrings, large stones nestled in a setting of tiny golden leaves.

"They're beautiful!" she said, then laughed. "It's hardly an original comment, but they really are. Thank you so much."

"A token of my admiration."

Once they were in the limousine, he kissed her avidly. "I could hardly keep my hands off you in that restaurant. You're so beautiful. I couldn't stand it. Every man in the room was looking at you."

Kate felt a burning resentment. His unspoken thought, his reaction to the other men, was a proud gloating, "but she's mine!" He was buying her, already starting to feel he owned her. She knew it. That's the way the game was played. It was lucky that she, too, was playing a game, one in which she wasn't about to be a victim.

Jason, Page, David, and Allan met for lunch on Friday at The Regency Club, a prestigious members-only institution where privacy was guaranteed. The almost one thousand members paid an entrance fee of five thousand dollars for this privilege. The club was founded by real estate developer David H. Murdock, mainly because he wanted a place where he could get a decent meal *and* choose the clientele with whom he shared his repast. The other two prestigious clubs in town, The California Club and the Jonathan Club, were not known for their epicurean delights. When he opened his own club, Murdock hired chef Louis Outhier, owner of the French Riviera's three-star L'Oasis. The food was truly excellent.

Members here included such notables as Lew Wasserman, chairman of MCA; Paige Rense (one of about a hundred women members), editor-in-chief of *Architectural Digest* and *Bon Appetit*, and Armand Hammer, who reportedly became a less active member after Murdock announced at a dinner Hammer was attending that he wanted Armand's job as chairman of Oxy because he was getting too old.

Jason sat at a prime table near the window. Outside was the busy center of Westwood, and beyond the village, the UCLA campus.

After ordering their food, Jason gave his listeners a stock tip that was guaranteed to double their money, and then, when they had expressed sufficient gratitude, he got down to the real business.

"I have a little surprise for Stod and the Museum, but I'd like your help," he said.

David shuddered inwardly. The only time Jason needed help was when it involved money. Of course, he had helped both men make a fortune with insider information and was entitled to a favor or two in return. But even so. He withheld comment, however, sipping the excellent Burgundy instead.

Allan had a similar thought.

Page wondered why she had been invited.

"You know that the opening is scheduled for two months from now?" Jason continued. "Construction is right on target. You know also that I've committed some of my private collection."

Both men nodded. They had each given hundreds of thousands of dollars to the new wing, under Jason's urgings. Tax-deductible dollars, but dollars nevertheless. But their contributions had been nothing compared to his donations or the energy he had put into raising other moneys from his wealthy contacts.

Jason cleared his throat. "Well, to be quite frank, my collection doesn't meet the standards I think should be applied to the new wing of the Rex Museum."

The Jason Thomas Wing, Page thought, adding what Jason had humbly left unsaid.

"Some of your stuff is marvelous," David protested. "Why, the Gauguin is a wonderful piece."

"It's a minor work," Jason said dismissively. "I have something much more major in mind. Major. I mean major, with no equivocation." He paused to sip his wine, then continued. "I have been searching for just such a piece—an undiscovered treasure—for the past few months. Without success. My contacts in the art world have been unable to find anything that meets my standards."

"What kind of budget are you talking about?" Allan asked.

"Ah," Jason said, "the reason you are here. Gentlemen, I am prepared to commit five million dollars to this single work. I am asking you to each commit a further one million dollars. This will give us a world-class piece of art worth seven million dollars, an acquisition that will be the envy of every museum in the country, if not the world."

"A million dollars?" Allan said weakly.

"After all the money I've helped you make this year, I'm sure you could use the write-off," Jason said meaningfully.

"It's a considerable sum," David said.

Once again, Page wondered what she was doing here.

"Yes, it is. But so are the rewards," Jason said. "You couldn't buy publicity like this if you tried. And your contributions will be well acknowledged."

Jason turned to Page and smiled. "Which brings us to your part in this," he said, "Until now, I haven't let anyone know of my plan. I wanted to announce it as a *fait accompli.* However, as I am not having any luck finding the work I want as yet, I think that a bit of judicious publicity won't hurt. So I'd like to retain you to handle this project as an account. We can go over the details later."

"Thank you," Page said. In spite of their relationship, this was the first time Jason had actually hired her to do a job.

"I'll have to let Stod know of my plan and you can work with him on it."

"We can do it subtly," Page said thoughtfully. "A couple of articles in prestigious art magazines on the Rex that mention the donation you three will be making—once you find it."

"Exactly," Jason agreed. He looked at the two men. "Well, can I count on you two for a million dollars each?"

"I'll have to look at some numbers," Allan said.

"Yes, me too," David said. "However, I don't think it will be a problem."

"Excellent," Jason said. "I'll need your answers as soon as possible."

"Very exciting project," David said. "I imagine you have your people watching all the auctions?"

"Yes. The problem is prices are being bid up to extraordinary levels these days. The Asians have entered the market heavily. Last year the Japanese paid almost forty million dollars for Van Gogh's "Sunflowers." Ridiculous. Some works are going in New York and London for ten and twenty million dollars. I'd prefer to find a private seller, or perhaps an undiscovered work."

"Kate might be able to help," David suggested. "She's very knowledgeable."

"Ah, yes, your Miss Buchanan," Jason said. "That's a possibility." He smiled. "How is the romance?"

"She's a wonderful person," David said with a grin.

"And a real looker," Allan contributed with something close to a leer.

"I was very impressed with her as well," Page said, a trifle primly.

"I hope we see more of her," Jason added.

"Oh, you will," David promised.

"Well, shall we eat?" Jason asked. "I'm sure you'll enjoy your lunch."

He had accomplished his business. Both Allan and David would talk to their accountants and figure out the methods that would benefit them most. But they would come up with the money, regardless of any hesitation they were demonstrating now. He knew his men.

* * *

Madge asked Kate who had picked her up in a limousine the day before for lunch. There was a gleam of envy in her eyes.

Kate hesitated, then said, "David Ross."

"Really?" Madge asked archly.

"Well, I told you we had mutual friends in New York."

"Oh, a friendly lunch. Just reminiscing," Madge said sarcastically.

"Come on, Madge."

Madge got up from her desk and sat on the edge of Kate's. They had become good friends in the short period they had worked together. Madge had confided all her secrets to Kate after only a couple of days. She was a warm and funny person, Kate discovered, willing to share herself with those she liked.

"Give me all the dirt," Madge said with a wink. "Are you sleeping with him yet?"

Kate grimaced. "As a matter of fact, he's asked me to go away with him for a week. You breathe any word of this to anyone, Madge, and I'll murder you."

"Really? Where?" Madge asked avidly.

"Bali."

"My God, I thought Santa Barbara, or maybe Hawaii. But Bali! This has got to be serious."

Kate shrugged. "Could you spare me for a week? I know I've only just started here, and it's asking a lot to take off so soon. You wouldn't have to pay me, of course."

"When are you thinking of going?"

"I haven't made up my mind even to go yet. But since you bring it up, he has some time off in a few days."

"The man doesn't mess around, does he?"

"Apparently not," Kate said.

"Yes, you can have the time off. Things are pretty slow now."

"If I decide to go."

"If you decide to go," she added mischievously. "When are you going to decide to go?"

"I haven't. But if I do, you'll be the first to know. Thanks."

Madge grew serious. "That's a fast crowd you're going

to be moving with,'' she warned. ''And you know he's married, I assume?''

''Yes.''

''Well. I hope you know what you're doing.'' There was only concern in Madge's voice, no criticism.

''So do I.''

On Friday, Jasmine took her sister to lunch at the Hard Rock Cafe. With the vintage Chevy embedded in the outside roof of the Beverly Center and its kitschy fifties decor, it had become one of LA's hip landmarks, particularly for the younger crowd.

After watching Fay devour an enormous hamburger Jasmine bought her a Hard Rock Cafe T-shirt and then took her into the Beverly Center proper, four stories of shopping mall, jampacked with trendy stores and restaurants.

''I always heard what a bummer LA was,'' Fay said excitedly, her eyes darting to the eclectic window displays. ''But I love it here!''

''Well, that's just Bay Area talk. Past glories,'' Jasmine said. ''San Franciscans have never forgiven LA for becoming bigger and more important.''

''Wow! Look at that! That's cool!'' Fay said, pointing to a window.

It was a dress, cotton and lace, something similar to the style Madonna had made famous—underwear as evening gear. The accessories displayed with it were two three-quarter arm's-length lace gloves and a heavy black vinyl belt from which dangled a selection of phallic symbols.

''Come on!'' Jasmine said, going into the store. ''You're going to try it on.''

''It'll cost a fortune,'' Fay said dubiously.

''It doesn't cost a dime to try it on,'' Jasmine countered when they were in the store.

She gestured at a salesgirl and asked for the dress in size three.

''Wanna try it on?'' the salesgirl asked, her eyes flicking over Jasmine.

''She does,'' Jasmine pointed to Fay.

Fay took the dress into the changing room and came out two minutes later, a smile transforming her face. "What do you think?"

The built-in support bra pushed her small breasts together and up. Instant cleavage. The back was cut low, revealing a perfectly shaped body. She looked three years older.

"It's great!"

"God, Mom and Dad would freak if they saw this," Fay said.

Jasmine giggled. "Not something a nice Chinese girl would wear."

Fay rolled her eyes, then giggled as well. "But the guys will love it!"

"Let's buy it," Jasmine said.

Fay sobered. "It's one hundred and twenty-five dollars. It's so expensive. We can't!"

"Sure we can! Go take it off."

"It's too expensive!"

"I want to buy it for you."

"It's too much money."

"You like it, don't you?"

"I love it! It's so rad! But—"

"Go and change," Jasmine interrupted. "Don't worry about the money."

When Fay came out, the dress over her arm, Jasmine marched her over to the cash register. She paid for the dress with a credit card.

"There!" She handed the box to Fay. "You can go home tomorrow and shock the hell out of Mom and Dad."

"Maybe if I didn't wear the belt?" Fay said.

"What? And ruin the effect!" Jasmine sounded shocked. "You just keep the belt in your bag and put it on when you're out of the house."

When they left the store, Fay took Jasmine's hand. "I don't want to go home tomorrow. I like being here with you."

"I know. But you have to. For now. You understand that, don't you?"

"I know, Jas, but it's such a drag. You can't understand what I have to go through."

Jasmine gripped her hand tightly and stopped. "Of course I understand! Are you kidding? Why do you think I left? But now isn't the time. You've got to think this out and do it when it's right, for you and for them."

A group of five kids passed them. One of the boys carried a ghetto blaster, two of the girls danced as they walked.

"You didn't think about them," Fay said sullenly.

"I know. And that's the only thing I regret. If I had a chance to do it all over again, I'd leave on better terms. In spite of their faults, they love us. They don't want to hurt us, they just don't know any better. And they don't deserve to be hurt."

"Shit! They know what they're doing," Fay said defiantly.

Jasmine looked at the set jaw and the rebellious eyes and marvelled at the blind certainty of youth. She had been that way once. Now? Now if she ever stopped whirling around long enough to look, she knew she would find she wasn't certain of anything.

"Come on! Let's go and find some ice cream," she said. "I think there's a Haagen-Dazs store here."

CHAPTER ELEVEN

Allan was extremely irritated, and snarled into the telephone, "Listen, Billy. I don't give a fuck what you think he's worth. I know what he's worth to me. If you can get that much money for him from another studio, take him to another studio and try and do it. Okay? But don't waste my fucking time."

He glared around the room while the other man spoke, then curtly interrupted. "Hey, hey, hey, Billy, you know as well as I do that Hispanic actors are a dime a dozen in this town. How many Richie Valens movies are there, anyway? If I want to, I can get a new face for less money, one that wasn't killed off in a soap opera like your boy. You're just trying to hold me up. My offer's firm. Take it or leave it. Let me know by the end of the day. If I don't hear from you, we're going to proceed with someone else."

He listened for a moment, and then said, "Absolutely no fucking way. Not a dime more. You've heard the offer, that's what it is. Take it or leave it." He slammed the phone down.

His secretary Carol stood near the door, her eyebrows raised quizzically. A serene married woman in her forties, she had been with Allen more than five years, knew his every mood, and sometimes treated him like a small child. "A little rough on Billy, weren't you?"

"Shit! I should have reamed a new asshole on the asshole," Allan said.

But her implied rebuke reminded him of the realities of Hollywood, a town that survived on mutual back-scratching, run by people who owed each other favors. Billy Meyer represented a number of big stars that Allan would kill to have in one of his movies. His young Spanish actor, a has-been at twenty-three after being dropped from a daily soap opera, was simply a bargaining tool. Give the actor a job and maybe next time around Billy would return a favor by handing Allan one of his stars. It was never stated so bluntly, but that was the oil greasing the wheels in this town.

"Damn!" Allan said. "Call him back, offer him another twenty thou, tell him I reconsidered. Tell him I have an irritated colon, tell him my liver's acting up. Tell him anything, just smooth it over, okay?"

"All right," Carol said, showing no resentment at the command to put out her boss's fire.

"Who's next?"

"Maya Bell and Otis Turk."

"Oh, hell, she wants a part in *Domination,*" Allan grumbled. "Everybody always wants something."

"Hey, that's the name of the game," Carol said. "Shall I send them in?"

"Yeah . . . no, have them wait five minutes, then buzz me, then send them in."

"Sure, boss," she said, and left the room.

Allan got up from his desk, walked to the window, and looked down at the parking lot. He looked more dishevelled than usual. His suit jacket was thrown over a chair, his shirtsleeves were rolled up, and the back of his shirt was creased and rumpled.

What a day, he complained to himself. Fuck Billy, fuck Maya, and fuck Jasmine. Double fuck Jasmine, he thought bitterly, focusing on the source of his irritation. Damn woman had a young sister staying with her and wouldn't let him near her apartment. This was Friday and he still hadn't seen her. He was getting horny as hell. She had no right to do this to him. Yesterday he had exasperatedly called Jasmine and insisted on coming over.

Her response had been unsympathetic. "Where we going to do it, Allan?" she said tartly. "In the bedroom while she's in the living room? For Christsake, the girl's only seventeen."

"Hey, maybe she could watch us and learn something," he suggested sarcastically.

Jasmine had hung up, making him even more pissed.

Sometimes he hated his life. Juggling two woman often took more skill than he had. When both women were acting up it was even worse, becoming a prime waste of time and money. Jasmine was costing him a fortune, and then she wasn't there when he needed her. What the hell was he paying for? He returned to his desk, looked at a contract he was supposed to review, and tossed it back in the basket.

Things had been so much simpler fifteen or so years earlier, he thought self-pityingly. Back then, he'd been married, of course, but even though there'd been infidelities—

numerous infidelities if the truth be known—they had all occurred without any responsibility on his part. It was totally carefree cheating. There had only been one woman he returned to night after night, at the place they called home. The others were what were known as passing ships.

In the situation with Jasmine, it was like being married to two women. He supported her and he was responsible for her, much like a wife although, of course, he could let her go at any time without incrimination or obligation. But it was still complicated.

The intercom buzzed to announce his guests. He got up and walked halfway across the room to meet them.

The door opened and Maya swept theatrically in, closely followed by her agent, Otis. She headed straight for him without breaking her stride, an ecstatically pleased smile on her face, clasping his hands and kissing the air on either side of his cheeks. "So wonderful to see you, darling! It's been simply too long."

"You are looking very well, as always, Maya," Allan said. As indeed she was. Blond with long legs and a buxom chest, both barely covered by the short strapless glittering blue dress that clung to her body, she had a bow-shaped mouth and topaz eyes.

"Nice to see you, Allan." Otis stepped forward and shook his hand. Otis was a small thin man with bulging black eyes and the coke user's habit of constantly sniffing and touching his nose unconsciously with his finger.

"Please sit down." Allan waved an arm at the couch. He took an armchair while Maya sat at the end of the couch closest to him. He knew there would be three minutes of polite chitchat before Maya got down to business.

"Been keeping busy, Maya?" he asked.

"Oh, you know me, never a dull moment," she said with a trill. "I just saw your latest release, *Dog Days*. It's a wonderful film. You must be very proud of it. I'm sure it's going to do well."

Allan nodded. "Thank you. We have high hopes for it." In truth, the movie probably was going to die within a week. It had simply not found its audience. But these mishaps were never acknowledged, let alone discussed. Luckily, some intensive preselling to overseas distributors, cable, and video had already covered the bottom line. Any business it did now, no matter how bad, would be gravy.

"I thought the young girl was just marvelous," Maya gushed. "What was her name?"

"Ummm, Candy Barry. Yes, I think she has a good future ahead of her," Allan said, which was probably more, he thought, than could be said of Maya unless something drastic changed.

Her story was common. Although only in her mid-twenties now, she had lucked out by appearing in a feature film directed by someone who knew what he was doing when she was about nineteen and receiving good notices. She followed her success with another film, using a different director, and turned in a disastrous performance. Since then, she had done mainly inferior films or television guest appearances.

She was a beautiful woman, but no one had really brought out the ability she had shown at the beginning of her career. She had become a caricature of herself in many ways and of late had been typecast as a blond brainless bimbo, which was not a good career move. It left very limited opportunities. Probably much of it had to do with Otis who had "guided" her career for the last five years. His advice had apparently not worked.

They chatted for another couple of minutes, and then Allan said, "I understand you wanted to talk to me about *Domination?*"

"I love it," Maya said. "I read the script and it's wonderful. I think you really have a potential hit on your hands if you have the courage to cast it properly."

"I assume you have something to suggest."

She smiled brilliantly. "I want to play the part of Edna. I think it's right for me. I empathize with the part so much. I also want to work with Kellerman. I've always wanted to work with him. He's one of the best young directors around today. I think that with him I can turn in a performance that's going to knock their socks off."

Domination was the story of two couples. The character she wanted to play was literate and witty, not exactly the type Maya was famous for. In fact, she was exactly the opposite. Allan couldn't disguise his misgivings and shook his head.

Otis saw his reaction and jumped in. "Did you see Maya in *School of Hard Knocks?* She was wonderful, she was fantastic, she was fabulous. This girl has matured as an actress. She's finally coming into her own. She can do this part in her sleep."

As a matter of fact, Allan had seen *The School of Hard Knocks* at an industry screening and thought the film was a dog. However, one never knew how audiences would react. One thing was certain: Maya would not be able to play Edna in her sleep. It would demand more of her than she had ever given.

Otis continued, "We got a big media campaign going with this. When that movie comes out it's gonna take the box office by storm. We have *People* magazine interested in a cover for Maya. We have *Glamour* magazine interested in a cover. We have her booked on the *Today* show; we have her booked on all the local talk shows from *AM Los Angeles* down. Maya's face is going to be in the eyes of America, her name will be on their lips. And when they see this movie, she's also going to be in their hearts." Otis finished with a loud sniff, rubbing his nose with his finger.

"Well, that's wonderful," Allan said. "But somehow I don't see Maya in this part. It's not the type of thing she normally does."

"Sweetie, that's why we're called actresses." She leaned forward and put her hand on his knee. "I can do it, Allan, all I need is a chance. I'd even be willing to test for the part."

Allan's eyes fell to her cleavage, a rosy colored valley of promise. "I don't know, Maya, they've already considered a couple of actors, and I think there may even be a decision."

She gave his knee a little slap and withdrew her hand. "Come on, Allan, don't be naughty," she said girlishly.

"You know that a word from you will make them consider me. After all, you are financing the film."

"I don't usually get involved in these things," Allan protested.

She leaned and touched his knee again. "Allan, if you would get involved this time, I would be very grateful. I wouldn't let you down, I promise."

"Come on, Allan," Otis chimed in. "You owe Maya this one, after what happened last year."

"What are you talking about?" Allan asked irritably.

Maya gave Otis a warning look, but he ignored her. "*Amazon Forest,* that's what I'm talking about. You told Maya she had a part in that movie, and then when the decision came down, she was out."

"I did not tell her she had a part," Allan said coldly. "I told her that she would be considered. She was considered, and it was decided not to use her. I don't see that I owe you anything because of that. It's fairly normal procedure, don't you think?"

"Oh, of course you don't owe me anything," Maya interceded. "Don't be silly, Otis. I'd want Allan to recommend me for *Domination* because he felt I could do the job, not because he felt he owed me something." She uncrossed her legs then crossed them again, as if to emphasize her remarks with the rustle of pantyhose.

Allan couldn't help but look down at the sleek display. When he looked up, Maya had a small smile on her face, as if to show her pleasure at his admiration.

"All I want is a chance, Allan. Just let me test and see what happens. Give me that chance, and I'll be very grateful."

Grateful again, Allan thought. Her message was clear. Maya had a reputation for sleeping her way into parts. She also had a reputation for a mouth that could suck the foreskin off a man's cock. He couldn't help it, but his blood warmed at the thought.

"Well, I don't know," he said indecisively. "Maybe if we talked a little more about the part, and I could get your feelings on it . . ."

It was a charade and all three of them knew it. Allan looked at Otis. "Why don't you take a walk, Otis, and let Maya and I work this out. Maybe we can reach some kind of understanding."

"Oh, that would be great," Maya agreed. "Let's talk about it. Didn't you have some other people to see in the building, Otis?"

"Sure, sure." Otis got to his feet. "Yeah, I got some other people to see. I'll be back later for you."

Alone, they sat and stared at each other. Maya's glossy lips were slightly parted, her eyes expectant, waiting for Allan to make his move.

Why not, he thought. He hadn't done anything like this since he first began to sleep with Jasmine, but Jasmine wasn't here, and Maya was. Besides, he was as horny as a dog. It was one of those opportunities he'd be an idiot to pass up. Men around the world desired this woman, yet here she was offering herself to him.

He got to his feet, walked to his desk, and flicked the intercom. "Carol, I do not want to be disturbed. Understood?"

"Sure, boss." The voiced sounded distant through the speaker.

When he turned back to face Maya, she had already rolled the top of her dress down over her full breasts. Lazily, almost unconsciously, she put her finger in her mouth, then withdrew it and ran it lightly over her right nipple.

Allan felt himself getting hard as he stood there.

"Are you ready for my audition, Allan?" she asked, and laughed throatily.

"The bleeding stopped. We're not going to have to operate at this time."

"And what's the prognosis?" Page asked.

"I would categorize it as cautious optimism," Dr. Perkins said. They were standing in the hospital lobby. It was Friday afternoon and she had taken time off from work to visit Clara. Perkins had intercepted her before she went up to the room, saying he wanted to bring her up to date before she saw her mother.

"How is she doing emotionally?"

Perkins shifted his feet, looked down at the floor, and coughed. "She's, ah, doing all right under the circumstances. She's been through a scare, you know. I'm sure she thought she was about to die. And a woman of her age . . ." He left the sentence unfinished.

"But she's not as scared now?" Page asked.

"No, I think she's quite relieved. Of course she still is quite disoriented, and you shouldn't expect too much of her."

"And what's your next step, doctor?"

"I think we need to just observe her for a few days. As the bleeding has stopped, there is no immediate danger. I'd like to keep an eye on her for a little bit."

A noncommittal answer, Page thought, but entirely expected under the circumstances. "Well, thank you, doctor. I'll go and see her now."

"Um, please don't do or say anything to excite her," Dr. Perkins said. "More than anything, she needs to rest now."

"Of course."

She couldn't help but wonder how Clara would react to her. The recognition she had shown last time by using her name had been all too brief. Her mother had expressed her fear, accepted Page's words of comfort, and then had withdrawn again.

Clara was lying in bed, slightly propped up, her eyes glued to the television set on the wall. A daytime soap was playing. She looked slightly better than when Page had last seen her. A little color had returned to her cheeks.

"Hello, Mother," Page said, slipping into the chair beside the bed. She leaned over and kissed Clara's forehead.

Her mother ignored her.

"The doctor says you are doing much better. I'm glad to hear it. I was a little worried."

Still the silence. For Clara, the only life was in the figures moving before the flickering blue light of the television set. Page noticed that it was a hospital show, and just then her mother spoke, proving again some limited grasp of the relationship between reality and fantasy.

"The doctors aren't like that here, neither are the nurses," Clara said. "There aren't any handsome doctors like that. Here they all have pale skin, pouches under their eyes, and they are always in a hurry. They always look worried. The nurses are all so busy they don't have time to have a word with you."

"But they are treating you well, aren't they, Mother?"

"Are you a nurse?" Clara asked, looking at Page for the first time, her eyes blank.

Page didn't feel in the mood to rise to the bait. "No." she got up from the chair and walked to the window. It was small and square. Through it she could only see another high-rise building. Perhaps eyes were staring back at her, prisoners looking at prisoners, she thought heavily.

How unpredictable life was. If ten or fifteen years ago someone had told her she would be standing here staring through a hospital window in Los Angeles, a woman of her age alone for all intents and purposes, her mother sick and refusing to acknowledge her presence, she would have laughed.

There had been no premonitions of this moment. As a child in a house cluttered with belongings and willing servants, reverberating with her father's booming laugh, her mother still the same flustered person but cheerful and empty-headed, parading through the halls in new dresses and gowns, who would have guessed at the loneliness she was feeling at this moment? Her only problems then had been those of parental control, of petty disputes between friends over what to do next or how to present oneself. Even then those problems had appeared insurmountable, in spite of their minor nature. Perhaps, Page thought, life was simply a progression of growing problems that kept pace with you. As you grew, so did your problems. Perhaps in ten years the problems she now faced would seem petty and minor.

She doubted it. Now it seemed her survival was at stake. But hadn't the intrigues between friends, the need for freedom from parents, the urge to discover by herself who she was, threatened her survival?

And what had she found? An anxious woman on the wrong side of thirty. A woman who had created the very barriers she now sought to avoid. A woman who wanted freedom yet one who probably wouldn't even recognize it if she had it. A woman who had trapped herself, bound by the chains of her own needs and desires.

She turned and went back to the chair beside the bed, taking Clara's frail hand in hers. She wished she had someone, anyone who could hear her, help her. She found herself saying, "Mother. I wish for once that you could help me. God, I need some help."

Clara stared unblinkingly at the television set. Her mind, Page thought, was probably as vacant and innocent as when she had been a baby.

She had to leave. Duty had brought her here. There was no satisfaction for either of them, as far as she knew. Clara had lost her life when Page's father had blown his brains out, and since then, she had been marking time with no purpose, no intention, no direction. The only thing she had accomplished was to bind her daughter to her in some futile obligation on Page's part to gain approval and acknowledgment she neither needed nor, in truth, desired.

"Mother, I'll be back to see you soon. I'll bring you something to cheer you up," Page said.

"A gift?" Clara's eyes suddenly came alive and slid over to meet Page's. "I love presents. Do bring me a present. It will make me feel so much better."

"I will." She kissed her mother on the cheek, and then quickly rose and left the room.

Death is waiting for us all, she thought, each word punctuated like nails driven in by the sound of her footsteps on the hard tile floor of the long corridor. Not an original thought, but one which made her quicken her pace, breathe a little faster, and hope a little harder that somehow she would discover a way to find the freedom she sought.

* * *

Stodding Watson was so ecstatic he could hardly contain himself. With his hands in his pockets, he jiggled from foot to foot, as if needing to go to the bathroom, and said over and over again, "Five to seven million dollars? A work worth five to seven million dollars? Jason, I can't believe it. I'm overwhelmed. I'm beside myself."

"I wanted to present this to you as a *fait accompli,*" Jason said. "However, I haven't had much luck turning up a worthy work."

"Well, for that kind of money we could turn up three worthy works," Stodding said.

"I'd like only one. Something really substantial," Jason said. "Something that will really put the Rex on the map."

"I can put the word out as well. As you know, I have contacts throughout Europe and on the East Coast."

"That would be fine," Jason said. "However, I'm going to pursue my own avenues. Let's see what we can turn up together."

"Well, I have no doubt something substantial will appear."

"I put the word out to a number of reputable people and came up empty-handed," Jason said. "I've hired Page to do some articles which will divulge my intentions. I'm hoping the response will turn up something special. My intention is either to find a major Impressionist work or something earlier."

They were standing in Stodding's office at the Rex. Jason had left his office early and dropped in unexpectedly to make his announcement. To say that Stodding was amazed was to put it mildly. He still hadn't sat down behind his imposing French provincial oak desk.

"With that kind of budget, I'll discover something in no time," Stodding said.

Jason put his hands behind his back and took a few paces. "Stod, I want you to understand something. I want to choose this work. I'm going to find it and I'm going to announce it. This is *my* contribution to the Rex. I want that clearly understood."

Stodding, whose main contribution to the Rex was his fund-raising capabilities, and his ability to adapt to the situations it required, merely nodded. He wasn't about to look a gift horse in the mouth because of ego. He knew he'd have trouble with his curators: The one who specialized in Impressionism would want an Impressionist painting, his Old Master specialist would want an Old Master, and so on. Perhaps it was better this way. Internal politics wouldn't have to enter into it if Jason made the decision.

"I shall, of course, seek your expertise on the matter," Jason consoled. "However, as far as the public announcement is concerned, I want it made plain that I discovered the work and contributed it to the museum."

"That's only fair."

"I'm glad we understand each other."

Stodding suddenly got a cunning look on his face. "You really do want to go down in posterity, don't you, Jason?"

Jason did not answer the question. It struck him as impertinent. He nodded coolly at Stodding. "I'll be in touch. Have a good weekend. And let me know if anything turns up on your side."

Kate decided against Bali. It wasn't right to leave town for such a long time. If Jason Thomas had been going to Bali, she would have gone to Bali, but Thomas was here in Los Angeles, and that's where she should be, she decided. She needed to get closer to Thomas, not farther away from him.

Jason Thomas was uppermost on her mind these days. She found herself thinking of him while doing her hair in the bathroom, while cooking in the kitchen, while talking to a customer at work.

The problem of how to bring about justice, how to make him pay for Joel's death, occupied her waking thoughts. There was no violent solution available to her; she was unequipped and didn't have the stomach for it, anyway. She had to find an opening, a weakness, and build a plan that would breach his imposing protective wall. To do that she needed to know a lot more about him than she did.

* * *

On Friday night, as they were eating at The Bistro in Beverly Hills, Kate decided to tell David of her decision not to go to Bali.

"This restaurant was renovated last year," David said, "much improved."

He had made exactly the same comment the last time they were there, but she didn't point that out. In fact, she liked the restaurant immensely. It was a bright, cheerful place, with mirrors on the walls, fresh flowers everywhere, and an attractive pinkish carpet dominating everything. The service was attentive yet unpresumptuous. This was not a restaurant in which waiters would give you their names. David ordered the baby salmon, Kate the veal.

"I'm sorry. I've thought it over and I really can't come with you to Bali," she announced.

David put his knife and fork down carefully. "Why? It will be a wonderful experience for both of us."

"It's simply too soon. I've just moved here and I'm not ready to travel yet. Besides, it just really wouldn't be fair to Madge. I've only been working there a short time and to take off a week now wouldn't be right. It would place too much of a burden on her, and I can't do that."

David picked up his napkin and dabbed at the corners of his mouth. "Well, I admire your loyalty, but I'm terribly disappointed."

"So am I, but it's really not the right time."

"I was so looking forward to spending some time with you," David said. "These moments we have together, they just don't seem enough. I really want to wake up with you in the morning, have breakfast with you, have a shower with you, make love to you in the middle of the morning, have lunch with you. Just spend more time with you. You know what I mean?"

"Well, maybe we could just go away for a weekend. Some place that isn't so intrusive upon our time and obligations. Perhaps we could go to Santa Barbara or something. I've heard it's beautiful up there, and I haven't seen it yet."

"Well, something would be better than nothing," David said, putting a good face on it. "We could perhaps go down to Mazatlán for a weekend; it's a little more exotic than Santa Barbara. And a little more romantic."

"Sure," Kate said. "I've never been to Mexico. That would be fun. Plus the idea of us spending a couple of days alone is wonderful."

"All right. Let's see what I can work out. I'll let you know as soon as possible."

By tacit mutual agreement, they changed the subject.

"I had drinks with Jasmine the other day," Kate said. "I really like her. She's an interesting woman."

"Yes, I guess she is," David said. But he couldn't help ponitificating. "Of course she's an actress, and they are notoriously unreliable. I wouldn't get into a position of depending on her if I were you."

"We just had drinks," Kate said defensively.

"I'm sorry, I'm not intending to interfere. It's just that Jasmine is not the most stable personality I've ever encountered. She's very pleasant, of course, but she's been in Hollywood awhile and I suppose some of it's rubbed off on her."

"I like her. How are your other friends? What's his name, Jason Thomas?"

"Oh, he's fine," David said. "Now that you mention it, I was talking to him the other day and your name came up."

"Oh?" Kate asked, more casually than she felt.

"Yes. I brought it up. You know that he's one of the prime fundraisers behind the new wing at the Rex. The Thomas Wing, as it's going to be known. But he has an added caveat that he just announced to us the other day. He plans to donate an extraordinary work of art to the new wing. With the help of myself and Allan Silvers, he's prepared to pay five to seven million dollars for this work."

"How exciting. And how expensive," Kate said. "That would imply a major work of art."

David nodded, "Oh, yes. He wants to come up with something exceptional. Something that will attract attention around the world."

"That's wonderful. So, how did my name come up?"

"Well, I mentioned your expertise in art. You see, he's been trying to find this work for some time now without any success. And at our meeting the other day, he retained Page to start a small public relations campaign to make his intention known to the art world. Hopefully, this will bring some response to help him find his acquisition."

"It'll bring the flakes out of the woodwork," Kate said, unable to hide her incredulity.

"Exactly, and that's how your name came up. I suggested you as a resource. Someone who is an expert and might be able to help him sort through the responses and come up with this extraordinary work."

"Well, sure. Of course I'll be happy to help in any way I can. However, I'm sure the people at the Rex will have a lot to say about it."

"They already have their hands full. Besides, there's a lot of internal politics there and I think Jason wants to avoid that." David said. "I'm glad you're willing to help. I'm sure you'll be hearing from Jason about it."

Kate changed the subject and asked David about his business. The gyrations of the stock market had been troubling him, and for the remainder of the dinner, she heard his theories on the subject. After they had completed the main course, the waiter asked what they wished for dessert. Kate grimaced, saying, "I don't think so." But David contradicted her.

"You must try their mousse. It's very small but it really packs a punch. It's the best in town," he said, not waiting for her answer but waving dismissively at the waiter to indicate the order.

Kate resented his presumptuousness but nevertheless still had the chocolate mousse. She had to admit that it truly was an exceptional treat—creamy, rich, flavorful, filling her mouth with luxury.

But as they left the restaurant, the dessert wasn't what put the smile on her face. It was a thought that had been growing and growing for the last half hour. Perhaps she had found her opening. It had miraculously presented itself to her. Perhaps she had found Jason Thomas's weakness. The thought was still pregnant and growing. It would have to mature before it was born. But definitely gave her something to think about.

Fay couldn't help sobbing in the car during the drive to the airport on Sunday evening.

"I'm sorry," she said to Jasmine. "I don't want to make a scene, I just don't want to go home."

"That's all right, I understand," Jasmine consoled. "But it won't be so bad. It's never as bad as you think it is."

"Easy for you to say. You escaped."

"You don't have too much longer to go. In less than a year you'll be out of there if you want to. It's not a long time to wait. I know it seems long, but it really isn't. Enjoy yourself, enjoy your friends, enjoy school, and just try to get through home life without making waves."

"God, I wish I had your life," Fay wailed.

"My life? It's not that great, Fay, believe me."

"How can you say that? You're an actress. I'm the envy of every kid in class for having a sister as famous as you."

"Huh! Famous I'm not. I'm a middle-of-the-road actress who gets a job occasionally. And the parts aren't that great."

"But you're so good. Everyone says so. And so beautiful," Fay said adoringly.

Fay's worship disturbed her. It was like getting a prize for an examination after cheating. "I could be good if I worked at it. But let's be honest, I haven't worked at it," Jasmine said regretfully. "I guess I'm lazy, have things too easy. I don't want to disillusion you, little sister; I enjoy your admiration, but don't misplace it."

"I really enjoyed being here with you."

"And I enjoyed having you here," Jasmine smiled.

"Maybe I could come down again?" Fay asked with trepidation.

"Of course," Jasmine said. "After you've been home a little while, I'll talk to Mom and Dad and maybe you could come down here for Christmas vacation, or maybe for a weekend every now and then. It's not that far, just an hour by plane. And I'd be willing to pay the cost of the tickets. Maybe they'd allow that."

"That would be great," Fay said enthusiastically. "I wouldn't get in your way. I'd just sort of come down, and hang out and cool it."

"Okay, we'll see about it. Don't mention anything, just leave it to me," Jasmine said.

After a last tearful good-bye at the gate, Jasmine drove back to the city. She had enjoyed seeing Fay, she realized. She'd never had much of a family before. When she and Fay were growing up there was too large a difference in their ages for them to be much more than strangers. Now, suddenly, Fay was a young woman, old enough to be a contemporary, a friend.

It felt good to have a sense of family again. Although it had never occurred to her before, the absence of family had left a void in her life, a void that, to be truthful, her relationship with Allan hadn't been able to fill.

The thought depressed her. Fay was no longer here. All she had to look forward to was Allan.

CHAPTER TWELVE

Apparently having a hard time starting the week, Madge wanted to play hookey on Monday morning. "I've got tickets for a fashion show at Neiman-Marcus. Let's close up the gallery and go there," she said playfully. "It's three designers. An American, an Italian, and a Frenchman. It should be interesting. We can also have a bit of lunch."

"Are you sure? I'm not really dressed for it," Kate said dubiously.

She wore lightweight wool slacks of a soft brown that matched her low-heeled pumps. Not expecting much more than a slow day at work, she had also thrown on her favorite sweater that morning, an oversized pink cashmere pullover, and with it large, loopy pink plastic earrings. Although comfortable, which had been the original idea, she wasn't sure it was appropriate for a fashion show at Neiman-Marcus.

"Hey, I'm the boss and nothing much is happening today, anyway. So let's do it. Besides, I'm not dressed for it either." Madge wore a simple navy sweater and skirt, with flat white shoes and white beads around her neck.

"Okay, you're the boss," Kate conceded.

When they got there, Madge seemed to know most of the people at the show. Kate soon became totally overwhelmed by the blitz of names and faces she was introduced to. One thing was certain, judging by the appearance of these women, they were not middle-class housewives from the Valley.

When they were seated, Madge explained who some of the people were, responding to Kate's question about whether these women could really afford ten-thousand-dollar designer dresses, "Are you kidding?" Madge asked. "The lady I introduced you to—the blonde, Mabel Hartford?"

"You mean the one with rings on her fingers, bells on her toes, and the loud voice to go with it?"

"Yeah. Well, she can afford to be loud. She's the wife of James Hartford, who owns one of the biggest law firms in the city. She could write a check for twenty thousand or thirty thousand dollars for clothes without even blinking. In fact, it's demanded of her. In the circles she moves in, appearance is secondary only to the amount of money you have. And the other one you met who was with her . . . the brunette?"

"Oh, the thin, dangerous-looking one?"

"Yeah, well, she's married to Oliver Kesselman. He runs one of the biggest film studios in town."

"And they're all like that?" Kate asked weakly.

Madge sniggered. "Except for you and me, sweetheart."

The master of ceremonies stepped up to the microphone, told everyone how delighted he was to see them, and then said he would introduce a speaker before the show began. "Ladies and gentlemen, the chairperson for the Foundation for the Homeless, Mrs. David Ross."

Kate's temples began to pound, an involuntary fight/flight response to seeing her lover's wife unexpectedly. Pat Ross was not an imposing-looking woman. Rather plain and dumpy, she looked as if she might be more at home on a farm than with these smooth coiffured city ladies. Still, the beige-colored suit she wore didn't look as if it had been bought off the rack.

"I'd like to thank you for the support you've shown to the homeless foundation by appearing here today," she began. She seemed a little nervous, unaccustomed to public speaking. "As you know, the proceeds from your tickets, plus a portion of receipts here today, will go to the foundation."

A few more platitudes and thanks, a smattering of applause, and the microphone went back to the master of ceremonies.

Mrs. Ross returned to her seat, obviously thankful to be out of the limelight.

Kate tried to analyze her feelings. She was uncomfortable. This rather decent-looking woman was being betrayed by her husband and she, Kate, was largely responsible for it. She had no wish to hurt Pat Ross. Perhaps David had even lied about their relationship. Perhaps the woman loved her husband dearly. Perhaps, through her actions, Kate was mortally wounding her very way of life.

Kate stopped herself. There was no point in guilt. Guesswork like this invited it. She was involved in a war, and in any war innocent bystanders got hurt. Besides, if David Ross weren't with her, he'd be with someone else. She already knew that much about him. He was a born philanderer.

And then, with the thunder of a prerecorded orchestra, the show started, taking her mind off her discomfort.

The models began their parade down the runway, slinking and sliding in ways appropriate to the fashions they were showing. The Italian and French designers had tried their best to shock and surprise their audience. And they won.

Plenty of glitter and balloon skirts were topped with outrageous hats that could have passed for Easter baskets. Oohs and aahs and the occasional titter at some of the more revolutionary designs rose from the crowd.

The American designer had produced a more conservative line: beautiful clothing for the working woman—if she made over half-a-million a year.

"God, how can people spend that much money on clothes?" Kate wondered afterwards as they walked through the store. It struck her as obscene.

"It's easy when you have it," Madge said. "What else are they going to spend it on?"

"Well, with very few exceptions, they weren't that interested in spending it on the homeless," Kate said cynically. "This could have been a fundraiser for anything and they would have come."

"How did you feel seeing Mrs. David Ross there?" Madge asked cattishly.

"Uncomfortable." She was rescued from further discussion by an approaching woman who raised her hand in greeting. At first she didn't recognize her, but then she saw it was Page Peters, Jason Thomas's mistress.

"Oh, hi," Kate said, her voice flustered by the unexpectedness of the encounter. "How are you?"

"Fine, thank you," Page said. "Doing some shopping?"

"We just attended a fashion show." Kate turned to Madge and introduced the two women.

"Oh, I've been to shows at your gallery," Page said. "It's very impressive."

"Why, thank you. You do look familiar. I suppose I've seen you."

Page looked as elegant as ever. She wore a Calvin Klein black stretch dress, black stockings, and black patent shoes, all of it topped with a long, tailored yellow cashmere jacket.

It was altogether stunning. To complete the effect, she wore a large diamond pin near the neckline of her jacket. Page could have walked down the runway with the other models and elicited more applause than any of them.

"It's funny I should run into you," Page said to Kate. "I was thinking of calling you. I'm involved in a public relations project in the art field, and I was hoping that I could pick your brains and get a little advice."

"Sure, I'd be glad to help. Do you want to get together sometime?"

"That would be nice. If I remember, when we met, we were talking about having a drink together. What about this evening? Are you free? Or is that too short notice?"

"No, that's fine," Kate said.

"Would the Beverly Wilshire be okay?"

"Sure."

"All right. How about I meet you in the bar at five-thirty?"

They parted, agreeing to meet later that day. "What a beautiful woman," Madge said when they were out of ear-shot. "Who is she?"

"Jason Thomas's mistress."

"Mistress meeting mistress in Neiman-Marcus. What a strange world," Madge muttered half to herself.

It was a lucky meeting, Kate thought as they walked through the exit. Page had been next on her list as someone to contact, and she had been planning to call her. Events were falling into place.

Although not exactly consumed with guilt, a niggling voice tugged at Allan as he drove to Jasmine's apartment. To hear from his conscience was a rare experience and it disturbed him.

She had called that morning to say her sister had left the night before. She had wanted to let him know then, she said, but as they both knew, she never called him at home, which was where he spent his Sundays.

Allan had suggested leaving work early and visiting her in the afternoon, as he had an appointment that evening.

He had to take Elena with him to a studio party. Now, as he took Santa Monica Boulevard toward her apartment, he couldn't help but think back to his encounter with Maya the previous day. It had been delicious, satisfying, and Maya had more than lived up to her reputation. But it had also been crazy. Who knew where a woman like that had been, or what she was carrying?

His hands tightened on the steering wheel and he swerved to avoid a car that was changing lanes ahead of him. "Fucker!" he shouted, raising his finger.

Damn all women, he thought, they were nothing but trouble. Too bad he couldn't get on without them. What was strange was that the guilty feeling was directed at Jasmine and not his wife. Well, not so strange, he conceded. His infidelities toward Elena had been countless, but since being with Jasmine, he had been more or less faithful according to his standards. All he had done was cop a feel here and there, a little harmless flirting. Until now. Serve her right, he thought. She should have been there when he needed her. What was a man supposed to do, anyway? He pushed the thoughts aside. There was no purpose in flogging himself. It wasn't that serious, anyhow. It was simply a single encounter and had meant nothing.

Jasmine greeted him with her usual enthusiasm, throwing her arms around his neck, saying how much she had missed him.

"I missed you, too," he said, walking into the living room. He sat on the couch, took off his shoes, and put his feet up.

"Can I get you something?"

His throat was dry and he smacked his lips. "A beer would go down well."

The living room was in its usual state of disarray. Records littered the floor, the coffee table was obscured with half-opened magazines, and a glass from the previous night still stood on the end table.

"How's your sister?" he asked when she returned with a beer. "I didn't even know you had one. I never thought of you having a family."

"Ah, a deep dark secret of my past," Jasmine said lightly. "I was actually born once and had parents."

"Well, it was damn inconvenient," he said, his earlier resentment returning.

"Well, excuse me if I have a private life," Jasmine said, sitting beside him.

"Shit, it's not that. It's just that I think I'm a little more important to you than a sister you never see. What was she doing here, anyway?"

"She ran away from home. She had a fight with our parents."

"Jesus! Where is she now?"

"We talked and she went back."

"Well, I hope it doesn't happen again. I can't stand being away from you more than a couple of days."

"It was a situation I had to handle," Jasmine said sarcastically. "I'm so sorry it was inconvenient for you."

"Hey. I pay the bills here. I pay for your clothes, this apartment, for your car. I think that I'd be allowed to come here whenever I wanted to, wouldn't you?"

Jasmine drew further away from him, her back stiffening. "Sometimes you are really an asshole, Allan."

"Yeah, yeah, well I'm glad she's gone. I hope it doesn't happen again."

"It probably will. I invited her down here for Christmas vacation."

"Shit! So what are we going to do then?"

"What you usually do . . . spend Christmas with your family leaving me here alone."

"I see you. I saw you last Christmas. It's just on Christmas day that I was tied up with the family."

"Yeah, well, I'll have some of my family here on Christmas day and if you don't like it, stuff it."

"Okay," Allan said with a sigh. "I didn't come here to fight with you, I came here to make love to you. Let's drop the subject."

"No, I'm not going to drop it," Jasmine said fiercely. "You have to understand that I have a life of my own, too. Sure I like to be with you, and sure I'm available for you most of the time. But sometimes things happen that I need to do. Jesus, you make me feel like your fucking slave."

"I'm sorry, I'm sorry." Allan held his hands up in surrender. "You're right, I'm being an asshole. I just missed you. I'm jealous when you're not with me. I'm sorry, I apologize."

He looked contrite, sincere. She couldn't push it further. "I love you, Allan." Her voice was shaking. She was suddenly unsure of her position, her bravado deserting her. "It's just that you have to understand that I'm a person with my own needs as well."

"And I love you too, baby. And yeah, I understand. I'm sorry." Thank God that's over, he thought. But as he kissed her, that niggling guilt unexpectedly rose again.

Page was sitting below a gigantic painting of a thoroughbred horse in the lounge of the Beverly Wilshire Hotel.

Kate hurried over and apologized for being late. "I'm sorry," she said, sitting opposite her. "Somebody came into the gallery and I had to deliver my sales pitch."

Page was already drinking a glass of wine. "That's all right. It's nice to see you again. I don't mind waiting; this room's always interesting. A fascinating mix of out-of-towners and local color. What would you like to drink?"

"The same as you would be fine." Kate leaned back in her seat. "The day started off slowly, we even got to play hookey, but the afternoon just got frantic. It seemed that dozens of people came into the gallery."

"Do you like the job? From what I know of you, I'd think you'd be qualified for something more . . . I don't know . . . prestigious."

"Well, I like Madge a lot, and the job's fine for now," Kate said.

"But you don't plan on making a lifelong career out of it?" Page ventured.

Kate shrugged, "Who knows what the future holds?"

Page smiled wryly, "That's a question that's been on my mind a lot these days."

"What, the future?"

Page shrugged. "A single girl always has to worry about the future."

"Gosh, I wouldn't think you'd have to worry," Kate said disarmingly. "You have your own business. I understand it's quite successful."

Page smiled. "A girl said something similar to me on the beach the other day. As I told her, I suppose it's a matter of how much you want. Or what you want."

"And what do you want?"

Page was saved from answering. A burly man made his way from the bar to their table. He had pleasant features and wore a business suit, but even in the dim light they could see that his eyes were bloodshot. He'd obviously been sitting there for a few hours. "Excuse me, may I buy you ladies a drink?" He swayed ever so slightly as he stood and waited for their answer.

"Thank you, but no," Page said, her voice cool but polite. "We already have a drink and we're having a business meeting."

"Oh, I see. Well, sorry to disturb you," he said, and made his way back to the bar.

"A lonely out-of-towner on a business trip," Page commented.

"You're from the East Coast, aren't you?"

Page nodded. "New York, born and bred."

"How long have you been out here?"

"Oh, a couple of years here. I was in Texas for a bit."

"Do you miss New York?"

"No, not at all. I like living here. I like the climate, I like the people. What about you? Are you missing New York?"

"Oh, no," Kate said, "LA's great."

"You seeing David?"

"Yes."

"Well, with him you'll see the best LA has to offer," Page said.

Throughout the exchange, the two women measured each other. The sedate patrician, Page's face gave nothing away. Her eyes were interested but bland. Kate, a bolder beauty with a more fiery potential, seemed only friendly, but Page sensed there was more to her than she could see.

"A word of advice, if I may offer it," Page said.

"What?"

"Don't grow too dependent on David. You are obviously bright and I suspect ambitious. Dependency is a crutch ambitious women can't afford. The crutch becomes the handicap."

Kate leaned forward at the table, her eyes puzzled. "I'm surprised to hear you say that," she said. "It seems out of character. You're so cool, so assured. But first, I sense a regret in you. Second, what do you care about what I do?"

"You mean I appear cold and unfeeling?" Page said with a little laugh. "It's a pose, my dear. It's the face I present to the world. I like you. I liked you the moment I first met you. And I've been a part of this little coterie long enough to see what can happen to women in this group, in this city, in this world we live in today"

"Well, thank you. I like you too." And as Kate said it, she knew it was true. She genuinely did feel an attraction towards this self-assured woman. There was something elegant and pure about Page, or at least you knew there could be a purity to her. She was obviously a complicated woman and not to be taken lightly.

It was as if that moment of honesty had somehow broken the barriers down between them. The wariness, not seen but nevertheless present, disappeared, replaced by something more comfortable, warmer.

"What about you and Jason Thomas? What kind of a relationship do you two have?" Kate asked.

Page's eyes flicked away then returned. "Master and slave, what else?"

"You're not serious? You have your own income. You have a life of your own, a business."

"My successful business is very small," Page said wistfully. "Jason Thomas is very generous, very powerful, and very demanding. It's a situation I've become acutely aware of in recent days. You have to understand that when women like you and me get into this position, we are assuming the subservient role. Once we accept or take, we have agreed to that role."

"David doesn't support me."

"But he gives you gifts, doesn't he?" She read the answer in Kate's eyes and continued. "That's just a start. He will support you. Soon he'll suggest gently that you quit your job, that he pay your rent, that he buy your car, that he take you places, that you be available when he needs you, that your friends be his friends, that your life be his. It's preordained."

"It sounds like marriage," Kate muttered.

"Oh, no, if we were married and decided to end the game, we might walk away with half of what the men own. We end the game, and we definitely walk away with nothing. If they end the game, we walk away with nothing, depending upon the whims of their generosity. It's a vulnerable position."

"So what do you do about it?"

Page leaned back. "There's the rub. I don't know." Her mood changed, growing lighter. She smiled. "I'm sorry, I don't mean to depress you, it's just that this has been on my mind lately. I've sensed a certain sympathy in you and I suppose I don't have many friends, really. I don't get to talk about this stuff to anyone. I'm sorry."

"Don't apologize," Kate said. "I appreciate your confidences, and I really don't mind them. You are more experienced than I am and I also appreciate your advice. Listen, are you doing anything tonight? Maybe we could just have dinner here. I've just realized I'm famished."

"Sure. I'd like that. Do you want to eat now?"

"Eh . . . I don't know. Maybe another glass of wine. Anyway, you did want to see me about something else, didn't you?"

"Oh, yes," Page said, "I almost forgot. I'm doing a project for Jason, and I guess it's also for the Rex. Do you know about the art he's trying to purchase for the new wing?"

"Yes, David told me. It's very exciting, very ambitious, and very expensive."

"Don't worry, these guys can afford it. Anyway, I'm trying to plant some stories in various magazines, but the problem I'm running into is that they have a very long lead time. Magazines like *Art and Antiques* work months ahead, and I think Jason wants results sooner than three or four months down the line. I was wondering if you would have any suggestions. Art isn't really my field, and you obviously know a lot more about it than I do."

"Sure, what exactly do you want to say?"

"Well, something to the effect that . . . ah, well, it depends, of course, where it appears, but it will be something like Mr. Jason Thomas has announced that he is purchasing a major work of art in the five to seven million dollar range. A valuable work for the new Thomas Wing of the Rex, which is due to open in a few months. That would be one way, just a straight press release. The other way would be in an interview with Jason. Perhaps have him say something to the effect of 'What I really want to do is find an Old Master or Impressionist work for the wing. I am prepared to spend five to seven million dollars, but I want something that is going to add significantly to the already considerable prestige of the Rex.' That's the type of thing I'll do."

"Well," Kate said, "the art magazines, as you say, publish too far down the road. Your best bet would be to have it appear in a column of the *Sunday Times* Calendar Section in the art pages or in the View Section of the *L.A. Times,* and you can do similar things in the *New York Times*. I don't think it will be difficult; it's a significant announcement. And you'll get a deluge of response to it."

"That's what I figured," Page said. "I've been trying to reach Stodding Watson to get his input on this, but I've been unable to get hold of him. I think he's out of town for a couple of days."

"You realize you are going to get all sorts of weird and wonderful offers?" Kate said.

"That's not my problem," Page replied. "My problem is just to make it known. What happens then is up to Jason and Stod."

"Well," Kate volunteered, "let me give you the names

of some weekly publications that I think you should send your press releases to as well.''

Page withdrew a small notebook from her bag and began to write the names down as Kate gave them to her.

''All right,'' she said, snapping the notebook shut when Kate finished, ''that's the end of business. How about some dinner?''

''Mmmm, I'd love it. I'm ravenous,'' Kate said.

While they were eating, Kate returned to the subject of Jason Thomas. ''Why's he doing this? Spending so much money on the Rex?''

''It's his legacy,'' Page said. ''At least that's what he claims. I think he sees it as an entry into even more powerful circles.''

''Is he that calculating?''

''Jason calculating? He can make a computer look human.''

''Why are you with him? I don't understand it.''

Page gave her a sad smile. ''I'm fatally attracted to power,'' she said, making fun of herself. ''I'm like a moth that flies into the flame. I know it'll burn my wings, and yet I can't resist it.''

''It sounds as if you've had a realization about that, though.''

''Yes. But I wonder if it's too late?''

''How old are you?''

''Thirty-one.''

''Well, I'm only four years younger than you. Is it too late for me?''

Page smiled maternally. ''I don't think so. I think there's more to you than meets the eye.''

Again a flash of paranoia struck Kate, but it wasn't justified. This perceptive woman might know she was playing a game, but there was no way she could know the reasons or the end results.

Page giggled, a strange girlish sound coming from her. ''I think I'm a little drunk. Do you know, in addition to two glasses of wine before dinner, we've finished a bottle with dinner? I don't normally drink this much.''

"Well, I was just thinking of an after-dinner drink," Kate said. She wasn't feeling the alcohol at all. Perhaps Page had drunk most of it.

"How about a B & B—I so love the smell."

Halfway through their liqueurs, Kate casually broached the subject of Jason Thomas's search again. "You know, I was just thinking. Jason is looking for an Impressionist or Old Master work for this showpiece at the Rex. Just from a public relations viewpoint—and that's your business, I know—it seems that an Old Master would be the most prestigious."

"Really? Why?"

"Well, I was just thinking in terms of something like a Rembrandt. You know, there are no major Rembrandts in any of the museums in Los Angeles. The L.A. County Museum of Art has some, but they are not by any means major works. If he could come up with a major Rembrandt, it would be a real coup."

"That's a good point," Page said. "I'll mention it to him."

By the time they parted an hour later, Kate was satisfied. She had grown to understand Page and liked what she had found. She had gained, in some sense, Page's acceptance, and she had hopefully planted the seed from which her plan would grow.

The premier showing of Andora Dover's new film was a gala event. Obviously, the out-take scenes that had so amused Allan and his friends on the night of Selena's death were missing.

The media cannons had been brought to bear and the blitz was on. Andora had appeared on network television, plus every talk show in Los Angeles, to promote the new film. On opening night everyone was there, from the mayor to the heads of rival studios. Allan had invited both Jason and David and other members of the circle to the premieres and party afterwards at Spago's.

It was a wife-only night. Jason was there with Sharon and David with Pat. Allan's wife, Elena, well aware that he was almost the center of attention apart from the star, hung onto his arm and smiled at the paparazzi.

Just before leaving home, Jason had noticed Sharon's full-length mink. "Is that new?"

"Yes," she had said, stepping into the limousine, an innocent smile on her lips.

"When . . . how much . . . never mind, I'll talk to you about it later," Jason had muttered.

She felt triumphant. He had noticed the stab. He'd never admit to bleeding but the wound was there.

The film was, by all relevant accounts, a success. Oh, it wasn't an artistic masterpiece by any stretch of the imagination. But the great unwashed masses of America did not pay five dollars and up a head to see Andora being artistic. They paid their money to see the reigning sex goddess be exactly that. Which is exactly what they got. Even without the footage of Andora fucking her leading man, she was gloriously sexual in the film. She communicated sex, oozed it, dripped it, and pleased her audience.

"Great movie," the people said coming up to Allan at Spago's, a euphemism for a film that had a good chance to be a commercial success. In spite of the X-rated invasion, America was not yet blasé about the subject of sex, particularly if it was aesthetically presented.

"Are you pleased with the film?" Jason asked Allan. They were standing to one side of the room. Beyond them the flow of bodies and conversation had raised the noise level to a point just past bearable.

The wealthy, the glamorous, and those who wished they were, milled around like frenzied fish on a feeding binge. People nodded, shouted greetings, snubbed those they wished to, and approached those they desired to speak to in a Babylonic binge.

"It would have been better with the footage that we saw," Allan sniggered. "But I think it'll do just fine."

"Make it's money back?" David said, coming up to them.

"It already has. We're sold out in Europe and Asia; the rest is pure profit."

"I'm going to remember that when you pull some of your famous Chinese studio bookkeeping on your loyal investors," David said nervously.

"Hey, my friends are going to do just fine from this," Allan said. He took them each by the arm. "Want to meet the star?"

"Sure," David said.

Jason allowed himself to be led to the queen bee.

The workers were hovering around her in her moment of glory. She stood near the center of the room, a blond goddess enjoying her time of glory. She wore a floor-length velvet skirt and a very thin sequin and beaded blouse with a large V-neck. Every movement of Andora's arms bared one or the other of her shoulders as the blouse slipped down. A giggled "Oops!" accompanied each intentional mishap.

She smiled and bobbed and threw back her head, exposing her long lovely neck to the men surrounding her. Vapid, immature, irrationally egomanical though she might be, it did not matter. She wove her own kind of spell.

Allan cut through the crowd like a tugboat, Jason and David in tow.

"Sweetie, you were marvelous," he said, putting his hand on her shoulder, kissing the air by her face.

"I couldn't have done it without you. If you hadn't had faith in me? If you hadn't been willing to support me?" She didn't elaborate on those dire consequences, but broke off and looked at her audience. "He's one in a million, fellows. I owe him everything."

Allan laughed and indicated Jason and David. "You owe them too. They put money into the movie. They also had faith in you. Right where it counts."

"Oh, pleased to meet you," she said with a little curtsy.

Both men shook her hand, and then a man beside her said, "I particularly loved you in that scene in the boatshed. It was so sensual and yet so innocent."

"Oh, darling, thank you," she trilled, ignoring Allan, Jason, and David. "It was so difficult to capture the exact mood that was needed at the time. My leading man"—she waved a languid hand—"well, he did his best, but we did have to shoot that scene over a few times to capture the exact ambiance."

"I hate this Hollywood bullshit," Jason said when they were a safe distance away.

"Then why do you come?" David asked.

"I do have to take my wife out occasionally," Jason said stiffly. "She happens to enjoy this type of display."

His eye wandered across the room to where Sharon stood near the bar, resplendent in her new mink coat. She was listening attentively to an intense young actor, hanging onto his every word, lightly touching his hand for emphasis, leaning ever so slightly toward him, laughing joyously at his every humorous remark.

She had hired a new chauffeur, he had noted the day before. Perhaps it would keep her out of trouble for a while. Like they had all been, he seemed young, virile, and eager to please. For a time he would suffice, but he did not want to dwell on that. He turned to David. "Stock market's been going crazy. What do you think?"

David shrugged, "It's just a correction. A good buying opportunity. Some good bargains out there now."

Jason nodded, "That's my opinion as well. Some selective buying should pay off."

"Excuse me," Allan said. "I need to go talk to some people."

"The ladies seem to be enjoying themselves." Jason nodded his head toward Elena Silver and Pat Ross, who were standing among a small circle of people, the center of some animated conversation.

"Yes," David said, "I suppose everyone needs a night out occasionally."

"How's your new lady? What's her name? Kate?"

"Just fine, absolutely fine. By the way, I mentioned your search for a painting for the Rex, and she is perfectly willing to help in any capacity."

"Excellent," Jason said. "I might have to call on her. I have a feeling we are going to be overwhelmed with possibilities."

"A nice problem to have," David said.

"You do have the money available, don't you?" Jason asked.

"Of course. When you are ready to make your purchase just let me know, and I'll attend to it."

"Very good, I knew I could depend on you." Jason looked over to where he'd last seen his wife. She and the actor she'd been speaking to had disappeared. Damn! he thought to himself. Is she going to embarrass me here? And then with some relief he saw her on the other side of the room, still with the actor but joined by two young women and another young man.

He wouldn't have been as relieved if he could have heard her words.

" . . . and then I lay back on the bed and said, 'Have you ever fucked a woman in a mink coat before?' " The group erupted into hysterical laughter.

Jason watched her give a pretty turn, the mink coat twirling in the air. He hated these people, he thought to himself. Sycophants, hangers-on, opportunists, most of them had never worked an honest day in their lives. They flocked around the stars, hoping a little glory would rub off on them. As for the stars, they lived for these moments, needed them desperately. Their frail egos craved this kind of attention.

Pat Ross came up to them and touched David on the arm. A level-headed woman, Jason thought. Too bad she drank so much and was so damned ugly. "Are you going to be ready to leave soon?" she asked David.

"Whenever you like," he said, "just give me the high sign."

He should leave as well, Jason thought. Get out of here before Sharon did something to humiliate him. She was getting worse and worse. He never knew what to expect next.

"Shall we get together soon?" David asked. "Perhaps with our ladies?"

"That sounds good," Jason said. "I'll give you a call.

They shook hands and David wandered off to reclaim his wife.

A pretty young actress, slightly tipsy and flushed, came up to Jason. "Did you work on the film?" she asked.

"No," Jason said. "I simply had a financial interest in it."

"Oooo, a backer! I've always wanted to meet a backer." She took his arm. "Are you very rich?"

Jason was not amused. He freed himself. "You must excuse me. I have to speak to someone." He walked toward Sharon.

She was laughing, her head thrown back. "Excuse me," he said as he approached and drew her aside. "I'd like to leave now."

"Oh, but this is such fun! We can't leave now. The party's just getting warmed up."

"We need to leave now," he repeated, his eyes growing hard.

"Why don't you go home? I'll come later."

"How am I going to get home?" Jason asked, forcing patience.

Sharon shrugged. "Who cares? Take the limo or take a cab. I can get a ride."

He put his hand on her arm and gripped it, squeezing hard. He placed a smile on his face and said quietly, "We're leaving together now, Sharon. Let's go and pay our respects to Allan."

"Let go of my arm, you're hurting me." Her voice was getting shrill.

"Come on." He tugged her imperceptibly. To anyone else, he might have looked like a solicitous husband holding his wife's arm. But he was inflicting pain while he pulled her.

"You son of a bitch," she hissed. "I hate you."

"That's fine," Jason said smoothly. "We're leaving now."

CHAPTER THIRTEEN

Mazatlán was not what Kate had expected. Perhaps it was prejudice, or simply the unconscious acceptance of a thousand bad jokes about stomach flu, but she had always thought of Mexico as a Third World country, with all the attendant problems. But it wasn't.

In spite of the thoroughly modern luxury hotels on the beachfront, the city itself had been there since the seventeenth century and was charming. On the way to their lodging, they drove through the thriving Zona Dorado, or Golden Zone, with its dozens of shops containing leather goods, silver jewelry, and other handicrafts. Most people seemed to travel in the *pulmonias,* an open air cart with a fringed roof. The harbor area—the home of Mexico's largest fleet of shrimpers, she was told—was colorful and busy.

David had called her at work on Wednesday and suggested they leave for Mexico on Friday afternoon. After a hasty conference with Madge to get the time off, she had accepted.

They were staying in a luxury condominium, a short walk from the beach. The weather was faultless, the sand white, the ocean a deep rich blue. Eleven miles of gently sloping beach disappeared into hazy sunlight.

"Like?" David asked, joining her on the balcony a short time after they arrived.

"It's beautiful," Kate said. "It seems so far away from anywhere real."

David laughed. "Oh, it's real all right. It's just been created to pamper people like us who are willing to pay two hundred fifty dollars a day.''

David couldn't help mentioning money, Kate noted again. It was more than letting her know how much he was spending on her; it was almost a point of pride with him. I have it, look how well I can spend it, one part of him seemed to be constantly saying. And yet the other side of him, the less flamboyant side, the banker perhaps, carefully totaled up the check after every meal, and if there was a mistake of a few cents, he took great satisfaction in pointing it out to the waiter. A strange and contradictory man. Kind to her at the present but probably capable of great unkindness when things were not going his way. That was something for her to remember.

''Would you like a drink?'' David asked.

They were sitting in the comfortable living room, with a satellite television, a stereo system, and a fully stocked bar.

''A Mexican beer seems appropriate,'' Kate replied.

David had the same. They sipped their Dos Equis. 'It's not Bali, but it's nice,'' David said.

''It's wonderful,'' Kate said. ''Let's go down to the beach.''

David looked at her quizzically for a moment, and then said, ''First we have an appointment in that huge bed. It's been hard to keep my hands off you all day.''

He led her into the bedroom, which was dominated by a King-sized bed and another large-screened color television set.

Their lovemaking was over almost as soon as it began. Maybe the trip had been tiring, or maybe the beer had dampened him. David rolled away from her and muttered morosely, ''I'm sorry, I guess I was a little anxious.''

''That's fine,'' she consoled. ''We have all weekend. There is no need to rush anything.'' She couldn't help but wonder how many women had said the same thing.

''I'm a little tired. I think I'll take a nap.''

Kate sat up. He had done nothing to tire her. ''I'll go down to the beach and take a swim, catch some sun if you don't mind.''

"That's fine." David closed his eyes. By the time she had changed into her bikini, he was already asleep.

Down at the beach, Kate dropped her towel and dark glasses and ran into the surf, skillfully diving underneath the onrushing rollers. Compared to the East Coast, where she had sometimes swum, the water was like a warm bath. The temperature must have been in the eighties. She swam out to a point just beyond the breakers and then bodysurfed back to the beach.

Two young men in their twenties walked by, admired her lines, and shouted out a greeting.

"Hi," she said, then turned back to face the ocean, letting the foam wash over her feet.

She didn't feel like talking to anyone. Being alone was a luxury. She dried herself off and lay on her towel, but after five minutes of allowing the sun to soak into her, she grew bored and got up again.

Following the water line, she walked along the beach, her mind blissfully empty. A childlike pleasure enveloped her as she made patterns in the sand with her feet, splashed the water when the inclination struck her, and stopped to examine shells.

A jogger approached her, coming from the opposite direction. A fit-looking man in his thirties, in spite of graying hair, he slowed down as he approached, eyeing her appreciatively. As he reached her side, he began to jog backward. "Hey, I hope you don't mind the comment, but you are absolutely gorgeous."

"Thanks," Kate replied, unable to resist smiling at the compliment. But she kept on walking, her long legs eating up the yards, her mind still blank and untroubled. This was better than any therapy could be.

She must have walked at least two miles, because when she got back to the condo David was already up, a worried expression on his face. "I went down to the beach to look for you. I couldn't see you anywhere."

She fell onto the couch with a great exhalation of air. "I went for a walk. I must have walked miles."

"I wish you'd let me know where you are going," David reprimanded.

"I told you I was going for a swim," Kate said casually. "I'm afraid when I see a beach, I start walking. It's involuntary."

"Well, I just . . ." David stopped himself and, obviously trying hard to be pleasant, said instead, "I though we might go into town and walk around and have dinner. Would you like to take a shower?"

"Sure," Kate said, and went to the bathroom.

It was happening even sooner than she'd expected, she thought ruefully as she soaped her body in the jacuzzi. In spite of her casual attitude, she'd been well aware of David's chagrin. Ownership, she thought. An attempt to dominate her. It's what these men were all about. She remembered the conversation with Page and felt pity for the woman. But at least Page was aware of her position. She was a step ahead of most. From there she could do something about it.

But she wasn't supposed to have these thoughts. They could only occur beneath her disguise. She went back into the living room after showering and changing, gaily urging David to hurry up and get ready.

The town was a charming tourist trap, the people warm and friendly. Their seafood dinner was extraordinary. If the fish and shrimp had been any fresher, they would have swam away. By the time they returned to their condo at about nine-thirty, David had regained his good mood and, she soon discovered, his staying power in bed.

And so the weekend went. Sex, eating, drinking, swimming, sunbathing, and walking.

The sex was pleasant but unspectacular. The first time she had made love with David she had been sexually starved. The ensuing eruption had been physically as good as anything she had experienced. Since then, her body had taken it more in stride. Nothing exciting, but as exhilarating as a good exercise session.

The times she enjoyed most were when she was by herself, walking down the beach with no destination in mind, the smell of salty water filling her nostrils, the breeze blowing in her hair, the feel of sand giving way beneath her feet. She felt as much a part of nature as it was possible for her to be—a modern woman in a modern age, facing excruciatingly modern problems.

Jasmine was sitting alone on a Saturday afternoon listening to a George Michaels record when the phone rang. Her sister Fay was almost incoherent. "I don't know what to do, I don't know what to do," she kept repeating, sounding hysterical.

"What's the matter? What's happened?"

"Nothing," Fay said, "I just don't know what to do, Jasmine. Can you help me?"

Jasmine took a deep calming breath. "Fay, of course I can help you, but first you have to tell me what's wrong."

"I had—I had an operation. I'm bleeding and I don't know what to do."

Jasmine couldn't help it. The word *operation* conjured up disaster. "What kind of operation?" she asked anxiously.

"A kind of an—an abortion," Fay said.

"An abortion!" Fay hadn't told her anything about being pregnant when she had visited just a few days earlier. But now was not the time to question her. "All right," Jasmine said. "When did you have it?"

"This morning. I went to a clinic this morning and a doctor did it."

"Okay. Where are you now?"

"I'm at a friend's house. I told Mom and Dad that I'd be spending the night with her."

"Is she there now?"

"No. She said she'd be here, but she and her boyfriend had a fight and she left."

"Okay. Is the boyfriend there now?"

"No. He left too."

"So you're all alone?"

"Yes. Jasmine, I don't know what to do."

"Calm down, Fay. Why don't you call Mom and Dad?"

"Oh, God, I can't. I can't do that, I can't do that. Don't

make me do that. I can't do that." Hysteria leaped back into her voice.

"I'm not going to make you do anything, Fay. Tell me about the bleeding."

Fay explained that she was bleeding, and when Jasmine questioned her further, it sounded like a fairly normal flow of blood, something totally predictable after an abortion.

"Have you tried calling the doctor?"

"No. I don't want to call there. He was such an asshole and I'm just so upset about this. I did it, and I don't know if I should have. I wanted to but I didn't want to, and . . . I feel so horrible. I feel so ashamed. I thought it would be okay, you know what I mean? But I feel terrible about it."

Fay sobbed as she talked. Jasmine could hear the panic in her voice. Every word was difficult for her to get out.

Jasmine's heart went out to her frightened sister. She had made such a big decision for one so young. Jasmine wished she were right there with her, so that she could hold her and comfort her. The poor thing must feel so alone and so empty.

Fay continued to try to speak through her sobs, "My girlfriend said she would look after me, but then she left and now I'm here all alone, Jasmine, and I'm scared."

"All right," Jasmine said. "Do you know the address of where you are now?"

"Yes."

"Well, I want you to give me that address and I'm going to get on a plane and come up there. I'll be there in two or three hours. I'll get a cab from the airport and I'll come right to where you are. Okay?"

Fay sobbingly told her sister the address. "I'm sorry, Jasmine, I didn't mean . . . I don't . . . I . . ." She wasn't able to speak any longer through her tears.

"Don't worry, I'll be there soon. You just relax, take it easy. It doesn't sound like you have anything to be really scared about. It doesn't sound like you're going to bleed to death. It's perfectly natural to bleed after an operation like that. Just take it easy and lie down on the couch and take some deep breaths and rest your body. You just need to rest. I'll be there as soon as I can. Okay? Don't go anywhere. All right?"

"All right. Okay."

"Okay, see you soon, hang tight," Jasmine said, and hung up.

She packed quickly, two changes of casual clothing in a small overnight case.

She turned when she was at the door. Allan! She'd almost forgotten. She left a large note for him on the coffee table. For once she put the magazines in a neat pile so that he'd be able to see it. He was supposed to drop by for a short time and he had a key to the apartment, so when she didn't answer the door he'd come straight in.

It was just as well that the next day was Sunday—his family day. He was leaving on the "red eye" for New York somewhere around midnight on Sunday night, and he was going to be there for the entire week on business. So now was as good a time as any for her to handle this situation.

The first plane she could get on left LAX at four o'clock; it would arrive in San Francisco a little after five o'clock. She'd be arriving a little later than she had told Fay. She wished she'd had the foresight to get a phone number so she could call her and tell her. But all she had was the address.

During the flight she was tense and uncommunicative, in spite of the attempts by the man beside her to draw her into conversation. All she could think of was her poor sister, sitting in some apartment, afraid and very alone, feeling that she had done something terribly wrong and that retribution was being visited upon her.

She got a cab immediately at the San Francisco airport, breaking into a line and earning hostile glares from more patient travelers.

The apartment was in the Filmore District, a bad area that she remembered well from her own days of revolt against her parents and their mores.

"Is this it?" she couldn't help asking the cabbie when they pulled up.

"This is the address you gave me, lady," he muttered.

She peered out the window at a dismal three-story building on a dismal street. The streetlights in the immediate vicinity had been knocked out. Piles of rotting refuse blocked the sidewalk.

"All right," she said, and paid the cabbie.

Clutching her overnight bag, she went up the steps and tried to read the names on the mailboxes. There was no name on 2B, so she simply pressed the buzzer. The speaker apparently no longer worked. Jasmine heard a buzz as the door unlocked and she quickly pushed it open.

Inside, bare floors were littered with newspapers and flakes of peeling paint. A strong smell of mold and mildew permeated everything. She took the stairs two at a time and knocked loudly on the door to the apartment.

A bearded young man in his early twenties opened the door, regarding her with bleary eyes. "Yeah?" he asked.

"I'm here to see Fay," Jasmine said, pushing her way past him.

The apartment was a pigsty, sparsely furnished with frayed, tattered, and cracked remnants. The floor was covered with dust.

She saw a half-opened door and a dim light and entered the bedroom. Fay was lying on a mattress on the floor. The light came from a flickering candle. The orange crate on which the candle sat also held a half-eaten can of spaghetti and a banana peel.

"Oh God, Jasmine," Fay said when she saw her. "I'm sorry, I'm sorry."

Jasmine dropped her suitcase and sat on the bed beside Fay, hugging her sister, holding her head fiercely against her chest and murmuring, "It's all right, it's all right, Fay. You're going to be fine, you're going to be fine."

Fay drew back, her eyes bright with tears. "I'm sorry to call you. I didn't know who else to call."

"It's okay," Jasmine said. "I told you to call me any time, remember? And this is a time when you really should have called me."

"What am I going to do?" Fay asked.

"How's the bleeding?"

"I'm still bleeding a bit. The doctor told me I would, but I was just so scared."

"Come on, let's have a look at you. Just let me look at how much blood there is on the pad."

Fay pulled off her jeans and showed Jasmine the pad stuck to the inside of her underpants.

Jasmine saw her embarrassment. "Come on, kid, I bleed too, you know. It's nothing new. You know what the song says: Only women bleed?"

Fay managed a little giggle, and then began to relax.

At that moment, the young man appeared in the doorway. He leaned against it, a beer in his hand.

"Get the fuck out of here," Jasmine said, and then turned her head back to Fay.

He backed out of the doorway.

"All right, you're fine," Jasmine said. "There's nothing wrong with you. But I'm going to get you out of here. I'm going to take you home."

Fay backed away from her, skidding cross the bed. "I can't go home. I just can't. I'm not going to go home, I'm not going home."

Now was not the time to fight. The first thing Jasmine had to do was get her out of there. "I won't take you home then, not now. But we're going to get out of here. We're going to go check into a hotel somewhere. Somewhere that's nice and relaxed. Okay?"

"Will you stay with me?"

"Of course. I'll be with you every minute. I'm going to go call a cab. If you've got any stuff to get together, get it, and I'll be right back."

The man was sitting on the couch when Jasmine walked back to the living room. "Where's the phone?" she snapped.

He jerked his head. It was sitting on the floor.

"Where's her friend Debbie? What's she? Your girlfriend?"

"Man, she split, what a bummer. We had a little discussion and she got uptight and she got out of here."

"Some friend," Jasmine said with disgust. She picked up the phone and called a cab.

She went back into the room. "Time to go," she said. She put her arm around Fay and helped her walk.

"Thanks for your hospitality," she said sarcastically as they left.

They stood on the sidewalk and waited for the cab. Fay was cold. Jasmine could feel the thin body shiver against hers.

Finally, after about five minutes, the lights of a car approached and stopped in front of them.

Jasmine huddled Fay inside. "Miyako Hotel on Post Street," she told the cabbie.

When they arrived at the hotel she made Fay sit in the lobby, partially obscured behind a large potted plant, while she went to the front desk and booked a room. Fay looked a mess and she didn't want to have to answer questions.

"I want a suite," she told the clerk. "Two beds and a sunken Japanese bathtub."

She paid with a credit card, took the key, and then went back to her sister. Fay's face was pale and little beads of sweat were on her forehead. Her mouth was tight and she looked more exhausted than anything else.

"Come on." Jasmine took her arm with one hand and carried her small suitcase with the other. "Let's go get you in shape."

The room was spacious and comfortable, a remarkable contrast to the hovel in which she had just been.

Jasmine threw her suitcase on the bed and then began to unbutton Fay's shirt. The young girl sat unprotesting on the edge of the bed.

"We're going to get you in a nice warm shower," Jasmine said.

She turned the faucets on, adjusted the temperature of the water, completed undressing Fay, and then took her into the bathroom. The hotel supplied them with a fragrant liquid soap and Jasmine handed it to Fay.

"Oh, that looks great," Fay said.

"Okay, you get on in there and just relax, and I'll get

something from room service,'' Jasmine smiled. She saw that the frantic look was disappearing from Fay's face.

Jasmine ordered some food, an assorted tray of snacks, and a double Scotch. And for Fay, she ordered a Seven-Up and some hot tea. ''How long will it be?'' she asked the room service clerk.

''About twenty-five minutes,'' the woman answered.

''Make it ten minutes, and there's a twenty-dollar tip,'' Jasmine urged.

''Yes, ma'am!'' the woman said, and hung up.

She went back in the bathroom. Fay was leaning against the wall of the shower, her eyes closed. ''How are you feeling?'' Jasmine peeked through the shower door.

''Oh . . . better, I guess. It sure is nice.''

''Who is your friend that you were staying with?''

''Debbie? She's a friend from high school. She dropped out last year and went to live with this guy.''

''Not much of a life, from the looks of it,'' Jasmine said.

''I guess not. I thought it was cool. He's such a creep though. They got into this fight, shouting at each other, throwing things. She ran out crying, and then he left. He came back right after I called you.

''And she was supposed to be looking after you?''

''Yeah, I guess. But she wasn't thinking of me.''

Jasmine suppressed some caustic remark about her friend. Fay had to come to her own realizations. She was smart enough to do so, she was sure. All it would take was a little bit of time and a new environment, a chance for Fay to regain her own emotional equilibrium.

''Did the doctor at the clinic give you any pills?'' Jasmine queried Fay.

''Yeah, they're in my purse. He gave me some pain pills and said to take them if I needed to, and he gave me some antibiotics and said to take them.''

''Have you?''

''No . . . I . . .''

''Well, are you in any pain?''

''No, not really. Just feeling a bit tired and sort of beat up.''

"Well, don't take the pain pills if you don't need them, but I'm going to get the antibiotics and I want you to start taking them as soon as the food gets here. You have to have those, just to prevent any infection."

"Okay, I will."

"How did all this happen?" Jasmine asked.

"The usual way."

"The guy . . . did he know you were going to have an abortion?"

"No, he didn't even know I was pregnant," Fay said. 'I thought I would take care of it myself."

"Are you still going with him?"

"No. We just went out a short while. It wouldn't have done any good to tell him about it. He wouldn't have done anything anyway."

"And Mom and Dad? You told them you were spending the night with a friend?"

"Yeah."

"Why didn't you tell me?" Jasmine asked.

Fay's eyes teared up again immediately. "I wanted you to like me. I didn't want to give you problems and I guess I was ashamed. It's a stupid thing to do—to get knocked up. I just didn't want to tell you. I made up my mind to have an abortion and I was just going to do it. I'm sorry. I guess I should have told you."

"That's all right," Jasmine said kindly. "Don't worry about it. You called me and that was the right thing to do."

There was a knock at the door. Room service. Jasmine let the woman in. She rolled a cart into the center of the room and waited expectantly.

"All right," Jasmine said, remembering her promise. It had been exactly ten minutes. She went to her purse, took out a twenty-dollar bill, and handed it to the maid.

The woman thanked Jasmine and left.

She took the Scotch and the Seven-Up into the bathroom and sat on the toilet seat. Fay was standing on the plush bathroom carpet, beads of water dripping off her body. She had a very large soft towel wrapped around her back and shoulders. "Here, Fay, drink this and here's your first pill. I want you to take this now."

"What's this?" Fay asked.

"It's just a Seven-Up."

Fay took a large swallow and downed the antibiotic, then took another long drink. She realized she was very thirsty.

Jasmine laughed. "There's more where that came from. We'll get you in good shape before you know it."

Within the hour, clean and fed and calm, Fay was fast asleep. Jasmine sat in the living room and watched TV, wondering how she was going to handle her parents the next day. She had no inclination to hide what had happened from them, even though she knew there would be a bitter argument with Fay over her decision to tell them. They needed to know they were losing their other daughter and that something would have to be done.

The small house out on the Avenues near Golden Gate Park never changed. Outside, the same neat square of lawn, the same single row of roses, the same frayed armchair on the porch; inside, the sickly green living room furniture Jasmine had grown up with, the same dining room set where she had sat for innumerable meals.

Her mother, still always fretting and bustling around, seemed smaller and more bent, older than when she had last seen her. Her father seemed straighter, stiffer, more taciturn and dull, his flat face and unblinking eyes never changing expression.

Her arrival with Fay had totally flustered her mother, sending her into even more of a tizzy than normally. Her father had remained inscrutable, hiding his bafflement as he always did.

Jasmine's argument with Fay had been bitter when they had first gotten up that morning. But it had been short, and finally Fay had agreed that they should tell their parents. Jasmine's ultimate argument had done the trick. "It's the way that we can get you down to LA more often to visit me. I'll promise them to look after you and be a big sister to you."

Fay was not the only apprehensive one. Jasmine was not entirely together either, she realized as she sat in the living room, waiting for her mother to bring tea. The house filled her with the familiar sense of oppressiveness, that clawing, choking hold that she had known as a child, that had caused her to escape at the first chance.

Her father's lack of responsiveness was just that. It wasn't some Oriental serenity or inscrutability, as some people thought. It was nothing to be admired. He was a bitter man soured by life's unfairnesses. He had worked hard all his life but never found a reason to justify it. The rewards had never been great enough to fulfill him. He despised the people he served, the country in which he lived, the mores of his time, the backwardness of his ancestral country, the politics there and the politics here. Nothing pleased him. Nothing gave him pleasure as far as Jasmine could tell.

When she was a little girl, she remembered him smiling occasionally, but as she grew older, with the years, the smiles grew further and further apart, until finally she became aware at about the age of thirteen that her father no longer smiled. Her mother, if she thought back to the youngest years, had once been pretty, even cheerful. But her father's malaise had been a contagious thing and her mother too had been dragged down by it, consoling herself in life's daily problems, mountains she created out of miniscule molehills. She had become an ineffectual woman.

Her mother brought the tea and they sat facing each other in the small living room.

"Why don't you go to your room?" Jasmine said with a nod to her sister. "I want to talk to Mom and Dad alone." Fay rose obediently and left.

"Fay had an abortion yesterday," Jasmine stated, coming directly to the point.

"What?" her mother shrieked.

"How do you know?" her father asked.

"She called me in Los Angeles," Jasmine said calmly. "Naturally, she was upset, so I came right up last night and spent the night with her."

"At her friend's house?" her mother asked.

"No, I took her to a nice hotel where she could relax and be more comfortable," Jasmine said, leaving out all the particulars of Debbie and her boyfriend. There was enough bad news already.

"How could this happen?" her father asked.

"The way it usually happens," Jasmine said. "A boyfriend, one night, and a mistake. An accident."

"How dare she not tell us!" Her father's smooth face was marred by anger.

"Why should she? Why should she trust you?"

"We are her parents," her mother said.

"Yes, you are, but how long since you've sat down and asked her how she feels about her life, how she feels about her friends, what she's afraid of, what she needs?"

"She needs discipline," her father said, smacking the arm of his chair with a hand.

Jasmine stood and faced them both. "She does *not* need discipline. You gave discipline to me all my life and you've been giving discipline to her all her life, and it hasn't worked. You are just driving her away, just as you drove me away. Do you want to lose both your daughters?"

"I am the elder, I know what I am doing." Her father's voice rose probably exhibiting more passion that he had shown in ten years.

"Age doesn't always bring wisdom," Jasmine countered. "There isn't any love in this house. That's why I left and why you are losing her."

Her mother and father looked at each other then. A furtive glance, as if to admit that they could not argue with that point.

"What are we to do?" her mother asked helplessly.

Her father relapsed into his shield of silence.

"Help her. That's all you can do as parents, help her and protect her as much as you can."

She launched into her plan. Fay needed an elder sister, someone she could identify with and talk with. Frequent trips down to Los Angeles on weekends and holidays to visit her would help Fay build that relationship.

"If things continue the way they have been," Jasmine

said, "she's just going to get into more trouble. Who knows what it will be next? Drugs, drinking, trouble with the police, failure at school. I know one thing, if you don't loosen the reins a little bit, you are going to lose her, she'll run away again. And perhaps this time she won't come to me. Do you know how many teenaged kids there are wandering the streets of America? We can't let that happen to her."

Her father grunted, "You're talking about loosening the reins, I say we need to tighten them. Look what happened when we loosened the reins . . . pregnant at her age . . . an abortion."

"You tighten them any more," Jasmine said, "you'll choke her to death. She won't stand for that, I promise you."

Her father looked with disdain at Jasmine, "You talk about being a sister to her? What sort of a sister are you for her to look up to? You live in Hollywood, you live off men. You're nothing but a whore."

Jasmine paled under the onslaught but stood her ground. "What you think of me is immaterial. The point is I treat her well and she looks up to me. I also will not let her get into trouble. My life is not that bad. I don't know what you think it is, but I have the respect of my peers."

Her father just glared back at her.

Jasmine bullied and browbeat them for another half hour, finally gaining an agreement that Fay could visit her more often, and a promise that they wouldn't punish her.

When she finally got as much as she knew she could get, Jasmine excused herself and went to the bathroom. She felt drained, nauseous. She looked at herself in the bathroom mirror. Her face was pale; she felt like throwing up. She was going to throw up. She bent down to the toilet, felt her stomach heave, and vomited.

It was the pressure of handling Fay, the stress of facing her parents again, she told herself. But even as she thought it, she knew it was a lie. Some deeper, more intuitive female knowledge contradicted her.

A voice came from within her body and its message was clear.

"God damnit," she said aloud while she stared into the mirror. 'It couldn't be. God damnit," she repeated, "I think I'm pregnant."

CHAPTER FOURTEEN

When she returned to Los Angeles from Mazatlán late on Sunday night, Kate called Madge at home and asked if she could have Monday and Tuesday off to attend to some "personal business."

"Of course," Madge said, "take as long as you need. Is everything all right? Did you have a good time in Mexico?"

"Yeah, fine," Kate said. "Just some things I have to take care of, and of course I don't expect to get paid for my time off."

"Well, that's okay, but I want all the scoop on Mazatlán when I see you," Madge said, laughing conspiratorially, and hung up.

On Monday morning Kate went to the UCLA art research library in Westwood and began her investigations, delving into books dealing with seventeenth century art and, in particular, the works of Rembrandt. That night, her apartment littered with the notes she had taken, she began to draw charts and timetables, estimating costs and other facts that she needed to master to develop her plan.

She went to bed late, thoroughly exhausted, but she was unable to fall asleep. She was too excited and nervous and stared up at the dark ceiling for hours.

It would be expensive and dangerous, but it would wipe the smile off Jason Thomas's face forever.

* * *

Jasmine returned from San Francisco late on Sunday night. Hopefully she had handled the family crisis, not with a permanent solution, she knew, just enough to patch it over until the next one erupted. It was all she could do.

On Monday morning, at nine o'clock, she called her gynecologist and made an appointment for that afternoon.

She had felt nauseous again that morning but had not thrown up this time. Perhaps, she thought hopefully, it was just some kind of stomach flu. But then she remembered her body's message. Well, she'd find out soon enough.

Orson Taft's office was in Beverly Hills, on the third floor of a medical building. He had been her gynecologist for a year and she liked him. He was young, intense, bearded, hurried, but never harried, and never too rushed to treat her cordially. Unlike other doctors she'd had experiences with, he always treated her as a human being, not as some dumb object.

He greeted her and rose from behind the desk to shake her hand. "So you think you're pregnant?" he asked.

"I'm suspicious," she answered. "My period's a little late; and I've been getting morning sickness.

"Well, we'll know in a few minutes. Come with me." He led the way into the examining room.

Jasmine put on the silly little cotton dress with the open back and got onto the table. She placed her feet into the dreaded stirrups and felt him gently insert his fingers into her vagina.

He talked softly and quietly to her as he felt the size of her uterus. He told her that indeed it felt a little swollen, a little larger than normal. He pushed down on her belly with one hand, as the finger of his other hand felt the inside of her vagina. He merely grunted gently and raised his eyebrows.

She knew then what she didn't want to know.

They went back into his office. He sat behind his desk, leaned back, crossed his legs, folded his hands, and placed them on his knees. "Well, you certainly are pregnant."

"I am, huh?"

"Yep. Just."

"When would the baby be due?" Her palms began to sweat and she felt a butterfly begin gently to flap its wings in her stomach.

"Well, judging from the date of your last period and the slight swelling of the uterus, it looks like you're about three weeks, so figure a little more than eight months from now."

"And what about an abortion?"

"What about it?" Dr. Taft leaned forward with his elbows resting on his desk.

"What's the procedure? Can you do it here in the office, and how late can I have it? In other words, when do I have to make up my mind?" Jasmine was doing her best to stay calm.

"Yes, I can do it. But the sooner the better. The most you can possibly wait is when the pregnancy is at twelve weeks. The longer you wait the harder it is. You're undecided about what to do?"

"Yes," she said, looking straight into his eyes.

"I'm going to ask you some personal questions." He looked at her file. "I see your bills are paid by Mr. Allan Silver. I presume he's the father. The question is, is he willing to *be* the father of this child?"

"He's married to someone else. I don't know the answer to that question. But please don't send him the bill yet. I need to talk to him first."

"All right," he said, making a notation in the file. "I want you to call me if you have any questions, if you need to talk anything over, you need any kind of help. Understood?" Dr. Taft got up from behind his desk and walked around it to Jasmine's side as he spoke. He put his arm around her shoulders. He had soft warm hands, gentle yet strong.

"Thank you," Jasmine said. When she felt his hand on her shoulder she suddenly felt like crying. She'd expected that the test would be positive, and now it was a reality. Whatever decision she made would be irrevocable, would change her life.

During the drive back to her apartment Jasmine tried to analytically examine her options. She could get an abortion.

She could tell Allan that she was pregnant and get his blessing and support. Or she could tell Allan she was pregnant and not get his support and still have the baby.

She remembered her sister's sense of loss after her abortion, just two days earlier. That vacant feeling it had left her with, that sense of betrayal. She'd had friends who'd been through it, and Jasmine knew it was a common phenomenon and that indeed, as all things did, it passed. But she didn't want to feel that way.

Allan was in New York and she wouldn't be able to talk to him until Friday. He might call before then, but it wasn't something she wanted to discuss over the telephone. She needed to talk to someone and it wasn't just her doctor. She really needed a friend.

She thought of Kate. They hardly knew each other, yet she felt a connection, a deep sense of affinity with her. Perhaps she'd call her. Perhaps Kate would provide a sympathetic ear. In the meantime she would try and examine her own confused feelings.

Sharon Thomas had a new chauffeur. She had tried to hire Jim Morris, the parking lot attendant she had taken to the Beverly Wilshire, but as a student he could only work part-time, and no matter how desirable his body, she did need a full-time driver. Regretfully, she had given up the idea of hiring him, although she did have his telephone number and intended to meet him again sometime to repeat the delicious experience of the week before last.

The new chauffeur's name was Danny. He was of medium height, well-built, with a stocky torso and strong arms. His hair was dark, his eyes almost black, and he wore a gold crucifix on a chain around his neck. He was of Italian ancestry, he told her.

He was clerking at a small Beverly Hills gourmet grocery store when she met him. After ringing up her purchases, he had carried them out to her car. "Let me guess," she said as he unloaded the groceries into the trunk, "you're working here but you actually want to be an actor."

"Yeah, well, why should I be any different?" he muttered.

He had a great ass, she noted as he bent forward with the last bag. She put her hand on it, and he almost jumped. "Why don't I pick you up after work?" she asked with a sweet smile.

And so she had. She went back with him to his small apartment on Santa Monica Boulevard. A dingy cheap place, with thin walls and almost no furnishings, where she tested him out. He was energetic and competent. And still naked, lying on the bed recovering her breath, she offered him a new job.

He took it.

In the four days he had been working for her, he had turned out very well. Still enthusiastic and still competent. Now it was Tuesday, Jason had announced that he would not be returning home, and she was alone with Danny. They had made late-afternoon love in her bedroom. It had been quite a workout, and they were both bathed in sweat.

"Do you want to do a line?" he asked.

"A line?" she asked.

"Yeah, some coke."

Unlike alcohol, drugs had not been a mainstay of her life. She had tried marijuana a couple of times, but it had simply made her sleepy. Instead, she usually drank copious amounts of alcohol. Cocaine had always intrigued her but the opportunity had never presented itself. Jason despised drugs, and when drugs were present at events they attended, he always frowned on it. She had never felt comfortable enough to indulge the desire to satisfy her curiosity.

"What'll it do?" she asked.

"It'll get you high," he said, "What more do you want to know?"

"Okay, I'll try it."

He got out of bed and walked to where his pants lay on the floor near the doorway. Taking a white envelope from his hip pocket, he brought it over to the bedside table.

"Here. This is quality stuff."

He tapped the envelope until there were two small piles

of the glistening white crystals on the glass-topped table. Then he removed a straw and a blade from the envelope. He used the blade to arrange the piles into two long lines, then handed her the straw.

"You first," she said.

"Like this," he demonstrated. Holding the tip of the straw between thumb and forefinger, he lifted it toward his nose, put it against the line, sniffed up half of it, moved the straw to his other nostril, and did the same to the other half.

"Whoooo!" he exclaimed, and handed her the straw.

She did the same. At first there was just a tickling in her nose and an urge to sneeze.

"Don't sneeze," he said, putting his hand out and holding her nose in a pincher grip.

And then she felt the energy, a rush of it starting in her face and moving to her brain and then engulfing her entire body, an electrocution of force. She felt powerful, satisfied. For the first time since childhood, she felt she could do anything. "My God," she hissed.

"Cool, isn't it?" he asked with a satisfied smile.

She looked at his bright eyes and knew that hers were the same. "*Cool* is too . . . let's see . . . cool a word," she said. "This is explosive. This is fantastic. This is like nothing I've ever felt."

She looked at the black hair on his chest and touched it. It felt different somehow, more alive, more "present." She grabbed a clump of it in her hand and pulled him toward her, ignoring his yelp of protestation.

"Come on," she said, "I want to do it again. I want to feel what it's like now."

It felt like nothing on earth.

David sat in the living room with his wife, Pat, on Tuesday evening. She had her legs curled up underneath her while she read a book. He was bored and flicked the television channels with the remote. It was his own fault, he thought. He'd felt guilty about leaving Pat for the weekend. Although he was dying to see Kate again, he had decided to come home for a few nights in a row. As he planned to take Kate to dinner with Jason on Wednesday, it wasn't too great a sacrifice.

To make matters worse, it was barely six o'clock and Pat had already had three drinks that he knew of.

Pat looked up from her book, as if sensing his thoughts. "I had a letter from Pamela today," she said. "Did you see it?"

"No, where?"

"I left it on the table in the study."

"What did she want?"

"Money. She said her allowance isn't enough."

"Jesus, she already gets more than most people earn in a month," David complained.

"I know."

"What's she spending it on?"

"That I don't know." Pat closed her book and put it on the table beside her. "What are we going to do about her, David?"

David shrugged. "The same as we've always done. Nothing. What can we do? She's totally uncontrollable. She's undisciplined. She has no direction."

Pat's reply was unnaturally caustic. "And you, David, you are disciplined, I suppose?"

David bristled. "Yes. I believe I am. Why would you think otherwise? I conduct my life in a disciplined manner, my business, my home."

Pat sighed and picked up her drink from the table beside her. She took a long swallow before speaking. "Where do you think we went wrong, David?"

"What do you mean, went wrong?" David blustered.

Pat smiled sadly. "We have a daughter who has lost all direction. No, let me rephrase that—has never found her direction. We have a marriage that has never found a direction. I have a husband who doesn't speak with me, who merely tolerates my presence. You have a wife who drinks too much and a mistress who—who knows?"

"A mistress? What are you talking about? What is this? Have you been drinking more than usual?"

"Perhaps we should face our situation. Perhaps it would be better for all of us."

David put the remote control down and swiveled the chair to face her. "We have an exemplary life," he said. "We have everything we need. I have a good position. You are well respected in the community. All right, so we have a daughter who hasn't turned out quite the way we wanted her to turn out. It's not the end of the world. Our lives are good, fulfilling."

"It's useless," Pat said. "I can't talk to you."

"I don't know what you are talking about," David said. "I don't know what more I can do for you. I've given you everything. I've worked hard all my life to do that."

"What about your mistress, David? Is she young? Is she pretty? I'm sure she's younger and prettier than I am. I've never been pretty, have I? You never married me for my looks. What did you marry me for? My mind? I doubt it. My money? I don't know. I don't know why you married me. I don't know why we've been married for twenty years. Perhaps it's time to simply face the facts and go our separate ways."

"I won't hear of this!" David angrily got to his feet. "You've had too much to drink, and it's been a problem with you for a long time, and I think it's time to get some help."

Pat began to laugh, a low mocking chuckle. "Help for me, David? I'm the problem, aren't I? I'm always the problem. There's nothing wrong with you. I am the problem, your daughter is the problem, you are never the problem, are you?"

"I'm going to my study to get some work done," David said stiffly. "I suggest you stop drinking and get some food in your stomach."

Pat picked up her glass and regarded him over the rim. "What's the point? All food will do is sober me up, and then what will I do?"

David didn't hear her. He'd already left the room.

For a second it looked as if her face would crumple. But she forced herself to smile and drank her drink.

* * *

"Why don't you stop worrying about it now and just talk to Allan about it when he comes back?" Kate suggested. "I'm sure the two of you can work it out."

They were sitting in Kate's apartment, sipping a glass of Pinot Noir. It was late in the day. Through the open living room window, they could see a deepening dusk and hear the cries of busy homeward birds.

Jasmine had called earlier and asked if they could get together for a drink. Kate, who had spent most of the day doing further research at the L.A. County Museum of Art library, felt the need for companionship. She invited her to the apartment, saying, "We can have a glass of wine there and munch on something. I'll throw together some pasta." Jasmine had agreed gratefully.

Kate had accepted the news of Jasmine's pregnancy without any displays of dramatics. Apparently what Jasmine needed now was a calm head.

"No," Jasmine said of her suggestion. "I don't think that's the right way to do this. I don't want to go whining to Allan and telling him I'm pregnant and what do I do now. I want to go to him with a solution. I want to be able to say, 'Allan, I'm pregnant, and this is what I want to do about it. Will you help me?' I may feel unsure right now, but I'm not some helpless woman who has to cry on her man's shoulders and beg for help."

"I know you're not," Kate said.

Jasmine lifted her chin defiantly, "Well, in a way I am. I have been. I've depended totally on him up until now. But I don't want to do that anymore, not in this case This is something more important."

They both wore jeans and T-shirts, no shoes. Kate sat on the couch with her legs stretched out on it, Jasmine in the armchair, her legs crossed underneath her.

"What do you really want to do?" Kate asked. "I mean, what would make you happiest?"

Reflexively, Jasmine's hand went to her stomach and patted it. She couldn't help smiling when she said, "You know I think I'd really like to have this baby."

"And what do you think Allan would want you to do?"

Her hand went up to her hair, smoothing it back. "I think Allan will want me to have an abortion. He doesn't like . . . I don't know . . . I think he'd see this as just another complication in his life. He has a family and he loves that family. I think he loves me in his way, but not in that way."

"And you really think you want to have a child? A single woman in Hollywood?" Kate mused.

"I'm surprising myself," Jasmine said with a laugh. "I never knew I'd feel this way. But there's a life here," she said as she patted her stomach again, "and it's a feeling like . . . I don't know how to describe it. It's like nothing I've ever felt before. There is something so beautiful about it. It's as if my whole life has led to this moment. Now it's here and I don't know what to do."

"I think you do," Kate said. "I think you've already decided that you're going to have the child. And I think that's wonderful. All you have to do is work out the details."

"I guess it's the details that scare me," Jasmine said. "In truth, I really don't know how Allan's going to react. What if he just cuts me loose? What if he won't support me? What if he demands an abortion? I just don't know."

"You'll handle it," Kate asserted, "when the time comes. When these problems present themselves, one by one you'll handle them. You're not a dummy. You're a talented, able woman, and quite capable of handling a situation like this."

"Your praise is very generous," Jasmine sighed.

"It's true. You are those things. You've just never had to prove it to yourself before."

"How do you know me so well? We've only met twice. You seem to know me better than I know myself. You've certainly got more confidence in me than I do."

Kate grinned. "I'm not that smart, it's just that it's there to be seen. I'm observant enough to see it."

Jasmine shook her head disbelievingly. "I think you are that smart." She sipped at her wine, and then her hand went back to her stomach. "I've never admitted it to myself until the last day or so, you know, but I've always wanted to have a family. It's always something I thought would happen later, though. After I'd established my career, after I have enough money, after I'd meet a man who'd marry me. Suddenly it's here, and the timing seems all wrong."

"Perhaps not," Kate said, rising from the couch. "Perhaps the timing is perfect. Perhaps this is what you need now, and it's totally right." She moved toward the kitchen. "Come on, let's get some food together. As an expectant mother, you're going to have to watch your diet," Kate said with a giggle.

"Oh God," Jasmine groaned, getting up. "I never thought I'd hear those words. Is that what I'm going to be called from now on? An expectant mother?"

"Or a pregnant lady," Kate said over her shoulder. She grinned, "At least everybody will know you're not a virgin anymore."

Jasmine's mood grew lighter. She kidded around while Kate cooked, made jokes about Allan and her own predicament, attacked her food with gusto, and quizzed Kate shamelessly about her trip to Mexico.

"How was Mazatlán, anyway? Did you and David have a good time?"

"It was nice to get away," Kate said circumspectly.

Jasmine wasn't fazed. "Is he any good in the sack? I can't even imagine him taking his clothes off."

"Oh, he takes them off."

"You never know with guys," Jasmine said, shaking her head. "Sometimes the most conservative-looking ones are the wildest."

Halfway through the meal she suddenly looked up at Kate and said, "Thank you for being my friend. I guess I really needed one."

"I'm here if you need me. Don't forget that."

"That's exactly what I told my sister," Jasmine said. "I guess we all need someone, don't we?"

Except me, Kate thought. I'm out on a limb, acting totally on my own. But for this plan to work, I'm going to need some help sooner or later. I hope I can find it.

"I guess we all do," she said.

CHAPTER FIFTEEN

"I've been robbed," Elsa said.

Page was sitting in her office. It was noon on Wednesday, and the previous four hours had been hectic. She spoke into the telephone, "What do you mean, Elsa? When? What happened?"

"This morning. Two men came into my apartment. They robbed me."

"My God! Are you all right?" Page asked.

"They took my television set." Elsa started to cry.

"I'll be right over." Page looked at her watch. She had never heard Elsa cry before. "I assume you've told the police?"

"They're here now."

"Okay, I'll be over real soon." She hung up, grabbed her bag, told her secretary she'd be out for an hour or two, and took the elevator down to the garage.

As she drove up to Elsa's building, she saw two men get into a police car and drive away. She went upstairs quickly and Maria opened the door. "Are you all right, Maria?"

"God be thanked," Maria said.

Elsa was lying on her couch. "Oh my dear, I'm glad you've come," she said when she saw Page.

"Are you okay?" Page asked, walking over to her and looking down.

"I have been violated," Elsa said dramatically.

"Did they hurt you?"

"They took my television set, my VCR, my other television set in the bedroom, my radio."

"But did they hurt you?"

"No, no. They didn't. They violated my privacy. They violated my home."

"What happened?"

"The bell rang. Maria opened the door. Two men came in. They had flowers. Cheap daisies. A flower delivery, they said. They also had guns. They locked us in the bathroom and then stripped the apartment."

"Your jewelry?"

Elsa's eyes grew shrewd. "They didn't find my floor safe. They got a few trinkets from my bedroom, but nothing of consequence."

"Everything is insured, isn't it?" Page asked.

"Yes. I will not lose on it," Elsa said. "But it was so frightening. They waved these guns at us, started to shout, pushed us into the bathroom."

"You're lucky you weren't hurt. All you lost were a few things."

"My television," Elsa wailed. "What can I do without my television?"

Page couldn't help smiling. Fat and ugly Elsa, tear-streaked makeup, whimpering about her stolen television set. It was quite a picture. And yet, it occurred to Page that the relationship they had was more like mother/daughter than the one she had with her own mother. They helped each other, confided in each other, and could even chuckle at each other. They were friends, something she had never experienced with her own mother.

"You'll buy another one, Elsa. God knows you can afford it. Anyway, as you said, the insurance will cover it."

"Would you get an old woman a little schnapps in a glass?" Elsa wheedled.

"Of course," Page said, and went to the liquor cabinet. She brought the drink back to Elsa and handed it to her. It disappeared in one gulp.

"And another, please."

As Page walked back with a fresh glass, Elsa said, "Will you stay with me, my dear? I do not wish to be alone." She patted the overstuffed pink sofa.

"I have to go back to the office and I'm supposed to go out with Jason this evening," Page said. "Perhaps I could drop by before we go out and just see that you're okay."

"Could you come by after you go out? Could you perhaps spend the night here? I—I don't like the idea of being alone tonight."

Page thought for a moment. She noticed Maria in the corner of the dining room, still wide-eyed with fear, nervously pretending to be busy. She was wiping the already-shining walnut dining table. "That may be difficult, Elsa. Could you get Maria to spend the night?"

"Maria is useless." Elsa clicked her tongue derisively. "All she does is pray. But I suppose it will have to do if it has to."

"Look, let me call you or stop by. I'll let you know. Let me see how it goes. Perhaps I can work something out."

"All right, I appreciate it."

Page got to her feet, "I've got to get back to the office now. I'll call you, and I'll either look in on you after work, later in the afternoon, or later tonight. Okay? In the meantime, you can get on the telephone and order yourself a new television set. If you hurry, you can have it delivered in the next few hours."

"You think I can get it that fast?" Elsa cheered up immediately. "I'll get started on it right now. Perhaps all isn't lost."

"Well, Elsa, you wanted some adventure in your life," Page said, gathering her bag.

"Yes, but not this kind. This kind I can live without."

"Well, apparently we can't be all that selective when we make wishes," Page said. "I'll talk to you later, okay?"

There was a pile of telephone messages on her desk when she returned to the office. She pushed them aside unread. She would have liked to have helped Elsa by spending the night, but it would probably be impossible. Jason wouldn't enjoy the idea of being stood up. After going out, he would expect to come back to the apartment with her for a while, perhaps even spend the night. He didn't like his plans to go awry.

Page's secretary came into the office. "Did you see the message from the hospital?"

"What message?"

"A doctor. He's called you two or three times, something about your mother."

Page grabbed the messages again. Sure enough, there were three from Dr. Perkins asking her to call at once. All three messages were marked urgent. She called his office and the receptionist put her through immediately. "Dr. Perkins, this is Page Peters. What's happened?"

He sounded more assured on the telephone than in person. His voice was smooth and calming. "Your mother started bleeding again, Miss Peters. She should be in the operating room about now. I suggest you go to the hospital. I was just about to leave myself. I can meet you there and we can find out how the operation went."

"Is it dangerous?" she asked. "Is she in trouble?"

"Any operation for a person of her age and constitution is not safe," he replied. "However, she's in the hands of a very skilled surgeon. And I'm sure she'll be fine."

"I'm leaving now. I'll see you there."

She hung up and turned to her secretary. "Cancel my appointments for this afternoon and reschedule them whenever it's possible. And also would you—" She stopped. She'd have to call Jason herself from the hospital. There would be time to catch him at his office. "I won't be back today," she said, and swept out of the room.

Remembering something then, she spun around and retraced her steps to her desk. Yanking the top drawer open, she grabbed a small bag marked "Neiman-Marcus."

It took her fifteen minutes to get to the hospital, five to find a parking spot. She went directly to the reception area and asked the woman to page Dr. Perkins.

While she waited, she got a cup of coffee from a machine and sat on a plastic-covered chair. A couple near her held hands, speechless in the face of whatever it was they were there for. Close to them was an old woman who leaned forward on a round walking stick, brazenly staring at everyone who passed.

A young black man, in his late twenties perhaps, paced the floor of the waiting area, his hands gripped behind his back, his mouth moving every now and then as if muttering to himself.

Page hated hospitals. They were places where all fear and dashed hopes, disappointments, and resentments collided. They were monuments to mortality, a mockery of all the striving people did in their short lives. They were, to put it dramatically, the last stoplight on the highway to heaven or hell.

"Shit!" she said aloud, and went back to the desk. "Dr. Perkins, I asked you to page him," she told the lady behind the counter.

"I did, ma'am," the woman said. She was in her fifties, gray-haired, dull-eyed. "He's probably not here. Were you expecting him?"

"Yes, he was supposed to meet me here."

"Well, ma'am, he should be along shortly. Why don't you just wait a few minutes more."

Page turned to go back to the waiting area, and then saw Perkins coming toward her. He wore a business suit and his usual nervous expression.

"The operation's over," he said. "Why don't you come with me and we'll go talk to the surgeon. He's expecting us." He led the way through doors marked "No Admittance" and down a corridor past some rooms to an office marked "Dr. Gunther Schaab." He knocked and entered at the muffled "Come in."

Dr. Schaab was a middle-aged man with graying hair and a lined face. He stood up, shook Perkins's hand, and then Page's at the introduction.

"How is my mother?" Page asked, sitting at the desk.

"It's too early to say," Dr. Schaab said. "She's an old lady and these operations can be draining. We're going to have to watch her closely.

"What's her condition?" Page asked.

"Critical," Dr. Schaab said, and sat behind his desk. "I'm not going to mince words. Your mother may die, there's a fifty-fifty chance. I think now it depends upon her will to live."

Oh God, Page said to herself, what will? "Can I do anything?"

The surgeon shook his head. "Nothing. She is in intensive care and you can look in on her if you like, but that's all. Believe me, we're going to be watching her very closely."

"Dr. Schaab is one of the best surgeons in the city," Dr. Perkins interceded. "I'm sure he's done all he can and will continue to do so. Your mother is in very good hands."

"I'm sure," Page said. She stood. "Thank you, doctor. How do I get to intensive care?"

"I'll take you there," Dr. Perkins said. "I'd like to look in on her myself."

More corridors and swinging doors. Soft yet hurried footsteps, rumbling trollies, speeding gurneys, intent faces, and then they were there: Intensive Care.

"This is the ICU," Dr. Perkins said. It was unnecessary. They were both facing the sign. He pushed open the door and entered.

Page was surprised. It was a busy room, filled with scurrying bodies. The nurse's station near the door looked like the deck of the Spaceship Enterprise: glowing monitors, keyboards, tapes of printed paper spewing out.

Dr. Perkins spoke quietly to one of the nurses, and then jerked his head. "She's over there," he said to Page, indicating a bed near the corner.

Like the entire room, it was brightly lit. Somehow Page had expected subdued and muted lighting, and quiet, a more sedate atmosphere.

Clara was lying in the bed, a sheet pulled up to her chin, her thin arms on top of it, pierced by needles through which the IV dripped nourishing fluid. Her face was so pale. Paler than Page had ever seen a face, as if it had been drained of blood.

"Oh God," she choked. This was the woman who bore

her, her mother. The woman she had never particularly liked but who she now knew she loved on some level that defied understanding. It was something rooted deeply in her, something primeval, something she had no control over. She wanted to lift that silent head and press it against her bosom, but of course she couldn't. She couldn't do anything.

"What do you think, doctor?" she found herself saying.

Perkins's shoulders twitched. It might have been a shrug. "It's in God's hands."

Page turned angrily to him. "God never gave a damn about anyone, Dr. Perkins. If that's the best you have to offer . . ."

He met her glance and seemed to grow defiantly taller. "I can offer nothing," he said, his voice firm. "Medicine is limited in what it can do. So much depends upon the will of the individual, the health of the individual. These are things that medicine can't know. Believe me, we've done what we could. It's now up to her. She's going to do what she wants to do."

Page stared back into his eyes, and at that moment she knew her mother would die.

Jasmine's agent, Ted Shields, called her on Wednesday afternoon at three o'clock.

"Babe," he said, 'you wanna work?"

"What's the job, Ted?" she asked.

"It's a feature. It's being produced by Billings and Dorp. But the deal is that they had an actress for this part who dropped out and they need somebody fast and you need to get over there by four o'clock. Can you do that?"

"When do they start shooting?" How long would it be before her pregnancy began to show? she wondered. That was one question she'd forgotten to ask her doctor.

"Two weeks. They're really in a crunch. I think you can land this."

Two weeks. She was sure nothing would show. Two weeks, and then perhaps a twenty-eight-day shooting schedule. It should allow her plenty of time. Besides, an interview now would give her something to do instead of worrying about Allan's reaction to her news.

"I'll be there," she said. "Give me the information."

She was sure there'd be a confrontation with Allan, but she'd made her decision: She wanted to have this baby, and she'd spent hours rehearsing in her mind what she'd say to Allan.

She knew he'd be angry—angry at her carelessness, angry at her decision to have the child, angry at the inconvenience of losing her undivided attention. But she was quite willing to face his anger for the sake of this baby. Sooner or later, he'd see things her way, as he usually did.

In less than an hour she drove up to the office building on the corner of Sunset and Doheny. The casting director's office was on the sixth floor. She took the elevator up, gave her name to the receptionist, and sat in the waiting room.

After about five minutes, a thin young woman appeared, gave her a quick, nervous smile, and took her into the office.

There were two men there to interview her. One of them was enormously fat, a globe of a man with a balding head and a face that was wreathed in insincere smiles. The other was about ten years younger, in his late twenties, wiry and intense. He cracked his knuckles nervously while the other man spoke.

"Ah, Jasmine," he said, lumbering from behind his desk, his hand outstretched. "I'm Frederick Dupar, and this here is Cort. I'm so pleased to meet you. I'm an admirer of your work."

"Thank you," she said, taking his hand. His palm was wet.

"Please, please, sit down," he said, pointing to a couch. She sat and he went back behind his desk. "I suppose you've been told, we need an Oriental woman. Actually, she's supposed to be Japanese, but nobody will be able to tell the difference." He held up a cautious hand, "It's only a small part, you understand. You appear in three scenes and speak about twenty-five lines. I hope it's not beneath you."

"No, it's fine," she said. "Do you want me to read the part?"

He waved his hand dismissively. "I've seen your work. I know you can handle the part. Actually, you are kind of a girl friend of a gangster type. It's more the physical appearance that counts, to be frank, than the acting ability."

"I see," Jasmine said.

"Beautiful, isn't she?" Frederick said to his partner.

"Yes, I think she'll do just fine," Cort said. "If you'll excuse me, I have to make a phone call." He got up and left the room.

The fat man coughed. "As I said, it's more of a physical part. . . . Ah, I wonder if I could impose upon you to stand and walk around, so I could have a look at you."

"Of course." She was used to this phenomenon of being treated like a cow. She stood, walked to the center of the room, and twirled as well as any model. Then she turned back to face him.

He frowned. "The girl is a dancer. Do you dance?"

"Yes, I can."

He gestured again with his omnipresent hand. "Could I ask you to lift your skirt? She must have excellent legs."

"I have excellent legs," Jasmine countered.

"Yes, I'm sure you do." He laughed. "From what I can see you do, but I'd like to see a little more if you don't mind."

Jasmine lifted her skirt to mid-thigh.

"A little higher, please," he said with a wave.

She lifted it another inch.

"Now please turn around."

She turned, her back to him. There was a long silence, then she swung her head and said, "Is that enough?"

He was bent forward, leaning his chest against the desk. His hands had disappeared from view. But the motions of his shoulders gave her a hint of what he was doing.

She dropped her skirt, as if it had burnt her fingers, and stomped toward his desk. Sweeping her arm, she knocked paper tray, pen holder, coffee cup, and ashtray toward him in one forceful motion. He jerked back.

"You fucking asshole creep!" She turned and stalked out of the room.

I've got to change my life, she said to herself as she headed toward the elevator. I've just got to change my life.

Page sat beside her mother for about an hour, holding the small jewelry box from Neiman-Marcus in her hands. It contained a beautiful little broach, something her mother could treasure, even though she probably wouldn't acknowledge or remember where it came from.

But Clara didn't regain consciousness and there was nothing Page could do, so she left the box on the table by the bed and went back to the main reception area. She hadn't eaten since breakfast, she realized, so she got a candy bar out of the machine.

The room had filled up with an entirely new crew of waiting relatives and friends. The only one still there from before was the young black man, who still walked up and down, his hands clasped behind his back.

A new young couple had appeared and they, too, held each others' hands as they sat staring miserably at the floor. It was as if central casting kept on supplying the reception area with young couples.

Surprisingly, there was also a different old woman there. This one did not have a walking stick, but she sat knitting a sweater, muttering to herself as she counted the stitches.

A businessman in a suit tapped his feet constantly on the floor, looking angry, as if his being here was part of someone else's betrayal.

It was then that she remembered Jason. She was supposed to meet him at her apartment. She had intended to call him.

She went to the bank of pay phones nearby and dialed his office number. The secretary put him through.

"Hello."

"Jason, it's Page. How are you?"

"Fine, thank you. And you?"

"I'm okay, but I'm afraid I'm going to have to beg off our date tonight."

His relaxed tone changed. "Tonight? Such short notice? Why?"

"I have a personal emergency . . . ah . . . situation that I have to handle," she said. "I really wouldn't do this unless I had to. I hope you understand that."

"What kind of personal emergency?"

She had never told Jason about her mother's presence here, or even of her existence. She didn't have anything to hide, but she had always felt it best to keep her private life private and her relationship with him on another level. Now she was in a spot.

"Someone is in the hospital. I'm here now, and I have to stay here. It's a critical situation," she said.

"Anyone I know?" he asked.

"No," she said, volunteering no further information. It was the wrong move. He grew curious, wondering, no doubt, how he did not know a person so important to her.

"Who is it?" he demanded.

"It's my mother. She has diverticulitis."

"The mother you keep in the retirement home in Westwood?" he said. "Is she seriously ill?"

"Yes, as I said she's in critical condition."

"Well, I'm sorry to hear that. Can't you just leave for a few hours so that we can show up together? I told you days ago that we had a date on Wednesday night with David."

"I'm sorry for the inconvenience, but I don't think so."

"Well, why don't you call me in an hour and let me know what the situation is then? Perhaps you'll be able to slip away for a while."

Page repressed a sigh. He wasn't giving her much. "All right, Jason, I'll call you then."

"Good," he said. "I hope she's okay. I'll talk to you in an hour."

She listened thoughtfully to the click of the receiver, then after a second replaced her own. She stood there for a moment, his words sinking in. He knew of her mother! He knew she lived in a home in Westwood! How? She had never told him. It could only mean one thing. On checking up on her shopping habits, the bastard had had her followed. It was a disquieting feeling. One that made her feel both claustrophobic and naked.

"Damn!" she said. She looked at the time. She should go back and check on her mother. She began the long walk back to the intensive care unit.

The nurses had told her she could come and go, so she opened the doors and entered, heading directly for her mother's bed, her thoughts still on her conversation with Jason. She looked up when she was about fifteen feet from the bed and suddenly became aware that at least four people were clustered around her mother. And then she saw her mother's body jerk as if hit.

Page's hand went up to her mouth. They had electric plates on her mother's chest and were trying to bring her heart back to life. An oxygen mask covered her mouth.

One of the nurses saw her and disengaged herself from the group. She came hurrying over, took Page's arms, and turned her around. "You must leave now." She hustled Page toward the door.

"What's happening?" Page asked. "What's happening?"

"We're trying to resuscitate her," the nurse said. "Please just wait outside. There's a small waiting room across the hall."

"Oh, my God! Is there anything I can do?"

"Just leave, and let us get on with our job here," the nurse snapped, pushing Page through the door.

She stood forlornly in the corridor, lost and unexpectedly afraid. Of what she did not know.

After a couple of minutes, she saw the waiting room and entered it. She sat in one of the chairs and waited.

She found herself wondering when they had lost each other. It had probably been in 1982, when she had gone to Houston with her businessman. Her mother had never forgiven her for leaving her in New York. Maybe it had been a year later when Clara found out that Page was the man's mistress.

There had been an ugly scene during a visit back to New York, when Page had let slip that the man supported her.

"How could you? You're nothing but a glorified whore,"

Clara had said, her entire body trembling with anger. "I've had hard times, but I've never lowered myself to that."

"And that's only because I've looked after you through all these hard times," Page had replied, equally furious.

Their shouting had led nowhere. From then on, they had been polite to each other, but Clara had been distant. It was as if someone else had replaced her daughter Page, some stranger. Finally, her distance grew to such an extent that it led to complete non-recognition.

After ten minutes, Dr. Schaab entered. Page stood up. "Is she dead?"

He nodded gravely. "I'm sorry," he said. "I told you it was up to her. She decided to give up, I think."

"She gave up a long time ago."

"I'm sorry there was nothing more we could do. The blood pressure started dropping, she started hemorrhaging again, and then she went. We tried to bring her back, but—"

"But she didn't want to come back."

"Is there anything I can do for you?" he asked. It was a genuine kindness. She could tell by his expression.

She touched his arm lightly. "Thank you, doctor. No, there's nothing you can do for me now. But thank you for doing your best for her. You're right, though, it was her decision. I'm sure you did all you could."

He nodded.

"Are there arrangements to be taken care of?"

"Yes," he said. "Of course. But they need not be done immediately. Why don't you return tomorrow? You'll have to make funeral arrangements, of course."

"Can I see her?" Page asked.

"Yes, she's still in there. Come with me."

He led her back into the ICU. She went to her mother's bed and stood beside the body, looking down at it. It was true; there was no one there anymore. It was just a body now. The life force that had once been her mother had left.

"Thank you," she said to the doctor, picked up the gift her mother would never see now, and turned and left the room.

There were days when the gods were so bored they had nothing better to do than test human beings, Page thought. It didn't seem fair, but then what did?

There was no point in grief, she told herself as she walked down the corridor. Clara had gone, and it was the best thing for both of them. For the first time, they were both free. And now she was truly alone.

Jason waited five more minutes for Page's call, then flipped open his Rolodex and dialed a number.

"Ellen," he said when the woman answered, "how are you? Jason Thomas here. Good. I'm having dinner on the yacht tonight with a couple of friends, and I wondered if you would like to be my guest? Very good," he said. "Shall I send a car around for you? Seven-thirty shall we say? Excellent." He hung up.

He had provided the senator with Ellen Baker during the last party on the yacht. She was very proficient, and also very expensive. However, he was dining with David Ross and his young lady this evening, and did not want to appear bereft of female companionship. Without another woman present, it would be a lopsided gathering. Ellen would do just fine during dinner, and provide some diversion afterwards as well.

And Page Peters would pay dearly for standing him up.

"Jason invited us up to the house for drinks first, before we go to the yacht for dinner," David said as the limousine drove through the gates into Bel-Air. "He thought you might be interested in seeing his paintings. You should feel very honored. He rarely shows his private collection to anyone."

"Oh. Oh, I am," Kate said unable to keep a sarcastic note out of her voice.

David looked at her sharply. "He has a marvelous collection. Very valuable. I think you'll like it."

"I'm sure I will," Kate said more enthusiastically. "I'm really looking forward to seeing it."

Jason's house was predictably imposing, Kate thought,

as the huge iron gates swung open and they entered the driveway. She corrected herself: It wasn't a house, it was a mansion of two stories with huge pillars in front, a combination of Roman and Spanish architecture peculiarly unique to Southern California. The beautifully landscaped yard was big enough to be a park.

Kate was slightly disappointed when Jason opened the front door. She'd expected some venerable English butler. "Welcome, I'm glad you could make it," he said graciously.

"Thank you so much for inviting us," Kate answered.

After the two men shook hands, they all walked into the house.

The inside was just as impressive, with its tasteful nineteenth century European furniture and significant pieces of art on the walls. Kate's attention was immediately drawn to a cabinet of netsuke, miniature Japanese carvings in wood, ivory, antler, bamboo, and metal.

"Do you like those?" Jason asked proudly.

"You have some magnificent pieces here." She ran her eyes and a well-manicured fingernail along the glass case.

Jason nodded. "And a good investment, too. Last year a collection of netsuke fetched $1.36 million at Christies in London. A single eighteenth century ivory piece went for $48,000. I bought some of these ten years ago. They were bargains then."

"They're beautiful. I particularly like that one. The Buddha figure with the flute."

"Yes, it's very finely done," Jason said.

Kate stood back and scanned the walls. The paintings in this room were beautiful but unspectacular. Apparently this was not where Jason kept the main part of his reputedly invaluable collection.

He seemed to sense her thoughts, because he waved a careless arm at the walls. "These are nice pieces—some nice nineteenth century American work and a few minor Impressionistic works—but this isn't my main collection. Before I show you, what would you like to drink?"

"I'll have a glass of white wine, please," Kate said.

David ordered the same.

Jason went to a small bar off the living room, poured them each a glass of wine, and a Scotch on the rocks for himself.

"Page not with us tonight?" David asked, taking the drink Jason handed him.

"No, I have another friend who'll be meeting us on the yacht for dinner," Jason said smoothly.

Kate had been wondering the same thing. The mention of another friend, presumably another girlfriend, pricked her curiosity. Who was it and where was Page? Whoever it was, she wasn't welcome in this house nor was Page. Jason's home wasn't for his mistress or girlfriends.

"Sharon up in Santa Barbara?" David asked.

"Yes, she's gone up to the house there for a couple of days," Jason said. "Come on, let me show you my real collection."

He led the way down a flight of stairs to a large steel door. "I had this floor specially built below the house," he said over his shoulder as he fingered an enormous combination lock on the door, obscuring what he was doing with his body. Then he turned the large brass handle, swinging the heavy door open. "I have four rooms down here. All they contain is art and wine, which is, of course, another art."

Jason flicked a switch on the wall and a series of strategically placed lights glowed. Kate couldn't help but gasp at what she saw. "This is my Impressionist room." Jason smiled, pleased at her reaction. "It's my favorite." His eyes seemed to shine with possessiveness.

Slowly Kate wandered around the room while he looked on proudly. There was a Maurice Brazil Prendergast cityscape and a Mary Cassatt pastel—the two most valuable works. Then there were paintings by Gustave Loiseau, Raphael Soyer, Richard Earl Thompson, Claire Ruby, Edouard Cortes, Antoine Blanchard, and Alice Kellogg Tyler.

With the exception of the Prendergast (who some would consider a post-Impressionist) and the Cassatt, these were not major Impressionist works in the vein of Claude Monet or Paul Cézanne, but they were nevertheless extremely fine and of great value.

"That's amazing," Kate said, standing in front of a Thompson landscape.

"I have a few more in here." Jason led the way into the next room. The display also included a few choice pieces of sculpture. Kate recognized a de Kooning bronze and a couple of other sculptures by Tony Smith and John Chamberlain.

"You must be very proud of these," Kate said.

"It's taken years of work to acquire them," Jason replied. "I'm sure you appreciate how much effort it takes to gather a painting here, a painting there."

"Oh, yes," she said. She pointed at another smaller room that was still dark. "What's in there?"

Jason shrugged, "Nothing I'm particularly proud of. Some modern work."

"May I see it?" she asked.

He hesitated for a moment and then shrugged, "Sure." He went through the door and turned on the light.

There were about twenty-five paintings on the walls, all by the same artist. "Why, these are all Jack Patney's works," Kate exclaimed. "All of them."

"Yes," Jason said. "I suppose you could call it an investment. I spotted Patney about five years ago, before he became well-known, and began to collect his work at a very reasonable price. I'm donating six to eight of these pieces to the Rex. They'll be in a room of their own. Representative of modern work."

Patney was a modern Abstract Expressionist who had become extremely well-known only in the last year and a half, particularly in New York. A native New Yorker, Patney had managed, through a calculated publicity campaign, to get his name in every major art magazine in the country. Since then, he had begun to realize the fruits of his labors. Still, having six of his paintings featured in a single room in a major museum like the Rex would establish his career, probably tripling the price of his work almost immediately.

Kate didn't particularly like his paintings, but there were many people who did. Many of them with more money than sense, she suspected.

Jason noted her expression, "I know," he said, "it isn't exactly my style, either. But I should realize a tidy profit."

"You'll sell all of these?" she asked.

"All except the ones I give to the Rex. I don't want to keep them. I could put this room to better use."

"I'm very impressed." Kate turned and looked back into the other room. She took a few steps forward as Jason switched off the light, then stood by her side.

"I'm glad you like it," he said. "I thought you'd appreciate it."

"Didn't I tell you it was something, Kate?" David asked.

"Oh, I'm staggered," Kate said. "It's marvelous to be able to own so many beautiful paintings. . . ."

"Well, as I said, I worked for them," Jason declared.

Was that a defensive note in his voice? Kate wondered. Did Jason Thomas feel guilty about his wealth? No, he was far too arrogant.

"Let's finish our drinks, and then we'll go to the yacht for dinner,"Jason said.

He carefully locked the huge door, which Kate now saw was at least six inches thick. His entire gallery, all those rooms, were actually a huge safe. They went back upstairs, finished their drinks, and then took their separate cars to the yacht.

"Well, what did you think?" David asked, holding her hand in the back of the limousine. "Were you impressed?"

"Very. It's a magnificent collection," Kate said sincerely. It truly was. Probably the combined value of all the work was in the millions of dollars.

"It's worth a fortune," David said enviously.

"Do you own much art?"

David smiled ruefully. "Not in that league. I try and buy less expensive stuff, you know, up-and-coming artists like Breer, who you exhibited at the gallery. Hopefully, they'll increase in value as the years pass."

"Well, Breer's work certainly will," Kate said.

As she spoke, something tugged at her mind. Some mathematical equation. A series of facts that would add up to a realization. But David spoke again, interrupting her thoughts.

"I'm afraid you have to be very knowledgable to invest in art of that magnitude," David said. "I just don't have the time. Jason's lucky. He has the help of Stod at the Rex. I think that over the past few years Stod has guided his purchases to a large extent. Anyway"—he released her hand and put his on her leg—"there's more to life than art. Like love and sex, for instance." He leaned over and kissed her deeply on the neck.

Kate giggled, hiding her irritation. She had had a thought, something about Jason, and David had distracted her.

They reached the marina at the same time as Jason and walked up the gangplank to the yacht together. When they entered the lounge, a woman rose from a chair and greeted them, kissing Jason on the cheek.

"You remember Ellen, don't you?" Jason said. "From the party here?"

"Of course," Kate said, smiling at the attractive woman of indeterminate occupation, the one with the loud laugh and spectacular legs.

"Nice to see you again," David said. If he was surprised, he hid it well.

"Well," Jason said, "another drink before dinner?"

As they sat down to a dinner of tender beef teriyaki, tempura, sushi, and a choice of either sake or wine, Kate asked curiously, "Do you have a Japanese chef?"

"There are two chefs on the yacht," Jason said. "One is French, the other Japanese."

"Believe me, the French chef is just as good as the Japanese," David said appreciatively, smacking his lips as he tasted a piece of yellowtail sushi.

Dessert consisted of intricately carved fruit—oranges, melons, and kiwi fruit. It was while she was enjoying the cool freshness in her mouth that Kate realized what she had been trying to piece together.

It was all connected. Jason, Stodding Watson, the Rex, Jack Patney, and Breer. The Rex had been about to buy at least half-a-dozen Breer paintings for a special room, she remembered Madge telling her. Watson had initiated the purchase and then abruptly changed his mind. It was a great disappointment. Breer would have been established as a major modern force or at least one to be contended with in the art world, probably tripling the price of his paintings. But it hadn't happened. When pressed by an angry Madge, Watson had finally admitted that a wealthy donor to the museum had objected to the purchase of the Breer paintings: Jason Thomas.

Now it became very clear Thomas had nixed the Breer deal. He had wanted his own Patney paintings as the museum's choice to represent a modern artist, and not out of admiration for the man's work but simply to increase the value of the rest of his collection, which he intended to then sell. What a cold, calculating bastard, she said to herself. He was willing to sacrifice one artist's career for his own motives, which had nothing to do with art but simply with profit. As a fervent admirer of Breer's work, it seemed doubly vicious to Kate.

She pushed her anger aside and smiled absently at something Jason was saying. The mask. She had to keep wearing the mask. One day, one sweet day she would remove it and Thomas would see his nemesis.

After leaving the hospital, Page had driven toward her apartment. Halfway there, she realized she didn't want to be alone, remembered that Elsa too had not wanted to be alone, and she headed for the older woman's apartment.

They were sitting in the living room now, Elsa's gorgeous new forty-inch television playing quietly in the background. Elsa was on her third schnapps of the evening and was growing philosophical.

"I think it is a good thing your mother is gone." Her chins wobbled as she nodded to herself.

"What do you mean?" Page asked, sipping her second gin and tonic and beginning to feel it.

Elsa grimaced. "These ties, sometimes they are artificial. I think that in some way your mother bound you and now you are free of that. That's from your side. From her side, what was she doing here? She was just holding on. I think she died before."

Page nodded. "You're right. I feel a sense of relief, I can't help it. I know I'm not supposed to, but it's there."

"Not supposed to!" Elsa snorted. "The demands of society sometimes don't make sense. They don't coincide with our own needs to survive. Those are the demands of the group. But you and I, we're individuals. We have our own demands. If you feel that way, feel it and enjoy it."

"I'm sad for her though," Page said. "I'm sad that these last years have been so, I suppose, damn miserable for her. And I'm sad that she resented me and that we never really made our peace, although I think perhaps for a moment there we might have. But it's true, she was old, she wanted to die. So I suppose I should just congratulate her and wish her well wherever she is."

"Good," Elsa said. "Good."

"The question is, what am I going to do now?"

"What you've been doing," Elsa said. "What else?"

Page shook her head, 'It's not enough. I'm going to have to change something. I don't know how much longer this thing with Jason will last. And when it ends, I don't know what he'll do."

"Well, it's good that you're thinking of that. One has to think defensively. Although, of course, it's even better to think offensively."

"I have, but so far it's a blank."

"It'll come," Elsa said, "just wait and see. Something will happen. You create a need and something will turn up to fill it."

She picked up the remote control and began to flick the TV channels. "I thank you for coming to spend the night with this old woman," she said, not looking at Page.

"Why, Elsa, you're all I have left," Page said with a smile.

"It'll be my turn next," Elsa said morosely. "I'll be the next to go."

Page laughed. "Elsa, you'll probably outlive me. I wouldn't worry about it if I were you."

"I'm not worrying. I'm just facing the facts. I'm getting old, like everybody else. One day I'm going to die."

"Then what'll I do?"

"You'll carry on as people always have," Elsa said. Her voice strengthened and she added fiercely, "All I ask is that you do it well, better than most. I have faith in you, my child. I always have."

Page found herself staring numbly at the floor. She couldn't say anything to Elsa's encouraging words. They seemed too incongruous. Perhaps seeing the face of death had done it to her. Or perhaps it was because the tentacles of her situation were gripping too firmly, fixating her in a position from which she longed to free herself. Whichever it was, Elsa's extraordinary confidence in her seemed misplaced. Tonight she was feeling smaller and more insignificant than she had felt for a long time.

CHAPTER SIXTEEN

Kate's research had turned up a name that jangled her memory when she first saw it. Jacques Chiroc. A wealthy Parisian art dealer for many years, Chiroc had fallen from grace during a major scandal seven years earlier. He had catered to the affluent of Europe, and also to a series of wealthy American clients, who apparently had more knowledge of money than of art. It was discovered, through luck more than anything, that what Chiroc had been selling them as nineteenth and twentieth century masterpieces were excellent, virtually undetectable forgeries.

If one of his clients, a wealthy San Francisco Nob Hill matron, had not decided to donate her Van Gogh sketch to the Whitney, where a zealous curator questioned its authenticity, Chiroc might have gone undiscovered for years. The Whitney curator used modern tests to prove the work a forgery. This set off a string of discoveries that left at least a dozen red-faced and poorer American buyers, who had purchased "major works" through Chiroc's Paris gallery. The French frown on any activity that sullies the national reputation, but few are more serious than those involving art, and Chiroc served five years in jail, in the process losing his reputation and status as an art dealer.

A thoroughly disreputable character, Kate knew, but she needed to find him.

At seven A.M. on Thursday morning, Kate called Bernard Lithgow in New York. She had only met Lithgow once and doubted that he would remember her. He owned a thriving art gallery on Forty-second Street. But he also had a reputation (and this is how she had heard of him) among the more reputable dealers as a dishonest man. In fact, Lithgow had bought three of Chiroc's paintings and sold them. Because his cries of innocence and victimization were numerous and influential, he avoided prosecution. She had met him once at a gallery opening and remembered him as a short, overweight, swarthy man, with folds in his neck, black eyes, and a smile that was too eager to charm.

When she called New York at ten o'clock, a time at which he was hopefully just opening the doors of his gallery, a secretary answered.

"Mr. Lithgow, please," Kate said, putting on her most obnoxious accent. "This is Mrs. Daphne du Maret calling from San Francisco."

The phoney but aristocratic-sounding name must have had some effect, for a moment later Lithgow came on the phone. "Bernard Lithgow, here," he said.

"Good morning, Mr. Lithgow. I wonder if you could be of assistance to me," she said. "I'm trying to contact someone in Paris and I believe you might know of his whereabouts?''

''Yes?'' His voice grew slightly less friendly when he realized she wasn't a potential customer.

''I'm trying to contact a Mr. Jacques Chiroc. I believe you had some dealings with him in the past.''

''That thief!'' Lithgow said. ''I got taken by him, that's what happened.''

''Be that as it may. I do need to contact him and I wonder if you could give me an address or telephone number.''

Lithgow calmed down and asked, ''Why is it you need to speak to Chiroc?''

''That is no concern of yours,'' Kate said. ''However, I do understand that you are a busy man, and if you are able to supply me with this information, I shall immediately send you a check for five hundred dollars to cover your time and expenses.''

''I see,'' Lithgow said thoughtfully. ''Well, why don't you send the check and call me after I've received it?''

''Mr. Lithgow, do you know who I am?'' Kate asked cuttingly. ''I need this information immediately. If I say you'll receive a check, you will receive a check. My husband is John du Maret, chairman of Cal-West Petroleum, president of the Danning Newspaper Group, owner of Novata Computers, Inc., and I am not used to being kept waiting.''

''Well, uh, I'm . . . I . . . uh, I didn't mean to imply . . .'' he began to sputter.

''Please give me the information if you have it. You shall receive a check via express mail.''

''Well, of course,'' he said more respectfully. ''If you could just hold on a moment?''

''Certainly.''

He came back to the telephone a moment later. ''I, ah, don't know how up-to-date or accurate this is, but it's the best I can do, I'm afraid. Chiroc used to have offices at 15 rue Jean Jacques Rousseau, Paris 1, the telephone number would be 214-3476.''

''Thank you very much, Mr. Lithgow,'' she said, writing the information down.

"And if I can be of any further assistance, please call on me," he said.

"Thank you," she said, "I certainly shall," and hung up.

She would send him his money. Not in the form of a check that bore her name, but she'd send him a money order. For a moment she was tempted not to send him anything. He was a weasel, a dishonest one. But she wanted no flurries, no calls to Chiroc, no suspicions. She had promised money and she would send it.

The next problem was to contact Chiroc. She looked at her watch. It would be five P.M.—a nine-hour time difference—in Paris now. It was worth a try, but she had to call from a public phone somewhere. She didn't want an international call appearing on her telephone bill. Hurriedly she grabbed as many coins as she could find and drove up the street to Melrose Avenue.

There was a phone booth, one of the remaining few that actually had doors on it, outside a small liquor store. She parked, went into the store, got some more change, and walked to the booth. Hastily she dialed the operator and placed the call.

The telephone rang at the other end. She shivered in the chilly morning air, shifting her feet in an attempt to keep warm. After several moments, a gruff voice answered, "*Bon jour.*"

"Monsieur Chiroc," she said.

"Yes, it is I," said the voice in heavily accented English.

"My name is Mrs. Daphne du Maret, and I would like to hire your services."

"What is it you wish, Madame?"

"I'm not prepared to discuss it over the telephone," she said. "Can you come to New York?"

"Come to New York for someone I do not know?"

"I shall pay you well. All I wish to do is to consult with you on a matter."

"Why do you not come to Paris and visit my office?"

"That isn't possible," she said. "I would like it if you could fly to New York immediately. Perhaps next weekend?"

"What is this matter about that you wish to consult with me?" he asked persistently.

"Monsieur, I *cannot* discuss it over the telephone. I need one hour of your time in New York. A conversation. A name. That is all."

"Ah," he said.

"What will your fee be for this, Monsieur Chiroc?"

"Five thousand dollars, and expenses," he said, without a second's pause.

"That's ridiculous! For an hour of your time, I'll offer you a fee of twenty-five hundred dollars plus expenses."

"Madame, I am quite content to stay in Paris. The weather is very nice now."

Damn, she thought. He knew she needed him, and he was willing to gouge her. "All right, I shall send you a check for one thousand dollars now and pay the rest when we meet."

"Half now," he said, "and half when we meet."

"No," she said firmly. She had to remain tough on this point. "I want to make it well worth your while to decide to make the trip to New York."

"Madame, how can you say such a thing? I give my word I shall meet you."

"One thousand now, four thousand in New York," she said, her tone leaving no space for argument.

"Very well. Where shall we meet?"

"I want you to check into the Warwick Hotel. Do you know where it is?"

"Of course," he said, "I've stayed there. It is behind the Museum of Modern Art, no?"

"Yes," she said. "Check into the Warwick, I will contact you there on Sunday morning, shortly after ten o'clock, New York time. Now, may I have the address where I should send the money?"

"Of course," he said, and gave her the address she already had.

"Very good," she said, "I shall see you on Sunday," and hung up.

Kate went back to her apartment and made a fresh pot

of coffee. She stood in the kitchen while it was perking, examining her checkbook. The expenses were already beginning and there was no way she could cover them. She'd be able to come up with the initial thousand dollars that he wanted, but she only had about two thousand dollars of her original nest-egg left. She'd have to move into the next phase of her plan sooner than anticipated. In the meantime, she'd go to her bank at ten A.M., withdraw a thousand dollars in cash, and send Chiroc an international money order which she'd purchase at another bank under her new pseudonym—which was rapidly becoming comfortable.

She laughed at the thought. She was beginning to think of herself as Mrs. Daphne du Maret, wealthy San Francisco matron. God, she thought, the whole thing was unbelievable. It sounded like a plot for *Mission Impossible,* the old television series. And yet, she reminded herself, it was very real—as real as life and death, to be honest. Again she shivered. Her apartment was warm, but she nevertheless clutched her coffee mug hard in both hands.

She'd send the money order to Chiroc by "next-day" courier, so he'd get it tomorrow. And then she'd have to raise the rest of the money to be able to take it with her to New York.

She called the gallery and left a message on the machine for Madge, saying that she'd be late, and then, after a quick shower and a bite to eat, went to the bank.

The business at the bank went smoothly. She withdrew her cash, went across the street to another bank, got an international money order, and placed it in an envelope with Chiroc's name and address on it. She didn't want her real name or address to appear on the package, so instead of calling the courier company to come for a pickup, she went to the Beverly Hills headquarters of Worldwide Company, handed the package over the counter and paid the delivery fee in cash.

Shortly after eleven, she arrived at the gallery. After greeting Madge, she picked up the telephone and called Page.

* * *

Page was having a rocky day. Before arriving at her office, she stopped at the hospital and completed the paperwork dealing with Clara's death. Then, as soon as she arrived at work, she called a funeral home and made arrangements to have her mother's body cremated. "What? No ceremony?" the man had asked disbelievingly.

"No. No ceremony." She absently stared out her office window. Smog was obscuring the Hollywood Hills. Page was not a religious person and refused to see why she should suddenly become one.

Now her secretary buzzed her to say that Jason was on the phone.

Last night, she had only remembered when arriving at Elsa's that Jason had wanted her to call him within an hour of their last conversation to let him know whether she could make it to dinner or not. With Clara's death she had completely forgotten, and by the time she remembered it was far too late.

She took a deep breath and leaned forward on one elbow, resting her head on her hand. "Hello, Jason," she said, picking up the phone.

"Good morning, Page. I trust you had a good evening?"

"Not particularly."

"Neither did I. I got stood up."

"I'm sorry, Jason. I know I said I'd call you, but what with one thing and another it just didn't happen."

"I'm well aware of that," he said. "You're proving to be somewhat unreliable."

Page's nerves were jangled. "I apologize!" she said irritably. "What more do you want?"

"Don't snap at me, Page."

"I'm sorry," she found herself saying again. It seemed to her as if she'd said it half-a-dozen times already in this short conversation. But was she really sorry? It didn't matter.

"How is your mother?" Jason asked.

"She died last night," Page said wearily, "that's why I didn't call."

"I'm very sorry to hear that. However, a simple telephone call would have been appreciated."

"Yes," Page said. What a cold bastard, she thought.

"I would hate to have to tell all the clients I've recommend to you that you've become unreliable." The threat was blatant.

"I haven't become unreliable, Jason," she replied, adding caustically, "Luckily my mother only gets to die once."

A pause. "I'll be unable to see you tonight," Jason said, as casually as if nothing had just happened. "Perhaps tomorrow?"

"Yes, that would be fine," Page said, somewhat relieved that the conversation was ending.

"All right, I'll drop by your apartment around seven. We can go out to dinner or stay in."

"Whatever you like."

"Good, see you then."

She sat at her desk, feeling the anger bubble inside her. She didn't need sympathy from Jason because her mother had died. She didn't expect that from him or anyone for that matter. It wasn't necessary. But she could have used some understanding. Or course, from Jason that was probably too much to expect. He understood only that he needed to be obeyed.

He'd threatened her without a trace of subtlety or ambivalence, making it once again very clear that not only could he cut her off as a mistress, but he could virtually destroy her business and source of livelihood. It took a long time to build up a business, even one that involved only a handful of clients. If Jason pillaged her roster and soured her clients, she'd be left with not even enough income to pay the overhead on her office.

The hell with him, she thought bitterly. She should just cut herself off and take her chances, move if she had to, start over again. But that was a rash thought. She hadn't built up her finances over the last few years just to spend them all in one year on mere survival. She couldn't do that. She didn't know what she could do.

Her secretary buzzed her again and said that Kate Buchanan was on the phone.

Page almost didn't take the call. She was still seething, but then she remembered how understanding Kate had been and picked up the telephone. "Hi," she said, "how you doing?"

"I'm fine. I was wondering if we could get together this evening?"

"This evening? I—I—I don't know," Page mumbled. She didn't feel much like getting together with anyone. And Jason had "given her a night off," so to speak. A perfect opportunity to be alone and ponder her problems.

"I have a proposition to put to you," Kate said. "It's not just a social call. I think you'll be very interested."

"Oh, really?" Page said, already interested. "Okay, let's meet. Where?"

"I'm supposed to meet David at eight. Perhaps we could meet earlier, have a drink?"

"Sure."

"Somewhere quiet and gloomy?" Kate said with a laugh. "Do you know of a place like that, where we won't see anyone we know?"

"There's a place off Fairfax, Molly Malone's, an Irish bar. It's not at all classy, you understand, but the walls happen to feature an artist's work that I like very much. It's just sort of a neighborhood pub. Why don't we meet there at six?"

"That would be fine," Kate said.

A proposition was what Page needed. She'd always felt there was something curious about Kate. Perhaps she'd find out now what it was.

Molly Malone's, one of a few authentic Irish pubs in Los Angeles, was small, dim, and made for the serious Irish business of drinking.

Page was seated at a small table facing the bar, sometimes turning around to look at the oil sketches of world figures and neighborhood characters that covered the walls. The works had been done by an artist who had a sure, deft hand.

To her left was an area where a couple of men were throwing darts. On their right a juke box blared.

"Hi," Kate said, sliding breathlessly onto the bench beside her. "How on earth did you discover this place?"

"Just luck. I like it for the very reason you suggested. I don't know anyone here and am never likely to."

"What are you drinking? The wine's probably awful, right?"

"I'm afraid so," Page said. "That's why I'm drinking a gin and tonic."

"I guess I'll have the same," Kate said.

Page got up and stepped to the bar to order the drink for Kate. She brought it back to the table.

"So how are things going?"

"So, so, I guess."

Kate examined her face. "You look a little peaked."

"In fact, I'm a little exhausted. Emotional exhaustion, I guess." She brushed a stray hair off her forehead with her graceful fingers.

Kate looked at her over the rim of her glass. "What's going on?"

"Well, my mother died yesterday and I—"

"Oh, Page, I'm sorry!" Kate started to reach out a hand to touch her but changed her mind. Some people demanded sympathy, but Page wasn't the type.

"Thanks." Page looked up and managed a small smile. "It's okay, really. It wasn't a total shock, and it's a relief that her suffering is over. It's just amazing what an emotional drain that can be."

"Do you have any other family?"

"No."

"Alone in the world, just like me."

They sat silently for a minute. Page looked around the room at the paintings.

Were those tears glistening in her eyes, or was it just the light? Kate wondered. She broke the silence. "Page, has Jason been a help to you through this?"

"No, just a problem really. He's been very demanding of my time, as usual." Page sounded almost embarrassed to admit Jason's lack of support, but her voice was also weighted by sadness.

"Sometimes I feel these men think they own us," Kate said resentfully.

"Of course they do. Jason does. Right now I feel like he has me in a vise and he's trying to squeeze," Page said.

"What I have to tell you is related to that," Kate said. "But I didn't know about your mother. Are you sure you want to discuss business now?"

"Absolutely," Page said, her voice firm.

"Let me ask you a couple of questions first," Kate said. "I promise your answers won't be divulged to anyone, okay?"

"What, kind of questions?" Page asked, a little taken aback by Kate's approach.

"Well, from what you've told me already, my instincts say that you're looking for a way to get more—more money, more freedom. That you'd like to be wealthy enough not to have to depend upon the whimsical generosity of someone like Jason. Would that be correct?"

Page nodded slowly, her eyes speculative. "You could say that."

"I also sense that things between you and Jason are a little shaky, that you don't feel on a firm foundation in that relationship, perhaps that you don't even like the man much. Would those suppositions be correct?"

"Perhaps," Page said warily. "But you're treading on dangerous ground."

"I know I am," Kate said. She also knew that she was taking a tremendous risk by approaching Page, but she felt she didn't have much choice. She needed her. And, she felt, the only way to snare her was to appeal to her self-interest.

"I have an investment opportunity that might help you," Kate said. "You can achieve a number of objectives for a fairly insignificant amount of money. You can walk out of it with some real wealth. But to do this, you are going to have to help me take Jason Thomas to the cleaners."

"What?" Page exclaimed. She'd been listening attentively and with great interest up to the point of the word "wealth." However, the mention of Jason's name in connection with it had thrown her. "Jason is involved in this?"

Kate hesitated. At this moment, everything would be placed at risk. Would her instincts about Page prove correct, or would she blow the whistle?

"First, before I tell you more, I have to be assured that I can trust you," Kate said.

Page smiled. "And how will you know that?"

"Because I want you to see how this is going to serve your interests and I want you to understand very clearly that it won't be to your benefit to tell Jason what I'm doing. I'm being frank with you, I'm not playing games here. This is a serious matter."

"You're making me very nervous," Page said, "but go on."

"Jason cares for nothing except his own power," Kate said quickly. "He'd throw you aside if he needed to, to protect his own interests. I'm offering you a chance to protect yours. You can walk out of this a rich woman."

"I know, probably better than you, that Jason is a very dangerous man," Page warned. "That fact gives me pause."

"I know he is. But nobody will ever know of your part in this," Kate said. "All I need from you is an investment. And I have to know that I can trust you. I want to make this very clear. If you told Jason about this, what would you get? An expensive gift? Some stock? A few new clients? You'd still be in the same precarious position that you're in now. It's untenable for a woman like you. You have to understand that. I'm offering a deal that you can walk out of with probably about two million dollars."

"You don't have to tell me my position," Page snapped. "I know it all too well. Believe me, it's been very much on my mind."

"I know it has, and that's why I felt I could approach you with this," Kate said. "But before I continue, I need to know in principle if you're interested."

"I'm not interested in suicide missions," Page said. "To

be frank with you, I'm afraid of Jason. This talk of taking him to the cleaners scares me."

"Believe me, suicide isn't among my plans, and I'm not minimizing Jason's effectiveness."

Page drank some of her gin and then said, "Why don't you tell me what this is all about?"

Kate took a deep breath. It was time to gamble. If she took the next step, there would be no turning back.

She began her story. "My name is Kate Buchanan, as you know. What you don't know is that my brother's name was Joel Buchanan," Kate began. "Joel Buchanan, who was also known under the stage name of Joel Buck, was a musician in a local band. Joel, the only remaining member of my family, fell in love with the wrong woman. A woman by the name of Angie Cox."

Page put her drink down on the table and narrowed her eyes. "I know the name."

"Yes, Angie Cox was Jason's mistress before you were. Jason found out that Angie and Joel were in love. He sent some of his men around to Joel's apartment, and they threw him out of a fourth-story window. Killed him. He was murdered."

"How do you know this?" Page asked, her voice tight. "How can you prove this?"

"I can't prove it," Kate said grimly. "But I knew he was murdered, I just didn't know who was responsible. Angie Cox filled in the details. Jason admitted the whole thing to her before he threw her out."

"What happened to her?"

Kate gave Page a hard look. "She's suffering the fate, the nightmare, of all mistresses. She's now a hooker in West Hollywood. Jason threw her out without a penny. Nothing, She had to make a living, she was qualified for nothing, and that's what she's doing. That's what every woman who considers herself a professional mistress faces."

"So you're after Jason?" Page said. "I knew there was something about you. I just knew it."

"Jason Thomas is my target," Kate said. "I intend to bring him to his knees."

"How can you do that?" Page asked skeptically. "It's like one man taking on an army."

"There's no way to touch him legally," Kate said. "I can bring about my own kind of justice, though, and that's what I'm doing. But to do it, I need your help."

Page looked away, silent now.

Kate watched her. She had plunged into a very frightening reality by telling Page the truth. She hoped to hell that Page wouldn't run scared at this point.

Page finished her drink and stared into the empty glass. "I believe you. I believe that Jason could be responsible for your brother's murder. He's a ruthless man, a dangerous man. And he has people who would do things like that for him."

"Will you help me?"

"Maybe. Tell me what you're planning to do," Page said.

"What if you say no?"

"That's the risk you're taking, isn't it?"

"If I tell you my plan, *if* you think its workable, and *if* the returns seem large enough for you versus the risk, would you betray Jason? That's what I have to know before I tell you more," Kate said.

They stared into each other's eyes silently, each weighing the other.

"Would you?" Kate urged, breaking the silence.

"In a second," Page said.

Kate told her everything.

Kate got back to her apartment at quarter to eight. She had fifteen minutes to change, and then she was going out with David to the screening of some new film, an invitation gained through Allan no doubt.

She was elated by the outcome of her meeting with Page. When it came right down to the bottom line, the excellence of her plan had allayed Page's not inconsiderable fears. Page had grilled her like an interrogator on every aspect of it, looking for weaknesses and flaws.

Furthermore, Page was nothing if not a hardheaded business woman and her perspective on financial matters had given a far more realistic edge to Kate's plan—a plan that had both intrigued and ultimately captivated Page.

Traveling to New York and paying this man's fee were just beginning expenses, Page had said. "You're going to need a lot more money than that. Probably more money than I have available right now."

"I don't have any other sources to turn to," Kate said.

Page smiled, "I do. I have a friend, Elsa, a very wealthy old woman."

"Can we trust her?" Kate asked.

"I'd trust her with my life," Page said.

"That's good enough for me. But you understand this is a speculative venture?"

"Only too well," Page said. "But when the potential return is this high, speculation is the name of the game. There are risks involved. I think that with your background and expertise, not to mention your motivation, you will be able to take care of your part in this. There is some luck involved, of course. But maybe for once the gods will be with us."

"I'll need money tomorrow," Kate said.

"You'll have it. Enough to cover the four-thousand-dollar fee, his expenses, and your airfare."

Just before they left the bar, Page gave Kate a warning. "My involvement in this can only be financial, you understand that, don't you?"

"That's all I need," Kate said.

"Even so, we're going to have to be very careful to cover the tracks of the money. I don't want any trace of money passing between you and me. I found out that Jason's been having me followed recently. I don't know if it's happening now. I don't think so. I've been very careful. But we can't take any risks. I don't think we should see each other too often, or if we do, we've got to be very careful about it."

Kate nodded. "I'm going to cover every fingerprint, every footstep. I'm not planning to leave a trail. Don't worry," she said.

Kate had overcome a major barrier: her limited finances.

She also had an ally now. Someone not only to help, but to give her support.

She looked at her watch. David would arrive in ten minutes. He was always punctual; she knew she could count on that. She didn't even have time to shower. Quickly she went into the bathroom, took her washcloth, and gave herself a French bath. Then she perfumed her body and dressed in a long, casual skirt and a matching mauve cashmere sweater.

Promptly at eight o'clock the doorbell rang. "Hi," David said, kissing her on the cheek.

"Hi, David. How are you?"

"Oh, just fine, just fine. Are you ready to go?"

"Yes. Just let me grab a shawl." She threw a shawl over her shoulder and came back to the door.

"The screening starts in half an hour. I thought we'd have a late supper afterwards."

"Oh, that would be wonderful," Kate said. "I'll probably be hungry by then. Where are we going?"

"It's a new Fifties diner, started by the same guy that owns Hamburger Hamlet, but you're liable to see everybody and anybody there after eleven."

"Sounds like fun," Kate said.

They reached the front door and stepped out. David's limousine was parked across the street. He took a ring of keys out of his pocket and dangled them in front of her. "I thought you might like to drive."

"The limo?"

"No, not the limousine. This," he said, pointing.

Directing in front of them was a small black Toyota MR-2.

"I don't understand," Kate said.

"I thought it about time you got rid of that rental car and had something decent to drive. This is it."

"Really? You bought this for me?"

"Leased it," David said. "But it's yours to use."

"Gosh, David, thank you."

"It's the least I could do after such a wonderful weekend in Mazatlán."

She hugged him, then turned to look at the car again. "We're going to go in this?"

"As long as you drive. I'll leave the limo here. I've told my driver he can take off for a few hours."

"David, this is so generous of you," Kate said hesitantly.

"It's only the beginning." He put his arm around her waist. "There's nothing I like more than taking care of you."

As she climbed into the car, Kate felt a pang of guilt. By the time her scheme had come full circle, David too would suffer.

Allan stamped his feet like a little boy. "How can you be so fucking stupid?"

Jasmine was unperturbed. His reaction was exactly what she had expected.

They were sitting in her apartment on Thursday evening. Allan had just returned from his East Coast trip and stopped off there on his way home from the airport. He had burst in, exclaiming how much he had missed her. She hugged him, kissed him, sat him down, and gave him her news.

Allan had bolted to his feet, as if suddenly realizing he was sitting on pins.

"It was simply a miscalculation," Jasmine said calmly. "You're right, though, it was stupid. But it happens and it's happened. Now I'm here facing you, pregnant."

"Jesus," Allan said, running his hand through his hair. "Now what?"

"Well, that's what we need to talk about."

"You can get an abortion, right? I mean it's easy to do that these days, isn't it? It's legal, isn't it? I mean you can just go to your doctor, and in ten minutes he can handle it and your problem's over, right?"

"That can be done," Jasmine said evenly. "But it's not what I want."

Allan's head swiveled around. "What do you mean?"

"I want to have the baby."

Allan began to pace. "You can't. That's impossible. That's crazy. There's no way you can have the baby. You're going to get an abortion, that's all there is to it. There's no way you can have a child."

"Allan, sit down and calm down. Come here, sit next to me. Let's talk about this." She patted the couch.

He came obediently, dropping heavily onto the couch. "Jesus," he said again, "I don't believe this."

"Allan, I don't want to have an abortion. I want this baby. I've thought it over carefully. I'm not getting any younger and I've always wanted to have a child. All right, this was an accident—a dumb one—but this is the result and I'm willing to live with it."

Allan threw his head back on the couch and rolled his eyes at the heavens. "Jas, I already have a family, you know that, right? I don't need another one. I don't need more complications in my life. You understand? This is a complication, this is a *major* fucking complication."

"It doesn't have to be. Nothing has to change."

"Ha!" Allan scoffed. "Your sister comes here for three days and that's a major complication. What the hell do you think it's going to be like with some little brat running around here with a snivelling nose all the time? How often am I going to see you? What time are we going to have to ourselves? What are we going to do when you are pregnant six months from now? Who am I going to fuck then? No. No way. It's out of the question."

"Allan, it'll just be a temporary interruption. I've had a little morning sickness but now that's even gone and I feel wonderful. And after a few months things will return to normal, as far as our time together is concerned."

"Oh, Jesus, what books have you been reading?" Allan asked scornfully. "All kids are beautiful, all puppies are beautiful, all kittens are beautiful. They are also a pain in the ass, especially once they grow up. Trust me, I know. I've been through this. You don't want to have a baby. What about your career?"

"What about my career?" Jasmine asked. "Where is it now? Practically nowhere."

"You want a career?" Allan said, leaning forward to press his point. "I'll get you a career. I've gotten you exactly as much work as you wanted, lady. You want more work, I'll get you more work. You want to become a star, I'll make you a star. Just don't ask me to become father to this kid. I'll do anything else, not that. I have enough headaches with my own kids."

"Goddamn it, Allan! This is your kid. Your own kid. Who do you think the father is? This is yours and mine. That's the only difference—that I'm a part of it, and not Elena. All I expect from you is some support."

"I'm married to her. I'm not married to you. Keep that in mind." Allan got up and began to pace again. "No, this is not going to happen, Jasmine. You are going to go and have an abortion. I'll get you the name of a great doctor and he'll take care of it for you."

"I'm not going to have an abortion!" Jasmine said vehemently.

"Yes, you are. I say you are, and you are!"

Jasmine shook her head mutely.

Allan stopped and faced her, his hands on his hips. "Hey! Who pays for this?" he demanded. "Who pays for this apartment? Your clothes? Your food? Your jewelry? Your car? Your insurance? Your medical bills? Your hospital bills? Who pays for this?"

"You do," Jasmine said quietly.

"You bet I do!" he said, punching his chest with his thumb. "I do. Yep, I do. And I'm not going to pay for a baby. You either do what I say, or all this"—he swept his arm to indicate the entire room—"stops! Right here and now! It ends, it's over, it's finished. It's gone. The car, the apartment, you name it, it's gone."

"You're threatening me," Jasmine said dangerously.

"I'm giving you an ultimatum: Either you do what I say, or it's over between us. I'll cut you off without a goddamn stinking dime."

He was bluffing. He'd never do that to her. They'd been together too long. He loved her, in spite of the pregnancy.

He couldn't be so callous, thoughtless, and cruel. But she wasn't about to test him.

"Be reasonable, Allan. Think about it," she pleaded. "This baby really won't affect our relationship. It's going to add something to it. Sure I'll be pregnant, and maybe we won't be able to make love on occasion, but that shouldn't matter. There's more to our relationship than just sex, isn't there? Anyway, after she's born, things will be just like they were."

"You've got to be kidding," Allan scoffed. "You've never been pregnant before. I've seen Elena pregnant twice. It's craziness. It's two years of craziness after the child is born. No sleep, you're up in the middle of the night. You're running yourself ragged, you look like shit. You don't have time for me. Every time the baby snivels, you are running to the doctor. When the baby is healthy, you are oohing and aahing over it. Give me a break, Jasmine. This isn't what I'm paying for."

Jasmine began to lose her patience, "Paying for. It always comes down to what you're paying for, doesn't it, Allan? Just like you own me or something."

"I'm paying money, I expect value," he said curtly.

"Fuck you, Allan!" Jasmine snapped. "You're an asshole! I'm not your chattel, your slave. I have a life of my own, I have rights of my own. And I have a body of my own, and I'm not about to cut into my body and get rid of this child. I want this kid. If you don't like it, fuck you!"

"Fuck me, huh? Fuck me? What happens when I cut you off? Fuck me, then what?"

"So cut me off!" she screamed, now in a total rage. "I don't give a shit what you do. If you're going to be an asshole about this, I'll take care of it myself. Why don't you get the fuck out of here and leave me alone so I can plan my future? I should have known better than to think I could count on you."

"Sure, sure," he said, "if that's what you want. Hey,

far be it from me to impose on your time, you stupid bitch. Wallow in it. See if I care."

"Get out, Allan. Just get out!" she shouted. "Leave me alone, just get out of here. Go!"

"Hey," he said with a shrug, "your choice, babe." He turned and walked out.

Jasmine burst into tears. What had she done? And what would she do now?

CHAPTER SEVENTEEN

"I love it," Elsa said, "I love it. I just love it." She waddled across the room and adjusted a crooked painting on the wall. Page hadn't seen her so physically active in a long time.

"Well, you did express the need of a little adventure, Elsa," she said, smiling.

"And what an adventure!" Elsa said with a grin "I've never really liked the way Jason treats you, Page but I didn't feel it was my place to say anything. In truth, I would like to see Mr. Thomas with egg all over his aristocratic face. I'd pay for it."

"You will," Page reminded her. "That is why I'm here. Money." It was Friday. She had given Kate a little over five thousand dollars in cash earlier in the afternoon and had stopped in to visit Elsa after work.

"An investment, my dear," Elsa corrected her, "an investment. A high-risk investment, but the returns . . . Oy!"

"No guarantees," Page said.

Elsa waved her hand disdainfully. "It's worth the effort. If you girls can do this, it's worth the effort."

"So I can count on you?"

"Whatever you need just let me know."

"We're going to have to cover our trail," Page cautioned.

"I have cash," Elsa said. "A lot of it. I don't trust banks with everything I own. Cash can't be traced."

"You realize from what I've told you that I hardly know this woman. I met her a short time ago."

Elsa leaned back on her couch. "One of the things I admire about you, Page, are your instincts. They are very fine. I don't think they are wrong very often. If your instincts about this woman are good, then that's enough."

Page nodded. "That's what I decided, and they are. I like her. I have a good feeling about her. And I checked out what I could. There was a Joel Buck, and he was killed. The police called it a suicide—a fall from a window. But she explained to me how Jason's men threw him out of that window. It checks out."

"Very good, very good." Elsa clapped her chubby hands together. "Even though your instincts about her are good, you still do your homework. I'm proud of you."

"Well, there's a lot of money involved. My position with Jason could end at any moment. I'm using my savings for this. It may not seem much to you, but it's a major investment for me."

It hadn't been easy. After agreeing to Kate's plan, she had been plagued by doubts. They were three women taking on Jason Thomas, for Godssakes! If they failed, they would pay for it. Oh, God, would they pay for it!

Kate's plan was good. Hell, no, it was brilliant! But like any plan, it had its vulnerable points. Things could go wrong. And if they did, they would suffer. It wouldn't just be a mistress turned out on the street, it would be jail. Justified though their actions might be, the law would not take kindly to Kate's project.

But if it worked? God, not only would it bring about a kind of justice, but it would solve all Page's problems!

That fact, together with a kind of weird faith in Kate and the "rightness" of what she was doing, had finally decided Page. It was worth the risks.

"How much have you put in already?" Elsa asked, interrupting her thoughts.

"Oh! A shade over five thousand dollars, nothing much. There's going to be more travel, more fees, and then of course the major fee."

"How much are you willing to put in?" Elsa asked.

"I'm willing to put in as much as twenty-five thousand dollars. I feel that the investment justifies that sort of exposure."

"Put in ten thousand dollars," Elsa said. "After you've put in ten thousand dollars you call on me, I'll cover you from there on out."

"Thank you," Page said simply.

"No, no," Elsa contradicted her. "I should be thanking you. This is a good one. This brings new life to this old body. This is the adventure I wanted. I want to know everything. You'll keep me posted every step of the way?"

"Every step," Page promised.

"Good. I like this. I really like this."

Kate told David on Friday night that she had just started her period and needed a few days to herself. "I'm afraid I'm one of those women who has a difficult time of it for a couple of days," she said. "All I want to do is be alone, uninterrupted, and lie around like a sponge, soaking up a few books and a little television. Kind of hibernation."

"Well," David said doubtfully, "I'm sorry I won't see you this weekend. I was looking forward to it. I had the whole day on Sunday set aside for you. I was hoping we could take a little trip up the coast."

"David, can we do that next week? I really am starting to feel bad and I just need a couple of days' rest."

"Of course, of course," he said. "I'll talk to you next week."

* * *

She caught the "red-eye" out of LAX on Saturday night, leaving her answering machine on in case David called. She arrived in New York in the morning and caught a cab from JFK into Manhattan. She carried over five thousand dollars in cash: four thousand for Monsieur Chiroc, enough to pay his hotel bill, and enough to cover incidentals. If all had gone well, he would be waiting for her at the Warwick. She wouldn't go there, but would call him and arrange a meeting place.

She couldn't help but feel a sense of excitement as the cabbie took the tunnel to Manhattan. In a way, she missed the bustle of New York—expensive, cramped, frantic, insane though it might be. It was a vital place, a city in which she'd spent many happy and productive years.

The Warwick Hotel was on the corner of West Fifty-fourth Street and Sixth Avenue, but she had the cabbie drop her off at the Plaza Hotel overlooking Central Park. She called Monsieur Chiroc from a telephone in the lobby and arranged to meet him in the Oak Room restaurant in twenty minutes. He sounded relieved to hear her voice and said he would be there.

From the lobby she went to a woman's restroom, where behind closed doors she withdrew from her briefcase a blond wig and a pair of dark glasses. When she emerged a few minutes later, she was a different woman. It seemed melodramatic, she knew, but it was better to be safe. As she had promised Page, there would be no fingerprints, not even a trace of a footstep.

With her gracefully cut and obviously expensive business suit and her impressive diamond earrings, she looked the part of Mrs. du Maret.

Monsieur Chiroc turned out to be an oily little man with a black pencil moustache, balding temples, and curved bushy eyebrows. His clothes were on the dowdy side. She had told the maitre d' she was expecting him, and Chiroc was shown to the table. "Madame du Maret," he said, limply taking her hand.

"Please sit down, monsieur. I am very glad you could be here." She noticed he wore four thick gold rings on the fingers of his right hand. "I trust your trip was comfortable?"

"*Oui,* but the Warwick is not what it used to be. I stayed here many years ago, and it was a luxury hotel then." He spread his palms, "Such is the way of the world. Things change."

"Would you like to eat?" she asked.

"No, not at this time. Perhaps some coffee and a pastry."

"I'll have the same," she said.

When the waiter came, Chiroc gave the order. "You have brought the balance?" he asked, folding his hands and leaning forward.

She withdrew an envelope from her bag and placed it carefully on the table beside her. "Yes."

"So, what is it you wish to know?"

"I wish to contact the most skilled forger of paintings in Europe. Someone who could do a perfect copy of an old master," she said quietly.

Chiroc raised his formidable eyebrows. "But how should I know of this?"

"Don't play games with me. I know your reputation well. I know why you're here; you know why you're here. It's not the time for evasion. All I want is a name and an address and a way to contact the person."

Chiroc leaned back and drummed his fingers on the table. "An old master? That is difficult, very difficult. There is a man I know. Unfortunately, he is unavailable now. He languishes in a French prison." He looked at her shrewdly. "Which painting is it you wish done?"

Kate shook her head. "That's not material; you don't need to know that."

Again Chiroc spread his hands, "Madame, if this is a criminal act we are talking about here, I need to know enough to protect myself."

"You won't be in any danger, as this is not a criminal act," she said. "It is for a private collection. All you are doing is providing me with a name. There is nothing criminal involved as far as you are concerned. A name, and you receive five thousand dollars. It sounds like a fair exchange."

"Yes, well . . . there are people," Chiroc said thoughtfully, staring down at the table.

"It would be even better if you give me two names," she interrupted, "so that I have a choice."

"Yes." Chiroc looked up at her. "I know of two men. One in Germany; his name is Hans Dickopf. He could do the job, perhaps. But he is getting old and would probably be very expensive. He is in Munich. The other one is in Spain; he's American." Chiroc shook his head. "Very talented. The best I have ever seen, particularly with the old masters. But I think he is retired, even though he is still a young man." He withdrew a small notebook from his pocket. "The German, I can give you an address and telephone number in Munich. The American, I can tell you where he is, but I do not have an address."

"Which would you recommend most highly?"

He shrugged. "The most difficult, of course, the American. He is the best. He did some work, a little work, some years ago and, as I said, displayed great talent. However, I believe he grew squeamish and retired from such activities. Perhaps if you met, perhaps if the commission were large enough, there are many perhaps. . . . "

"What is his name and where is he?"

"His name is Marcus Devereaux and he lives on Ibiza. Do you know that place?"

"No," she said. "In Spain, you said?"

"It's an island off of Spain. You've heard of Mallorca, I presume?"

She nodded.

"It is a neighboring island. Not as well-known. But a beautiful place. Smaller than Mallorca, quieter."

"How would I find him there?"

"That I do not know. Perhaps if you asked at some of the art galleries there, they would know. I'm afraid I cannot give you more information than that."

"And the German?"

He gave her an address and telephone number in Munich.

"The German would be easier," she said.

"Yes, but I doubt he would be as good."

She tapped the envelope with a red fingernail. "Monsieur Chiroc, if neither of these men are suitable, will you be able to produce other names?"

"Possibly, now that I know what you are looking for."

"Very good. I shall pay you your fee now, as agreed. However, if neither of these two men are suitable, I shall approach you again and expect you to supply me with more names at no further fee."

"That is agreed," he said, his gold-laden right hand creeping forward on the table.

She lifted the envelope and dropped it into his now-upturned palm. "Thank you very much for your time." She pushed her chair back.

"You will not finish your coffee?" he asked.

"No, I have other business. Good day."

She walked down Fifth Avenue and abruptly entered a large toy store. Going into the ladies' room, she took off her wig and glasses, threw her coat over her arm, and emerged as Kate Buchanan.

Hailing a cab, she asked to be taken to JFK. She would catch the next flight back to Los Angeles. Her business here was done.

On Monday morning Jasmine received a hand-delivered letter from the company managing her apartment building. After uncomprehendingly reading the bureaucratic legalese through once, she read the letter again. It stated that since Mr. Allan Silver had ceased paying the rent, she should telephone and advise them as soon as possible whether she wanted to rent the apartment under her own name.

She was dismayed. This was no hovel. Although she had, in fact, never asked Allan how much the rent was, she figured it was probably about two thousand dollars a month.

An hour later, a car dealer called to inform her that he would be sending someone by to pick up her leased car as soon as it was convenient, as the lease had been cancelled.

Allan was actually doing it, she thought grimly. He was cutting her off. Probably her credit card had already been cancelled, and there would be no allowance, that was certain.

She got out her bank book and sat at the kitchen table. Banking had never been her strong suit, and the checkbook hadn't been balanced for about six months. There'd been no need; she'd always had plenty of money. Now, she struggled through, adding the columns. By the time she finished an hour later, she realized she had a grand total of $1,384 left in the world.

She had saved nothing. With money as plentiful as it had been, she had essentially spent it as quickly as it came. All she had of value were some expensive pieces of jewelry worth a few thousand dollars, which she probably would be able to sell for a fraction of their retail value. Other than that, there would probably be some residual checks trickling in over the next few months from various television and film appearances, but not enough to support her in the manner to which she had grown accustomed. She realized for the first time that she was desperate.

There was only one way to face the situation and that was head-on. She called Allan at his office. His secretary said politely that he was not in but promised to give him the message that she had called. She needed to talk to someone, so she called Kate at the gallery.

"Oh, hi," Kate answered. "How did it go with Allan?"

"It was a disaster," Jasmine said. "We screamed and fought. I lost my temper, kicked him out, and he's cut me off without a penny."

"You can't be serious," Kate said. "Cut off everything?"

"Every dime," Jasmine said glumly. "I don't know what I'm going to do. I really need to talk to someone. Can we get together this afternoon or this evening?"

"I'm seeing David this evening. But that's a little later.

You could stop by my place right around five-thirty or six o'clock.''

There was a short embarrassed silence from Jasmine, and then she said, ''I don't think I'm going to have a car by then. The leasing company is repossessing it because Allan's cut off the lease.''

''Jesus! Well, fine. I'll stop by your place when I leave work. I'll probably leave here around five o'clock. What's the address?''

Jasmine gave it to her. ''I hope I'm not imposing on you. It's just . . .''

''Forget it,'' Kate cut in. ''What are friends for?''

As soon as she hung up, Kate called Page, told her that her trip had been successful, and asked if she could stop by her office about four-thirty.

''Sure,'' Page said.

''You need to talk to me about your PR campaign for Jason, don't you?'' Kate said meaningfully.

''Right,'' Page said. ''I'll tell Jason you stopped by.''

''Good.''

Kate was tired, still suffering the effects of bi-coastal jet lag, but she struggled bravely through the day, fighting back the fatigue. At four o'clock she asked Madge if she could leave a little early.

''Sure,'' Madge said. ''You look a little peaked. Is everything okay? Feeling all right?''

''I guess,'' Kate said. ''Just a little woozy. If I just head home and take it easy for a while, I'll be fine.''

''Well, don't hang around here,'' Madge said.

Twenty minutes later, she pulled into the garage of Page's office building. When she was shown in by the secretary, Page greeted her warmly, rising from behind her desk to shake her hand, and then closing the office door behind her.

''Sit,'' she said, pointing to a couch. And then she sat down as well. ''So, you got a name?''

''Yes, I do. He's in Ibiza, an island off Spain. I'm going to need to fly there soon.''

''How are you going to get away?'' Page asked.

"I'll be on a business trip to New Mexico or Arizona, or something like that."

"I see. So you'll need money for that trip?"

"Yes. What's the latest on the new wing's opening?"

"From what I gather from Jason," Page said, "it's scheduled to open when he has his painting. That's going to be the high point of the evening—the unveiling."

"Have they been getting much response yet to their queries?"

"Nothing of any value from what I can understand. I talked to Stodding this morning and he said there were a couple of minor Impressionist works. But when I pointed out that if they got a Rembrandt, the Rex would be the only museum in town with any significant work of his, he was quite thrilled with the idea of getting an Old Master, particularly a Rembrandt.

"Good, that's great," Kate said. "Okay, I also came to see you for another reason. It's Jasmine. She's in real trouble. Allan's cut her off completely."

"Really? What did she do?"

"She got pregnant."

"So?" Page said with a small shrug of her shoulders. "She can have an abortion, can't she?"

"She wants the child," Kate said. "Allan, of course, wants her to have an abortion."

"She refused?"

"And he's cutting her off till she, quote, 'comes to her senses,' unquote. She's actually quite destitute. He's stopped payments on her apartment, taken her car back, cancelled her credit card, no allowance. She has very little money."

"So why are you telling me?"

"Because I think we should help her," Kate said. "I'd like to help her just because I like her, but I also think she'll be able to help us."

"Jasmine?" Page said with a grimace. "I don't know if she's together enough to help us."

"I think you'd be surprised," Kate said. "I see more to her than most people do, I think. She's just a woman who hasn't had to use her intelligence. It's there. It's dormant."

Page nodded. "Well, I'm not sure about that, but I respect your judgment. Why are we going to need her?"

"Neither you nor I can travel much, and this is going to involve a great deal of travel. You can't be away from your business or Jason, and David will get suspicious if I'm away too often. Jasmine is now free and clear, unattached, and from what she's said feeling physically strong. We can have her do the traveling for us."

"Hmmm," Page said thoughtfully. "You're right, that may come in handy. Do you think we can trust her?"

Kate snorted. "She doesn't owe Allan anything. He wants to take her baby from her. She's been cut off and she needs money desperately."

Page nodded again. "So what do you want to do?"

"First, I want to figure out a way to help her," Kate said. "I'm going by to see her now. She needed someone to talk to. I'd have her come stay in my apartment, but it's a little small, number one. And number two, I don't want to appear to be taking sides in this thing, and David of course is around there fairly often and he'd know that she was staying with me. The same would be true of you. We have to remain impartial observers in this whole thing between Jasmine and Allan as far as the men are concerned. We don't want to attract any suspicion of any kind. Do you have any ideas?"

"Elsa," Page said. "My friend Elsa, who incidentally is going to help us as well with the money, she needs company. She has a maid but she doesn't live in. And she has an enormous apartment. There is a spare room in it. Jasmine could use that and keep Elsa company too. Let me call her about it, okay?"

"Can you do it now?" Kate asked. "I'm going to see Jasmine, and I'd like to be able to offer her an alternative to her situation. I'm not going to tell her anything about what's needed from me yet. Let's just give her the help she needs."

"Good." Page got up from the couch, went to her telephone, and dialed Elsa's number. "It's busy. I'll call again in a few minutes."

Kate looked at her watch, "I've got to go. Can you call me at Jasmine's?"

"Sure," Page said. "Let me just make sure I have her number." She flipped through her Rolodex and said, "Yeah, here it is. You'll be there in what, fifteen minutes?"

"Yeah, probably."

"Okay, I'll call you there in about twenty minutes."

"Good," Kate said. "I'll take off now."

"I'm glad things are proceeding well," Page said.

"Yeah, they are. I have some problems though." Kate hesitated before going out the door. "This man in Ibiza, all I have is a name. I don't know where to find him. I'm going to have to track him down. That's problem number one. Problem number two is that he's retired and I'm going to have to persuade him to do this."

"Were you able to get a back-up name?" Page asked.

"There's someone in Munich."

"Well, if Spain doesn't work out, you'll be on your way to Munich."

"Yep, I guess so. I'll keep you posted about when I'm going."

The two women said good-bye.

Jasmine was distraught when Kate arrived, pacing around her apartment, her face flushed, her normally perfect make-up a little runny from her earlier tears. Her apartment, which Kate had never seen before, was messy.

"I don't know what to do," Jasmine said to Kate soon after she arrived. "I keep thinking he's bluffing."

"It seems a pretty serious bluff," Kate said.

"I tried calling him twice and left messages, and he hasn't called back."

"Well, I'm assuming that he hasn't cut the line completely. Maybe he's just trying to make you sweat. When he calls back in a day or two, he'll ask you if you changed your mind."

"That's what I figure," Jasmine said. "If I say I have and I'll have the abortion as he wishes, then everything will be all hunky-dory again. Fuck him. I'm going to have this baby whether he likes it or not. If he doesn't want it, it's mine."

"Good, I'm glad to hear it," Kate said.

The telephone rang. Jasmine answered it and said, "It's Page for you."

Kate took the phone and, after listening for a moment, said, "That's wonderful, I'm glad to hear it."

She wrote down a name, address, and telephone number on the pad beside the phone.

"Super," she said. "I'll talk to you later."

Kate went back to the armchair in which she had been sitting. "Listen, I have proposition for you, although no one must know about it. I have somewhere for you to stay."

"Really?" Jasmine said. "Your apartment's a little small."

"No, not there. It's a friend of Page's. Her name's Elsa. She's an older woman, very wealthy, has an enormous apartment, and would really like company."

"Page did this?" Jasmine asked disbelievingly. "I thought she despised me."

Kate shook her head. "She's willing to help. I went over and talked to her just before coming here. She just talked to Elsa."

Jasmine looked flustered. "I can't pay much as far as rent goes."

"I don't think that's going to be necessary. As I said, she's wealthy and she needs company. I think she'll be really pleased just to have you there."

Jasmine glanced around the room in confusion. "I appreciate it, I really do. What am I going to do with all this stuff?"

"Box it," Kate said. "Box it and store it for the time being. We'll find out how much space there is at Elsa's, and you can take whatever you need, I guess. And as for the rest of it, you can store it until things straighten themselves out, which they will. I promise.''

''You think so?'' Jasmine asked.

''Yes, I do.''

Jasmine began to cry. She hid her face with her hands and shook her head. ''You are being so kind to me I don't know what to say. Why are you helping me like this? Why are you being so nice?'' Jasmine asked, looking up.

''Because you need help,'' Kate said. ''Because some time I may need help, and I'll call on you.''

''Fair enough,'' Jasmine said, a smile breaking through her tears.

''One thing: I don't know if the men are going to stand together on this,'' Kate said. ''But Page and I don't want to be in the middle of it. We don't want them to know that we're helping you at all. There's no telling how they would react.''

''Yes, that's probably wise,'' Jasmine said.

''David will probably ask me if I've heard what happened, and I'll tell him yes, that you called me and told me that you were upset. But that's all. I won't say anything about helping you or where you're staying or what you are doing.''

Jasmine allowed a crafty smile to creep across her face. ''This is cool. This is actually good. Allan is going to freak out when he finds that I've moved out of here. He won't know where I am or what I'm doing, and he won't be able to stand it. Believe me, I know him well enough to predict that.''

The smile fled again as she looked wildly around the room. ''How am I going to do this?'' she asked. ''How am I going to get my stuff over there? How am I going to pack, put things in storage? My God, I don't know where to start.''

''This is no time to act like a helpless female,'' Kate said caustically. ''You'll handle it just fine. Don't forget you're about to become a mother. From now on, you're going to have to use your intelligence.''

Jasmine looked sheepish. "I guess so. I guess it's just habit, isn't it?"

"Probably."

"Well, you're right, it's a habit I'm going to have to change, starting right now. I'm going to start packing tonight, and I'm going to move to Elsa's in the morning. I'll give her a call in a little while."

"Good." Kate looked at her watch, "I've got to run now. You call me if you need anything. But keep in mind that I don't want the men to know that we're talking to each other much. I don't want anybody to know. You understand that, right?"

"Sure," Jasmine said.

Kate stood. "I guess I'll talk to you tomorrow then."

Jasmine hugged her. "I really appreciate what you're doing. You know that, don't you?"

"Yep," Kate said. "See you later."

As soon as David entered her apartment, he asked how Kate was feeling. Then he said that he had spoken to Jason earlier in the day.

"Jason says that Allan and Jasmine have split up," he said.

"Yes, I heard," Kate said.

"The dumb girl went and got pregnant, from what I understand. Naturally that upset Allan considerably."

"She was a little upset herself," Kate said. "She wants to have the baby, he wants her to have an abortion. And apparently he has cut off all financial support to her."

David was sitting on the couch, his jacket and tie off, his shirt unbuttoned. He sighed. "The two things you have to know in life are your strengths and your weaknesses. You don't lay your weaknesses out there and invite people to walk all over them. Jasmine's not a very bright girl."

Kate held back an angry retort. "Well, it's none of our business, I suppose."

"That's right. It's between Allan and Jasmine."

Later, while they were eating dinner, he asked how she

was enjoying her new car. "It's beautiful," Kate said. "It runs like a dream."

"It should," he laughed. "It cost fourteen thousand dollars. This is no econo-box, even though it's small."

So, she thought to herself, he'd managed to mention the price. It was totally predictable. Also predictable was the fact that slowly, from now on, he would attempt to encircle her with his possessiveness. The car was the down payment. There'd be a few more down payments, and then he'd feel that he owned her.

Sure enough, a subtle change was already occurring. While they were drinking coffee, he said, "I want you to come to Santa Barbara with me next weekend." None of the tentative lover was there. No "Would you like to?" or "Would it be possible?" Simply, "I want you to."

"I don't know if I can," Kate said calmly. "There may be a business trip in the offing."

"Out of town?"

"My trips usually are. I may have to go to New Mexico for the gallery."

"When, and for how long?"

"I'm not sure yet. The arrangements haven't been made. But I'll let you know as soon as I know."

"Hmmm," he grunted, and sipped his coffee.

After a moment, he said, "You know you don't have to keep that job. I'm perfectly willing to help you out financially if you'd like to leave it."

"I enjoy it," Kate said.

"But if you quit, we'd have more time—you'd have more time," he said. "It's not as if working for Friars is something important—a major contribution to the world or anything."

"It's what I do. I'd feel useless sitting around all day eating bonbons."

"It's just that I don't want it to interfere with us."

"*Your* business won't interfere with us?" she asked sarcastically. "You won't be going on any business trips? Your family won't interfere with us? You won't have certain obligations to your wife?"

"Well, yes, of course I will," he said disgruntledly. "But that's necessary. What I do is important."

Kate shook her head. "And what I do isn't?"

"That's not what I mean, Kate. I make large amounts of money. It can buy you that car, pay for this apartment, pay for even a nicer apartment, pay for your clothes, and there'd still be plenty left over for everyone."

Kate smiled ruefully. "I'm afraid money isn't the only important thing in my life—" she started to say.

David interrupted, "Besides, if I went on a business trip, you'd probably be able to come with me if you weren't working."

"David, I'm not ready to quit my job yet," she said stubbornly. "Why don't we drop the subject?"

He saw that this was leading to their first argument and backed down. He smiled, "You've got to admit that money's nice to have though, isn't it?"

"Sure, I enjoy having it. Nice dinners, nice cars, nice trips. Yes, it's very nice, but I also enjoy my work."

"Well, I won't pressure you," he said. "I didn't mean to belittle what you do; I'm sure you're very good at it. It's just that I want to be with you more."

"I understand," she said, and let it drop.

When they made love after dinner, she felt no physical satisfaction whatsoever for the first time. In fact, it left her feeling slightly soiled. It was all so mechanical, so without meaning. She simply went through the motions, hiding her true feelings, pretending to enjoy his attentions.

She was irritated at herself as she lay open-eyed in the dark room, David quietly snoring beside her. This was no time to weaken, no time to have compunctions. She had to see this through to the end, to play the game like a pro, until the final whistle.

On Tuesday morning, Kate approached Madge with her plan. She'd thought about it during the previous night, wondering how to handle it, and had come up with a strategy. It was about eleven o'clock, and they were drinking coffee in the office. No one had been in the gallery all morning, and the phone had rung only twice.

"Slow, isn't it?" she said.

"Any slower and we'd be swimming in molasses," Madge replied.

"Madge, I think you should just think of me as a part-time employee," Kate suggested, as if the idea had just occurred to her.

Madge wasn't fooled, not for a second. She looked across at Kate. 'You want more time off, don't you?"

Kate laughed. "I can't con you. Yeah, I do. Something's come up. I not only need time off, I need your help. I need you to lie for me."

Madge began to look interested. 'This has got to be about a man."

"Right," Kate admitted. "I need about a week. There's someone—" she paused, "someone else I have to see, and I don't want David to know."

'Ho, ho," Madge said, "double dealing on double dealing. The mistress cheating on the master who's cheating on the wife. What a book, what a book. Your life's so exciting, Kate, and mine is so boring, but I'm getting a vicarious thrill out of all this."

Kate smiled. "I need an excuse to be out of town for a while. I'd like you, if David calls, to tell him the same story that I'm going to tell him."

"And what's that?"

"I'm telling him that I'm going to New Mexico. That I'm appraising some paintings for an insurance company, which were destroyed in a fire, and also to find some new artists for possible showing in the gallery."

Madge clapped her hands, "A good story, a good story. I couldn't have dreamed up a better one myself. He's not likely to call here, though, is he?"

Kate twisted her mouth wryly. "I wouldn't count on it. He's becoming quite possessive."

"I see he bought you a car," Madge said.

"Leased," Kate replied blithely. "But mine to use as I wish."

"Are you enjoying yourself?"
"I have my moments," Kate said.

CHAPTER EIGHTEEN

There were arrangements to be made. Packing, tying up loose ends, and not the least getting to Ibiza.

Kate discovered there were no direct flights from Los Angeles to Ibiza. She called TWA and found that they could fly her to Madrid, where she would have to wait twelve hours before catching a flight to Ibiza via Iberia, the Spanish airline. The next logical step was to call Iberia. Unfortunately, they only had two flights a week and the wait was only forty minutes shorter in Madrid than TWA. Back to TWA.

Because of the fact that she was not booking thirty days or a week ahead, the fare was over a thousand dollars for a round trip. Time was running against her now and she couldn't quibble over a few hundred dollars. In fact, time had become the single most important element in her plan. At any moment Jason could find a painting that satisfied his needs. She made arrangements to leave the following day, Wednesday, in the morning.

David was one of the loose ends she had to tie up.

She called him at his office and told him that she had to leave the next day for approximately a week.

"You don't know exactly how long you'll be gone?" he asked.

"No, it depends. This appraisal stuff can take a while, plus I have to look at some new artists."

"Well, all right," he said. "Afraid I won't be able to see you tonight, so we won't get together for a while."

"I'll miss you," she said, because it was required of her.

"And I'll miss you as well. Call me if you can, okay? Do you know where you'll be?"

"No, I don't have that information yet. If I get a chance I'll call you, though, at your office, of course."

"All right. Have a good trip. And by the way, think about what I said about quitting that job."

"I will," she promised, and hung up.

Her next problem was to get cash from Page. They couldn't be seen together, not now. Not more than they had already.

"Let's meet at Elsa's tonight," Page said when she called. "I'll have the money for you in cash then. About five thousand dollars, and there's more where that came from if you need it."

"That should do for now," Kate said. "I have no idea what the expenses are going to be. It depends upon what's going to happen when I talk to the artist."

"Understood," Page said. "I'll see you tonight at around eight." She gave Kate the address and hung up.

The atmosphere that night at Elsa's apartment was almost partylike. Jasmine had moved in and excitedly showed Kate her bedroom. It was twice the size of the room in her previous apartment. Page was there, and Elsa reclined like a queen on her couch, while they hovered around her.

Jasmine and Elsa apparently got along famously. "Elsa says my sister can come and stay with me whenever she likes, as well," Jasmine told Kate. "There is a roll-away bed that I can put in my bedroom."

"I enjoy having young people around me," Elsa said. "Jasmine for one, and then she has an even younger sister who will visit sometimes."

It was understood by Page and Elsa that Jasmine was not yet to know of their scheme, and so it was not openly discussed. At one point, when Jasmine left the room, however, Elsa drew Kate to her side and said, "Your adventure has breathed new blood into this old body. Is all going well?''

''Yes,'' Kate said. ''So far so good.''

Kate found she liked the shrewd Elsa. She reminded her of a retired Madame, that traditional cliched figure of a woman with a heart of gold beneath the tough exterior. Elsa, in turn, found Kate both charming and beautiful. Kate knew that because the old woman said it twice.

A little later, Page coolly withdrew a manila envelope from her purse and handed it to Kate, saying, ''Here are the press releases on the painting.''

Kate put it in her purse without looking at it. She knew that it was stuffed with hundred dollar bills.

At nine o'clock, Kate said she had to leave. ''I'm going on a business trip tomorrow,'' she announced. ''I have to go to New Mexico for the gallery, so I'll be away for probably about a week. Anyway, I need some sleep,'' she said, then left.

In the morning, she arrived at LAX almost two hours ahead of her flight time, parked in the long-term parking lot, and took a shuttle to the terminal. She hated checking luggage through, particularly when it involved changing planes. So she stuffed as many clothes as she could into a suit carrier and the rest into a small carry-on. Consequently, the check-in time was done in minutes. She spent an hour waiting in the lounge before boarding the flight. And then she was soaring high above Los Angeles, speeding towards Europe and a new phase in her quest.

For once Kate had managed to sleep on an aircraft, and she arrived in Ibiza feeling fairly refreshed. She took a taxi from the tiny ''international'' airport to the port town, also named Ibiza and the capital of the island, asking the driver to recommend a suitable hotel.

In the early evening light she could see it was a charming town, built on a hill sloping down to a beautiful blue-water harbor. On top of the hill, overlooking the town and harbor, was the cathedral and acropolis. Somehow, the whitewashed buildings packed on top of each other up to the high horizon looked familiar to Kate. Perhaps, she thought, I've been here in another life.

The pension was small, inexpensive, and comfortable, located in the older walled part of town. There was nothing fancy to it, but it was clean, the owners were friendly, and they spoke English.

She took her luggage into her room, with its wooden bed, sink, and water jug, and then enjoyed a refreshing shower down the hall in the communal bathroom. She dressed in jeans, T-shirt, and a floppy hat, and wandered down the hill to the main area of town near the harbor.

The tourists were still in evidence, filling the tables of the sidewalk cafes: Scandinavians, French, Germans, English, and Americans. There was more than a fair share of remnants of the sixties, long-haired Americans surreptitiously handing joints to each other across the small metal tables. More interesting to her were the lissome blond Danish girls, trying to appear bored and blasé, the dark Italians trying to imitate the Americans, the intense Germans, and the English looking down their noses at all the inferior races.

She took a table at a small cafe and ordered *cafe leche.* It was strong and invigorating. She had changed five hundred dollars into pesetas at the airport and she paid the waiter, fumbling over the change.

Within minutes she was approached by a tall, lean American. His hair fell down to his shoulders, and he wore torn blue jeans and scuffed Reeboks. "Hey, how you doing?"

"Just fine," she said.

"Just arrived, have you?"

"Yes."

"How long you here for?"

"Just a few days. I needed a break."

"Oh yeah? Where you from?"

"New York," she said.

"Huh. I left there two years ago, I don't think I'll ever go back."

"You been here all this time?" she asked.

"Nah, I was in London for a while, Copenhagen, Amsterdam. Been here for about six months."

"Just hanging out?"

"Yeah, it's as good a place as any. What's your name?"

"Daphne du Maret."

"Well, hi, Daph. I'm Jack."

"Pleased to meet you," she said.

"Need any dope?"

She shook her head. "I'm relaxed enough already just being here."

He shrugged. "Well, if you do, you can score through me. I have what you need. You name it, I got it."

"I'll keep that in mind." Then she asked him, "You know somebody here named Marcus Devereaux?"

Jack frowned, "Devereaux, Marcus . . . Marc? Nah, don't know anybody by that name. Why? Who is he?"

"Friend of a friend," she said. "Someone in New York told me to look him up and thought he might be here. I guess not."

"Nah," he said. "I know everyone here."

"Are there any good art galleries on the island?"

He waved down the street. "There are three of them right down there. I don't know how good they are. Art's not my bag, you know what I mean?"

"Yeah, well, I'll check them out," she said.

He looked her up and down. "You want to get together later?"

"No," Kate said.

He shrugged and stood, "Well, good talking to you. See you around." And he wandered off looking for his next victim.

She finished her coffee and decided she'd visit the galleries in the morning. Right now, she needed sleep more than anything, she decided. Fatigue over the last few days, which had involved a trip to New York and back, and now a trip halfway across the world, was catching up with her. She needed to be alert and awake for what she had to do. It would pay to take the time now to sleep.

* * *

Kate slept until nine the next morning. After a quick shower, she dressed and went out for breakfast. The sun was shining brilliantly, although a small breeze was whipping whitecaps out in the harbor. The air smelled salty and wonderful.

She went to one of the sidewalk cafes and ordered croissants and coffee. While she ate, Jack, the local pusher, walked by. He gave her a nod of recognition but did not stop, for which she was thankful.

When she finished breakfast, she returned to the galleries she had seen the previous evening. Only one of them, Traditions, was open. It looked like the typical tourist trap, with harbor scenes and other seascapes badly done yet picturesque enough for people to buy as memories of a vacation on the island.

A fat bearded man behind the counter peered at her over his glasses and said, in an English accent, "May I help you?"

"Just browsing," she said politely.

"Well, if you need anything, do call on me."

'Oh, there is one thing," she said brightly.

His head rose slowly.

"Do you know someone named Marcus Devereaux, an artist, I believe? A friend in New York asked me to look him up."

"Don't know anyone by that name," he said, and returned to his newspaper.

She spent another three minutes in the shop, gazing aghast at the hideous paintings, and then left.

Apparently Mr. Devereaux was keeping a fairly low profile, if he was even going by that name. Well, she'd just have to keep on trying.

By noon, she had tried the other two galleries, with no luck, and a fourth gallery on the other side of the town square. Nobody knew Marcus Devereaux, or if they did, they weren't telling her. All she had gained from her endeavors were the names of four other galleries, two of them at Santa Eulalia del Rio, a town on the other side of the island. In the afternoon she took a taxi there.

Ibiza was no emerald isle, she decided as she looked out the window. The few patches of green stood out like jewels in a tray of stones. But most of the island, except for fig trees, carob trees, and olive groves, was brown and seemed even more so because of the old stone walls the farmers used to mark their boundaries.

Of the two galleries, one was owned by a Frenchman who was even more uncommunicative than the Englishman had been. He didn't even bother verbally answering her question, just shook his head.

The last gallery was run by an American, as effusive as the Frenchman had been withdrawn.

"Hi, my name is Bart Stone." He greeted her with an outstretched hand as soon as she entered the shop. He was slim, tanned, probably in his mid-thirties, with a broad, friendly face. "What's your pleasure, ma'am? American, aren't you?"

"Yeah, from New York," she said.

"Oh, New York, land of the free, home of the brave . . . how pleased I am not to be there."

"You've been here awhile, I take it?" she asked, amused.

"Four years, four years of happiness and bliss, being my own man. I lived in New York once, an ad director. I added ten years to my life coming here, maybe twenty."

Kate looked around the store. The caliber of art here was higher than what she had previously seen. Some excellent landscapes, a few modern abstract pieces, and some excellent bronze and wood sculptures. "Your stuff is better than most on the island," she acknowledged.

"Ah, you have the eye," he said. "Yes, it is. Unfortunately, it's not what the tourists want. They prefer paintings of four-masted ships and waves pounding against rocks, or perhaps a little sidewalk cafe scene."

"Yes, I noticed," Kate said with a laugh. "But I assume you make a living."

"As much as I need. Once you've been here a while and know how things work, you can live pretty cheaply."

"Do you know someone named Marcus Devereaux?" she asked.

It was as if a hood dropped over his face. He pursed his mouth, furrowed his brow, and said, "Devereaux? Devereaux? Marcus Devereaux? Lives here, does he? No, don't know anyone by that name."

"Are you sure?" she asked, certain that he was lying.

"Oh, yeah, I'd remember a name like that. French, is he?"

"No, American," she replied. "An artist. I figured that if anyone would know him, you would."

"No, I don't know anyone by that name," he said, and changed the subject. "See anything you like?"

"I'm just looking around. I'm not a serious customer, you know."

"What's your name?" he asked.

"Mrs. Daphne du Maret."

"Well, pleased to meet you. Staying in the port, are you?"

"Yes, at a small pension, The Catalan, I believe it's called."

"Oh, yes, I believe I know it. Nice place, nice place. What line of business are you in?"

"Oh, I dabble in a few things," she said evasively.

"Uh huh, I see."

There was a minute of silence, and then he said, "This guy you're looking for, what's his name? Devereaux? Friend of yours is he?"

"No, we just have some mutual friends. Somebody just wanted me to look him up," she said. "Nothing important."

"Yeah, I see. Well, if I happen to run across him, ah . . ." he laughed, "if he walks in, ah, in the store someday, I guess I know where to find you."

"Yeah, I guess you do. Well, thanks for letting me browse. I'll be seeing you."

"Sure," he said, "enjoy your stay."

When she stepped out into the street, Kate found it hard to suppress her excitement.

"Yeah," she said quietly to herself, she'd finally struck a nerve, she could swear to it. Bart Stone knew exactly who Marcus Devereaux was. He might have good taste in art, but he was a bad liar. Not only that, but he'd found out all he could about her without being too blatantly obvious. What it would result in, she didn't know, but at least she'd stirred the pot.

She found another taxi and rode back to Ibiza and the pension. There was not much else she could do now but wait. Devereaux knew where she was and that she was looking for him. He would either bury himself deeper, or his curiosity would send him looking for her.

It was ten-thirty. Kate had just had a late dinner, as was the Spanish custom, and was walking back across the square toward her hotel. The meal had been wonderful, a kind of paella with shrimp and mussels, accompanied by a half carafe of a hearty red wine from Barcelona.

In spite of the excellent meal, she felt disappointed. Nothing had happened yet. No reaction from Devereaux to her search. She had just crossed the square and entered a darkened street, where the headlights of a car approached from behind her. Automatically, she stepped from the road to the curb. The car stopped beside her and the door opened.

"Mrs. du Maret," she heard. She bent forward to see gallery owner, Bart Stone.

"Good evening," she said.

"Would you get in, please?" he asked.

"The car?" she asked, acting stupid.

"Yes, I have somewhere to take you. The person you are looking for will see you."

"Ah," she said, entering the car and closing the door behind her. "The person you don't know," she said ironically.

"Don't be dense, Mrs. Du Maret," Stone said, his earlier amiability absent. "He wants to know your business in looking for him. And, incidentally, I don't see a wedding ring."

"Ah, yes," Kate said sweetly. "I'm a widow."

"Had to hock it, I suppose," Stone said. From that point on he was silent.

They drove out of town, north she thought, and then they took a winding dirt road, another road off it, another road off that, and by then she was lost. They bumped their way for another mile or two, and then came to a stop outside a large stone house.

"In there," he said.

Kate suddenly felt nervous. "You're not coming in?"

"It's none of my business. I'll be back in an hour or two to pick you up and take you back to your hotel."

"Well, thank you," she said uncertainly, and got out of the car.

It was a large house, she noted, as she walked up the flagstone path, larger than most on the island. It looked as if it had three or four bedrooms, plus other rooms.

Except for a soft front porch light and a dimmer light shining from a window, the house was in darkness. She went to the heavy wooden door and knocked. The sound of her knock echoed back from stone walls and floors, and then she heard footsteps approach.

The door swung open and a man stood there.

"Mrs. du Maret," he said, "I believe you've been looking for me. Please come in."

He was a tall man, perhaps six feet two inches. Some would call him lean, she supposed, but to her he looked thin. Long arms and thin sensitive fingers. Brown hair fell over his forehead, and below it were dark brown eyes, a slightly large but straight nose, and a wide firm mouth. His eyes examined her with an imposing intensity. He turned and led the way into a large, comfortably furnished living room, where a fire burned in the fireplace. She noticed that he walked gracefully, almost like a dancer.

"Please sit down." He indicated an overstuffed couch.

She sat, but he remained standing. He put his arms behind his back and looked at her. "May I get you something to drink? Some wine perhaps?"

"Yes," she said, "a glass of wine would be fine."

"I'll be back in a moment." He walked out a door at the side of the room.

She looked around the room. There were two excellent pieces of sculpture, one of them reminding her of something she'd seen at Bart Stone's gallery. A long shelf along one wall held about two hundred books, many of them large art-sized tomes. On the walls were about five paintings, only one of which she vaguely recognized as the work of a European Impressionist. But they were all excellent pieces. The furniture was simple, functional, but looked old. A Persian carpet covered the concrete floor. Mr. Devereaux was apparently a man of impeccable taste.

"Here you are," he said, appearing in front of her and holding out a glass of red wine.

"Thank you."

He sat at the opposite end of the couch, lifted his glass, and said, "To life."

She raised her glass and sipped it. It tasted like rubies.

"Now," he said, lowering his glass, "why are you looking for me?"

"I have a business proposition for you, a commission."

"How did you find me?"

"Through a Mr. Chiroc in Paris."

Devereaux shook his head. "I'm afraid you're wasting your time. I'm not interested in that proposition. I'm no longer in that business."

"You haven't even heard it," she protested.

"I don't need to."

"Don't you need money?" she asked.

"No."

She didn't know what to say next. His words left no room for her to maneuver. What argument could she use? She looked down and noticed that her wine glass was almost empty. In her nervousness she must have gulped it.

He was watching her, a slightly ironic smile on his lips. "Would you like more wine?"

"I think I'd better have some coffee," she said. "I had wine at dinner and I think I've had too much . . . if you don't mind."

"Not at all," he said, "I'll make some."

Again he rose and disappeared through the side door. Apparently there was a room there and another one beyond it, because she saw the glow of a light come on in the distance. She got up and walked around the room. There was a chill in spite of the fire.

She peered through a darkened doorway at the end of the room. It looked like a study. There was another door leading from it, a light peeping through a gap near the floor. Curious, she walked to the door and opened it. It was an enormous studio, with a glass window opening it to the sky and light. There were easels, blank canvases, the smell of paint permeating everything and, yes, paintings—completed, half-completed, just-begun sketches, which sent a shock from her toes to her head.

She knew now why Ibiza had seemed so familiar. She had seen a painting of it.

"What are you doing in here?" a voice said harshly behind her.

She turned quickly. Devereaux stood in the doorway, a grim expression on his face.

"You have no right to come in here. Please return to the living room."

She didn't answer, instead stepping forward and looking at the painting on the easel. A landscape, a small bay on an island, a fishing boat, a sense of serenity, and yet in the rising waves, the feeling of nature's power.

"My God!" Kate exclaimed.

There was another painting against the wall that had been completed. A small village with a dirt road running through it, a sidewalk cafe, and old men in black sitting at the small tables, sipping on glasses of some unknown nectar.

She turned to face Devereaux.

He was looking at her curiously now, the anger replaced by puzzlement. She must have looked strange. Something of what she was feeling must have been translated into her body and face, for he asked, "What is it?"

She opened her mouth to speak, and then closed it. It

was impossible, yet here it was. "You're Breer. You are Breer. My God! Marcus Devereaux is Breer!"

"I want to tell you two stories," Kate said. "They are both about a man named Jason Thomas."

They were sitting in the living room, each holding a hot mug of coffee. Devereaux/Breer, as she now thought of him, had his feet up on a heavy wooden table that looked as if it had been carved from a piece of driftwood, all of its imperfections polished and highlighted to form a beautiful mosaic.

She was responding to his question of "How do you know my work; I'm not exactly world famous?"

"The first story," she continued, "concerns a talented painter by the name of Breer, a rising star in the art world, not because of gimmickry or outrageousness, but because he has that rare ability to put feelings on canvas and evoke them in his viewers. Breer was becoming quite well-known and his work was increasing in value. He approached a gallery in Los Angeles, Friars, to show his work. The owner, Madge Bernstein, was only too pleased, as she had been an admirer of his for some time.

"But then a breakthrough happened for Breer. The Rex Museum, an extremely prestigious museum in Los Angeles and indeed the country, learned of his upcoming show. The director, Stodding Watson, told Madge that in the new wing of the Rex currently being built, they wanted to feature a young, modern, up-and-coming artist. In that room, he suggested, there would be six to eight Breer paintings, featured by themselves as an example of contemporary art with roots firmly bound in tradition.

"Madge was ecstatic, and when she got word to Breer, through the circuitous route with which she communicated to him, he too was excited. This single stroke of fortune would increase his exposure, his credibility, his reputation, and probably triple the value of his work. It was one of those rare opportunities that many artists deserve but seldom get.

"The new wing of the Rex is going to be called the

Thomas Wing, named after its main benefactor, Jason Thomas, a multimillionaire who lives in Los Angeles. When Thomas heard of Watson's plan to have a Breer room, he immediately opposed it. Instead, he wanted another contemporary artist featured in that room, a man by the name of Jack Patney. Watson, in spite of his admiration for Breer's work, complied. You don't say no to a man who's given millions of dollars to your museum.

"Why did Jason Thomas do this? Perhaps he didn't like Breer's work. No. As it turned out, he was an admirer of Breer's work. The reason he did it was because, as a major collector for the past five years, he has been collecting Jack Patney's works, almost from the moment they first appeared at bargain-basement prices. He now has a collection of somewhere between twenty-five and thirty of this artist's works, works he does not particularly admire or care for, works that he considers purely an investment.

"Jason Thomas knows that if this artist's works are featured at the Rex, their value will increase tremendously and that in the gallery in the basement of his home in Bel-Air, even after donating six to eight of the Patney paintings to the Rex, he will be sitting on a small fortune—the remaining twenty to twenty-four Patney paintings.

"It isn't that Thomas needs the money—God knows he has enough of that. It is something derived from that peculiar need of some of the rich—the need to say they've won, that yet again they have beaten the odds.

"Breer's opportunity to advance in recognition and status as an artist—a well-deserved opportunity—was denied. It was denied because of the arrogance, greed, and manipulation of Jason Thomas."

Marcus stared back at her, his thoughts hidden except for a slight tightness to his mouth. "So that's what happened."

"Yes."

"Damn! I knew it was something. Madge Bernstein just said they changed their minds. She never told me why."

"She didn't know why. All she knew was that Jason Thomas had nixed the deal. She had no clue why."

"God, I hate people like that," Marcus said fiercely. "The vultures of the art world, we'd all be better off without them." He looked at her again with that intense gaze. "Who are you? How do you know all this?"

Kate looked down at her empty coffee cup. "Do you have more coffee?"

"Yes, of course. I'm sorry." He took her cup and disappeared into the kitchen. A moment later he returned, and handed the refilled cup to her. As he leaned forward, his eyes met hers. "I'm beginning to think you are a very remarkable woman."

"Well, thank you. Let me tell you the second story. It's about a young woman named Kate Buchanan and her brother who went under the stage name of Joel Buck—a shortened version of Buchanan, of course."

She told him the story of Joel and Angie. How Jason had found out Angie, his mistress, was having an affair, how he had sent men around to dissuade Joel and how they had murdered him. She then recounted how a distraught sister, who had lost the only surviving member of her family in this brutal murder, swore to take revenge and how she had come to Los Angeles to insinuate herself in Jason Thomas's social circle, by becoming a mistress to one of Jason's friends.

"And you are Kate Buchanan?" Marcus asked, interrupting her for the first time.

"Yes, I am."

"And I figure in your plan of revenge?"

"Yes, you do."

"How?"

She put her cup down and leaned back on the couch. "The Thomas Wing of the Rex is a monument to Jason Thomas's arrogance. It's the monument that will gain him entrée into the highest levels of society, levels that have been unaccessible to him in spite of his great wealth. It will bring him respectability and notoriety. I think it means more to him than anything he has ever done. In spite of his great achievements in business, they have not been unselfish. This seemingly benevolent act, the donation of huge sums of money to build this new wing, money of his own and money that he has raised from acquaintances, is something that would gain him a level of admiration he's never had.

"To top it off, Thomas has decided, as a showpiece of the new wing, to donate a seven-million dollar work of art, a masterpiece. One that would immediately make the Rex, and more particularly the Thomas Wing, one of the greatest museums in the country. He doesn't have this work yet. He's searching for it, and I intend to provide it for him."

Understanding lit Marcus's eyes, and a small smile appeared on his lips. "And this is where I come in, isn't it?"

"Yes. I want you to forge Rembrandt's "Christ" of 1662, for me and for Jason Thomas. I'm going to sell it to him for seven million dollars, and then on the night that the museum opens, when this masterpiece, the only major Rembrandt in all the museums in Los Angeles, is unveiled, I'm going to arrange for it to be revealed as a forgery."

Marcus erupted with a short burst of laughter. "You *are* a remarkable woman," he said, admiration in his eyes.

"I'm a woman," she said. "Perhaps if I were a man, I would have simply killed Jason Thomas. But that's not the kind of revenge I'm capable of. I think that this will bring about a different kind of justice. Thomas will be the laughing stock of the art world. This will puncture him where he is most inflated—his pride and arrogance."

A silence lengthened between them, each occupied with their own thoughts.

Kate wondered anxiously as she waited. He had two motives for helping her. One was to get his own revenge for the manipulation and misuse of power Thomas had shown as far as Marcus's own career was concerned. The other was to help her. But she was a stranger. Perhaps simply, when it came down to the bottom line, the aesthetic and the poetic justice of her plan would win him over.

"Will you help me?" she asked finally.

Marcus shrugged. "I don't know. You're asking me to commit a criminal act."

"From what I understand, you've done it before," she said brazenly.

He looked at her quizzically, then smiled. "Yes, I have. But I was younger then and more foolish."

"Why?" she asked. "Why did you do it?"

He grimaced. "I lived in Paris, I was a starving artist—literally starving. My paintings weren't selling and I needed money. I was also angry. I thought my work was good. I thought it deserved recognition. I despised the art establishment, with their airs and false expertise. I saw this as a way to gain financial rewards and to strike back. I knew I could fool them all." He shrugged. "As I said, I was younger then."

He rose and walked across the room, his hands behind his back, his lithe body graceful. "I'd learned my art the old-fashioned way, by duplicating the masters. I would spend time in the Louvre. I did Vermeer dozens of times. I did Rembrandt's works over and over again. I did Van Gogh paintings repeatedly, until I could duplicate the masters perfectly. This was the grounding of my art, the roots. From there I could master my own medium and create my own vision. But I had the basics."

He paced five or six steps forward and then turned, pacing back in the other direction while he spoke. "When I was approached with the scheme to produce some forgeries for what, at the time, was a magnificent sum of money, it seemed as if everything in my life had led to that capability and led to that moment. And so I did it. My motives were survival and revenge. I can no longer justify them. I did it for a year and then I quit, and swore I'd never do it again. Revenge is not as sweet as it appears. Sometimes it can leave a bitter taste in your mouth." He looked over at her. "I hope you know that."

Kate sighed. "I've thought about it, but it's something we all have to find out for ourselves, I guess."

"Yes," he said. "In truth, however, your motives are

far purer and more selfless than mine were. Perhaps your revenge will be sweeter than honey."

"Will you help me?" Kate asked.

He walked toward her and then stopped two feet away, his hands still behind his back. Marcus looked down at her, a smile dancing in his eyes. "How can I refuse? Yes, of course I will. I'll help you."

"Why?" she found herself asking. She had to know.

"Because Thomas deserves it. As I said before, his type are like vultures. They don't deserve to own art of any caliber," he said grimly. Then he chuckled. "And also, I must admit, because your plan tickles me. There's a certain element of poetic justice in it that appeals to me."

Kate had never admitted to herself that this moment would be one of the most important in her life. Her whole plan, all the work she had done, depended on it. She had dreaded the thought of him refusing her. She had wondered even if a refusal would have taken the wind completely out of her sails and sent her cowering back to Los Angeles, perhaps even to give up her plan of revenge. Stress had been stretching her feelings, the mystery of not knowing what would happen.

Now she couldn't help herself. She leapt to her feet, threw her arms around his neck, and kissed him on the mouth.

Marcus kissed her back. They drew apart, laughing and breathless.

Marcus's eyes held a new kind of warmth, and at that moment she realized he was one of the most attractive men she had ever met.

The moment was interrupted by the sound of an approaching car and the sweep of headlights across the front of the house.

"It looks like your ride back to town is here," Marcus said.

Was that a note of regret in his voice? she wondered.

"Well," he said, immediately turning businesslike, "I assume that you brought some research materials with you?"

"Yes, they're in my suitcase at the hotel. I have some photographs."

"I'm going to want to go over every step of this with you. I'd like to know the whole plan. I don't want any slipups, although I'm sure you've covered everything very well. I'd still like to know exactly how you are going to achieve your goal."

"Okay," she said, "I'll go over it with you."

"Good, well, let's have Bart take you back, and then he can bring you out here in the morning, if that's all right?"

"Sure, and thanks."

"My pleasure."

They went out into the night to the waiting car.

"Hey, Bart," Marcus said, "can you take the lady to her hotel?"

"Sure," Bart said. "I hope you guys had a good visit."

"Would you bring her back in the morning?" Marcus asked.

"No problem. Hop in, Mrs. du Maret," Bart said, and opened the door.

There were no questions on the drive back to town. Instead, Bart kept up a running monologue about life on the island. It suited Kate just fine. Her mind was too full as it was.

CHAPTER NINETEEN

At ten o'clock the next morning Bart Stone picked Kate up at the pension. In the car, she was relaxed enough to notice for the first time that it was a dilapidated old English Morris Minor. He drove down the bumpy, winding island roads with carefree abandon, one hand on the wheel, the other out the window, his eyes constantly scouring the countryside and her face as he talked nonstop throughout the entire journey.

The trip seemed much quicker than last night and she surmised that he had taken her on a purposefully circuitous route to confuse her about the location. However, such fears had disappeared and in about ten minutes they were at Marcus's house. She saw now that it was surrounded by large fig trees, with a small but colorful flower bed in front.

Marcus stepped out of the front door to greet them, waiting for her on the porch. He was wearing a long Morrocan caftan, a colorful robe that fell to his ankles. She stepped out of the car, and with a cheerful wave, Bart took off in a cloud of dust.

"He's quite a character," she said as she walked up the steps, a manila folder under one arm.

"A good friend," Marcus said. He turned. "Come on, have you had breakfast yet?"

"Oh, I had a cup of coffee and a croissant."

"Well, how about an omelette?"

"Mmmm, sounds good."

He led the way through the living room, through another small storage room, into a large airy kitchen.

"I've been coming to this island on and off since the sixties. When I first came here I was so broke I couldn't afford any of this. The first house I stayed in consisted of one room. At one end was a bed, at the other end a fireplace. I cooked on the fireplace. The only water came from a well outside, and there wasn't a toilet."

"How did you handle that?" she asked.

"There was an area outside filled with cacti. That's where people had been fertilizing the ground for generations."

"But you liked it well enough to come back."

"Oh, yes, but as I grew a little older, I became more used to the creature comforts, so gradually over the past few years, I've built this place up into something I'm more relaxed in. The modern conveniences like electricity and plumbing were something I found I couldn't really do without anymore."

She couldn't tell his age. He could be anywhere in his thirties. It wasn't that he had a baby face, but there was an innocence to it and a lack of that heaviness that comes with age. "How old are you?"

"Thirty-six. I first came to Europe . . . oh, maybe when I was eighteen, or seventeen, but it was in '69. This was one of the first places I visited."

"And you've lived in Europe since then?"

"Well, pretty much. I've been back to the States a few times. I went back once for a couple of years in the mid-seventies, but somehow I didn't feel quite at home there. And then, as my painting grew more serious, I realized how much I loved this island. It has a certain solitude that is available if you need it. But then in tourist season, of course, there are all kinds of diversions."

She watched while he skillfully mixed ingredients and told her more about the island. "Ibiza is known as an island of peace. It has been occupied by half-a-dozen cultures—the Phoenicians, Carthaginians, Greeks, Arabs, Romans. But somehow whenever they came here, they grew peaceful. At one time, the Carthaginians, Romans, and Greeks, who were lopping each other's heads off elsewhere in the Mediterranean, all coexisted peacefully here."

"What do they attribute it to? The weather?" Kate asked.

"They say it's because of the non-toxic soil on the island. Its purity. No poisonous plants or animals can grow here. The island's astrological sign is Scorpio and once they even imported scorpions, but they didn't reproduce and died after a generation. That's why there are so many cemeteries on the island, if you noticed. People used to have their bodies sent here for burial. The flesh wouldn't corrupt as fast in this soil and they'd go to heaven quicker, they believed."

He served the omelette, which was delicious, moist, and fluffy.

"Mmmm," she said, after the first mouthful. "You can add cooking to your artistic abilities."

"A hobby of mine," he said proudly. "What about you? What's your background?"

"Nothing very exciting. My parents died when my brother and I were pretty young. I went to school—art history—got a job in New York. Worked in acquisitions and authentications, got pretty good at it. Then Joel died . . ."

"Any men in your life?" he asked casually.

She shook her head. "No. There was a college romance, but it didn't work out. And there have been a few affairs here and there. And you can't count the man I'm now sleeping with."

"I was wondering how you felt about that?" he asked.

"I try not to. It's something that's necessary," she said shortly.

"You are a very determined woman."

"Yeah, some people say pigheaded."

"It's a good quality," he approved.

When they finished eating, he swept the dishes off the table and put them in the sink, saying, "We'll do those later. Now let's have a look at what you've got. Come on into the studio."

They went into the studio and she opened her folder on a large drawing table. "Here we go," she said. "These are old pictures. This painting disappeared from view after the Second World War. Some of these pictures were taken in the twenties, some in the thirties, and some in the forties, luckily."

"Color?"

"I've two color ones. The problem is, I don't know how accurate the printing was."

"That's all right," he said, "Rembrandt worked with a limited palette, which I know well. We'll be able to duplicate the original colors."

He removed the first photograph from the folder and held it up. "God, what a work," he said admiringly of a painting of Christ.

"That's why they call him a master," she said. "As you know, he did a number of 'Christ' paintings through the years, but this is considered one of the greatest."

"Well, it's not going to be easy, but it is doable. The key is in the pigments."

She nodded.

During different periods of history, certain pigments were available to artists. In authenticating older paintings, experts examined the layers of pigments that were used and compared them to what had been discovered in existing paintings. There couldn't be any divergences; they had to match exactly, in color and type, in order of layer.

"Do you know much about forgery?" he asked as he studied the pictures.

"I did some research."

He told her more. The forgery of art had been an art in itself for centuries, he said. "The single-most productive art faker of the nineteenth century was a gentleman by the name of Reinhold Vasters. He's one of my favorites," he said with a grin. "Vasters's specialty was luxury objects, such as gold cups of the fifteenth through seventeenth centuries—beautiful vessels of carved rock crystal mounted in gold or silver gilt—placques, pendants and other jewelry, precious stones and other items. He did tons of the stuff."

"What happened?" Kate asked.

He put the pictures back in the folder and closed it. "Vasters's forgeries would probably have never been discovered except for his habit of keeping working drawings of his fakes. When he died in 1909 his effects were auctioned, and these drawings finally came to rest at the Victoria and Albert Museum and half a century later were discovered, leading to the reattribution of many works in famous museums around the world."

"I think there was one of those at the Met."

Marcus laughed, warming to his subject. "I think that more forgeries have been discovered through the forger's desire for recognition than anything else. We all want to be recognized as artists. Why else would Vasters carefully preserve his working drawings?

"There was an Odessa goldsmith named Israel Rouchomovski, who made the 'Tierra of Siataphernes' and then sold it to the Louvre in 1896 as a rare Greco-Scythian goldwork. Rouchomovski would never have been caught except that he went to Paris and announced to the press that he was the Tierra's real maker. The Louvre was not amused."

Kate knew, both from her own experience and her research, that in the 1980's, due to the rise of scholarship and technical methods of detection, many famous works had undergone reattribution, a term used in art circles to describe corrected authorship.

In the seventies, in fact, the Metropolitan Museum of New York declared one of its own works a forgery. It was a small sculpture of a horse, a bronze from ancient Greece. A museum official "unmasked" it. Then in the mid-seventies, investigation by conservators revealed that it was indeed between two and four thousand years old.

It was also true that many of the changes in attribution didn't involve forgeries but came from recognition that a student of a master was really the author of the work. Even now scholars still had trouble between Van Dyke and Rubens. A Raphael in the Getty Museum had proven to be a copy. Controversy over the Getty's "Annunciation," attributed to fifteenth century Flemish painter Dirk Voutes, still continued. Some believed this to be a modern forgery, but the Getty stuck to its belief of its authenticity.

She knew Rembrandt's works were also involved. In 1986, two Rembrandts at the Met were questioned by the Foundation Rembrandt Research Project (FRRP), a committee of five Dutch scholars. These were portraits supposedly done in 1632. Doubt had also been cast on a Rembrandt in the Frick collection, "The Polish Rider." Reattribution had become a constant and embarrassing process.

"How long will it take you?" she asked. Once again her mind turned to the factor of time, that onrushing vehicle.

"Probably a couple of months," he replied. "I might have to make a quick trip to Holland. I'll find an old canvas of the era, perhaps one of Rembrandt's pupils. It won't be too expensive. Any other materials that I don't have can be shipped to me by air very quickly."

Kate cleared her throat. She hadn't discussed money with him. She had, of course, been prepared to pay very handsomely whoever did the forgery. But she was embarrassed about mentioning it and blurted out, "Well, what about money? What do you need?"

"Money?" He raised an eyebrow. "I don't need anything."

Kate's embarrassment began to show. "Well, you know, we were prepared to pay the person who did the painting," she stammered. "And we still are, of course, but it . . . ah . . . well . . ." She couldn't finish speaking, she didn't know what to say.

Marcus smiled at her discomfort. "I don't think that's going to be necessary. I'm not doing this for money, but for satisfaction. That's payment enough."

"Well, at least let me pay any of your expenses," she said.

"If it makes you feel better," he said with a shrug.

"And," she continued, "there is also going to be the matter of seven million dollars when this is all over. It's going to be split among the participants. And like it or not, you are now one of the participants."

"If it makes you feel better," he said again.

"You're not making this easy for me."

"Money's not important. What's important is that I'm helping you with what's important." He laughed.

He attacked the folder again, rifling through the photographs, quickly examining them. "You did some good research. But I think I might have to do a little more. Maybe a quick side trip to The Hague."

"Is there anything I can do there?" she asked.

"Better I do it myself. I know what I'm looking for."

"Well, if there's anything I can do, let me know."

"Let's go have some coffee and you can tell me exactly how this is going to work."

They went back to the kitchen, grabbed a mug of coffee

each, and went out to the porch, where four chairs were arranged in a semicircle. The sun was already hot. His house was on a slight rise and from it she could see a beautiful bay. He was only about half a mile from the water, separated from it by a grove of what looked to be pine trees.

''It's a beautiful place,'' she said.

''Yes, it's one of the quiet spots on the island. Solitude is necessary when I'm working.''

''You like islands, don't you?'' Kate noted. ''Your paintings that I saw, many of them seem to be island scenes. Do you travel a lot?''

''Yeah, I try to travel a few months every year. I like the Mediterranean, so I've traveled extensively from the Greek islands to the Spanish islands. But in the last few years, I've also gone down to the South Pacific, Australia, Indonesia, places like that. It gives me a new perspective. You can't keep painting the same picture anyway.''

''I'd love to travel like that,'' Kate said. ''I've always wanted to. I just haven't had much of a chance.''

''Until now,'' he reminded her.

''Yes, until now. Which brings up the business of where the plans stand now,'' she began.

Marcus listened attentively while she described the sequence of events, without interrupting her. When she finished she looked over at him inquiringly.

He hesitated and then said, ''It's a good plan. But there are a couple of points. One is how we communicate from now on. A lot of the success of this plan depends on nothing being traced back to you or any of the other participants. Security has to be very high.''

''I know,'' she said. ''Do you have any idea?''

''Privacy is my specialty,'' he said with a grin. ''Nobody knows who Breer is, right?''

''Right,'' she said. ''How do you do it?''

''I have a friend, someone I trust implicitly, in Venice, California. That's how I do my business in the States—through him. I think that we should use him as a conduit between us as well. I'll give you his name and telephone number, and I'll write to him and let him know that he'll be passing messages between us.''

''Someone you've known a long time?''

''He used to live here and in Paris, an artist.''

''Okay, what else?''

''The money. Taking payment from Thomas. You mentioned a Swiss bank account. Do you know how you're going to handle that?''

''I haven't worked that out yet,'' Kate said.

''You'll need somebody here to do that,'' Marcus offered. ''And probably that will be me.''

Kate hesitated for only a fraction of a second. Here was a man she had known for barely a day, and she was going to entrust him with seven million dollars, the spoils of their revenge. ''That would be fine. We'll work it out.''

''Good,'' he said. ''Now, here are a few more details. . . . ''

An hour later they finished their discussion. Marcus had spotted flaws in the plan that neither she nor Page had noted. It had been a productive meeting.

''I'm feeling much more secure about it now,'' she said.

''It's beautiful,'' he said. ''It's poetry.''

Kate spread her hands. ''Well, now what?''

He got up. ''Now let's take a walk down to the water. There is a beautiful cove down there that I want to show you.''

The cove was nestled at the bottom of steep cliffs, the water calm, unbroken by waves. Even from a hundred feet up, she could see the rocky bottom through the transparent blue of the shallow water.

''How do you get down there?'' she asked nervously. All she could see was a tumble of rocks and some steep faces.

''There's a way, but you'll have to let me guide you.'' He held out his hand and she took it. He clasped it firmly and led her to a path that she hadn't noticed before. ''There are a couple of spots that are pretty slippery,'' he said over his shoulder. "But just watch your footing and you'll be fine."

She slipped only once on a stretch of loose shingle and let out a frightened gasp, but the strength of his hand steadied her. In less than five minutes they'd reached the bottom.

The rocky shore was littered with seaweed and driftwood, most of it bleached white by the sea and the sun. At the top of the cliff there had been a slight breeze, but here the air was still. They walked down to the water and stopped at its edge. Only then she realized she was still holding his hand. Almost regretfully she released it.

"It's lovely here," she said.

"My special place. I don't think anyone else ever comes here. Sometimes in summer, when the nights are really hot, I sleep down here. There's a cave."

She turned to where he was pointing and saw the opening in the face of the cliff. "How far back does it go?"

"Not far. It's really just a pocket in the rock. I think it goes back maybe fifteen feet."

"Do you swim here?"

"Yeah, I snorkle here sometimes. There are some nice fish to be found out there."

"Oh, you mean with a speargun, like a real man?" she kidded.

"Afraid so. It's one of my hobbies," he admitted.

"How's the water now?"

"It's starting to chill, but it's bearable. You want to go in?"

"I'd love to," she said. "It's hot down here. But I don't have anything to wear."

"So?" he said with a shrug.

"I will if you will."

Within minutes they were both naked. His body was entirely brown, more muscles than she had first thought. But there wasn't an ounce of extra weight on him. It was lean, fit and, she thought, extremely sexy, particularly the way the dark hair of his pubic area crept up toward his belly button.

"Come on," he said, heading for the water. "Last one in's a geek."

He hit the water while running and, about ten feet out, where it deepened, dove in. Kate was more cautious. She walked in slowly and found that it was cold. It wouldn't do to hesitate, so she broke into a run and dove in after him, the shock of the water almost driving the breath from her body.

Marcus grinned when he saw her reaction. She came sputtering out of the water. "Can you open your eyes under water?"

"I can try," she said.

"Come over here. There's a deep pool I want you to see." He swam with strong strokes for about fifteen yards, and then stopped and treaded water until she caught up with him. "Right here."

They both went under the water. Kate opened her eyes and saw that the pool was probably twenty feet deep, a mosaic of color and vibrant life. There were small fish, anemones, seaweed, and other plant life. She almost forgot she had to breathe, so captivated was she. Then she felt the pain in her chest and rose to the surface, gasping. He came up a moment later.

"Beautiful, isn't it?"

She nodded, unable to speak.

"We'd better head back to shore. The water's pretty cold." He swam beside her, and then they reached the shallow water and emerged into the warm sunlit air.

"Brrr." Her body felt like ice.

"You'll warm up in a minute," he promised.

She turned and looked back out at the water. She suddenly became aware that she was wearing no clothes. "How are we going to dry ourselves?" she asked, turning toward him.

He was looking at her, a thoughtful expression in his eyes. "Just put our clothes back on. They'll be dry by the time we get back to the house."

They went back to the pile of clothes and she bent down to pick up her jeans. As she put them on she knew, without looking, that he was watching her. When she looked up, he was standing right beside her.

"You are a very beautiful woman, Kate Buchanan," he said quietly. And then he lifted his hand and ran the tip of his forefinger down one of her shoulders. They stared at each other mutely. She had no feelings, no thoughts, only a sense of deep contentment. And then, in unspoken agreement, they ended the moment and both dressed.

As he had promised, by the time they reached the house, she was dry and warm.

"Time for lunch." He rubbed his hands energetically together. Lunch consisted of fresh bread, cheese, and a light red wine. They ate it in the shade of an old oak tree on the side of the house.

"I'm worried about the time factor," Kate said, in between mouthfuls.

"I know it's dicey. We don't want him to find something else in the meantime. I'll have to get my pigments, grind my own, but the main problem—"

"—is drying the painting," she interjected.

He nodded.

"How are you going to do it?"

"Ve haf our vays," he said, laughing, then added, "it's a problem. Normally it takes oils a year or so to fully dry, and this painting's going to have to be glazed, of course, and then polymerized to make it look aged. But I have developed a heating system, which will dry it in a short period of time. I have kilns behind the house for that. There are also siccatives, which are drying oils that I can use. They are very tricky, though. They have to be used very sparingly. Otherwise they can ruin a painting. But during my short but illustrious career, I did develop the use of these to a high art, even if I may say so myself."

"I hope so," she said, with concern in her voice. "There can't be the slightest tackiness to it."

"Yeah, yeah. Don't worry about it, I'll take care of it. The main thing is what happens if Thomas finds something before I'm done."

"I know. I'm going to have to speed the process up.

We're going to have to let him know of the existence of this painting before you're finished with it, and then stall his viewing of it."

"So I'm really on a deadline," he said.

"Yes. We can only stall him for so long. It can't be unreasonable, or anything that will raise suspicion."

"I'll do my best. You can count on it."

"And you feel you can handle the forgeries of the signatures we need?" she asked.

"I'm an artist. I can forge any signature on earth. That's the least of our worries."

"And what's your greatest worry?"

"When I get to see you again."

He leaned forward on the grass, put one hand behind her head, and drew her toward him. They kissed. Their mouths seemed to melt. "When are you leaving?" he asked.

"I was thinking of going back as soon as I'd concluded my business. I was thinking of leaving tomorrow."

He took her hand, "Then we'd better make the most of the time we have." He stood, pulling her to her feet, then put his arm around her and led her into the house.

She wasn't even aware of undressing. After a while she knew only that they were both naked and that his mouth was everywhere on her. They explored each other, not just with hands and mouths, but as if each were trying to enter the other with the totality of their bodies.

This was different. She was not having sex with a man because she was obligated to; she was making love to a man because she wanted to. It was so unlike what she had done with David that it felt like a different activity. In fact, it was different from anyone she had ever been with.

They giggled and laughed and groaned. They whispered endearments and shouted their pleasures. They were unabashed, proud of the pleasure they could bring to each other.

When finally, after an interminable time, when neither could stand it any longer, he entered her. She wrapped her legs around him, as if trying to squeeze the life from his hips, and bucked like a wild thing.

They both felt like music, rising on endless octaves to a crescendo of sound and sensation until finally they were free of all form, looking down on their thrashing bodies, joined in some far deeper manner, beyond normal understanding.

There was a spiritual aspect to their lovemaking that went beyond words. A merging of two beings until they were one. Until they knew instinctively what each was feeling, thinking, where and what each had been and where they both were going. It was a unity so profound it transcended thought.

It was late in the afternoon when they finally fell asleep in each other's arms, and the blood-red sun fell into the horizon of the ocean.

Kate did not leave the following day. She couldn't bear to. But the day after that, she said her good-byes to Marcus early in the morning, and then waved at the solitary figure on the porch until she could no longer see him, as Bart Stone drove her to the airport.

Something in me has changed, she thought. She looked down from the airport at the tiny island, now just a shoal in the deep blue Mediterranean. They hadn't spoken of love; they hadn't needed to. But she knew that she had fallen in love with Marcus and with the island.

This had been a year of remarkable change. She had changed when she lost Joel. She had felt a void inside her so deep that she felt she could have disappeared in it. Now, she'd found something else, and she felt so full, so replete, that she thought she could disappear in this feeling.

Ibiza faded into a hazy sky. Now she had a job to do. It was time to put aside thoughts of love and the future and concentrate on what she was doing.

CHAPTER TWENTY

"How did it go?" Page asked.

She was sitting with Kate and Elsa in Elsa's apartment. They had found out that Jasmine had an audition to attend on Tuesday afternoon and arranged to meet there. Kate had arrived back late on Sunday night and slept virtually the entire day on Monday.

"Perfectly," Kate said. "He's working on it now."

Page congratulated her. "Well done. Was it difficult to persuade him? I assume that you are talking about the man in Spain, the one who had retired?"

"Yes, the one in Spain, and no, it wasn't difficult to persuade him."

"What's his fee?" Page asked, getting right to the point that concerned her most.

"No fee," Kate replied.

Both Page and Elsa looked up sharply at that. "What do you mean, no fee?" Page asked.

"Well," Kate explained, "he didn't want a fee and . . . ah, so I said I'd cut him in for a percentage of what we made, and he said, 'Fine.' "

"How large a percentage?" Page asked.

"I don't know. We never discussed it," Kate said. "Um, I just sort of assumed that all the participants would share. He doesn't care, he really doesn't. When I proposed that he get a cut, he just said, 'If you insist,' or actually his words were, 'If it makes you feel better.' " Kate smiled at the memory.

"Now wait a minute," Page said. "I don't trust anyone

who works for nothing. What's the deal here? What's going on?"

"Marcus Devereaux, the man that I met," Kate said, "paints under the name of Breer. He had a showing recently at our gallery. You may have heard of him."

"I've heard the name," Page said.

Kate explained how Thomas had ruined Breer's chance of appearing at the Rex.

"Ah," Page said, somewhat consoled, "so he has his own revenge to gain."

Kate shrugged. "I think that's a small part of it. I just think he likes the whole idea of this."

Elsa gave her a shrewd look. "Kate, is there something going on here that you have not told us about? Something between you and this man, Devereaux?"

"Oh, yes," Kate said blithely. "We love each other."

"What?" Page asked.

"I know it sounds ridiculous. We were only together for a few days. But we love each other. I don't know what else to say."

"Bravo!" Elsa exclaimed, her face wreathed in smiles. "If anything will triumph, it's love."

"I don't believe this," Page said. "You struck me as a very levelheaded woman. And here you are just . . . I don't know."

"Sorry to destroy your illusions, Page, but the fact is we fell in love. The time, whether it was two days, three days, three weeks, three months, had nothing to do with it. It's just something that happened. Surely you understand that."

Page shook her head. "I've never been in love."

"Well, I hope that one day you will be," Kate said.

"I have, and I think it's wonderful," Elsa added. "You and this man, you are a team now, no?"

"Yes," Kate replied.

"Good," Elsa said. "Then we are an unbeatable combination."

"I don't understand it," Page said exasperatedly. "But

if you're happy and everything is going to proceed as we planned, then I'm happy."

"It will," Kate said. "We have a few details to attend to, though, so let's get down to them. For one thing, it's time to get Jasmine involved. How's she doing?"

"Very well," Elsa said. "I think she likes to be here. But the poor girl is worried about her future. I think the baby is becoming a reality to her."

"Then it's time for us to put her mind at rest," Kate said. "I'll come to see her tonight or tomorrow and put the proposition before her. There are some things we need her to do soon. Oh, and I'm going to need some money to get them done."

For the next hour the three women huddled together and went over each step of the plan. They were going to leave nothing to chance.

Jasmine arrived just after Kate and Page left. Elsa greeted her cheerfully. "There was a call for you."

"Oh? Who was it?" Jasmine asked, putting the groceries on the kitchen table.

"It was your man, Allan Silver."

After days of silence, Jasmine had finally called him that morning and left Elsa's number with his secretary. Apparently her lack of communication had accomplished its purpose. Although in a strange way, she no longer knew what the purpose was. For some reason she had enjoyed being away from Allan, on her own again. "I suppose I'll call him."

"Here, let me finish putting the groceries away," Elsa said, waddling over to her. "You go and use the telephone in the living room."

Jasmine sat on the couch beside the telephone. She wore blue jeans and a cotton T-shirt. For some reason in the last few days, the urge to wear silk had diminished.

She picked up the phone and called Allan's office. His secretary, civil for once, put her through immediately.

"Yeah, hi," Allan said. "How you doing?"

"Fine, thank you," she answered. "You called?"

"Hey, you called me. I was just returning your call," Allan said.

"Oh, yes, that's right," Jasmine replied. "Um, I was calling you to find out if you are willing to support this child?"

"What? What are you saying?"

"If you are willing to support the child, financially?"

"Jasmine, haven't you got the point by now?" he said sharply. "I don't want a child. I don't want you to have this child. If you persist in having this child, you're not going to get a dime from me. But on the other hand, if you do what I told you to do and get rid of it, things can return to normal. You can move back into your apartment, you can have your car back, your credit card, your allowance, and everything will be just like it was."

"Except for the wound, huh?" Jasmine said.

"Wound? What are you talking about? These operations are simple. They just go in there and they scoop it out."

"God, I don't know why I ever thought I loved you."

Allan's voice grew gentler. "Well, I love you and I miss you, and I just wish you'd come to your senses. How you going to survive without me? Think about it. Get real."

"Get fucked," she said, and hung up.

"Ugh!" she said, walking into the kitchen.

"An unpleasant conversation?"

"He's such an asshole," Jasmine said, wonderment in her voice. "I never realized it before, but he's such an asshole."

"Ah, well, men," Elsa sighed, in a single phrase indicting half the human race.

"Yeah, well, they say you can't live with them and you can't live without them. I think I'm going to try living without them and I think I might even enjoy it."

"It's just one man," Elsa pointed out. "Keep that in mind. They're not all like that."

"I know. The damn problem is I like men," Jasmine said.

"It's just a matter of time before you find the right one."

"Oh, yeah?" Jasmine scoffed. "With my stomach sticking out? I'm a prime catch. A single woman with a child. They're going to be falling all over themselves trying to get to me."

"You might be surprised," Elsa said. "There are some men to whom that is not important, or perhaps to some it is important in a good way."

Jasmine sat at the kitchen table, put her elbows up, and buried her face in her hands. "I don't know," she said. "There's a lot I don't know. Right now I'm kind of scared about the future. I don't know what I'm going to do or how I'm going to manage. It suddenly seems to be a big world out there."

"Were you worried about that when you first came to Los Angeles, little more than a child?" Elsa asked.

"No, I wasn't. But I was younger then. Stupider."

"Perhaps you were smarter, more hopeful," Elsa said.

Jasmine smiled. "Maybe. Maybe I was more willing to work for what I wanted then. I guess I can do that again if I have to."

"You bet," Elsa said. "And besides, I have a feeling that something's going to turn up soon. Something you don't expect. Something good."

"Really? Like what?"

"I don't have a crystal ball, my dear," Elsa said. "You will just have to wait and see. Now, you did say you were going to cook dinner tonight. Chinese, was it?"

"That's what I said."

"Well, that'll be good. I'm sick of Maria's cooking."

"Jesus, I've only been here a few days and I'm already sick of Maria's cooking," Jasmine said. "Why do you think I volunteered?"

Elsa laughed until she shook. Then she walked to Jasmine and put her hands on her shoulders. "It's very nice to have you here, my dear. It's like a breath of fresh air. Don't worry about the future, whatever you do. The future will take care of itself."

"Okay," Jasmine said, standing up. "How about I

worry about dinner? That's about as far enough into the future as I'm willing to look."

"Very good," Elsa said. "I'll go watch television while you cook."

Stodding Watson met Jason for cocktails at Jason's club. He was there to give his progress report, notable for its lack of progress. A fact that left him feeling somewhat dubious about the meeting. Jason always expected progress. They shook hands and sat in a small booth.

"Well, how's it going?" Jason asked, not beating around the bush. "What happened with the Monet?"

One of Jason's contacts had approached him about a Monet waterlily painting for sale in New York. He had asked Stodding to check it out.

Stod shrugged. "It's a wonderful painting. It's probably worth three million dollars; they're asking five."

Jason scowled. "I'm not really interested. I don't want to see another damn waterlily painting. There are enough of them around anyway, probably better. What else is there?"

"We came across a Cezanne landscape. It's worth two to three million dollars. The Art Institute of Chicago is selling it."

"What do you think?" Jason asked.

"I don't think it's an important enough painting," Stodding said.

"What else?"

"There are some Picassos on the market. They are worth between two and three million each. There's also a Georges Braque cubist work, which is worth somewhere between three and four million. Other than that, there really isn't much."

"That's too expensive and the others are too cheap," Jason growled. "Stod, I have seven million dollars to spend on a major work of art. I want a major work of art. And I want to spend the seven million dollars. You do understand that, don't you?"

"Of course." Stod said. "But one of the things that

makes a work of art major is the fact that there aren't that many of them around. We're just going to have to wait until something turns up."

"I don't like waiting," Jason said. "Go out and find it."

"I'm doing my best," Stod said testily. "If you don't like the way I'm doing it, why don't you go out and find it?"

"I might just do that. Page's PR is starting to appear and I think there's going to be some response from that."

"Well, I'll be only too happy to help you out as needed," Stod said. "Something will turn up, believe me."

"The wing's going to be ready to open in two months. I hope something turns up before then."

"We can always delay the opening a little."

"I know, but we can't delay it for too long. I guess a month at the most. Otherwise it will start looking obvious."

"Agreed," Stod said, "and we can't have that."

"All right, continue your work and I'll do the same."

"I have a feeling it's just going to be a problem of sorting out the dross."

"I hope so," Jason said. "Now what would you like to drink?"

Sharon Thomas stood next to the telephone and listened to it ring. She was calling the chauffeur's room, but there was no answer.

"Damn him!" she said, and slammed the receiver back on the hook. The bastard had been getting more and more irresponsible in the last week. There were times she sensed, beneath his slightly mocking exterior, that he was even being insolent. He was probably sunbathing beside the pool. He seemed to be doing that more and more these days. Tightening the belt of her robe around her waist, she stalked through the living room and out to the patio. Sure enough, there he was, spread-eagled on the concrete.

"Danny!" she shouted.

He lifted his head and looked at her, but other than that he didn't move.

She walked over to him. "You do work for me, don't you? I mean, you are my chauffeur, right? And you are supposed to come when I call, right? I do pay you."

"What?"

"What do you mean, what?"

"What do you want?" He rolled over onto his back and looked up at her. "Is there something I can do for you?"

She wanted to leap into the air and land on him with her feet. But instead she clenched her jaw and swallowed. "I need a lift. Do you have any coke?"

"No, I don't," he said, regarding her through lazy eyes.

"Well, can you get some?"

"Yeah, I suppose so. You'll have to give me some money though."

"Sure. How much do you need?"

"How much do *you* need?" he asked.

"Enough for the next five days."

"Give me five bills and I'll see what I can do." He rolled back onto his stomach.

"Now," she said. "I want you to get it now."

"Just a few more rays, then I'll go."

"Now!" she shrieked.

He rolled over and sat up. Her face was livid. "All right, all right, don't wet your pants! I'll go now. I'll be back in an hour or two. Just take it easy, okay?"

"Just hop to it. I'll be waiting." She turned and walked back to the house, hating him and hating herself.

"I met your brother," Jasmine said. Her almost-white face looked as if it were about to collapse.

It was Wednesday and they were sitting beside each other on Jasmine's bed in Elsa's apartment. Kate had just told her who she really was.

"You did?" Kate asked.

Jasmine nodded. "Joel Buck. Angie introduced me once. We went out one evening together to a club to hear them play. Angie told me that he was her lover and—and . . . oh God!" She burst into sobs.

Kate put her arm around Jasmine's shoulders. "Jasmine, what is it? What happened?"

Jasmine looked at her with dull tearstained eyes. "Angie told me never to tell anyone. That it would be dangerous. But one night—one night I mentioned to Allan that Angie had a secret lover. Oh God! Perhaps Allan told Jason. Maybe I'm responsible for what happened!"

"You can't know that," Kate said gently. "And you can't do that to yourself. Even if that did happen, which I doubt, you are not responsible for what those men did. They decided to do it. You had nothing to do with it."

"I feel terrible," Jasmine sniffled.

"It's all right."

"Those bastards!" Jasmine's mood suddenly shifted from grief to anger. "They think they can do anything, that they can get away with anything, that they can buy and sell anyone. I wish there were something we could do to teach them a lesson. Is there no way you can prove that Jason had your brother killed? Where's Angie now?"

"When Jason kicked her out, Angie was left with nothing," Kate explained. "The last time I saw her a few weeks ago she was working as a hooker in West Hollywood, with a big cocaine habit."

"Jesus, nobody deserves that."

"Well," Kate said carefully. "there is something we can do. There is something I'm doing. And if you want, you can help."

"What?" Jasmine asked, her eyes clear now.

Kate explained her plan.

When she finished, Jasmine was silent, taking it all in, trying to give it some perspective. And then a smile lit up her face. "I love it! I love it! You thought of this? You did all this? Oh my God, I love it! How can I help?"

"Page and I are limited to how much we can travel. She's tied to Jason and I'm tied to David. We can't evoke any suspicions by disappearing for long periods of time. You, on the other hand, are tied to no one. You are a free agent. We'd like you to act as our courier. It's going to involve some international travel."

"I'll do it," Jasmine said. "Just let me know where and when."

"The other thing to keep in mind, Jas, is that by helping us you become a part of our group. That means you're going to walk out of this with a lot of money if we pull it off."

"I could use it." Jasmine looked curiously over at Kate. "Elsa told me that something would turn up. This is what she was talking about, wasn't it?"

"Yes."

Jasmine giggled. "I feel like a member of the Four Musketeers."

"One for all and all for one," Kate said, and then she added, "Oh, by the way, I need you to fly to Buenos Aires in a couple of days, as soon as I get the material I need."

"Is that Brazil?" Jasmine queried.

"No, Argentina."

"What am I going to do there?"

"Mail a letter."

"That's it?"

"Not quite. You also have to set up a post office box for us in Buenos Aires and hire somebody to forward mail from there to an address I'm going to give you here in LA—Venice actually. But don't worry. We'll go through all of this before you leave."

That night, Kate saw David. They were going to a party being given by Hollywood producer Corbett Blanchard. Allan would be there and so would Jason, David told her during the limo ride to Bel-Air.

The house was one of those huge California Spanish mansions, blazing with lights. The road wound around a circular patch of grass, and as guests arrived, uniformed valets opened their car doors and showed them to the front door. Then they took the cars to that netherworld where all guest cars go.

As soon as they entered, Kate felt underdressed in her

simple black dress and strand of pearls. This was designer country. Women wore opulent works of art or shockingly modern monstrosities. The men, as did David, for the most part wore dinner jackets. By California standards this was a very formal affair. David introduced her to the host, a huge hearty man with graying hair and a salt and pepper beard, and to the hostess, a small trim blonde at least twenty years his junior. She had a high-pitched voice and a distracted manner. She looked unimpressed by Kate's clothes and, after a perfunctory "hello," wandered away.

"Drinks are over there," said their genial host, waving an arm at the next room where at least a hundred people milled around.

"How do you know him?" Kate asked as they walked in.

"I helped get some investors together for one of his films," David answered.

"Did you invest money yourself?"

"No way!"

"How did the investors do?" she asked.

"Didn't make a dime, but he bought this house. That's Hollywood."

Allan saw them and came over to say hello. He shook David's hand, kissed Kate on the cheek, and said, "How are you two lovebirds?"

"Fine," David said, "just fine. You here alone tonight?"

"Are you kidding?" Allan said. "Just look around at the stuff in this room. I came alone, but I promise you I won't be leaving alone."

There were indeed an inordinate number of attractive young women milling through the crowd. Starlets, no doubt.

"Well, would you like a drink?" David asked Kate.

"Yes, a glass of wine would be fine."

David shouldered his way through a small circle of people, while Allan remained at her side. "Have you seen Jasmine?" he asked, his eyes nervous.

"No. I talked to her on the phone some time ago, but I haven't seen her. Why?"

"Oh, just wondering," he said, "wondering how she's doing. She's left her apartment . . . she's staying with some friend somewhere."

"I see," Kate said noncommittally, then added, "I thought it was over between you two."

"Well," Allan shrugged, "the woman's being difficult. Maybe we can still work it out."

"Well, good luck," Kate said, thinking, "Fat chance."

David returned with their drinks. "Do you want to meet some people?"

"Sure," Kate said.

They wandered through the room, stopping every now and then to say hello to various people. Almost everyone there seemed to be in the money business or the film business. Snippets of conversation caught her ear as they progressed through the room.

" . . . he wouldn't know a good script from a pimple on his ass."

" . . . she gives the best head in town."

" . . . I got some great coke out of it. Do you want to try some?"

" . . . they wanted a cross-collateralized project but I said, 'Fuck you' and took it over to Twentieth."

" . . . listen I've got a great idea for a movie. These two broads, they live in Vegas, see . . ."

" . . . would you give your telephone number to a stranger?"

David introduced her to another producer, Irv Caplan, who looked Kate up and down. "You should be an actress, honey."

"Oh, no," she said, "I have no talent whatsoever."

"Who's talking about talent?" he said. "With your looks you wouldn't need it."

"Thanks, but I think I'll pass," she said.

"Some broad," he said with a short burst of laughter at David. "Half the women in this room would do anything for a part; this one's not even interested."

"She's an art expert," David said with some pride. "She works in a gallery."

"Art, hey? Is there money in it?" Caplan asked her.

"For some people," she said.

"Never could understand people who spend thousands on a painting. You put it up on a wall, and after a week you forget to look at it."

Their host came by. "Having a good time?" he asked them all, and disappeared again before they could answer.

She also met Blair Campbell, an actress she'd always admired. Blair was now in her fifties. Her face was still smooth, but there were telltale wrinkles around her neck and something hard in her eyes that had never been apparent on film. There was rasp to her voice. "You look like an intelligent young woman," she said to Kate. "What are you doing here?"

"I was brought," Kate said.

"You make it sound like you were kidnapped, carried in on a horse."

"In a manner of speaking. Why are you here?"

"I come to these things because I'm bored," Blair said. "But they only make me even more bored. Every now and then something different happens though."

"Are these people your friends?" Kate asked.

Blair laughed genuinely at that. "This is Hollywood, honey. There are no friends. Half of these people here are shrewd assholes and half of them are dumb assholes. The shrewd assholes take advantages of the dumb assholes. They're here to get reamed. It's victims and victimizers."

"Blair always talks like this," David said. "Nobody minds."

"Yeah, at my advanced age people don't pay attention to what I have to say," Blair said derisively. "Hollywood's a young town now. Anyone over thirty isn't worth shit."

"Excuse me," David said, and drew Kate away.

"Why did you do that? I liked her," Kate protested. "I was enjoying talking to her."

"She just makes trouble," David said. "Best to leave her alone."

Jason must have just arrived because he came over and said hello to them. Page stood beside him. Wearing a white crepe turtleneck full-length gown with a diamond stickpin on the neck, she looked totally at home in this uptown crowd.

"Hello, Jason," David said, shaking his hand. "Page." He kissed her on the cheek.

Jason greeted Kate but did not kiss her.

"Hi, Page," Kate said.

Page touched Jason lightly on the arm. "Kate has been very helpful in this PR I've been doing."

"Thank you very much," Jason said. "Did you hear? There's going to be an article in the Art section of the *Times* on Sunday."

"Oh, very good," Kate said.

"Excellent," David chimed in.

"You should start getting quite a response," Kate said. "Have you had much yet?"

"Nothing of any value," Jason said. "But I'm sure we will."

David's face suddenly froze. He was looking over Jason's shoulder. "Oh, Jesus Christ! Jason?"

The tone of his voice alerted Jason, who quickly turned his head. A tall blond woman was bearing down on them. It was Sharon Thomas.

"Excuse me," David muttered, turned on his heels, and walked quickly away. Kate was left standing there with Jason and Page.

"Why, Jason, honey," Sharon said, coming up to them, "what brings you here? With two women, what's more?"

"What are you doing here, Sharon?" Jason asked.

Sharon giggled, her eyes bright. "Well, I happened to see the invitation lying on top of your briefcase, honey. I saw that it was addressed to both of us, so I thought I'd show up. It seemed like a fun idea. And it looks like fun. I'm glad I came. Who are the ladyfriends? Which one of them is yours?"

"Sharon," Jason started warningly.

"It must be this one here," Sharon said, narrowing her eyes at Page. "You always did have a thing for classy-looking broads." She swung her head at Kate, "Or maybe it's this one here. You always did have a thing for sluts too. Actually, girls," she said, lowering her voice conspiratorially, "Jason has a thing for anything with a hole between its legs, if you get my meaning?"

Jason's face was white. He grabbed Sharon's arm and hissed, "You're leaving."

"Oh, no, I'm not!" Her voice rose, and she threw the glass of booze in her right hand directly into Jason's face. "Bull's-eye!" she shouted.

Increasing rings of people were watching them. It was like a stone that had been dropped into a pond.

"Jason Thomas," Sharon was shouting now. "Big deal! Multimillionaire, respectable citizen, mother-fucker, nothing more than a cheap hoodlum in a business suit! Jason Thomas, unmasked!"

Two burly waiters appeared out of the crowd. Calmly, they each grasped one of her arms and swung her around, marching her toward the door. "And what about Mr. David Ross?" she shouted over her shoulder. "Is he here with his wife? You're all the same, you mother-fucking bastards. You're all the same."

And then she was gone.

Another waiter appeared at Jason's side and handed him a towel. He dabbed at his face, unable to speak, his hands shaking with rage and embarrassment.

David came back to Kate. "I'm sorry," he said. "I couldn't be seen by her with you. God! What a bitch. What a scene, what a disaster! What could have got into her?"

"I presume that's Jason's wife?" Kate said. She, too, had been shaken by the outburst. But she was calming down quickly. Page, on the other hand, had turned several shades paler.

"Jason, are you all right?" David asked.

Jason seemed to return from a distant point before answering, "Yes, yes, thank you. I'm fine. Please, all of you, excuse that interruption."

"Not your fault," David said.

"Unfortunately it's my wife, my responsibility. I think I need a drink."

"I'll get you one," Page said.

"No, I'll come with you."

They wandered off toward the bar.

"I think we should leave," David said to Kate. "I hate scenes like that."

"Whatever you wish," Kate replied.

"Well, let's stay another half hour and then go. Is that all right?"

"Fine," she said.

Blair Campbell came up to them, a vicarious glint in her eyes. "Well, that was worth staying around for. Was that his wife?"

"Excuse me," David said. He took Kate's arm and pulled her away. "I can't stand that woman. She thrives on trouble."

"Perhaps it's all she has left," Kate said. "Has she made any films recently?"

"Her? I doubt it. She's been over the hill a long time."

"She used to be such a wonderful actress," Kate said.

"Used-to-bes don't count in Hollywood," David said cruelly.

It was true though, Kate thought, looking around the room. You could see who was being courted and who was not. Who was "hot," "tepid," and "cold." You could tell the excitement an individual generated by the number of people around them, by the patronizations, by the displays of power, and in a sense by the magnetic fields around each individual. They either repelled or attracted. For the most part the reigning kings and queens were young, but there were endearing exceptions. People whose charisma was timeless; emperors, perhaps, and empresses. There were very few of them here, however.

As soon as the limousine cleared the outer gates, David

leaned anxiously toward her. "Do you think Sharon saw that I was with you?"

"No, I don't think so."

"God, I hope not! She could really make trouble for me. She's a vindictive woman. Totally irresponsible."

"I'm sure she didn't. She thought that perhaps I was with Jason," she said.

"Really?"

"Yeah, she couldn't decide which one of us was with him."

"Oh, thank God!" David said with relief. "That's one problem off my mind then."

After a few minutes, he seemed to realize how selfish and callous his behavior had been and began to treat her with overdone deference. "Is the car running well?"

"It's perfect," she said. "After all, it is new."

"Yes, yes. I was thinking of taking you shopping some time in the next few days."

"Shopping? For what?"

"Some new clothes. I thought maybe as a gift I'd take you to Neiman-Marcus and you could indulge yourself in a new wardrobe."

"Oh," she said, not knowing what else to say to this propitiative generosity.

"Would you like that?"

"Yes. As long as it's just a couple of things," she said with a sinking heart.

All night, she had been dreading this moment. She knew that David would want to sleep with her tonight and the thought filled her with dismay. Up until now she had been able to separate herself from the act of sex with him. But since Marcus . . .

She loved Marcus. Not this jowled old man with his money, which he thought could buy anything. His selfish tunnel vision. His insensitivity. His greed. His misplaced pride. His thinning legs and growing belly. The thought of sleeping with him, of acting out his fantasy, of pretending, filled her with revulsion. Not toward him, but toward herself.

When they reached her apartment, he got out of the car with her and said, "I can only stay a short while."

"I'm tired, David," she began to say.

"That's fine," he said hurriedly, "I won't stay for long," and took her arm.

They went upstairs, and she opened the door while he stood behind her. Her fingers trembled slightly and a rock sat in the center of her stomach.

"I've missed you so much," he said, as soon as they entered. He kissed her and she could smell his aftershave lotion. It clogged her nostrils.

"Let's go to bed," he said urgently.

Kate didn't know what to do but comply, and she went into the bedroom followed by him. She took her clothes off and sat on the edge of the bed, watching him struggle with one of his shoes.

"That was really embarrassing," he said as he undressed. "Poor Jason. God knows what he must have felt. I wouldn't want to be Sharon when he gets home tonight."

What about poor Sharon? Kate thought to herself. How embarrassed was she to see her husband with another woman or two? Perhaps she had been too numb to feel anything. She looked as if she'd been stoned out of her mind. Kate had seen enough people on cocaine in recent years to recognize it in their eyes and grandiose gestures.

"Does she use drugs?" she asked.

"God, I doubt it," David said. "Jason can't stand drugs, wouldn't allow them in his house."

Jason might not know everything about his wife, Kate thought.

David knelt on the floor in front of her, picked up one of her feet, and kissed a toe. Then he kissed her shin, then her knee, then he buried his face between her thighs and ran his tongue over them, up toward the bushy triangle, the mysterious darkness of her womanhood.

"Oooo," he said, pulling her legs apart, and then lifting his hands to feel her breasts and push her back until she was lying there, open and inviting.

She looked down at her, with his busy tongue and his

grunts of delight, and felt nothing. Nothing at all. It was as if she were outside her body, looking down at actors on a stage. The two bodies going through the required age-old motions.

She was dry in there, dry as a bone. Mercifully, David did not notice. And soon, in spite of her disinterest, her body took its own path and began to lubricate itself as it was required to do. He got up then and put his arms under her legs, lifting them and entering her, and thankfully, it was soon over.

He lay there for a short while, murmuring endearments to her, and then he looked at his watch and saw that he had to leave. He ran into the shower and cleaned his body so that no evidence of their tryst would be apparent to his wife. Then he kissed her, thanked her, and said, "That was wonderful, wasn't it?" and left.

Kate felt bruised, betrayed by herself. She got up and walked to the shower, and stood in there soaping and scrubbing her body again and again at least an hour, in a futile attempt to clean herself of everything.

She returned to her bed with white wrinkled skin and a waterlogged soul and cried herself to sleep.

CHAPTER TWENTY-ONE

Kate received a telephone call at the gallery on Friday.

"Miss Kate Buchanan?" the caller said.

"Yes, speaking."

"A package for you," he said, and hung up.

The first shipment had arrived from Marcus. After work

she drove to Venice, staying away from the clogged freeway and taking surface streets to the seaside community.

She had memorized the address Marcus had given her and found it on a small street of wooden bungalows, three blocks back from the beach. She stopped outside 1342 and, after looking around, went to the front door and knocked. A small red-haired man opened the door. With his bushy red hair, pinkish skin, bulbous nose, and bright blue eyes, he looked exactly as she imagined a leprechaun would look.

"Kate?" he asked.

"Yes. Billy?"

"Come on in," he said. "I have a package for you from our mutual friend."

The house, which probably consisted of only one bedroom, a living room, and a kitchen, was a shambles of old furniture, driftwood, half-finished canvases, and cardboard boxes.

"Sit, sit," Billy gestured. "I got to find it."

Kate sat on the couch beside a long-haired gray cat, who opened its eyes, regarded her for a second, and then went back to sleep.

"That's Sheba," Billy said. "Sheba, that's Kate."

Sheba opened her eyes again and then closed them.

"It's here somewhere," Billy said. "It just came tod—ah, here it is." He returned from the other side of the room with a manila envelope and plunked himself on the couch beside her, a ball of nervous energy.

"I don't know what it is, and I don't want to know. Anything Marcus does is Jake with me. What is it?" he asked. Then he broke into a laugh to show that he was only kidding.

"Have you known Marcus long?" Kate asked, curious how two such disparate characters could be friends.

Billy scratched his head and furrowed his brow. "Long? I suppose so. Yes, I suppose in terms of years we've known each other a long time. Met in Paris. Long time ago. Lived together for a while. Met in Spain again. He's a good friend, Marcus. Helped me out when I needed help."

"Oh?" Kate said, prompting him.

"Junkie. I was a junkie back then. Used to shoot up anything that would fit in my veins. Used to burn dirty Turkish opium in a teaspoon and shoot even that up. I shot up speed, heroin, you name it, I put it in my arm. When there weren't any holes left in my arm, I put it in my leg."

He laughed again. "Marcus helped me. Tied me up, he did. Top floor of some dirty apartment in Montmartre. I screamed for days. He didn't have an ounce of pity, the bastard. Made me quit cold turkey. Then he took me away from Paris down to the south of France. Got me some sun, some food, talked some sense into my head. Saved my life. I'd be dead now if it weren't for him. I can't do enough for Marcus."

"He's a very special person," Kate said.

Billy snorted. "Special? He's an angel. Walking amongst mortals, dressed like a mortal, talks like a mortal, but an angel—sent down for people like me."

"Are these your paintings?" she asked, gesturing at a group of unfinished canvases, an incomprehensible jungle of color.

"Naw," Billy said. "I don't do that shit. I buy these canvases from a friend down the street. He starts paintings and never finishes them. I buy them and just overpaint."

"What kind of work do you do?" she asked.

"Come on, I'll show you," he said, getting quickly to his feet. He led the way out the back door. There was a small shed behind the house, a garage once perhaps. He opened the door, flicked on the light switch, and stepped inside.

Where the house had been chaos, this was orderly. Two easels, paints neatly laid out, books carefully aligned on four shelves, materials on a table, a drawing table with sketch pad, canvases carefully stacked.

"I do portraits," he said, waving at one of the easels.

The painting was of a young woman, a pensive expression on her face, sitting on a colorful merry-go-round horse. It was beautiful. "You are very, very good," Kate said. "That's something else."

Billy beamed. "Yeah, I know. I'm good at this. This is what I do. I conjure up souls and I put them on canvas."

"Do you show anywhere?"

Billy shook his head. "Nah, all commissions. I don't get to keep any of them to show."

"But you make a good living doing this, I assume?"

"I charge doctors, dentists, and lawyers three or four thousand dollars for a portrait. The people I like, I do it for free, or a meal, or a gift, or whatever they want."

"God, they're fantastic." She turned to him and said, "Billy, do you want to show?"

He jerked back his head, as if she'd just asked him an obscene question. "Sure I want to show. But I'm not about to go traipsing down La Cienega Boulevard and Melrose Avenue and downtown Los Angeles with a portfolio, showing some jerk what I can do. Showing some jerk something I can do that he can't, and I'm asking him if he thinks it's okay to put up on his wall? The hell with it."

"But you could show if you wanted to? You could get enough of your paintings back on loan to have a show?"

"Yeah, I guess I could."

"Billy, I can't do anything now," Kate said, excitement entering her voice, "but in a few months when I've completed what I'm doing and the dust has all settled, could I help you put on a show? You see I know a gallery that would love your work. It's just that I can't do anything about it right now. But I really think your work should be seen, it's so fine."

Billy looked at her as if seeing her for the first time. "How long have you known Marcus?"

"A few days. Why?"

"And you guys are in love with each other, aren't you?"

Kate was shocked and flustered. "Ah, me? Marcus? How do you know that?" she blurted out.

"An educated guess." Billy smiled.

"Well, that was some guess," she said. "But you're quite right. We are in love."

"Good," he said. "I like you."

"I like you too."

"All right! Now we like each other, and in a few months, if you still want to do this, let me know."

"Okay," she said.

"Now, you're going to want to open that package, aren't you?"

"Yes."

"Well, let's go back to the house."

They went back inside the house. She sat on the couch again and looked at the package.

"You want some tea?" Billy asked.

"Sure, what kind do you have?"

"Tea. I only have real tea. There's Ceylon tea, there's Darjeeling tea, there's Assam tea, and then there are weeds—weeds are flowers—and thyme, and they have names like 'Sleepytime' and 'Red Zinger.' They're not tea. Do you want some real tea?"

Kate laughed at his diatribe. "Sure."

"Okay. You have a look at your letter from Marcus and I'll make us some tea."

She opened the envelope. It contained only two pieces of paper. The first page said in a bold, black ink scrawl: "I love you and I miss you, Marcus."

The second was a typewritten letter addressed to Daniel Feinstein in New York, one of the art brokers whom Jason was using to find his precious painting. The letter read:

"Dear Mr. Feinstein:

My name is Otto Dressler. And I am, as you will find, legal owner of the 1662 'Christ' painting by Rembrandt.

At this time, due to certain circumstances, I wish to sell this painting. I understand that you are a reputable broker who can assist me in this matter. The price I wish for this magnificent work of art is ten million dollars.

When you complete the provenance of this painting, you will see that it has been in my possession since 1938, at which time I legally bought it from the Cohen family in Munich, Germany.

Unfortunately, due to misunderstanding and the slanderous accusations of certain people regarding my activi ties in the Second World War, which were, I might point out, the honorable activities of a soldier, I am not at liberty to come forward and place myself in the public eye, therefore I must conduct this procedure under an umbrella of strict security.

If you feel that you have a market for this painting available at this time, you may contact me at the address on the envelope.

Documentation for this painting is available.

I remain, yours sincerely,
Otto Dressler''

The signature at the bottom of the letter was bold and, Kate surmised, (if Marcus had done his homework as she suspected), probably perfect.

''Here's your tea,'' Billy said, coming into the room.

Kate folded the papers again and placed them in the envelope. ''Thank you.''

They chatted for another hour. She enjoyed herself tremendously. Billy was vivacious, intelligent, cosmopolitan, and above all a true artist. She looked forward to renewing their acquaintance at a calmer time.

When she got home she burned Marcus's note to her. It pained her but she had to do it. She left the letter from Otto Dressler in the envelope. Jasmine would have to carry it to Buenos Aires and mail it as soon as possible.

Kate drove immediately to Elsa's apartment. As soon as she entered the living room, Elsa took one look at her and said, ''It's time, isn't it?''

''Yes. Where's Jasmine?''

''In the bedroom.''

Jasmine was sitting in front of a mirror, fooling with makeup. ''Hi! How's everything going?''

''You have to make a trip,'' Kate said.

''The letter came?''

''Yes. I want you on a plane on Sunday so that you're there for business on Monday morning.''

''Oh God!'' Jasmine said, bending her knees, clasping

her hands, her face radiant with excitement. "Isn't this somethin' else!"

Kate wanted to smile, but she couldn't. She was too nervous. Everything was moving along, but so much depended upon Marcus's skill, a skill she had no firsthand knowledge of. A skill she entirely depended upon. Soon it would be put to the test.

She fumbled in her bag. "Here is your ticket." She opened up the paper airline pouch and said, "Los Angeles to Buenos Aires and return."

"Oh God, this is so exciting," Jasmine said, totally unperturbed by any of the complexities.

"Your flight leaves on Sunday morning, early. Don't bother packing much," Kate warned. "It's a quick trip."

"What language do they speak there?" Jasmine asked. "Is it Portuguese or is that in Brazil?"

"That's Brazil," Kate said. "They speak Spanish in Argentina."

"Oh, good, I can speak a little bit. That'll be helpful."

"All right, now let's run over what you have to do. The first step is to find an agent to act on your behalf, a lawyer. You'll be able to get some names at your hotel. He has to understand that for whatever exorbitant amount of money he wants to be paid, he will guarantee you complete confidentially. His job will be to open a post office box, forward any mail we get under the name of Dressler to the address here in Venice and, when you arrive on your next trip with the painting, to have it shipped by a shipping agent to the address we will provide."

"I got it, Kate. Don't worry."

"Okay, I think we're all set."

Kate went into the living room where Elsa was sitting. "Elsa, when Page comes by this evening, she will be leaving some samples of Jason's signature with you. They'll be copies of checks that he has written to her in the past. Thank God, Page keeps records like a martinette."

"Page is very organized," Elsa said.

"Oh, there's one more thing I have to tell Jasmine." She went back into Jasmine's room. "Jasmine, don't forget that when you mail the letter back here, you have to put the Argentinean box number on the front of the envelope. Have our agent's secretary type it in for you."

"Okay," Jasmine said, "I've got it all. Don't worry about a thing."

"I'm not," Kate said. "Have a good trip. I'll see you when you get back."

She said good-bye to Elsa and left. She was worried, she admitted to herself. There were so many things that could go wrong and so much depended on Marcus, who was four or five thousand miles away. Well, all she could do was proceed one stop at a time. Her job was to make certain each step was the right one. Worrying wouldn't help.

Kate needn't have worried. Jasmine left on Sunday, did exactly as she was supposed to do, and returned on Tuesday to report her mission accomplished—and some exhaustion.

"I didn't get to see Buenos Aires at all. I took a cab from the airport to the middle of downtown, went to the hotel, did my business within a block of the hotel, took a cab back to the airport, and left. It is an enormous city. It looks like fun."

"You'll have another chance to enjoy it," Kate told her. "You're going to have to go back as soon as the painting's done. We're going to ask you to fly to Spain and then to Buenos Aires and then back home through Mexico City."

"Will I be spending any time there then?"

"Yes," Kate replied.

Jasmine patted her stomach. "I've got to get all the traveling in now. Pretty soon, I'll find it hard to walk across the room."

"How's it feeling?"

"It's growing," Jasmine said with excitement. "I feel her growing inside me."

"I notice you call the baby a 'her.' Do you know something we don't?"

"Of course," Jasmine said. "I'm the mother. I know it's a girl."

"I hope this traveling is not too hard on you," Kate said with some concern.

"No, I'm doing fine. Like I told you, I feel great."

Kate looked at the calendar on her watch. "All right, that letter should reach the dealer within a week, and I expect that his reply is going to be very prompt. You did arrange for any mail that arrives at that box to be sent by air courier to the address here, right?"

"Yes, it's all arranged. The lawyer there, Senor Alverez, is going to check it daily, starting on Friday. Anything that's received there we'll get the next day."

"Great." Kate gave Jasmine a hug. "You did a good job, Jas."

"Maybe I should have been a spy," Jasmine said. "I'm cut out for this kind of work."

Allan was now going crazy. It was Thursday, and he'd called Jasmine four times. Twice when she was not at home and twice after that. Each time an elderly woman with an accented voice answered, and the last two times she told him that Jasmine did not wish to speak to him.

"Where are you?" he asked the last time. "Where is this place?"

The woman had hung up.

He mentioned this during a brief conversation with Jason. "I can't even find out where the bitch is."

"What's the number?" Jason asked.

"Why?"

"Because I can probably have my people get an address for you and a name."

Allan gave him the number.

"I'll call you back," Jason said.

Allan was missing Jasmine—and the sex. He'd gotten laid a few times recently, but it was dangerous in this day and age, and wearing a condom was a drag.

Hell, he shouldn't have been so hasty with her. He knew how stubborn she was. Okay, if she wanted to have the baby, he could have continued to argue the point with her and at least gotten five or six months of good fucking out of it before dumping her. That was the problem with the two of them: They both flew off the handle too quickly.

Two hours later Jason called him back. "She's staying with a woman named Elsa Bennet. This is the address. It's a penthouse off Wilshire in Beverly Hills. Funnily enough, Elsa Bennet happens to be a friend of Page's."

"Really?"

"Yep. I'll have a few words with her about that."

Well, that was Jason's problem. He thanked him and hung up. He looked at the time. He'd go over there right now and see if he could talk some sense into her.

Allan felt his anger mount as he drove over the hill into Hollywood and toward Beverly Hills. The bitch was really putting him through the wringer. Really making him pay for it. And after all he'd done for her. Supporting her for all this time, helping her get parts. Where was gratitude these days?

He tried to suppress his resentment. He had to, or else he would just get into a fight with her and blow the whole thing again. He'd have to be nice. He'd have to manipulate her, which was something he had been able to do on occasion. She wasn't the only one with that skill.

He came to the street and peered at the number he'd written down on the memo pad. 1655. It was a large condominium building, perhaps six stories high. She lived in the penthouse with this woman, Elsa Bennet, whoever she was. He parked on the street, half a block away, and walked back. It was a high security building with no entrance. He pressed the buzzer marked "Penthouse" and waited for a voice to come from the speaker. "Yes?"

It wasn't Jasmine.

"Yes, is Jasmine in, please?"

"Who is this?" the voice asked.

"Allan Silver."

"She does not wish to see you, Mr. Silver. Will you please stop bothering us?"

The speaker clicked off. He peered through the glass window in the front door and saw a guard sitting at a table. He banged on the door.

''Yeah?'' came a voice through the speaker.

''I need to see someone in Elsa Bennet's apartment,'' Allan said.

''So why don't you buzz her?''

''I did, but—Hey, come out here so I can talk to you,''

''No way, buddy. If you buzzed and they're not there, I can't let you in.''

''I just want to talk to you,'' Allan said. ''There's a twenty in it for you.''

The speaker clicked off and a moment later the door opened. The guard was in his mid-thirties, and Allan noticed he had dirty fingernails.

Allan took a twenty out of his wallet and held it in his hand. ''Listen I've got to speak to the lady who's staying with Elsa Bennet. She's my girlfriend, and we've had an argument and I just want to talk to her.''

''Twenty bucks isn't worth my job,'' the guard said.

Allan took out his business card. ''Shit! I'll give you a hundred bucks and a higher-paying job. I'm president of Elixer Studios.''

The guard looked at the card and at Allan's expensive woolen suit, then shook his head. ''Can't do it. If I let you in and you go up there, there's still no way you're going to get in. It's like Fort Knox up there. They just had a robbery a few weeks ago.''

''Let me try,'' Allan said.

''No trouble, though? ''

''No trouble,'' Allan promised.

''All right,'' the guard said, and held out his hand.

Allan put a hundred-dollar bill and his business card in the outstretched palm.

''There's the elevator,'' the guard pointed. ''Penthouse suite.''

Allan took the elevator, which opened directly in front of Elsa's penthouse door. He rang the buzzer.

''Who is it?'' said a voice to his right. Another goddamn speaker.

''Allan Silver. I want to see Jasmine.''

"Mr. Silver, Jasmine doesn't want to see you. I'm asking you to leave, otherwise I'll call the guard."

"Look, I just want to talk to her," he pleaded.

"She doesn't want to talk to you."

"Look, I won't even come in. Just let her come to the door and talk to me through the door," he suggested.

"I'll ask her, but I don't think she wants to talk to you."

He waited thirty seconds, then a minute. Then a minute and a half, two minutes. He pressed the buzzer again. A voice spoke on the other side of the door.

"What do you want, Allan?"

"I wanted to talk to you, that's all."

"So talk."

Allan cleared his throat. "Jasmine, maybe I was a little hasty. I've been thinking about it."

"You mean you approve of me having the baby?"

"No, I don't, but I know how stubborn you are and there's nothing I can do about it."

"So?"

"So, let's get back together."

"It's too late, Allan. I've discovered I like being away from you."

Allan swallowed. "You can't mean that, Jas. I love you, you love me."

"You love yourself, Allan, and that's not enough for me. Now, would you leave me alone, please."

"Jasmine, listen to reason."

"Go away, or I'm going to call the guard."

"Listen, let's get together, let's talk this over, let's have some lunch, let's have dinner or something."

"Forget it. Now leave me alone. I don't want anything from you. I don't want to see you or talk to you. Just go, Allan."

Allan lifted both his hands and began to beat them against the door. "Jasmine, let me in! Let me in! We've got to talk," he shouted.

"I'm calling the guard," she said.

He banged harder on the door. It was useless. He

couldn't reach her. There was nothing he could do. Not now.

The elevator opened behind him and the guard stepped out. "I'm sorry, sir, but I'm going to have to ask you to leave. The lady's been complaining."

"Yeah. Okay," Allan's shoulders slumped. "I guess there's not much else to do."

He stepped into the elevator with the guard. As they went down, the guard said. "Is that offer of a job still open, sir?"

Allan looked at him—a loser, probably illiterate. "Fuck, no! I wouldn't hire anyone who takes bribes!" He stepped out of the elevator.

The guard had been right, the place was like a fortress. If he wanted to talk to Jasmine, he'd have to find some other way to do it. On the other hand, maybe she wasn't worth all the trouble. Maybe he should just find someone new. It wouldn't be that difficult. Hell, he knew a hundred young women who'd love to be kept in return for their sexual favors. The thought cheered him up.

Two days later, Jason had arranged to spend Saturday evening with Page. He arrived promptly at seven-thirty, took the Scotch she handed him, and got straight to the point. "I understand that you've been helping Jasmine out."

"What do you mean?"

"She's staying with Else Bennet. She's a friend of yours, isn't she?"

"I . . . yes," Page said, her heart thumping against her chest. She could feel her blood vessels changing shape. My God, she thought to herself, has he been following me? "How do you know about Elsa Bennet?"

Jason frowned at her. "Some time ago I had you followed, just to make sure you weren't pulling any more little shopping stunts on me. Your visit to Elsa Bennet was noted. My people gave me a sheet on her."

How dare you, Page wanted to scream, but instead she

said, ''Jasmine needed a place to stay and Elsa had some space, so I arranged it. What's the big deal?''

''The big deal is that you are not to interfere in these matters,'' Jason said harshly. ''Jasmine was being unreasonable and Allan was quite within his rights to reprimand her.''

''You call cutting off a pregnant woman from all support a reprimand?''

''It's a little discipline, and she needed it,'' Jason said.

''I'm sorry, I don't agree.''

''I'm not paying you to agree, but to obey. I want her out of there.''

''It's not within my power to do that,'' Page said. ''She and Elsa are now friends. Elsa wouldn't kick her out even if I asked her to.''

Jason grunted, ''Well, I hope you've learned your lesson. I don't appreciate your meddling in these affairs between the guys and their women. It's not your business.''

''The woman was pregnant and scared. It was simply a compassionate gesture. All I did was give her a roof,'' Page said mildly.

''She has money?''

Page shrugged. ''I have no idea. All I did was give her a place to stay.''

''Don't help her anymore. Is that understood?''

''Yes.''

Resentment boiled inside her. But for once she could afford not to show it. Jason would be getting his just dues soon enough.

The main problem was the danger his disclosure posed. If both he and Allan now knew where Jasmine was, Page and her ladyfriends would have to be very, very careful. She had to talk to Kate about it as soon as possible.

''When would you like to eat?'' she asked, closing the matter.

''After I finish my drink would be fine.'' He, too, seemed willing to end the discussion.

* * *

On Sunday morning Page called Elsa. "Why didn't you let me know that Allan knew where Jasmine was?"

"He didn't get in," she said.

"That's not the point," Page insisted. "The point is that Jason also knows where Jasmine is and knows about you and our relationship."

"That could be trouble," Elsa said.

"You bet your ass," Page responded with an edge to her voice. "If anything like this ever happens again, let me know as soon as you can. We can't afford to take chances."

An abashed Elsa promised she would.

Next Page called Kate at home and told her what had happened.

"That could be very dangerous," Kate said immediately. "We've got to check it out."

"What do you mean?"

"We've got to find out if Allan is having Jasmine watched."

"How can we do that?"

"Have Elsa hire a private detective to watch Jasmine for two days, to see if she's being followed. And make sure that Jasmine goes out during that time."

"Good idea," Page said approvingly. "I'll take care of it."

She hung up and called Elsa back. "I have someone very good that I've used in business matters before," Elsa said. "I'll call him first thing tomorrow."

Elsa's man must have been very good, because in the next two days Jasmine didn't even see him—and she looked for him. But more to the point and much to their relief, he reported to Elsa that Jasmine was clean. "There's nobody on her tail," he said when he called her.

"We still have to be extra careful now," Kate said when Page told her. "I don't think I can go there anymore. And Jasmine—I'm still a little concerned."

"Tell you what," Page said, "we'll have him check her

weekly, to make sure that Allan hasn't got somebody following her.''

''Won't that be expensive?'' Kate asked.

''It's all part of the cost of doing business,'' Page said. ''Call it insurance.''

Ten days after Jasmine's return from Buenos Aires, Kate got another call from Billy saying he had something for her, and that evening she drove down to Venice.

''Hi, Billy,'' she said with genuine pleasure when he opened the door.

''Kate, how are you?''

''I'm just fine, thanks. And you?''

''Top of the world, top of the world. There's a letter here from Buenos Aires, which I assume is for you.''

''Yes. May I see it?''

The house looked exactly the same—the same magnificent disarray, the same cat on the couch. ''Ah, now let me see. Where did I put it?''

Kate shuddered inwardly, hoping to God that Billy didn't lose one of their important communications one day.

''Ah, here it is! On the table right where I put it.'' He came over and handed it to her. He gestured to the couch. ''Sit, sit.''

As she began to open the envelope, he said, ''Cup of tea?''

''Yes, that would be great.''

''All right,'' he said, and disappeared.

Inside was an envelope addressed to Otto Dressler at the Buenos Aires box number. She opened it. It was a letter from the dealer.

He thanked Dressler for his letter and said he would be most interested in seeing the painting, as there was a potential buyer. *''I've investigated the ownership of this painting,''* the dealer wrote, *''and have discovered that you did indeed buy it from the Cohen family in 1938. I am also well aware of your need for secrecy in this matter. However, in order to proceed further, I must examine the painting and hereby request that your representative bring it to New York or send it to me with the documentation.*

Please advise me as soon as possible what arrangements you will be able to make."

"Bingo!" Kate said aloud.

"Good news?" Billy asked, returning with their tea.

She folded the letter and put it back in the envelope. "Yes, you could say that."

Billy handed her the cup and sat opposite her. She held the envelope out toward him. "I need this sent to Marcus, overseas express mail or by courier."

"First thing in the morning," Billy replied. "He'll have it in two days, maybe three."

"That'll be fine," Kate said.

As soon as Marcus received this letter, he would send another letter from Dressler back to the dealer. They had anticipated this response and had carefully drafted a reply.

This time, it would be mailed from Switzerland. In it, Dressler would say that he had received Feinstein's letter just as he was leaving Argentina to go to Europe. Unfortunately, he would be there for at least two weeks. However, as soon as he returned, he would contact the dealer regarding the arrangements for him to see the painting. This strategy would not only avoid the difficult problem of sending another letter from Buenos Aires, but it would also buy them some time.

"So, Kate," Billy said cheerfully, interrupting her thoughts, "what have you been up to?"

"Nothing much. How about you? Working on anything new?"

"I'm doing a new portrait."

"A commission, I hope."

"No, a girl I met on the pier. Just gorgeous. I had to paint her."

"Can I see it?" she asked.

"Oh, sure," he said, trying to hide his pleasure. "come on back."

As she followed him out, she couldn't help but admire his unquestioning loyalty toward Marcus. A valuable friend, and a nice man. Maybe one day, when this was all over, she'd introduce him to Jasmine. She tried to picture the two of them together. The Irish leprechaun and the Chinese princess . . . Stranger things had happened.

When Jason heard the news about the Rembrandt from his dealer, he immediately called Stodding. They met at Jason's club for lunch on Monday.

"You have some news?" Stod asked as soon as they sat.

"Been approached by Feinstein in New York. He's received a query from a man in South America, totally unsolicited. It's not as a result of anything we've done."

"Oh?" Stodding said.

"The man, a gentleman by the name of Otto Dressler, wishes to sell Rembrandt's 'Christ'."

"Which one is it? There have been a few," Stoddingsaid.

"My man's been tracing the provenance," Jason said. "It was owned for many years by Jews in Munich—the Cohen family. However, in 1938, when the Nazis were already in power and the Jews were being sent to concentration camps, the family, which was not without influence, wanted to get out of Germany. They found it very difficult to get an exit visa. It was continually denied. They approached an acquaintance of theirs, a Capt. Otto Dressler. Dressler was a Nazi on the rise in the hierarchy and not without influence himself.

"They had a magnificent art collection and, in particular, this Rembrandt, which Dressler, of course, knew of. Dressler made a deal with them. He would buy the Rembrandt and, in return, provide them with an exit visa. When it's a question of art and life, there are very few people who are going to choose art. The Cohens sold Dressler the painting. Dressler kept it in his possession until 1945, at which time he was a major with responsible duties in the SS.

"By the time the Americans arrived in Berlin, Dressler had disappeared. He was what they call a war criminal and was sought by the British, American, and Russian authorities, not to mention in later years Jews like Simon Weisenthal. He is still very much a wanted man. However, he has contacted us and is willing to sell us this painting. His asking price is ten million dollars."

"Well, I don't know," Stod said dubiously. "A Rembrandt, but—"

"Yes, a major Rembrandt, from what Feinstein says. A work that nobody has seen since 1945."

Stod shook his head. "There could be problems of ownership if he stole this painting from this—"

"No," Jason cut in irritably, "he didn't steal it. He legally bought it. And there are, one assumes, legal papers in his possession, but the record shows that he bought the painting. He bought it for a pittance, but he bought it. And received a bill of sale and legally owned it. And, in fact, as late as, I believe, '42 or '43, it was shown in German museums as his legal painting."

"Well, then," Stodding said, relief in his voice, "I see no problem. The only problem has been that some of the treasures stolen by Nazi officials during the war—and there were tons of them—had problems of ownership later on, people claiming that these paintings were stolen from them. But in this case, if it is indeed a clear-cut sale, I don't see a problem. Do we get to see the painting soon?"

"My man's written back to him and asked him when we can see it." Jason banged a fist into the palm of his left hand. "I'm excited, Stod. I think this is it. A major Rembrandt. Nobody has one here. I think we might just pull off a coup with this one. Particularly the fact that it's a painting nobody has seen for more than forty years."

The waiter came to the table and asked for their order. Jason immediately stopped talking. He asked Stod what he wanted.

"I think I'll have a roast beef," Stodding said.

"I'll have the fish of the day, whatever that is," Jason said, turning his attention back to Stodding as the waiter walked away. "Do you think we'll get much criticism about whom we're buying this painting from?"

"You'd better talk to your PR person about that," Stodding said. "I don't know. I imagine there will be some."

Jason grimaced. "If it comes up, we'll position it as a cultural rescue. Here's a painting that's been hidden away in South America somewhere, kept out of public view, denied to the public for more than forty years, and we've rescued it. Whom we buy it from, we never have to say."

"That's true," Stodding said. "The price, who we bought it from, is strictly our business. We're a private foundation, we don't have to reveal these things. And talking about the price, do you think we'll get him down from ten million?"

"I'm sure we will. He approached us, remember? The man must need money to part with this treasure after all this time. Perhaps some specific need's arisen. When you're talking about ten million dollars, seven million dollars, the difference isn't that great. I'm sure we'll be able to come to terms."

"We have to examine the painting very carefully," Stodding said. "We'll have to keep in mind that this is a disreputable source."

"He's the man that bought the painting," Jason said. "He's had it for forty years. It's a well-known painting, with well-established antecedents going back to Rembrandt's time. The dealer says he's tracked all the owners."

"That's good," Stod said, "but we'll still have to check it out. We do that with any major purchase."

"Fine, fine," Jason said dismissively. "Do what we have to do. In the meantime, my man's written back to him and we should hear from him soon. We'll then move ahead. How's the building coming along?"

"We're just about complete. We could open in a couple of weeks if we had to," Stod said.

"Well, let's hold off any announcement until we have this painting in our hands," Jason ordered.

"Of course."

The waiter returned with their meal. He put the plates down in front of them.

Jason raised his glass of wine, unable to hide his elation, and said, "To Rembrandt Van Rijn."

"To Rembrandt Harmenszoon van Rijn," Stod corrected him.

CHAPTER TWENTY-TWO

Both Kate and Page felt as though they were treading water. Day merged into day. Kate saw David, and Page saw Jason.

Their only motivation was to make everything seem normal. To raise no suspicions. To maintain the status quo. They both worked at their jobs during the day and met with their men at night, when they were required to do so.

Page spent a weekend with Jason on his yacht, together with some of his business associates, and sailed to Catalina.

Kate went to Santa Barbara with David on the same weekend. They stayed at the Biltmore and walked on the beach, and she tried to forget what she was doing.

David again approached her about going to Bali with him, but she begged off with the excuse that she was just too busy at work.

"Maybe in a couple of months," she said.

Every five days or so they hired the detective to follow Jasmine. Apparently she was still not being followed.

It was with some relief after about ten days that Kate learned from David that Allan had a new mistress, an actress by the name of Shelly Pointer—young, blonde, hungry, and eager to please. Hopefully, this would take his mind completely off Jasmine.

While all this was happening, both women found that for much of the time their thoughts turned to a small island off Spain, where a man was painting a picture. So much depended upon his skill and reliability. Worse, Kate found that she missed him terribly.

Jasmine called her sister to find out how she was doing. She hadn't spoken to her for a few weeks and was wondering how she had been coping with home life and the aftereffects of the abortion.

"I'm fine," Fay said, "but I'm glad you called. I tried to reach you but your phone's been disconnected. Is everything okay? Can I come and visit you this weekend?"

"Hold on," Jasmine said. She looked over at Else. "Would it be all right if my sister came for a visit this weekend?"

"Of course. The more the merrier," Elsa said.

"Can I use your car to pick her up?"

"Yes."

"Fine," she said into the telephone. "Let me know your flight and I'll come and get you. It'll be great to see you. This is my new telephone number. I'll explain everything when you're here."

When Jasmine picked her sister up at the airport, Fay looked at her curiously but didn't comment. When they were back at Elsa's apartment, and after introductions had been made and they were alone, Fay cocked her head to one side and finally said, "Jas, you look different somehow. What's happened? What have you done?"

Jasmine had been nervous about this moment, although she had known that she wouldn't be able to avoid it. The nervousness came from how her news would affect Fay.

The kid looked fine, but who knew what scars she carried as a result of her abortion? These things were traumatic. But Jasmine plunged ahead. There was no other way to go.

"I'm pregnant," she said.

"Wow! Really?" Fay said. "Who's the father? That guy, Allan?"

"Yes."

"So where is he, and why are you staying here, anyway? What happened to your apartment? What's going on?"

"We had a disagreement. I left. It's over between us."

"So . . . are you going to have an abortion? Or what's the deal?"

"No, I'm going to have the baby," Jasmine said. "That's what the argument was about. He wanted me to have an abortion, and I said I wouldn't."

"Really?"

"I've always wanted a child," Jasmine said. "I'm old enough now, responsible enough. And I figured I wanted to keep it."

Fay looked at her thoughtfully. "Are you happy about it?" she asked finally.

"Yes, Fay, I'm very happy about it."

Again silence from Fay.

And then Jasmine saw what she had feared cross her little sister's face. A cloud of sadness and loss.

They were sitting side by side on her bed. Jasmine reached over and put her hand on top of her sister's. "Don't worry, you'll have your chance. You have so many years left."

Tears appeared in Fay's eyes. "It's been so hard to stop thinking about it. I keep wondering if I did the right thing. Maybe I should have done what you're doing and had the child. Maybe I should have had the guts to keep it."

"If it's any consolation, I think you did the right thing," Jasmine said. "Our situations are very different, Fay. I'm a lot older than you are. I don't have many chances left for children. You're so young. You have so much to do first before you settle down and have a family. How could you have looked after a child now? It would have affected your life so deeply and cut you off from so many things that you really have to experience still. Surely you can see that."

"Yes, I know. It makes sense," Fay said. "It makes complete sense and yet somehow the feeling that I've lost something is so strong that I don't know . . . it just makes it's own kind of sense."

"But I know, as sure as the sun rises, that that feeling will pass. It's natural to feel that way. You did lose something, but that feeling will go. And you will have a chance when the time is right to create that feeling again. And you'll know that it's right because you'll be happy then."

"I hope so." Fay turned and hugged Jasmine. "But I am happy for you, I really am. I think it's great."

"Thanks, kid."

Fay drew away as a realization dawned. "My God! I'm going to be an aunt."

"You think that's weird?" Jasmine burst out. "I'm going to be a mother."

They collapsed on the bed into giggles.

It was a good weekend. Fay was doing better at home and at school. Apparently her parents had taken Jasmine's cautions to heart and were doing their best, in their own clumsy way, to give her a little more room in which to breathe.

"Come again," Jasmine said when she took her to the airport.

"I will, and when you have the baby, I'll come down and help you look after it," Fay said.

Jasmine felt fortunate. Things had changed so much in recent weeks. She had a family now and friends—both of which she had lacked for such a long time.

Jason had just arrived at Page's apartment to pick her up when his buzzer went off. They were about to go to the Music Center to see some touring ballet company.

''Damn,'' he said, and went to the telephone.

The service gave him an urgent message to call his family lawyer, Paul Stanford.

''Sorry to bother you,'' Stanford said when Jason reached him. ''We've got a minor emergency on our hands.''

''What is it?''

''It's your wife. Sharon's been picked up for driving under the influence of drugs.''

''Drugs?''

Page looked up from her chair.

''What do you mean?'' Jason continued. ''She doesn't use drugs.''

''Well, she was flying higher than a kite, and I'm afraid the police also found a small quantity of cocaine in the car, in her bag.''

''Oh Jesus,'' Jason said. ''So what now?''

''I'm at the police station, getting her out. Do you want to come down here?''

''Hell, no. I don't want to see her. Just handle it. Are there any media down there?''

''Not that I've seen. But they'll get ahold of it.''

''Shit!'' Jason moaned. ''This is all I need. Just get her out of there and take her home. Is there any way we can nip this thing in the bud?''

''You mean with the police?''

''Yeah, so it doesn't reach court.''

''No way, Jason. Don't even try it.''

''A few honorariums in the right hands?'' Jason insisted.

''I don't even want to hear this. There is no way you can do that with these people. It will just get you in deeper.''

''What'll she get for this? Did she injure anybody?''

''No. No injuries. Except for a tree and her car. It will just be a slap on the wrist and a detox program.''

''But it'll get in the press?'' Jason asked. ''Right?''

''We might just get lucky and they could miss the whole thing.''

Jason laughed bitterly. "I doubt it. The *Times* would love to get my ass. After all, I am a media rival."

"Maybe there's someone you could talk to there."

"Yeah, there might be. Professional courtesy and all that. I don't know. It's a long shot. I guess I'll see what I can do. You'll take care of things down there, right?"

"Sure, the process is under way."

"All right. I'll think this over and talk to you about it tomorrow. Thanks for calling. Bye."

Jason hung up. "That stupid bitch!"

Page knew better than to ask what had happened. But he sat down beside her and told her. "It's just one thing after the other with Sharon. Not content with that scene at the party, now she's gotten herself picked up for using cocaine."

"Is this her first offense?" Page asked.

"Of course. I don't know when she started doing this. She's never used drugs."

Perhaps living with Jason would lead anyone to drugs, Page thought. The stress of it would be enormous for most people.

"Well," she said, "if she's a first offender, she probably won't get into much trouble."

"That's not the point," Jason said angrily. "The point is, I don't need the publicity right now. Not with the new wing about to open and all the publicity that will bring. God, you're in PR. Surely you can see how destructive this can be!"

"What are you going to do?"

"I don't know," Jason muttered. "The first thing I should do is kill the bitch."

Page didn't know whether he was joking or not. She decided to remain silent.

"Well, I'm not going to worry about it now," Jason said after a pause. "Let's go see this ballet. I'll tackle this in the morning. Maybe something will come to me in the night."

They began to walk toward the door. Jason looked admiringly at her and said, ''By the way, as usual you look very lovely tonight.''

Page wore a floor-length black velvet suit, with her ever-present diamond pinned to the neckline of the jacket.

She couldn't help but admire Jason's ability to block something out of his mind once he'd decided to do it. However, in the coming weeks, this ability of his would be put to the true test. Little did he know what was in store for him.

Jason didn't have as much time to ponder the problem as he'd anticipated. The next morning the story broke in the *Los Angeles Times*.

It wasn't a big story—about five column inches in the Metro section. But it clearly stated that Sharon was the wife of Jason Thomas, and at least two paragraphs explained exactly who he was.

Jason was livid. But there was nothing he could do about it. As a participant in the media process himself, he knew well how it would work from now on. His name would forever be linked to Sharon Thomas's arrest for cocaine use. Even when the stories appeared lauding his accomplishments and announcing the Thomas Wing, there would be a sentence, perhaps a paragraph, explaining that some weeks earlier Mrs. Sharon Thomas was arrested for cocaine use.

He had spent the night with Page and didn't read the story until he reached his office. He immediately called the house to speak to Sharon. But there was no answer. It was probably just as well she wasn't around to answer any media telephone calls either. He'd have to reach her soon and let her know that if anyone did reach her, her only answer would be ''no comment.''

Next he called Page at her office. ''I've had an idea,'' he said to her. ''I want to run it by you and see what you think.''

''Sure, Jason.''

"I want to donate a hundred thousand dollars to the Betty Ford Center. Can we get some good media play on that?"

"Yeah, I'm sure we can. Why don't you have your own corporate PR people handle that?"

"I will," he said, "I just wanted your opinion. You think it's better that I just forget this thing or that I do something like this?"

"Well," Page said, "you may forget this but the media won't. It's going to come up again and again. You know that, don't you?"

"Yes, I do."

"Well, if it keeps on coming up, it wouldn't hurt to have the next sentence state that you immediately gave a hundred thousand dollars to the Betty Ford Center."

"That's exactly my idea," Jason said. "I'm glad you agree. Thanks."

It wouldn't eradicate the problem, but it would certainly put a better face on it, he thought, pleased with himself. He'd make the arrangements with his accountant immediately.

That evening he went home and confronted Sharon. She was strangely sedate, even repentant. "I'm sorry, Jason" were the first words she said.

"It's too late for sorry," Jason said. She was sitting on the patio watching the dying sun. He pulled up a chair beside her. "How could you do something like this? Do you understand the scandal?"

"I don't care about the scandal," Sharon said, some of her fire returning. "What I care about is that I nearly killed myself last night. I hit a tree at sixty miles per hour, in a twenty-mile-per-hour speed zone."

"Shit, maybe it would have been better for everybody if you'd killed yourself," Jason said callously.

"Yes, I'm sure you think that, Jason. But I didn't and I won't give you that pleasure."

"I should divorce you," he said disgruntledly.

"You won't do that."

"No, I won't. But here's what I want you to do. I want you to check into the Betty Ford Center tomorrow and go through whatever program they have for drug users. The judge will want you to do that anyway. Be better if it's done before the trial. It'll look better."

Sharon rubbed her face. "I could use the rest."

"Good," he said, rising. "Then it's settled. I'll make the arrangements first thing in the morning. You can have whatever chauffeur you have these days drive you there."

"Yes," she said.

Jason went into the house, leaving her alone on the patio. She rubbed her face harder. She wished she had some cocaine. She was feeling so low, so useless, so stupid. A hit would make her feel better, she knew. But the thought terrified her. She'd become cocaine's mistress in such a short period of time, and she had almost died. She didn't want to die. She'd decided that when she climbed out of the shattered car.

Her chauffeur had had the night off, so she drove instead. She'd taken about seven or eight lines, and some crack. She'd never been so stoned in her life. She had felt invulnerable. But it was all a lie.

She'd been planning to go to a rehabilitation clinic anyway. It would be good to get away from Jason and her problems for a while. Perhaps it would even give her new strength. Strength to do what ultimately she'd have to do for her survival, if indeed she wanted to live. And that was to divorce Jason, to leave him, to seek a somehow better, more productive life. If only she had the courage to start the search.

She sighed. All she'd have to do was find the strength. Something she'd never been able to do before.

A sense of helplessness descended over her. She sat on the patio until the sun went down.

The days passed. Kate got one message from Marcus saying that "things were proceeding well."

Page mentioned that Jason was tremendously frustrated because the seller of the Rembrandt had left Buenos Aires for Europe and they were unable to contact him. He'd even wanted to fly immediately down to Argentina, but Stodding had talked him out of it, saying it would be best if the painting was sent to New York and examined there by his experts and perhaps others. He'd counseled patience.

Their lives continued their normal patterns, but the undercurrents of expectation were intense. Kate felt like a sedate country hiker waiting for a storm to break.

CHAPTER TWENTY-THREE

"Call for you, Kate," Madge said, appearing in the doorway of the gallery where Kate was with a customer.

The customer was very interested in a sculpture and it looked likely that Kate would make the sale. She almost turned to Madge to ask her to take a message, then she realized that she shouldn't do that.

"Excuse me," she said to the man. "I'll be just a moment. All right?"

She went into the office and picked up the telephone. "Our friend says that everything's ready," Billy said, and hung up.

Kate felt a surge of adrenaline course through her. She stood there, unable to move for a moment, her ears, chest and, it seemed, every vein in her body pounding away. She took a deep breath and then another. And then a third.

"All right!" she said quietly to herself and went back into the galley.

The customer bought the sculpture, much to Madge's pleasure. As soon as he left, Kate called Page.

"It's ready," she said. "We all have to meet tonight." She had stayed away from Elsa's apartment, just in case it was being watched. Now it was unavoidable that they all meet there.

"I'm going out this evening," Page said, "but I should be back around eleven."

"I'm supposed to as well," Kate replied. "But I'm going to cancel. I've got too much to think about now. Why don't we meet at Elsa's at midnight?"

"It's dangerous," Page said. "What if someone is watching the place?"

"Our man says not."

"He says she isn't being followed. But he says he can't guarantee the apartment building isn't being watched."

"Is there a back entrance?"

"Yes, an alley in the back. Let's do that. I'll make arrangements for Elsa to have Jasmine let us in. Park some distance away on the other side of the block and walk down the side alley and up the back alley. I'll meet you there at twelve."

"Are we being paranoid?" Kate asked.

"Safe," Page said.

Next she called David. "David, I wonder if we could cancel tonight?"

"Why? Is something wrong?" He'd been planning to take her to a screening. David loved the glamour of Hollywood screenings, even though half the movies they'd seen in recent weeks had been terrible. "I don't go there for the movies," he once explained to her. "I go there to be seen, because many of my customers are there."

"I think I've got a touch of the flu," Kate said. "I just don't feel good. I think I'll just go home and have a hot drink and get to bed early."

"You sure you can't make it?" he wheedled.

"I really don't feel like it."

"Well, all right," he said ungraciously. "I'll call you tomorrow and see how you're doing."

''Good, thanks for understanding,'' she said.

That evening he called her at nine, ''Just to see how you're doing,'' he said. But she had a nasty feeling that he was checking up on her. She'd noticed a jealous trait rising lately. He disliked it intensely when other men looked at her. And at parties, when men talked to her in his absence, when he returned to her he always asked what they had been saying.

''I'm fine,'' she said. ''I was about to fall asleep. I just turned the lights off.''

''Good,'' he said. ''I just wanted to see how you were doing. I hope you feel better tomorrow. Good night.''

''Good night.''

At eleven-thirty she left for Elsa's apartment. She parked in the block behind the building, as Page had suggested, and walked down the darkened alley on the side, hoping there'd be no transients jumping out from beneath cardboard boxes. She turned left at the alley, running behind Elsa's building, and stood outside the gate. There was no sign of Page.

A minute later she heard muffled footsteps and saw Page turn the corner. They grinned at each other.

''Hi,'' Page said. ''I thought I was going to be late. Jason just kind of hung around.''

Kate looked at her watch, ''You're on time. I was a couple of minutes early.''

There was a noise on the other side of the gate, and then it swung open. ''Hi, guys.'' Jasmine hugged them both. ''Come along this way through the back door.''

They followed her into the building and took the elevator upstairs. Elsa greeted them warmly. ''So it is now time, hey?''

''Do or die,'' Jasmine said.

They sat in a small circle in the living room. Kate took tickets out of her purse and handed them to Jasmine. ''Here you go. LA to Madrid, to Buenos Aires, to Mexico City, to LA.''

''And the money?'' Jasmine asked.

Page opened her purse and handed her a bundle of cash. "There should be enough here to take care of everything."

"So," Kate said, unable to keep the nervous tension out of her voice, "Marcus will meet you at your hotel in Madrid. He will have a suitcase to give you. The painting will be sewn into the bottom of the suitcase, so that it remains flat. Take your clothes out of your suitcase and put them in his, and give your suitcase to him."

"Got it," Jasmine said.

"You'll fly with the painting to Buenos Aires. I don't think you'll have any trouble with customs. They are more interested in people smuggling stuff out of the country than in."

"And if I do have any trouble," Jasmine said, waving the money, "some of this should take care of it."

"Right," Kate said. "They are notoriously bribable down there. But I really don't think you'll have any problems. Once you get there you need to have the painting framed. Our lawyer . . . Senor Alverez, I believe you said his name was?"

Jasmine nodded.

"He will be able to arrange for the painting to go to an art shipper and have it sent to the dealer, Feinstein, in New York, whose address you have."

"Right," Jasmine said.

"Now, if there are any questions when you take the painting to be framed, just tell them it's a cheap copy, okay?"

"Sure," Jasmine said.

"And you stay there while it's being done. Don't leave the painting alone for a second."

"Got it," she said.

"Then have them wrap it in paper before you take it to the lawyer's office. I don't particularly want him to see what it is."

"Right."

"He'll make all the arrangements with customs and get the painting shipped to Feinstein. I want you to stay there until the painting is shipped, just to make sure everything goes smoothly. But don't go into the shipping office. You mustn't be seen. You must stay with him till you know the painting is gone. Then you hang tight. Two days later you start checking the mailbox.

"We're going to get a counteroffer. Dressler is asking ten million and we know that Jason's willing to spend seven, so we're going to get a counteroffer for seven and you are going to send a cable accepting that offer and giving the number of the Swiss bank account. And Marcus will give you all that information about the bank account in Madrid."

"Right."

Page asked a question: "This Mr. Alverez, he showed no curiosity as to who you represented?"

"He was only interested in the color of my money," Jasmine said. "He didn't ask any questions at all."

"Well, if he does," Kate said, "remember you just say that you are representing a German gentleman, who wishes to remain incognito. And that silence is what we are paying him for. He is not to mention you under any circumstances and is only authorized to say that he is acting on behalf of a German gentleman."

"Good, what else?" Jasmine asked.

"All we have to do is pray that Marcus has done his work well," Kate said. "I wish I had a chance to see the painting myself, before it goes to Jason, but I don't, so we just have to depend on Marcus."

Elsa interjected, "He's going to provide the documentation to go with the painting as well, isn't he?"

"Yes, he'll give Jasmine that too. She will ship that with the painting."

"And he's arranging for a friend to open a Swiss bank account in the meantime?" Elsa asked.

"Yes. A friend has been carefully chosen. He'll open the account and do what has to be done after the money arrives."

"Good," Elsa said.

"Well, guys?" Kate asked, looking at each of them.

Page lifted the corners of her mouth into what passed for a smile. "Like you said, now we pray."

Jasmine left as scheduled the following morning. Elsa had taken the precaution of having her private detective follow her. He reported back that she had not been shadowed by anyone except him.

Kate spent the day in a semi-comatose state. Even Madge noticed her distraction and asked if she was feeling well.

"I'm sorry," Kate said, sitting in the gallery office. "I just have something on my mind."

"Well, do you want to take some time off perhaps? Would you like to take the rest of the day?" Madge asked, concern in her voice.

"I think I would. I could use a little time for myself."

"Go for it," Madge said. "You've been working your ass off lately anyway."

Kate picked up her bag and jacket. "If David calls, why don't you just tell him you've sent me out on an errand."

"Sure. I'll call your home and leave a message on your machine if he calls."

"Thanks, Madge." She felt a rush of affinity for her friend, leaned forward, and kissed her on the cheek.

"What's that for?" Madge asked, surprised.

"For being a friend," Kate said. "Thanks."

Madge watched her speculatively as she left. Kate had seemed to be under a lot of pressure in the last few weeks. Maybe being someone's mistress wasn't as easy as it looked.

Kate got into her little Toyota and found herself on the Santa Monica Freeway driving toward the beach. She took the Lincoln Boulevard exit and drove to Billy's house. She needed to be with someone who wasn't involved in any of this. Not her work, not the men she knew, not the painting.

There was no answer when she knocked on the door, so she went around to the back, thinking he'd be in the studio. He was, busily slapping paint onto a large canvas.

"Kate," he said, looking up with pleasure. "Nice to see you."

"I'm sorry. I'm disturbing you, aren't I?"

"Yeah, but I like it, that's why I don't get all that much work done. I encourage people to drop in uninvited. It breaks up my day. Want some tea?"

"Sure."

He put his paintbrush down, looked critically at the painting, and shook his head. "Good thing you came in. I think I was going in the wrong direction here." He bustled past her, a nervous ball of energy, and led the way back to the house.

"So what's new?" he asked, putting water in the kettle and placing it on the stove.

"Nothing much, just life," Kate said. "It tends to be one thing after the other."

"Ain't that the truth. Come on, let's go sit on the front porch," Billy said when the tea was done. "It's a beautiful day today."

They went and sat on a weatherworn couch. Between the houses, there was just a faint glimpse of ocean to the west.

Billy sipped his tea, and then said, "Is something troubling you, Kate?"

She looked at him, surprised. "Does it show?"

He jiggled his head, the equivalent of a shrug. "A little."

Kate was silent. The truth of the matter was that she *was* troubled. It wasn't just the stress of what she was doing, the duplicity of it, the necessity to maintain a front. It was her very motives that were suspect. She had been wondering of late if it were all worthwhile. Would her revenge leave a bitter taste in her mouth? With David, she had seen Jason off and on in recent weeks, forming an opinion of the man.

In spite of his outer display of strength, inside Jason Thomas was a weak and frightened person. His apparent strength was just an attempt to head things off at the pass. He was the type of man who saw enemies everywhere, although he would never admit it if the concept were placed before him. His power, his entire motivation, probably throughout his life, had been born of an attempt to entrench himself so that these "enemies" wouldn't get him. In fact, as she had mulled this over in her contemplative moments, she had realized that, to all intents and purposes, Jason was insane. A man who operated solely by delusion.

She had met people like that before. They saw everyone else as rivals. They had what was admiringly called the "competitive edge," and seeing everyone as a rival they did their best to incapacitate them, usually in a covert manner, before they could be harmed by them. This type of person was usually a critical individual. One who tended to belittle the efforts of others because *those efforts threatened him.* Any success by someone else, no matter how small, was a threat to his survival. If that wasn't insanity, what was?

The problem was, though, she'd come to realize, the hate that she'd originally felt toward Jason had changed into pity. Was it worthwhile taking revenge on someone like this? Was it worth all this effort, placing so many people at risk for someone like this? She didn't know the answer to that question, and that was what was troubling her.

"Billy, do you believe in revenge?" she asked finally.

Billy blinked twice. "Revenge? No, of course not. It's a waste of your time. I believe in karma. If someone's wronged you, sooner or later they're going to pay for it. You may never ever have the pleasure of knowing how that happened, but they'll pay. I know that."

"So you just have to sit back and take whatever abuse others heap on you?"

Billy laughed uproariously. "Sit back—hell no. You dodge the bullets, kid. But then to waste your energy shooting back, that's something else."

"Well, what about justice?" she asked.

"Ah, well, that's different. Justice is a tool that we have in society. It's available to us in some degree. It's hard to get it, but it's there. And I suppose we should avail ourselves of it. But you have to know the difference. There is earthly justice and then there's spiritual justice. Spiritual justice comes with karma. Earthly justice—well, sometimes we can do something about it.''

''And do you think we should?''

Billy looked at her sharply. ''Depends if you are willing to pay the price,'' he said. ''There's a tag on everything. But I wouldn't let it become a mission that interfered with my painting. Not worth it.'' He laughed again. ''But I suppose if you can do it without sending your own karma back a few lifetimes, hell, more power to you.''

What would come out of this? Kate wondered. Jason would receive his comeuppance, but he would experience no remorse, that was certain. What would come out of it that was constructive?

Billy didn't interrupt her thoughts. Instead he sipped silently on his tea.

There were positive things that would result from her quest: Jasmine and Page would both be affected positively. Jasmine had already shown an appreciation of a new-found freedom and ability. For Page, the whole episode would result in the financial independence she sought.

And what about me? Kate thought. She had found Marcus, and Marcus had found her. When you looked at that, at the impossibility of it, the incongruity of it, it was of earth-shattering importance—to them at least. The chance of it happening was equivalent to the chance of two stars flying from each end of the universe and colliding at some point in space. And yet it had. And surely that most wonderful, most miraculous event justified all her efforts.

She reached across and put her hand on Billy's shoulder. ''Thanks, Billy,''

Billy gave her an elfin grin. ''Come on, we do it all ourselves. I just happened to be passing by.''

Two days later, Kate got a call from Billy at her apartment. It was unusual. His instructions were always to call her at the office.

''Yes?'' she said, answering the phone.

"It's me," he said. "I need you to come over here now. There's something here for you." He hung up.

Luckily, she was alone. David had some board of directors meeting to go to that night. She worried all the way during the drive to Venice. Had something gone wrong? Was there some emergency? She was expecting no packages. Why did Billy want to see her? What could have happened?

She flew down the freeway and, less than twenty minutes after his call, pulled up outside Billy's house. She got out of the car, slammed the door behind her, and trotted to his front door.

When the door opened she stood transfixed, her mouth gaping for what seemed like forever.

Marcus stood there. He smiled, waiting for her to react.

"Marcus."

He grabbed her arm, pulled her inside, and closed the door. Then he took her in his arms and kissed her.

"Marcus, what are you doing here?" she asked when she broke away and could breathe again.

He grinned. "I weighed the risks and decided to come. I had to see you, I couldn't stay away. I met Jasmine in Madrid and gave her the painting, and then it seemed just like a short hop to come over here, so I decided to do that."

"Oh, I'm glad you did. I'm so glad." She kissed him again. They broke apart from each other, laughing.

He ran his hands through her hair, pulling her head against his chest and hugging her. "God, I missed you."

She found herself biting his shoulder. "I missed you too. I can't tell you how much I missed you."

He pulled himself away, took her hand, and led her to the couch. They sat beside each other, pushing Sheba, the cat, aside.

"Did everything go okay?" she had the composure of mind to ask.

"It went fine."

"How did the painting turn out?"

Marcus laughed. "The painting is absolutely magnificent. It's my masterpiece. It's better than Rembrandt. But it looks exactly like him. You don't have to worry about it. It's perfect."

"Oh God," she said, falling into his arms again. "I'm sorry. I *was* worried about it. I've been so worried about it."

"I know," he said, into her hair. "It was tricky, but it worked."

She drew away and looked at him quizzically. "What the hell *are* you doing here?"

Marcus laughed again. "I wanted to make love to you. What else can I say?"

"Marcus!" she exclaimed. "The documentation, Swiss bank account . . ."

Marcus patted her knee, "Don't worry, it's all taken care of. Everything's under control. All we have to do now is make love."

"Now?"

"I have some Polaroid pictures of the painting if you want to see them," Marcus said slyly.

"Now?" she said again. "Where's Billy?"

"Billy is elsewhere," Marcus said with a self-satisfied smirk. "He has lent us his abode for the evening. Indeed, for the entire night."

"The entire night?"

"The entire night," he repeated.

"Hallelujah!" She leaned forward and with one deft movement, clasping the top of his jeans with one hand and his zipper with the other, she unbuttoned and unzipped them. She fell forward and buried her head in his groin, taking gigantic bites into the area until she found what she was looking for. And then she growled.

"Help," Marcus groaned.

She slid off the couch until she knelt in front of him. Looking up, her eyes glowed. "Do you remember the last time we made love?"

Marcus nodded.

"I haven't been able to stop thinking of it." Kate lowered her head and pulled out his penis, taking it in her mouth, and she felt it harden and grow.

She lavished her tongue on it, taking as much of it in her mouth as she could, and tried to draw the vitality, the life from it.

"You can't do this. I haven't made love since I saw you last. I'm going to explode before we've even begun."

He pulled her up by the shoulders and kissed her. She could feel his penis against her stomach. Their mouths clashed, their tongues fought, their bodies tried to enter the other through layers of clothing.

They broke away, their breathing harsh and ragged.

"The bedroom," Marcus said. He stood up, his pants falling to his ankles.

Kate giggled. "Lift your legs," she said, and pulled them off. "Now the bedroom."

They almost ran.

The bedroom was miraculously tidy compared to the rest of the house. Perhaps Marcus had cleaned it before she came, Kate thought in a fraction of a second.

And then she was tearing her clothes off and he his, and naked they met, coming from opposite sides of the bed. He kissed her and bit her breasts and her stomach, and then his head was there, and his hands were there and he pulled her apart, and his mouth was there on the little pearl, tugging at it, biting and sucking it.

She felt that they had hardly begun, yet already she was coming. And she tried to pull away but he wouldn't let her. He kept his mouth there, until she let out little screams and felt her juices flow like countless fountains. And only then did he rise and kiss her and slowly enter her.

It was beautiful. Again she felt herself rising, an intensity of sensation, clasping her and clasping him, spreading through her body, and just then he pulled out and she said, "Oh what?"

He disappeared and then she felt his hand on her hips. Then he turned her over and made her kneel on the bed, standing beside it and entering her from behind, and plunged harder and harder into her until she could no longer stand it, saying things to him that she could not remember afterwards. And he said things to her and then again he left her and again she said, "What?"

He fell on to the bed and said, "Now it's your turn. I'm suffering from jet lag."

She got on top of him, looking down at his face and half-closed eyes, at the mouth curving into a smile, at the strong jaw that opened and closed with the rhythm of her movements. And then it was too slow and she felt she had to hurry, and she lowered herself and whipped her hips against him, and he said, "Oh God," and she said the same thing.

They each said something then that was both utterly meaningless and yet meaningful, and she could feel him spurt inside of her, filling her with his love.

She lost herself then. Lost in a deluge of passion that soaked him and the bed below him. And again they both shouted, until finally she fell against his chest, limp, drained, and totally satisfied.

Kate and Marcus walked along the beach, shoes in their hands, jeans rolled up, skirting the edge of the water line. It was morning. They had finally fallen asleep at about three A.M. but had woken at seven, remarkably refreshed.

After a leisurely breakfast at a small cafe, they had walked down the beach.

"I like it here," Kate said, skipping to avoid a wave. The water was cold. "Everybody in New York thinks that LA is the airhead capital of the world. It hasn't turned out to be that way. People here work hard and play hard. They enjoy both more."

"Yeah, I like it too," Marcus said. "If I lived in the States, I'd probably live here. I grew up not far from here, you know."

"They say native Californians are an endangered species," Kate said.

"Yeah, well, I was born in West LA and grew up there."

"Your parents—where are they now?"

"My father died about six years ago. My mother remarried and she's living in San Diego with her new husband."

"Do you ever see them?"

"Not very often. We each have our own lives now. She's a nice lady though. We get along fine. I drop her a line every now and then. What about your parents? What happened to them?"

Kate looked out at the waves. There were some early surfers, black wetsuits glinting just beyond the breakers. "They died in an auto accident when I was about eight. Joel was a couple of years older. We went to live with an aunt in Concord, New Hampshire. She didn't really want us, but she felt obligated to take us. She was my mother's sister. In fact, I think Joel persuaded her to take us, rather than to let us go to a foster home. He promised her that he'd look after himself and look after me, and he kept that promise. He was always a kind of a brother and a father to me."

"So it was the two of you against the world?"

"Yes. Our aunt died when I was about eighteen, I guess. Joel was already playing music in a band by then, making a little money. He took care of me, made sure I went to college, helped me when I ran out of money, although for the most part I worked my way through college myself. But Joel was always there for me. Someone to talk to. Until . . ."

"Well, now you have me," Marcus said, slipping an arm around her shoulders, pulling her against him. "I was wondering," he said hesitantly.

"What?"

"Well, when this is all over, if you like LA so much, will you want to come back to Ibiza with me?"

They had stopped and were facing the ocean. In the distance they could see the surfers coming in now. "I like LA, but my heart's in Ibiza," Kate said.

"Is that a yes?"

"I'm not sure. I don't know what I'd do there. I'd have

to do something. I'm not much good as an idle kept woman."

"Well, I have an idea," Marcus said.

"You do?"

"Yeah. Bart Stone has been talking for years about selling his gallery, you know. I think that if somebody just made him a good offer, he'd probably do it."

"Really? Do you think so?"

Marcus nodded. "It's something to think about, anyway."

She put her arm through his, turned him around. "We'd better start heading back or we'll end up in San Diego." Slowly, they began to walk back. "It's tempting. The only problem is I find it difficult to think of the future now. Until this is over . . ."

Marcus did not press her any harder. The idea would gestate in its own time.

When they got back to the house, Billy was there. He greeted them and said, with a quick glance at their glowing face, "Did you guys have a good night?"

"A splendid night, Billy," Marcus said with a sly sidelong look at Kate. "Thanks for the use of your house."

"Any time,"

"Well, thanks. How about we throw you out again tonight?" Marcus asked.

"Sure," Billy said with a shrug.

Kate noticed there was an easy familiarity between the two men. They had obviously been friends for a long time and used the shorthand that friends develop over the years—a gesture, a look that said more than any stranger could understand.

She realized she hadn't even asked Marcus how long he'd be staying, and she did so now.

"I'm flying back tomorrow," he said. "I don't think I should hang around here for too long, not now. I also have to be back there soon. There are still things to be done."

She was disappointed. But he was quite right. They couldn't take a chance on being seen together by anyone. "Yes, I suppose so," she said regretfully.

"But we'll have today and tonight."

"I have to go into work for a while today, but I can come back this evening." She turned to Billy. "Are you sure you don't mind, Billy? You know we could always get a motel or something."

"Wouldn't hear of it," Billy said. "Don't worry about me. I have friends to stay with."

They hardly slept that night. Once again, it was a revelatory experience for them both. At one point, Marcus, leaning on his elbow and looking down at her, said, "I didn't think anything could be better than last night. But this was."

And it was true. It was like they were climbing a mountain, going higher and higher, each moment together more rarified, providing them with greater vision of the plains below them.

"All my life I've been half a person," Kate told him. "With you, I'm whole again."

Marcus laughed at that. "That's funny," he said. "Billy said exactly the same thing about me today. He said ever since he'd known me, I'd been incomplete and that you made me complete."

They finally fell asleep shortly before dawn, their bodies entwined.

CHAPTER TWENTY-FOUR

Daniel Feinstein called Jason on a Tuesday. "I have good news. The painting is on its way from Buenos Aires."

"When will it arrive?" Jason asked.

"Tomorrow. I received a cable from Mr. Dressler confirming all the arrangements. It's being shipped. I'll have it here for your viewing the day after tomorrow. Will that be suitable?"

Jason glanced quickly at his calendar. "I'll make it suitable. There's nothing I can't change."

"Very good," Feinstein said. "Will there be some people from the Rex?"

"Yes, the director, Stodding Watson, will be with me, plus his head curator. Watson's also tentatively approached an expert from the Hague in Holland. I don't know if he'll be able to make it on such short notice. But I'll find out today."

"Very good. That's probably an excellent idea," Feinstein said.

"Shall we say your office at ten A.M., the day after tomorrow then?" Jason asked.

"I look forward to seeing you."

Jason immediately called Stodding. "Stod," he barked, "the painting's going to be here tomorrow. We get to view it the day after. Pack your bags."

"Excellent, excellent," Stodding said, reflecting back

Jason's infectious enthusiasm in his own voice. "I'll have Peter Moore, my head curator, come with us, of course."

"Good. Call the guy in Holland too. What's his name?"

"Van Nierden." Stodding added doubtfully, "I don't know whether he'll be able to come on such short notice."

"Offer him anything," Jason said. "I'll spring entirely for his bill. First-class air, best hotel in New York, and any fee he wishes."

"Perhaps he'll be able to make the time," Stodding said, with a trace of irony.

The next call was to David. He told him what had happened, and then said, "Will we have your portion of the funds available if we need them?"

"Yes, I don't see any difficulty with that," David replied.

"Good. I may need to act fast on this. We'll authenticate the painting, then make a counteroffer immediately. I assume that once it's accepted—as I'm sure it will be—the funds will need to be transferred very quickly."

"Well, just let me know when you need it," David said, adding, "that's very good news Jason."

"Yes, isn't it?" Jason said cheerfully. "I've been doing my own research on this painting. It's one of Rembrandt's masterpieces. A very, very fine piece of work. Well-thought-of. Shown in the best art museums in Germany during the war, too."

"Well, good, and congratulations."

"Thank you, thank you."

He called Allan, who did not sound quite as enthusiastic. "It's a million you said you needed. Right?" Allan asked.

"That's right, Allan, I've been counting on you for that."

"Yes, well that should be fine," Allan said, after a slight pause. "The way I've worked it, half will come from the studio and half will come from me. It'll be a corporate donation from the studio. I've cleared it with New York."

"However you want to work it, I don't care, as long as we get the million."

"Will you give me a few days' notice before you need it?"

"That's what I'm giving you now," Jason said. "I have a feeling we'll need it before the end of the week."

"Well, all right," Allan replied. "I'll set things in motion now."

Jason smiled grimly to himself when he hung up. He knew Allan well. It wasn't that he didn't have the money or couldn't get the money, it was just that he hated parting with it. That was all right. He could be as resentful as he liked, as long as he did it.

Jason's final call was to Page. "You can call off the PR," he told her.

"You have enough responses?"

"I think we have *the* response. The Rembrandt from South America is being flown into New York."

"Oh, that's wonderful, Jason!"

"Yes, I'm going there day after tomorrow with my battery of experts and we'll check it out, and if it's in good condition, et cetera, we'll be buying it."

"Well, if you buy that painting, you're not going to have to worry about media space," Page said. "It's going to be a major story."

"I know," Jason said, with much satisfaction.

Page called Kate. "Our friend has sent the package."

"What's the response?" Kate asked.

"Hook, line, and sinker. He'll be viewing it in two days."

Kate gripped the receiver tightly in her hand. "Anything else?"

"He's taking experts along with him, even flying in somebody from Holland."

"I see," Kate said. "Well, thank you. Let me know if you find out anything else."

After she hung up, she fought her fear of the experts, of the unknown entity from Holland. She had to have faith that Marcus had done his job well. If anybody could pull it off, it would be him. All they could do now was wait and see.

Allan arrived at the apartment he was renting for Shelly Pointer and threw himself into a chair. It had not been a good day. First had come Jason's request for a million dollars, and then the figures had come in on the studio's latest release. A twenty-two million dollar film that looked like it might, if they were lucky, make three. The board in New York was not impressed by figures like these. He knew there'd be trouble—questions, trips back and forth, veiled threats and maybe worse.

Shelly was sitting in a chair opposite him, doing her nails and babbling on about her day. "I tried out for *Thirtysomething* today. I think I might get the part. It's just a walk-on, but it's work."

Shelly was twenty-three, blonde, with long legs, slightly on the thin side, knock-out breasts, full lips, a voracious wide mouth, and a greedy glint in her eyes. She was hungry for success and totally unbashful about it.

Allan grunted. "Pour me a drink, will ya?" As he spoke he realized that he'd never had to ask Jasmine. Somehow she'd always anticipated his every need.

"Just hold on a minute, I'm doing my nails."

He got up, went to the cabinet, and poured himself a vodka, and then he went into the kitchen and slopped orange juice into it.

"There," Shelly said, admiring her nails. "They're perfect."

"God, what a day," Allan said, leaning his head back in the chair.

"Did you pour me a drink?"

"No," he said glumly.

"Don't worry, I'll get it." She went to the liquor cabinet to pour herself a Scotch.

She did have nice legs, Allan thought, watching her. And when she moved, her braless breasts bounced most appealingly. "Come here."

She came and sat on the arm of the chair, and ran one hand through his hair. "Allan needs cheering up."

"It's been a hell of a day."

"Well, you came to the right place."

He put a hand on her leg and kneaded her thigh. "Ummm," she said, "that feels good. Maybe you need more than cheering up."

"Whatever you got, I need."

"I got this." She leaned forward and kissed his neck. "And I got this." She took his hand and pushed it hard against a breast. She slipped off the chair and stood in front of him. "And I got this," she said, picking up the end of her skirt and pulling it up to her waist, showing tanned legs and pink panties.

Allan reach out and grabbed her ass and pulled it forward, until his face pressed against her panties. "That's what I want." He tried to bite his way through them, and she said something in a soft voice. "What?" he asked, moving his head back.

"I'm having my period," she said again.

Allan let his hands drop. "Oh shit! That's all I fucking need."

"That's all right. I can still make you happy. Come on." She took his hand, pulled him up, and led him into the bedroom.

She slipped her skirt off but kept her panties on. In a moment she had his clothes in a pile on the floor and told him to lie back on the bed.

"This'll be good," she promised.

She scooted down until she was kneeling between his legs, then she dropped her head forward, running her long hair across his chest and down his belly and over his cock. And then she wrapped it in the blonde hair, grasped it with her right hand, and pumped him.

Allan began to groan. She stopped and moved her hair away, taking his penis in her mouth and tonguing it fiercely. And then when he groaned again, she stopped again.

"I know what you like," she murmured, and pushed

her thirty-eight-inch breasts together with his penis in between and kneaded it through them. Suddenly she let go and rolled over to lie on her back. "Come on," she said, tugging at him.

He straddled her, his penis sticking out like a tower. She pulled it between her breasts and then again pushed them together. "Come on, baby, fuck my tits."

And he did, while she moaned with apparent delight until finally he came, leaving a pool of semen on her chest. He rolled away and lay beside her, his penis already shrinking. Somehow it had not been as satisfying as he had wished.

He lay there for a minute and felt her hand on his chest. She leaned over and nibbled at his ear. "Was that good?"

"Yeah, it was fine."

Another moment of silence, and then a tentative, "Allan?"

"Yes."

"You know, I really need a new car. This thing I'm driving now is just dying on me, and it's really not right for my image. I mean a Volkswagen . . . please! I need something snazzier, something more sophisticated. Can you help me out?"

"Oh, Jesus," Allan groaned.

Everybody wanted something from him, and for some reason, he felt he had nothing to give.

Jason used his corporate Lear jet to transport them to New York on Thursday. With Stodding was Peter Moore, his head curator, a man in his early thirties, with long hair, glasses, and an intense academic manner. Jason couldn't stand him. Moore tended to be pendantic about his art. Every question resulted in a lecture. He spent an hour of the trip talking about Rembrandt.

"He died a pauper," Moore said with some satisfaction. "Lost his house, essentially everything he owned. It was his own fault. He spent money as if it came from a bottomless well. There was a time when he had it all, and he just totally blew it."

Moore then backtracked to how Rembrandt, a youth from the provinces, had become a student at the University at Leiden.

Jason, who had read all of this before, drank two Scotches and then fell asleep for the rest of the journey.

By the time they made it into Manhattan from the airport, it was evening. They checked into their hotel and Jason immediately called Feinstein at home.

"Daniel, has it come?" he asked, not bothering with customary greetings.

"Yes, I have it."

"And what do you think?"

"I think it's wonderful," Feinstein said, "but I should leave that judgment up to your experts."

"Will it be ready for us to see tomorrow?"

"Yes, just come to the gallery."

"I'll see you at ten," Jason replied.

He rose at seven and made a number of business calls to managers of some of his holdings in Florida, North Carolina, and Louisiana. At eight, he went downstairs and had eggs Benedict for breakfast. About halfway through he was joined by Stodding and Moore.

"Have you spoken to our friend from Holland?" Jason asked.

"Yes, I just called him," Stodding said. "He arrived last night and I gave him the address of the gallery and he'll meet us there at ten."

"Very good," Jason said, then he buried himself in *The Wall Street Journal.*

At 9:45 they took a cab to the gallery on East Seventieth Street. Daniel Feinstein met them at the door and ushered them through it with handshakes.

A small, slightly bowed man with white hair, in his mid-sixties, Feinstein had a reputation as an expert on eighteenth and nineteenth century European and American art. The gallery reflected it, with paintings and sculptures of the period.

"Well, Daniel," Stodding said as they walked through

the softly carpeted gallery, "I assume you've seen the painting?"

"Yes, yes, I have," Feinstein said excitedly.

"And what do you think?"

"I think it's a magnificent work—beautiful."

"We're expecting someone else," Jason interjected.

"Oh, yes, Professor Van Nierden. He's here already," Feinstein said. "He arrived just a few minutes ago."

The painting was in a large back room, sitting on an easel, draped with a cloth. A tall, thin man with pointed beard and thick horn-rimmed glasses was standing six feet from it, looking as if he could barely restrain himself from leaping across the intervening space. This was Van Nierden. Stodding, who had met him before, made the introductions. Van Nierden spoke excellent English with a thick Dutch accent.

Feinstein rubbed his hands together. "Well, gentlemen, shall we?"

It was a rhetorical question. They all watched silently as he stepped up to the easel and withdrew the covering cloth.

The face of Christ stared back at them. It was a half figure. He held a staff, his hands crossed around it. He was bearded, with a thin moustache. His hair, parted in the middle, fell across his shoulders and down his chest. A hood of some kind partially covered his head.

They all moved slightly forward.

Van Nierden was the first to break the silence. "My God, it is magnificent."

Peter Moore leaned forward from the waist and peered at it. "Excellent condition for its age," he concluded.

"Remarkable," Stodding said.

The three experts then began an excited chattering among themselves, ignoring Jason and Feinstein.

" . . . marvelous contrast. A trademark of Rembrandt's."

" . . . the master draftsman."

" . . . they say the model was a young Jew."

" . . . yes, he was one of the first artists to derive his

Christ face by studying the faces of Jews. Before that they generally had classic Greek or Roman faces."

". . . look at the simplicity of the brush strokes."

". . . you see the influence of Caravaggio with his use of light and shadow."

". . . he has created boundless space."

". . . look at the varying textures."

. . . and so on.

"Well, gentlemen," Jason cut in impatiently. "What do you think?"

"He did at least eleven Christ paintings around this era," Van Nierden said. "This is certainly one of the finest."

"Yes, but is it genuine?" Jason asked.

Van Nierden shrugged, "We must do tests. We must take the painting out of the frame. We must take a microscopic sample of paint from the edge of the support system and submit it to chromotography." He looked at Feinstein, "You have ultraviolet light here?"

Feinstein nodded.

"We must put it under the light."

Stodding chimed in, "I've spoken to the conservation department of the Metropolitan and we can take the painting over there for x-rays as well."

"Excellent, excellent," Van Nierden said. "Our first step will be to look at it under magnifying glasses."

"How long will all this take?" Jason asked.

"About two hours, here," Van Nierden said. "And then we shall take it to the Metropolitan."

"And there?"

"Another couple of hours, Jason," Stodding said. "Listen, why don't you leave us to it? And by early afternoon we should have the verdict."

"Yes, that's probably a good idea. You are all too much like mother hens, clucking around an egg, for my stomach. Shall we meet back here at two-thirty?"

"That sounds fine," Stodding said. He looked at Van Nierden, who nodded absently, his eyes fixed once again on the painting.

"Yes, yes, two-thirty."

"Very good," Jason said. "I shall see you gentlemen then." Feinstein walked Jason out. "What do you think, Daniel?" Jason asked. "Is it worth seven million dollars?"

"He's asking ten," Feinstein said. "It's probably worth that."

"I'll want to offer him seven. No higher."

"Well, let's authenticate the painting first, and then we'll take care of the money."

"Excellent." Jason turned in the doorway and shook Feinstein's hand. "I'm very grateful. You've done a fine job turning this one up."

Feinstein grinned shyly. "It just walked through the door. I didn't have much to do with it."

"Nevertheless, I'm grateful," Jason said. "I'll see you later this afternoon."

He hailed a passing cab and asked the driver to take him back to his hotel. Looking at his watch, he saw that morning would soon be starting on the West Coast. He'd be able to make business calls and take care of some outstanding matters. He could easily keep himself occupied for the next four hours.

And yet, as the cab bounced over the bumpy Manhattan streets, he couldn't help but feel anxious. This was the painting he'd been looking for. He knew it in his gut. He could only hope that his experts found nothing "wrong" with it. He was tired of waiting. It was time to unveil his building—and his paintings. From concept to completion, this entire project had taken more than three years. Finally, the end was in sight and the rewards that would go with it.

Promptly at two-thirty, Jason arrived back at the gallery. He entered the front door and saw Feinstein talking to a customer.

The gallery owner excused himself and hurried over to Jason. "They're not back yet," he said.

"What could be keeping them?" Jason asked.

"These things take time. They should be here soon."

"How was the examination they did here?"

"They seemed to have no misgivings that this is a genuine Rembrandt. But let's see what the x-radiography shows up at the Met. They'll probably also do a microscopic analysis of the pigment structure and perhaps a chemical analysis of the pigments. It takes some time. Why don't you just look around the gallery, or if you wish you can sit in my office, and they should show up soon."

"I'll just look at some of your paintings here," Jason said.

He walked through the gallery, his hands behind his back, hardly seeing the paintings he was pretending to look at, his mind already rushing ahead to the unveiling of Rembrandt's "Christ" before everyone and anyone who mattered in Los Angeles on opening night of the Thomas Wing. There would be applause. He would be modest and unassuming. There would be congratulations that he would brush off or simply acknowledge, and there would be envy that he alone, of all the moneyed and powerful people in Los Angeles, had the vision to create this wing and to find this magnificent work of art.

The doors opened and he turned quickly to see Stodding, Moore, and Van Nierden enter. Their faces gave nothing away as they approached him. But then Stodding broke into a grin as he got closer and held out his hand.

"Congratulations," he said, shaking Jason's hand. "Looks like we have a genuine Rembrandt to buy."

"Everything checked out?"

"Yes. The chromotography, the spectroscopy, the x-rays, everything checked out. The x-rays showed that there is an underpainting."

"Is that unusual?" Jason asked quickly.

"No, not at all. It's a similar figure of Christ but a slightly different position. Apparently he painted that and then changed his mind. The age of the canvas, everything checks out. Oh, and there's also been about three inches cut off the bottom," he added.

"Really?" Jason asked, concern on his face.

"Yes, it's documented as happening sometime in the

thirties, I believe, when the painting was reframed. Back then the bottom was found to be damaged and they sliced that off. That's not unusual with old masters. They constantly trimmed through the centuries."

"I see," Jason said. "Daniel, our offer's going to be seven million. Payable in cash anywhere in the world, immediately. Will you take care of that?"

"Yes, of course. I'll get a cable off right now," Feinstein said.

"Excellent. I'm going to be flying back to Los Angeles in a couple of hours. You can call me there and let me know the outcome, and we'll make the financial arrangements over the telephone."

"Very good," Feinstein said.

"This is going to be a wonderful acquisition," Stodding said enthusiastically. "The finest Rembrandt in Southern California will be at the Rex," he looked at Jason's face and added, "—in the Thomas Wing."

Jason smiled greedily. He couldn't help it. He was feeling as smug as he'd ever felt in his life.

Before he left New York, Jason called Page with the news. He sounded more excited than she'd ever heard him.

"Congratulations," she said. "When will you have the painting here?"

"As soon as the financial arrangements are concluded," he replied. "It should take just a couple of days. It's marvelous, Page. Wait till you see it. It's going to bring great prestige to the Rex."

"Well, I'm looking forward to it. When will you be back?"

"We'll probably get in around six or seven, LA time." I guess I won't see you tonight but maybe tomorrow."

"All right," she said.

As soon as he hung up, she called Kate at the gallery. "Kate, Jason just called from New York. He's going to buy the painting." There was a silence at the other end. "Kate? Kate? Are you all right?" Page asked.

Finally a faint voice came back, "I'm so relieved. My God, I'm so relieved."

Kate stood alone in the office at Friars Gallery, staring dully at the telephone in her hand. She had almost fainted at Page's words. The rushing influx and intensity of feelings had almost been too much to bear. The walls had started to disappear into red dots, and a clamminess had covered her face.

She took a deep breath. We've done it, we've done it, she said to herself, and then she actually started to feel the sense of triumph and elation. "My God, we've done it!" she said aloud this time.

Marcus must have done a magnificent job. Thomas and his battery of experts had fallen for it.

There was still the final act to be played. The one that would end in Thomas's humiliation. The one in which justice would finally triumph.

Feinstein called Jason at home on Saturday. "Dressler has accepted your offer of seven million dollars."

"Excellent, excellent," Jason said. "Very well done."

"Thank you. He wants the money deposited in a numbered account at Credit Suisse in Zurich."

"No problem," Jason said. "Give me the information and I'll have my people do it immediately." He wrote down all the particulars and then thanked Feinstein again.

He had taken the precaution the day before of having both David and Allan transfer their funds to him. Naturally, Allan had complained loudly about parting with so much money. But he had come through as Jason had known he would. The funds were being held in an escrow account at his bank. It would now be a simple matter to transfer them to the Swiss bank.

The painting was his.

On Monday, David called Kate. "I've been invited to the Rex this evening by Jason. He's going to give us a sneak preview of the new Rembrandt, if you're interested in seeing it.''

''Oh, that would be wonderful,'' Kate said. ''What time?''

''We were going to meet there at seven-thirty and then go out to dinner. He's inviting Allan as well. As you know, the two of us have been the most supportive of the new wing and, of course, helped pay a significant amount for the Rembrandt.''

''Okay, do you want to pick me up?''

''Yes, I'll pick you up at your place around seven.''

''Perfect,'' Kate replied. ''I'll see you then.''

She had to hurry to the airport. Jasmine had sent an unsigned cable to Elsa, telling her what time she was flying in. Her last job had been to send the cable with the Swiss bank account number to Feinstein, and then pay the lawyer his remaining fee. She had stayed another couple of days and was now flying back. Kate had volunteered to pick her up.

She waited at the Tom Bradley International Terminal for forty-five minutes after the flight landed, while passengers cleared customs and immigration. Around her were Indian women in saris, Arabs in flowing robes, Sikhs with long beards, Chinese, Japanese, South Americans, people from around the world talking in thirty or forty different tongues.

And then she saw Jasmine come through the door, and Kate ran over to her.

''How did it go?'' was Jasmine's first question. There had been no communication to her from them. All she knew was that Jason had offered seven million dollars, which she then sent a cable back accepting.

''Perfectly,'' Kate said. ''They examined every inch of that painting. Marcus must have done a wonderful job.''

They walked through the bustling terminal, Kate carrying Jasmine's suitcase.

''I like Marcus a lot,'' Jasmine said. ''God, what a score you made! Such a sexy guy.''

''He liked you too.''

"Were you surprised to see him?" Jasmine asked.

"It was a shock."

"Yeah, he told me in Madrid that he was heading over here for a couple of days. I assumed you guys got together."

"Yes," Kate said, thinking back to the short time they had had. It had been idyllic, wonderful. A glimpse of the future they would have together perhaps. "How are you feeling?" she asked, looking Jasmine over.

"I feel fine, but a little tired." Kate saw there were dark rings under her eyes.

"Well, all you need to do now is relax. You did a really good job. We all appreciate it."

"Did the money make it to Switzerland?" Jasmine asked.

"Yes, Billy called this morning and said that he'd received a call from Marcus, saying the deal was done."

"Are we all rich?"

"Well, let's say we're all very well-off," Kate replied.

"All right!" Jasmine said.

"All right," Kate agreed. Laughing, they left the terminal and walked across the parking lot.

Jason led them through the new wing. The carpets were down, the walls were painted, and the art was already hung.

"This is the room with my Jack Patney paintings," he said with a casual wave of the hand as they passed it.

Page was there and so was Allan, although his new woman, Shelly Pointer, wasn't with him. David, walking beside Kate, asked him where she was.

"Are you kidding?" Allan said. "The girl doesn't know art from paint-by-numbers. She's great in the bedroom, but there are just some places I can't take her."

Kate and Page exchanged a sly surreptitious glance. Allan was beginning to find out what he'd lost by dumping Jasmine.

They came to the room that presently housed the Rembrandt. Jason stopped dramatically outside the door and turned to face them all. "This is the first time you've seen the wing, isn't it?" he said to Page and Kate.

"Yes," Page said.

"What do you think? Are you impressed?"

"Very," Page said.

"It's quite unique," Kate replied.

"Cost thirty-seven million dollars," Jason said. "And I couldn't have done it without their help." He pointed to Allan and David. "The fundraising they helped with, the contacts they provided, and the support that they've given me has resulted in this magnificent building."

"Bravo," Kate said.

"But," Jason continued, "they've also helped me with what you are about to see. They've each contributed a million dollars toward this seven million dollar painting. This masterpiece by one of the greatest masters of all time."

He stepped into the room and walked over to a painting that was hidden behind a screen on wheels. "This is Rembrandt's 'Christ.' " He pulled the screen aside to reveal the painting.

Christ, staff in hand, stared back at them with gentle, compassionate eyes.

"It's fabulous," Page said, sincerely.

"What a work," Kate said, mentally tipping her hat off to Marcus.

"It's beautiful," David said.

"It's smaller than I thought," Allan said. "That probably works out to about three hundred thousand dollars a square inch."

Jason laughed. "It's priceless. It was a steal at seven million. Do you know a Van Gogh went for fifty million last year in New York? This painting will be worth that much one day."

"Will you keep this covered until the opening next week?" Kate asked.

"Yes, but there will be a velvet curtain, not this screen. And it won't be in here, of course. The painting will be on the far wall of the main hall. They'll be unveiling it at the opening,'' he said. ''It should create quite a commotion. We haven't let any of the media know exactly what painting we found yet.''

''Well, that's one way of making sure they all show up,'' Page said with a smile.

''I've been getting calls from newspapers and magazines from all over the country,'' Jason said. ''So has Stodding. Wanting to know if we found the painting that we were looking for. All we've said is yes, it will be unveiled at the opening. These guys are salivating.''

''Well, it should be a grand night,'' Page said.

''Yes,'' Jason said pompously, ''it'll be the pinnacle of all my efforts.''

''I'm sure it will,'' Kate said. ''I'm sure it will.''

CHAPTER TWENTY-FIVE

It was a black-tie night the likes of which the Los Angeles art community hadn't seen since the opening of the museum of Contemporary Art in 1986. The men wore tuxedos, the women gowns. Bob Mackie, Carolina Herrera, Bruno Magli, Ralph Lauren, Margaretha Ley, Issey Miyake, Ungaro, Sonia Rykiel, Guy Laroche, and a dozen more of the world's top designers were represented by the bejeweled women at the event.

A thousand people cruised in and out of the various rooms, examining the building and the new acquisitions.

In the main hall, champagne and wine flowed while guests milled around the huge buffet created by notable

Los Angeles chefs. There was sautéed prawns, truffled pasta, oysters in their shells, and caviar. It was an international feast, with carpaccio, the Italian raw beef, trays of sushi and tempura, spicy Szechuan pork strips, Belgian endive, tiny pieces of Chinese grilled duck, hot Indian masala, Sumatran grilled chicken called Ayampanggang, and Mexican charro beans. A spread to satisfy the most jaded palate.

Among the crowd was Mayor Tom Bradley and his wife Ethyl, a sprinkling of senators and congressmen, Hollywood super-agents and, of course, stars. Andora Dover was there, as were dozens of other famous Hollywood names. Less glamorous, but no less wealthy, were Beverly Hills plastic surgeons and dermatologists, who had become rich and famous by catering to the rich and famous, bankers, real estate millionaires, old Pasadena families, new multilevel marketing magnates. And there were even people there who knew something about art. Many of the guests were donors, their names inscribed on a brass plate on the front of the building.

The media was well represented, with television crews from *Eye on L.A.*, *Two on the Town*, *Life Styles of the Rich and Famous,* and all the news channels. Reporters from *The Los Angeles Times*, *The Herald Examiner*, *The Valley News*, *Los Angeles Magazine,* and a dozen other newspapers and magazines milled through the crowd.

The conversations, Kate thought as she wandered through the crowd alone, were either enthralling or trivial, depending on your point of view. Those in the film business talked about film, politicians talked politics, the businessmen talked business, art collectors talked art. Opinions about the new building and the art it housed appeared to be divided. She passed one woman who whispered to her husband, "This wing is so cold. I always thought that art should be shown in a more humanitarian atmosphere." While another woman said, "The space in here is magnificent. It detracts nothing from the art, it adds to it."

The room showing Jack Patney's paintings seemed to have its share of admirers and detractors. "Why show so many paintings by such a trivial artist?'' she heard one man mutter. While from others she heard appreciative oohs and aahs.

But the conversation on everyone's lips at one point or another concerned the mystery painting. Everyone wondered what it was, the consensus being that if it was anything less than absolutely splendid, it would be perceived as a total flop.

Page walked by and winked at Kate without stopping. Kate wished that Jasmine and Elsa could have been here. They deserved to be, but of course they hadn't been invited.

David, Allan, and Jason all had their wives with them. However, Kate and Page both had legitimate reasons for being there, the former as an employee of a major gallery in Los Angeles and the latter as a public relations practitioner.

If Sharon Thomas saw them, she gave no hint. Apparently she was on leave from the Betty Ford Center for the event. Kate had to admit that she looked one hundred percent better, poised and gracious and comfortable in her surroundings.

Madge came up to Kate. ''What do you think?''

''I think it's very nice,'' Kate said noncommittally.

''It's not a friendly building, is it?''

''No, but it's impressive, and I suppose that's what was intended.''

Stodding Watson, who had known Madge for years, came over to say hello. ''Well,'' Madge asked, ''do you think your new wing is a public success?''

''They seem to like it,'' Stodding said. ''Either that, or the food. It's only the first step, of course. What's more to the point is whether the donors will continue to be involved in the less glamorous job of funding programs and operations and further acquisitions once the buildings are open. We've got fifty thousand square feet of exhibition space to look after here.''

''That's where your genius will come in, Stodding,'' Madge said.

"It's always a problem," he replied. "Well, excuse me. Gotta go work the room."

"Ah, the chains of responsibility weigh heavy on Mr. Watson," Madge said as he walked away.

Jason was apparently having the evening of his life. He held court near the door of the Patney room, surrounded by a group of admirers. Tall, lean, even more handsome than normal in his well-cut tuxedo, he seemed to reflect just the right amount of pride and modesty.

Curious, Kate moved over to the group. She wanted to hear what he was saying.

"I've always felt that those of us who have been fortunate enough to gain much have an obligation to return some of it to the communities in which we live," he said, directing his remarks mainly at film agent Van Jackman and his wife, Debbie.

"Well, you've certainly made those ideals a reality," Jackman said admiringly.

Jason brushed the compliment away with a wave of his hand. "I've just taken the first small step," he said, somehow making it sound like a step for mankind. "The continuing viability of this building will depend upon the contributions of others."

Kate moved on. The man's hypocrisy sickened her.

David, who was standing with his wife among a small group of people, looked over at her, his glance heavy with meaning. Earlier that day he had telephoned to say he was sorry he couldn't attend the event with her. He had ended the conversation with the real purpose of the call, by saying, "By the way, if you see me, let's just pretend we've never met before. All right?"

"Fine," she said.

Well, soon that would be over, thank God. She'd be able to stop pretending. He had grown increasingly more possessive and insecure, a combination doubly irritating in a grown man. She had tried to see him as little as possible without being too obvious about it, citing the pressures of work as an excuse. He had reacted, of course, by being even more demanding. There were times when it had taken all her self-discipline not to blurt out to him that he was an idiot. It had not been an easy period.

Her thoughts turned to Marcus: gentle, strong, sweet, loving, talented, handsome. Marcus. She missed him so much that at times it was like a physical pain. It was as if something had been torn from her body. These were the costs involved in doing what she was doing, she told herself again. There was no point in feeling sorry for herself.

The moment was approaching for the unveiling of the painting. Kate figured that the crowd wouldn't wait much longer, even for a mystery.

Then she saw Stodding head down toward the end of the long hall where the veiled painting stood. A moment later Jason followed.

The painting was no longer hidden by a screen. A curtain protruded from the wall to mask it. A microphone had been set up in front of it, and Stodding now walked toward it.

He tapped it with his finger, coughed, and said, "Ladies and gentlemen, ladies and gentlemen, please may I have your attention?"

Heads swiveled, and the crowd began to move toward that end of the hall, anticipation in their faces and voices. Stodding stood at the microphone and beckoned people forward. A few feet to his right, Jason stood with David and Allan.

"Thank you," Stodding said. "Thank you." And he began his speech, welcoming them and thanking them for their support.

He held up his hand during the thunderous applause and said, "Many of you know Jason Thomas. We owe much to him. The existence of this magnificent new wing today is largely due to his generosity and unstinting efforts. I am sure many of you wished you had never heard of him as he twisted your arms for money. But Jason Thomas is a committed man. A man who gets things done, and once he announces a goal, he accomplishes it—to my eternal gratitude. In addition to all the work that he has done to create this wing, and his donation of many fine pieces from his personal art collection, which you have seen here tonight, Mr. Thomas has also donated a work of art so magnificent that it alone could occupy this wing. A work that reestablishes the Rex as a major force in the international art world."

He gestured toward Jason, "Together with his friends and associates, Mr. Allan Silver and Mr. David Ross, Mr. Thomas raised the sum of seven million dollars to purchase this invaluable work for the Jason Thomas Wing. And now it is only fair and right that Jason Thomas unveil this painting."

Again the applause. Jason stepped forward, stood in front of the microphone, and allowed himself a small smile at the audience. "Thank you, Stodding. Although my efforts to create this new wing have not been trivial, I think everybody here agrees that without the guiding hand of Stodding Watson, the Rex would not be what it is today."

He waited for the applause to die down. "This"—he gestured at the veiled painting behind him—"work of art is here tonight because of a long and arduous search. Many beautiful, valuable, and historically relevant paintings were seen in this search. But none were chosen. Until this was uncovered. I wanted something special for the Rex. I wanted something unique for the thriving metropolis of Los Angeles, and without tantalizing you further, I shall share it with you."

He stepped back and yanked the velvet cord beside the painting. The curtain drew slowly open. "Ladies and gentlemen, I would like to present to you Rembrandt's "Christ!"

Applause echoed through the hall. People jostled forward to try to see the painting. At that moment, museum attendants handed out small one-page brochures containing a picture of the painting, a description of it, and its historical relevance.

Jason stood there, a smile on his face. This was his moment. The moment he had worked hard and long for. It was happening exactly as he had anticipated it. He knew that it was not only the painting they were applauding, but him.

Stodding, his face flushed with excitement, stepped back to the microphone. He gestured at Jason and said, "Ladies and gentlemen, Mr. Jason Thomas." And again the applause broke out. Stodding stepped back, shaking Jason's hand. Both were grinning with pride and accomplishment.

Jason graciously then pointed to Allan and David and said, "Ladies and gentlemen, without these gentlemen this would not have been possible. Mr. Allan Silver and Mr. David Ross."

The two men took small bows as the crowd applauded.

"Ladies and gentlemen, this is a small painting and there are a lot of you here," Stodding said. "May I suggest that to see it you line up and move around in a circle in front of it. I'm afraid you will not be able to spend too much time looking at it, because of the numbers here. But, rest assured, it will be here for a long, long time. Thank you very much for attending."

The four men stepped to one side. Allan slapped Jason and David on the shoulder and shook Stodding's hand.

"Well, gentlemen," Jason said, "I think we did it."

"They love it," Allan said. "They love it."

Just then a uniformed messenger pushed his way through the crowd, a small package in his hands. He walked up to Stodding and said, "A delivery for you, sir."

Stodding looked at him irritably. "What do you mean, a delivery? Now? Are you nuts? Why couldn't this wait until business hours? What's this all about?"

"Our instructions were to deliver it to you when the painting was unveiled," the messenger said. He had a bushy moustache and wore thick glasses that distorted his eyes.

"Really?" Stodding asked, puzzled. He reached out and took it from the man. "What is this?"

"I have no idea, sir."

The package was a little over two feet long and four inches wide, and was flat, as if it held nothing more substantial than a sheet of paper. Stodding looked at it curiously, apparently unwilling to do more.

"So, open it, Stod," Jason said cheerfully.

He tore away the paper, revealing a long strip of canvas about three inches wide, lying on a sheet of cardboard backing.

"What?" Stodding began to say, and then he saw the note of black ink on plain white paper: "The bottom of your painting." It was signed "Otto Dressler."

"My God," Jason said, his voice still cheerful. "It's the three inches that were cut off the bottom of the painting!"

Stodding shook his head. "How can that be? That was done years ago. How could he ha—"

"Well, maybe he just had it," Jason said. "Maybe it went along with the painting all this time."

Stodding let the paper drop to the floor. He turned, holding the cardboard and canvas, and placed it below the painting on the wall.

His face turned ashen. "Oh my God!"

The crowd began to realize something was happening and stared curiously at the tableau.

"What is it?" Jason asked. "What's wrong?"

"The staff," Stodding said, "look at the staff."

It obviously was the bottom of the painting on the wall. It showed a continuation of Christ's figure and matched exactly—except for one detail. The staff that Christ was holding in the painting did not continue in an unbroken line as it should have on the bottom portion, which had supposedly been cut off. Instead it continued six inches over to the left.

"What?" Jason said. "What does this mean? What is this?"

Stodding turned to face him. He looked as if he'd aged in seconds. "Jason, I think that what this means is that we've been taken for seven million dollars. I think it means that this painting is a fake."

There was no way to hide what had happened. Everyone had seen it. Not only had everyone seen it, but it had been recorded on videotape by television crews. As soon as the uproar died down and the museum was cleared a half hour later, Stodding, some of his staff, Jason, David, and Allan took Rembrandt's ''Christ'' down from the wall and unframed it.

There was no doubt that the piece brought by the messenger, who had since disappeared, had come from the painting on the wall. The way the canvas had been cut matched exactly. There was also no doubt now that they were all looking at a magnificent forgery.

At first Jason was shocked into silence. Now he was furious. ''This is going to make us the laughing stock of the art world. How am I ever going to live this down?''

''How's the museum ever going to live this down?'' Stodding spluttered.

''Fuck the museum,'' Jason said unkindly. ''I'm the one that's out seven million dollars. I'm the one that got taken. Someone's going to pay for this, I swear to God someone's going to pay!''

''Five million dollars,'' David corrected him, his own anger showing. ''Keep in mind that Allan and I are out a million each.''

''I want the police informed of this immediately,'' Jason demanded. ''If they act quickly enough, maybe we'll at least get our money back on this deal.''

''From a Swiss bank?'' David asked derisively. ''That money probably didn't even lie in that account long enough to get warm. We'd better face up to it. It's gone.''

''We still have to inform the police,'' Stodding interjected. ''They may be able to find out who was responsible. I'll call the LAPD first thing in the morning. I know the person down there who deals with forgeries and stolen paintings. Good man.''

''Jesus Christ,'' Jason said, disgust covering his features. ''I can't believe this is happening.'' He looked at the assembled men. ''Did anyone see that messenger? What happened to him? What company was he from?''

Everyone shook their heads. ''He disappeared into the crowd,'' Stodding said dejectedly.

Jason went to a nearby chair and sat heavily in it. He buried his face in his hands. "God, I don't believe this is happening. How could this have happened? The experts—we had experts," he said, looking up at Stodding. "What the fuck did we pay that asshole from Holland for?"

"The experts can be wrong," Stodding said miserably. "It's happened before and it'll happen again."

"Well," David said, "there's nothing more we can do about it tonight. Not until we report this to the police tomorrow."

"Report this to the police tomorrow," Jason said, a short, bitter laugh coming from his mouth. "By tomorrow morning every policeman in the country will know what happened. It's going to be on every television station in the world." He laughed again, then put his face back in his hands.

"Come on, Jason, it's time to pack it in," David said, putting his hand on his shoulder.

"Leave me alone!" Jason's head shot up, his face contorted. "Just leave me alone!"

David shrugged and looked at Allan, who raised his eyebrows. They had never seen Jason fall to pieces before.

Slowly the group dissolved, leaving Jason alone, slumped in a chair, his thoughts turned inward in fierce destructive circles.

Back in his small Venice house, Billy took off the moustache and dropped it in the wastepaper basket. Then he wiped the coloring from his face and removed the messenger uniform. Tomorrow he would burn it all, leaving no trace.

Kate waited in a darkened corner of the parking lot behind the Rex. She sat in her little Toyota, the radio low, wondering if perhaps she might have missed Jason. It seemed that everyone else had left. But she could still see his Rolls Royce Silver Cloud. He had to be around somewhere.

Finally, after about a half hour, she saw the back door

of the museum open and a figure walk slowly down the path toward the lot. It was Jason, his hands behind his back, his head bowed in thought.

She turned on the engine and drove forward slowly. He didn't even raise his head until she stopped directly in front of him on the roadway. She lowered her window with the flick of a switch. "Jason."

His eyes were clouded in thought and he looked directly at her without recognizing her. He blinked a few times and then said, "Oh, it's you, Kate." He shook his head, as if to clear it, and said, "What a night." Then he looked at her more sharply. "What are you still doing here?"

Kate put her arms on the window and leaned forward until her head was partially out, her chin resting on her hands. "I wanted to tell you something."

"Yes?"

"Do you remember Joel Buck?"

"Who?" he asked, genuinely puzzled. Apparently the name didn't mean a thing to him at the moment.

"Do you remember Angie Cox?" she asked, her voice harder.

"Angie? Angie Cox? Yes."

"Now do you remember Joel Buck? The young man she fell in love with? The one that your persuaders murdered."

Jason had been distracted, but now he grew still and watchful, his eyes suddenly alert as he stared back at her without speaking.

"Joel Buck was a stage name," Kate said. "Actually it was simply an alteration of his last name. Could it have been Buchanan, perhaps?"

Still there was only silence from Jason.

"Joel Buck was my brother, Jason." She locked her eyes on his, not blinking, not backing away, unflinching.

Jason was the first to break the silence. "I fail to see why you are telling me this," he said, his voice even. "Right now I have more important things on my mind than some accident in the past."

"To you it might have been an accident. To me, well,

I lost the only surviving member of my family, a young man I loved very dearly. A young man whose hopeful future was cut off callously by a rich man who didn't like being crossed. I swore I would bring about some kind of justice."

"I regret your loss, but it has nothing to do with me."

"I'm not going to waste time debating that point," Kate snapped. "I know your responsibility in the matter. That's not why I'm here."

"So? Why are you here? And why have you chosen this moment to tell me who you are?"

"Because I want you to know that no matter how rich and powerful you are, no matter now encompassing your arrogance, you can't escape justice. Tonight, seeing your face at the moment you knew that that painting was a fake, was one of the sweetest moments of my life."

She watched the understanding dawn ever so slowly on his face. She watched his skin flush and his mouth open soundlessly as he realized what she had done to him.

"Yes," she said with a smile, "revenge *is* sweet."

The first sounds that came from his mouth made no sense. He spluttered, and then broke into a cough. Finally, wiping his mouth with the back of his hand, he said, "I . . . you . . . I'll . . . see . . . you'll pay for this. I'll have you arrested and thrown in jail. I'll ruin you. I'll make life so miserable for you, you'll wish you died with your brother."

Kate smiled again. "I don't know what you're talking about. And believe me, you'll have great difficulty proving otherwise."

"We'll see about that," he blustered. "We'll see."

"Good evening, Mr. Thomas." She rolled the window up, waved her hand at him, and drove away. In her rearview mirror she saw him looking after her, rooted to the spot.

It was time to go to Elsa's. There would be a party in progress. Page and Jasmine would be there. Together they would celebrate their victory.

CHAPTER TWENTY-SIX

On Monday morning at ten A.M., Detective Frank Morris of the Los Angeles Police Department arrived at the gallery to see Kate. He investigated fraud and burglary, he said.

Madge had not yet arrived, so Kate showed him into the office and asked if he'd like a cup of coffee. "No, thank you," he said, taking a seat.

He was a stocky man in his early fifties, with thinning gray hair receding at the temples and a bland unexpressive face. In spite of his unprepossessing appearance, his eyes were alert and Kate decided he wasn't a man to be taken lightly.

"What can I do for you?" she asked, sitting in Madge's chair opposite him.

"I hope you don't mind," he said, rubbing a hand over his chin, "but I have to ask you some questions about the forged Rembrandt which was sold to the Rex Museum."

"Oh, yes, how embarrassing that was for them," Kate said. "But what kind of questions could you ask me?"

"I'll get directly to the point, ma'am. Mr. Thomas seems to feel that you had something to do with it. He recounted a conversation he had with you after the event in which he said that you admitted involvement."

"Me? I have no idea what you're talking about. I didn't talk to Mr. Thomas after the event. When it was over, I left and went to visit friends."

"Would your friends be able to substantiate this?"

"Yes, of course." She gave him Elsa's name and phone number.

"Well, why would Mr. Thomas say something like this?" he asked, frowning.

"I have no idea. Of course, he must be under a lot of stress." Apparently, Jason had carefully edited their conversation, because so far there had been no mention of the fact that she was Joel's sister, or of his death. She decided not to be the one to bring it up.

Detective Morris scratched at his moustache. "I understand your area of expertise is authentication and acquisition."

"Yes, I worked in that area in New York."

"Well, as someone who knows about authentication, you'd also know a great deal about forgeries?"

"Sure, in my particular area, which is mainly the Impressionists. But that Rembrandt . . . I saw it twice and I had no idea it was a fake. Whoever did it, did an incredible job."

"Have you been out of the country lately, ma'am?"

"Yes, I took a short trip to Spain for about a week a few months ago. Why?"

"And what did you do there, ma'am?"

"Just lay in the sun," she said with a smile. "I needed a break from work."

"Did you see anybody special there?"

"No, there were just tourists. You know, people you meet on the beach, stuff like that."

"I see." He scratched his head. "Well, ma'am, if there is anything you could tell us that would help in our investigation, I surely would appreciate it."

"Well, of course I would, if there was anything," she said. "But I've nothing to contribute to this."

"I understand," he said, taking a card from his wallet. "Here's my card in case anything comes up."

"Thank you," she said, taking it from him.

She showed him out and returned to the office. He would call Elsa and find out that she and Jasmine had been there, after the opening. They thought it best not to mention

Page's presence. As for any other investigation on his part, he would find nothing. Yes, she had gone to Spain. And yes, she had stayed on the island for a few days. Yes, she had been trained in how to authenticate paintings. That was all he'd discover. Even if, through some miracle, he found out that she knew Marcus, it wouldn't lead to anything. Marcus had never been arrested or convicted. His forgery history was not known to the law. There was nothing to connect her with what had happened.

Two days later, Detective Morris met Jason in his office. Jason, leaning back behind his big desk, was blunt, "Well, what have you discovered, Detective?"

"A very sophisticated job, Mr. Thomas."

"I know that," Jason scowled. "But what have you found out?"

The policeman sighed. "A lawyer in Argentina who says he was acting for a German named Dressler. Dressler is nowhere to be found and, of course, hasn't been anywhere to be found since 1945."

"What about the money?" Jason asked.

"You know how the Swiss are about their bank accounts. But we did find out something interesting through a Zurich policeman we do business with. The account was opened by a Mr. Jason Thomas, a gentleman who fits your description."

"What?"

"That's what the bank manager said. Described you to a tee. Height, weight, coloring, accent . . . sounded just like you."

"That's impossible," Jason said weakly.

Morris sighed. "We've asked them to send a copy of the signature of this person calling himself Jason Thomas. Of course, they are willing to cooperate to some extent, considering that this is a criminal matter."

"And the money in the account?"

Morris shrugged. "It was withdrawn the day after it arrived."

"Withdrawn where? By who? Surely there are ways of finding it."

"You must understand, Mr. Thomas, the Swiss exist to hide the passage of money. I don't know if we'll ever discover where it went. But to answer the first part of your question, it was withdrawn by Mr. Jason Thomas."

"Somebody's been impersonating me," Jason said, slamming his fist on the table. "That's obvious. I was here all week! I couldn't have been in Zurich withdrawing money."

"Yes, that's probably true, sir. Looks like somebody has been setting you up. I'd be willing to bet even money that the signature is a perfect forgery of yours."

"Jesus!" He rubbed his forehead. A headache was coming on. "What about the woman, Kate Buchanan?"

"Miss Buchanan claims that she never spoke to you after the event. She has witnesses placing her elsewhere. There is nothing else to connect her with this. No evidence whatsoever."

Jason slumped back in his chair. "What are you going to do?" he asked finally.

The policeman got to his feet. "We'll continue investigating the matter, sir. Rest assured on that account. Whether we ever find anything, that's another question."

"You'd better," Jason snapped, "or you might find yourself without a badge, Captain."

"Good day, sir." Detective Morris turned and walked out.

Jason watched the policeman leave. He was seething, absolutely furious. And yet for the first time in his life, he felt helpless.

His secretary buzzed to say that Page was on the telephone. He hadn't spoken to her since the event. He had tried calling her yesterday and now she was finally returning his call. Taking her own sweet time about it, too. he thought.

"Page," he said, "I'll be over this evening."

"I don't think so, Jason."

"Why? What's happened? Are you going somewhere?"

"No, I just don't want to see you anymore."

"What?" he said incredulously.

"Our relationship, as it's called for lack of a better term, is over."

"What?" he said again. "You can't do that. What do you mean? Why are you doing this? What are you saying?"

"I don't want to see you anymore, Jason."

"You're dumping me?"

"Yes."

"Why, I'll ruin you, you insolent bitch. You think you have a business? By tomorrow you'll have a shambles."

"You do what you have to do, Jason. And I'll do what I have to do."

"Is that a threat of some kind?"

"Not at all," Page said calmly.

"What brought this about. Why this change of heart? What's happening with you?" he demanded.

"It became very evident to me on the night your wing opened that you are an idiot, Jason. A loser. Somebody took you for seven million dollars. I don't associate with fools. Good-bye," she concluded, and hung up.

Jason sat there dumbfounded, the receiver in his hand. "Jesus Christ," he shouted out finally, and slammed it down.

David stopped in at the gallery. Kate was busy with paperwork while Madge spoke on the telephone. She heard the front door open and got up to see who it was.

"Kate," David said, "I've been calling you for two days. Haven't you been getting my messages?"

They stopped in the middle of the room. Looking over David's shoulder, Kate saw four Breer paintings. One of an island that looked like the Ibiza she remembered. "I'm sorry, David, I meant to call you back."

"Why didn't you?"

"I wanted to tell you it's over between us."

"What do you mean, over? Why?"

"I don't love you," she said simply. "I don't want to be with you any longer."

"What's love got to do with it? I thought we had an arrangement."

"No, we didn't," she said. "You'll find out that yesterday I returned your car to the dealer from which it was leased. They should be notifying your office today."

"What on earth got into you?" he asked, confused. "Has this anything to do with Jason, who tells me that you were involved in the forgery? Naturally I can't believe it."

"Jason is insane," she said. "It's only your own thirst for wealth and power that's prevented you from noticing it."

"You can't talk to me like that!" he protested.

"I just did," Kate said.

"Now wait a minute," David said angrily.

"No, you wait a minute," she cut in. "You men are all the same. You think money can buy everything, even people. Well, you're wrong. You couldn't buy me if you were the richest man in the world. You are an insufferable prig, David. You are also a weak and pitiful man. A fact that your wife has probably had to live with for many years and a fact that your daughter probably realized at an early age. I don't want to see you again. The jewelry you gave me has been mailed back to your office. You should receive it tomorrow."

"I—" David said, and then closed his mouth.

"Good-bye, David." Kate turned and walked away. She heard the front door buzz as he went out into the street.

Page laughed when she told the other women about her conversation with Jason. They were sitting in Elsa's apartment, each with a drink in her hand. "God, it felt good," Page said, giggling. "To tell Jason that I was dumping him because he was an idiot, a boob, an incompetent," she broke into loud laughter, unable to continue.

"I wonder how he felt when the police told him that he

opened the Swiss bank account?'' Jasmine asked with a smile.

''Well, by now they probably would have found out that someone was impersonating him. Although I'll bet that signature is going to give them a few headaches,'' Kate said. ''It won't stick in the long run, but it sure will muddy up the waters.''

She put her glass down on the table. ''Which brings up the subject of the money. As you know, Marcus has taken care of it. Marcus's friend, the one who looks just like Jason, withdrew it, gave it to Marcus, who put it in another bank. And there it sits, to be divided five ways, after initial expense outlay has been deducted.''

''Somewhere over a million each?'' Jasmine asked, her eyes wide at the thought.

''You know what we discussed,'' Kate reminded them. ''We can't all get rich quickly. That money is going to have to trickle out to us, over a fairly long period of time. And when it does, it's going to have to all be in cash.''

''Tax free,'' Page interjected.

''We have to remain circumspect,'' Kate said. ''No trips to Switzerland. I'll administer the account as we agreed, and whenever someone needs cash from their portion, I'll take care of it.''

''From Ibiza?'' Jasmine asked.

''Yes, from Ibiza. That's where I'm going to be.''

''I hope one day I get to meet this man who swept you off your feet,'' Page said. ''Maybe I'll understand it then.''

''Maybe you will,'' Kate replied.

''Oh, you will,'' Jasmine said definitively. ''He's gorgeous.''

''Mr. Silver called Jasmine today,'' Elsa volunteered.

''Really?'' Page asked. ''What did he want.''

''Me back,'' Jasmine said. ''Baby and all. I told him fat chance.''

''I guess going out with Shelly Pointer has taught him to really appreciate you,'' Kate said, and laughed.

''Too little, too late,'' Jasmine said.

''And you, Page, what are your plans?'' Kate asked,

noticing how relaxed and casual Page seemed. She had released some of that stringent and probably compulsive control with which she usually managed her life. Probably freeing herself from Jason had been like taking a monkey off her back.

Page had removed her shoes and wiggled her toes lazily before replying. "I'm going to go back to New York. Jason will probably decimate my business here, so I might as well start over again there. I still have contacts in New York that I can renew. And this time I'll be able to afford to take on the clients that I want, clients that I would be proud to represent. I think I'll enjoy my job a whole lot more."

"And you will occasionally come and visit an old woman, won't you, Page?" Elsa asked her.

"Of course," Page answered with warmth. "I may even persuade the old woman to come and visit me."

"What about you, Jasmine?" Kate asked.

"Me? I'm going to have a baby," Jasmine said humorously. Then added, "In the meantime, I'm going to try to keep my career going. And then after she's born, I'll have my sister come down and live with me and help out, and really go for it this time."

"Well," Elsa said fondly, "that takes care of all of you, my dears. Fame, fortune, careers, families—and I wish you all find and keep love," she concluded, her glance resting on Page.

"To the future," Kate said, raising her glass.

"To the future," they all toasted.

The aircraft finished its climb and leveled. Seat belt signs flicked off, and in the back of the plane, smokers drew hungrily on their cigarettes. Kate leaned her head back in the seat, utterly relaxed. It was over.

It had worked out well for everyone she cared about. Page was free. Free of Jason, and financially free. Perhaps now she would be able to find the fulfillment she sought, without the fear of poverty hanging over her head and without the lack of confidence that drew her to men who would support her. With renewed self-esteem, she could now create the career she was fully capable of. In fact, Kate thought, with a silent chuckle, she probably wouldn't need a penny of the money. Page would find success without even utilizing the funds at her disposal.

As for Jasmine, she too had reached some kind of realization. She had found that she could live without being dependent on men, realizing that even alone she could create the life she desired. In the coming year, with the birth of a daughter, she would also learn responsibility.

As for Elsa—well, Elsa had had her grand adventure, which is exactly what she wanted.

Madge had been sad to lose Kate, both as friend and employee, but she was also thrilled to learn that Kate had fallen in love with a man in Ibiza. Kate did not mention her involvement in the Rembrandt forgery, but she vowed to herself to see that Madge continued to represent "Breer." It was the least she could do to return her friend's many kindnesses.

And what about me? Kate thought. What did I get out of this? And was it worth it?

It was hard for her to unravel the many tangled paths of events. There was no doubt she felt a sense of relief, a sense that she had fulfilled an obligation to Joel and not stood silently by while the wheels of injustice ground away. She had done what she felt she had to do, and it was true that it had given her some satisfaction. But in a sense it had been a destructive endeavor. She had brought a man to his knees, taken her pint of blood and left him there. Whether he had been worth all her effort was debatable.

But out of that act of revenge, she thought, staring out the window at a carpet of tumbling clouds below them, something far finer had been born. Waiting for her on a tiny island in the Mediterranean Sea was a man without whom her life was incomplete. When she landed there and he met her, a unified whole would be formed, and together they would make something beautiful.

In her mind she saw his raffish smile and felt his hands

on her shoulders, his lips on her mouth. Surely that memory, that promise, made it all worthwhile, she thought.

She chuckled out loud, attracting a curious stare from the man beside her. It didn't matter. None of it mattered. She was free. Free of the past. Finally free to create an unlimited future.

EPILOGUE

A month after the event Kate bought Stone's gallery on Ibiza, and it soon became the best-known establishment on the island. She married Marcus within six months. Occasionally they returned to the United States to visit friends but, for the most part, both were content to remain on the Spanish island, where he could paint and she could run the gallery and assist him in his career. With the help of her contacts and promotional know-how, he became an extremely successful artist.

Page ran a public relations agency in New York, specializing in fashion, and her clients included notable designers from Europe, Asia, and the United States. The agency made her very rich and something of a celebrity herself. She did not marry, but three years after the event she met a man she felt she could love and they lived together.

Jasmine came to Ibiza to visit Marcus and Kate three months after the event. Billy was there at the same time. This odd couple immediately hit it off, and when she returned to Los Angeles, Jasmine moved in with Billy. He stopped painting for a month to build a two-room addition to his Venice house. After the baby girl, Pearl, was born, Jasmine's sister moved down and stayed with them. True to her word, Kate did arrange a show for Billy at Madge Bernstein's gallery, and he finally started to make some money from his art. Two years after the event, Jasmine starred in a low-budget film that critically established her. She would never lack for work again.

Elsa stayed abreast of the video revolution and bought a fifty-inch television set. Her life was enlivened whenever Page visited her, which was every few months, when she called on clients on the West Coast.

Jason Thomas continued to succeed in business, but he never lived down the humiliation of that night. Nor did the police ever find the perpetrator of the crime that left him five million dollars poorer. Six months after the event, his wife Sharon divorced him. He did not remarry.

Sharon became a well-known figure in Los Angeles society. She devoted most of her time to crusading against drug abuse and fundraising for drug rehabilitation organizations such as Narcanon. She remarried happily three years later.

David Ross continued his life much as it had been before, except that his wife Pat committed suicide nine months after the event. He saw his daughter occasionally, but they never had much to communicate to each other. In the next three years she went through two husbands.

Allan Silver was fired by the board of Elixer Studios, six months after the event. He went into independent production—the elephants' graveyard for ex-studio executives.

Madge Bernstein's gallery continued to do well, particularly as she was the sole West Coast representative of the reclusive Breer's work.

Angie Cox received a newspaper clipping about the debacle at the opening at the Rex, two months after the event. Attached to it was a note that said: "For Joel." She remembered the determination on Joel's sister's face and wondered if . . . It gave her a good laugh, which she needed, as her life had not improved much.

Detective Morris of the LAPD, based on thirty years of experience as a cop, knew without a doubt that the beautiful Miss Kate Buchanan had been responsible for the fake Rembrandt. He also knew that she had been much too clever and that he would never be able to prove her guilt. In the final analysis, he didn't care. There was crime, and then there was *crime.* As far as he was concerned, Jason Thomas was an asshole who had deserved to be reamed.